*Unwin Critical Library*
GENERAL EDITOR: CLAUDE RAWSON

# MARTIN CHUZZLEWIT

# Martin Chuzzlewit

Sylvère Monod

London
**GEORGE ALLEN & UNWIN**
Boston         Sydney

**George Allen & Unwin (Publishers) Ltd,
40 Museum Street, London WC1A 1LU, UK**

George Allen & Unwin (Publishers) Ltd,
Park Lane, Hemel Hempstead, Herts HP2 4TE, UK

Allen & Unwin, Inc.,
Fifty Cross Street, Winchester, Mass. 01890, USA

George Allen & Unwin Australia Pty Ltd,
8 Napier Street, North Sydney, NSW 2060, Australia

First published in 1985.

*cc*

**British Library Cataloguing in Publication Data**

Monod, Sylvère
  Martin Chuzzlewit.——(Unwin critical library)
1. Dickens, Charles, *1812-1870*. Martin Chuzzlewit
I. Title
823'.8      PR4563
ISBN 0-04-800028-0

**Library of Congress Cataloging in Publication Data**

Monod, Sylvère, 1921-
  Martin Chuzzlewit.
(Unwin critical library)                302214
Bibliography: p.
Includes index
1. Dickens, Charles, 1812-1870. Martin Chuzzlewit.
I. Title.      II. Series.
PR4563.M37 1985      823'.8      84-24292
ISBN 0-04-800028-0 (alk. paper)

Set in 10 on 12 point Plantin by Columns of Reading
and printed in Great Britain by
Billing and Sons Ltd,
London and Worcester

# GENERAL EDITOR'S PREFACE

Each volume in this series is devoted to a single major text. It is intended for serious students and teachers of literature, and for knowledgeable non-academic readers. It aims to provide a scholarly introduction and a stimulus to critical thought and discussion.

Individual volumes will naturally differ from one another in arrangement and emphasis, but each will normally begin with information on a work's literary and intellectual background, and other guidance designed to help the reader to an informed understanding. This is followed by an extended critical discussion of the work itself, and each contributor in the series has been encouraged to present in these sections his own reading of the work, whether or not this is controversial, rather than to attempt a mere consensus. Some volumes, including those on *Paradise Lost* and *Ulysses*, vary somewhat from the more usual pattern by entering into substantive critical discussion at the outset, and allowing the necessary background material to emerge at the points where it is felt to arise from the argument in the most useful and relevant way. Each volume also contains a historical survey of the work's critical reputation, including an account of the principal lines of approach and areas of controversy, and a selective (but detailed) bibliography.

The hope is that the volumes in this series will be among those which a university teacher would normally recommend for any serious study of a particular text, and that they will also be among the essential secondary texts to be consulted in some scholarly investigations. But the experienced and informed non-academic reader has also been in our minds, and one of our aims has been to provide him with reliable and stimulating works of reference and guidance, embodying the present state of knowledge and opinion in a conveniently accessible form.

C.J.R.
University of Warwick,
December 1979

# CONTENTS

# PREFACE

*Martin Chuzzlewit* is not one of the Dickens novels that everyone reads and that every Dickens critic writes about at great length. The *Chuzzlewit* literature cannot compare, in point of quality or in sheer bulk, with the studies devoted to old favourites like *David Copperfield* or *Great Expectations*, or to the later, darker masterpieces (*Bleak House, Little Dorrit, Our Mutual Friend*).

Yet *Martin Chuzzlewit* proves extremely interesting as well as agreeable to reread again and again, to examine and analyse. It offers an extraordinary variety of aspects, and raises fascinating critical problems, without ever being obscure or difficult.

As will appear throughout this book, I am immensely indebted to the Clarendon edition of *Martin Chuzzlewit*, which was published at the end of 1982, just in time to enable me to make use of its authoritative text and to refer to its valuable findings. It is a pleasure to express my gratitude to the editor, Margaret Cardwell, and to the general editor of the series, Professor Kathleen Tillotson.

For information, advice and help of various kinds, I also wish to thank Micheline Larès, Robert L. Patten, Robert M. Polhemus, Michael Slater, Olivier Cohen-Steiner and, above all, Claude Rawson, whose generous efforts on behalf of this book have far exceeded his duties as general editor of the series.

Because the Clarendon volume is unusually costly, all references to *Martin Chuzzlewit* are identified parenthetically by chapter-number, followed by page-number in both the Penguin English Library and the Clarendon editions, in that order (except in Chapter 2).

*Paris, April 1984*                                                     S.M.

# CHAPTER 1

# Dickens's Pre-*Chuzzlewit* Days

A rough outline of Charles Dickens's childhood and youth following his birth on 7 February 1812, and of Boz's early career, may cast some light on the personality of the author who began to write *Martin Chuzzlewit* in 1843.

Recalling that the novel opens with an elaborately jocular genealogy, it may be useful to refer to Charles Dickens's ancestry, precisely because there is not very much – and nothing notable – to be said about it. When in later life the successful novelist adopted a 'crest', and had it reproduced on his bookplate and silverware, he was asked whether it had existed in the family. He replied, disingenuously, that he had never 'used any other armorial bearings than [his] father's crest', which was true in a literal sense, that is, he had never used any other; but John Dickens, Charles's father, had never used a crest at all, and the form of the statement was of course intended to suggest that John Dickens had indeed used *that* crest, and bypassed the question of his having had any right to it, or to any other.[1]

John Dickens, as an impecunious and moderately successful public servant in the Navy Pay Office, or later as a self-taught shorthand reporter, may have been a man of some talent and a boon companion, but being his son was nothing to boast of, and his own father and mother had been mere domestic servants (steward and housekeeper) in the house of a richer family.[2] John Dickens's wife Elizabeth, née Barrow, belonged to a family of higher civil servants, also connected with the Navy Pay Office, but whose reputation was somewhat tarnished by a case of embezzlement of funds.[3] Such data may not be the only source of chapter I of *Martin Chuzzlewit*. The example of Fielding's *Jonathan Wild* (book I, chapter II) almost certainly exerted an influence on the young novelist and reinforced his determination to deride genealogy.

The next point of interest to the student and reader of *Martin*

*Chuzzlewit* is the extent, or the limitations of the education received
by its author. About the education at home, there can be no doubt
that it was intellectually adequate and even stimulating. John Dickens
was a man of real intelligence, and he was eminently literate and
articulate, very much attracted by words and phrases. Elizabeth
Dickens, though she is supposed to have sat, unwillingly and
unconsciously, for the portrait of Mrs Nickleby, was certainly not a
fool. At one time she wanted to eke out the family resources by taking
in pupils. There is no evidence that a single pupil ever came to her,
but neither is there evidence that she would have been incapable of
coping with him or her if one had come. And young Charles must
have been further helped by the continuous process of mutual
education that goes on within large families (John and Elizabeth
Dickens had eight children, only one of whom died in infancy, so that
they actually brought up seven children). As to the moral and
practical aspects of the guidance received in the home, they were of
more questionable value. John and Elizabeth Dickens were improvi-
dent and tended to run into financial difficulties. It was mainly
through a reaction against their example that the future novelist may
be said to have been felicitously influenced by his parents.

Charles Dickens's formal education was consequently a haphazard
affair. Its early stages, in Chatham, seem to have been sufficiently
happy and efficient. However, there was a financial crisis when
Charles, who had been left behind for a few months, joined his
parents in London in 1823. He was not sent to school, but kept at
home as a kind of unpaid household drudge, though he went on
reading and thus to a certain extent teaching himself. But when the
crisis came to a head, in the spring of 1824, Charles went out to work
in a blacking factory run by a young cousin of his mother's, earning
his livelihood at the unripe age of 12, while the rest of the family soon
joined Mr Dickens in the Marshalsea, where he had been imprisoned
for debt. It was only some time after John Dickens's release (after
three months) that Charles was withdrawn from the factory and sent
to school again. For three more years (1824–7) he attended an
establishment called Wellington House Classical and Commercial
Academy, which may not have justified its pompous name by real
academic distinction. In 1827 he left school for good and, at the age of
15, became a paid office-boy.

Fortunately, Charles Dickens was an avid reader and a fiercely
ambitious and energetic adolescent. He may be said to have taken his

own further education in hand at its decisive stage. He was never given a chance to go to one of the universities (an advantage of which he was later to underestimate the value), but he did the next best thing by obtaining a reader's ticket to the British Museum Library at the earliest possible date (the day after his eighteenth birthday) and reading assiduously and greedily. Of course, by such methods he never became a man of impressive culture, but neither was he the ignoramus, the purely instinctive writer, the 'Heaven-taught' penman that his more supercilious reviewers tended to see in him.

From his childhood and adolescence, Charles Dickens emerged with some first-hand knowledge of poverty, hunger and the streets of London, a good deal of variegated information gathered from books, a sense of his own gifts (for acting, singing, and even dancing, rather than for writing, so far) and an iron-hard resolution to rise in the world – to rise, if not to fame, at least above want.

It did not take him long, after he had finally left school in 1827, to work himself away from the low-level jobs in the world of lawyers and towards journalism. The way he chose was like David Copperfield's, and like his own father's before him, that of self-taught shorthand reporting, at which Charles Dickens seems to have become remarkably adept.

His career as a writer began in 1833 with the publication of his first story, 'A Dinner at Poplar Walk', in the *Monthy Magazine*. Unpaid, and seeing only the dubious light of print in an obscure and ephemeral periodical, this event was nevertheless regarded by the budding author as momentous. And of course he was proved right in the event, for in the course of the next few years he wrote more and more stories and sketches, for which he found a market without too much difficulty in various newspapers and journals. By the early weeks of 1836 there was enough material for two volumes of *Sketches by Boz* to appear (supplemented later in the year by a further volume). The year 1836 was in several respects Dickens's *annus mirabilis*, or perhaps it was Boz's rather than Dickens's. Charles Dickens it was who married Catherine Hogarth on 2 April 1836, but Boz was his signature on the title-page of his first book. And it was as Boz that Dickens simultaneously began to write *The Posthumous Papers of the Pickwick Club*. He was so much bent on impressing the British reading public as Boz (or so ready to let the label stick to him) that the third, definitive and best illustrator of *Pickwick*, Hablot Knight Browne, felt compelled to hoist a similarly neat banner and called himself 'Phiz'.

The author of *Sketches* and *Pickwick* had thus been rushed by events into complete Bozification.

It would remain for him to de-Bozify himself. If Boz was in the main a writer of light comic tales, and quite content to be acclaimed as such, Charles Dickens could justifiably nourish higher ambitions. The story of the years between 1836 and 1842 in Dickens's literary career, or between *Sketches by Boz* and *Martin Chuzzlewit*, is largely that of the emergence of the full-grown Dickens from the chrysalis Boz. Again it was a spectacularly fast process. Without going into all the details, and without counting *Sketches by Boz*, which was not essentially new work, it is striking to find that Dickens's first five novels (*Pickwick*, *Oliver Twist*, *Nicholas Nickleby*, *The Old Curiosity Shop* and *Barnaby Rudge*), making up one (large) third of his fifteen (or fourteen and a half) novels, were produced in under six years, between 1836 and late 1841. The other two-thirds (ten, or nine and a half, novels) were to take him twenty-nine years to write.

The outward form assumed by *Martin Chuzzlewit* and the method of its composition and publication were directly influenced, like a great part of Dickens's writing career, by what happened in the early weeks of 1836. When the young publishing firm of Chapman & Hall were approached by the artist Robert Seymour, who enjoyed a respectable reputation as the author and etcher of sporting sketches, he came to them with a proposal for a series of 'cockney sporting plates', to be 'accompanied by letterpress and published in monthly parts', and they set about finding some young writer who might be interested in providing the letterpress (and capable of doing so efficiently). They did not at once bethink themselves of the author of *Sketches by Boz*, but they soon had their eye on him among others and it was with him that they eventually came to an understanding. One significant feature of the transaction was the young writer's reservations about his proposed subservience to Seymour's invention. In spite of the gap in age and fame between the two men, these reservations were expressed so forcefully that the arrangement was radically altered – it was in fact reversed – by the time publication began. When the first number of *Pickwick Papers* appeared, there was no ambiguity as to who was illustrating whom. The 'Papers' were 'Edited by Boz', 'with Four Illustrations by Seymour'. Another important fact was connected with the original Seymour–Chapman plan for the work to be 'published in monthly parts'. It would be idle to try to imagine what turn Dickens's career as a novelist might have taken but for Seymour's initiative.

Seymour disappeared from Dickens's career at once; between the first and second numbers of *Pickwick* he had committed suicide. Chapman & Hall remained understandably attached to Dickens's literary fate throughout his life. Though the connection went through an eclipse in the 1840s and 1850s (beginning with – and brought about by – *Martin Chuzzlewit*, as will appear in the next chapter), it was never completely interrupted and was definitively resumed in 1859 with *A Tale of Two Cities*. But, apart from Charles Dickens himself, the most permanent member of the partnership turned out to be the monthly number. Boz rose to fame thanks to the monthly numbers of *Pickwick Papers*; when Dickens died thirty-four years later he was engaged in writing the monthly numbers of *Edwin Drood*. In the meantime he had hoped, and tried, more than once, to escape the drudgery of writing a set quantity of material at regular intervals. The launching of the weekly *Master Humphrey's Clock* in 1840 was the first of these attempts; *The Old Curiosity Shop* and *Barnaby Rudge* were originally published in *Master Humphrey's Clock*. But, as on all similar occasions later, Dickens returned to the form which was both his favourite and the one best suited to his talent and temperament. Nine of the fifteen novels appeared first in monthly numbers. And such was their success that other Victorian novelists had to emulate them. The choice had been in great part due to accident and circumstance. Dickens's persistence and his successful use of the form showed that the accident had been on the whole felicitous and the circumstance skilfully exploited.

In theory, however, publication, and especially composition, in small monthly doses is inartistic. This mode has been adversely criticized because it does not enable the novelist to modify the beginning of his work in the light of its later development. Even the staggered publication of a story written in its entirety before the first instalment is placed before the eyes of the public is open to objection, since it imposes upon the artist specific constraints: each part must form a tolerably coherent whole; the breaks must occur at regular intervals; the reader's interest must be kept alive throughout. But when a novelist agrees to do what Dickens did constantly, that is, invites inspection of the early chapters, makes them public, while the later incidents are not yet written out and may still be no more than hazily conceived in his own mind, he forgoes the power of altering his story by means of cancellations; additions and twists are the only weapons thus left as his disposal. George Eliot, for one, always refused to adopt these procedures. Dickens, on the contrary, proclaimed that he held the advantages of the method to outweigh its disadvantages. This obstinate practical preference for the theoretically indefensible can be understood. There is no doubt that Charles Dickens worked better under the compulsion of immediate urgency: what the opening night of a play was to him as a producer of theatrical performances, the printer's deadline was to him as a novelist. It provided an inescapable stimulation and precluded dawdling, while not mobilizing his energies for too long at a time. Dickens adapted himself happily to the monthly rhythm (as he did, on the whole, to the daily organization of his work); a two-week stint of hard labour (carried out in the morning) would normally see him through. It is likely that, during that period of concentration, he would be supported by the prospect of a fortnight's relaxation, although in his case it is abundantly clear that relaxation would take the form not of idleness but of a change of absorbing occupations.

A second advantage of the periodical instalment was that it implied concentration and constriction and protected the writer from the temptation of letting himself go, of becoming long-winded. Experience taught Dickens that the weekly fragments were too demanding in that respect, while the monthly parts of thirty-two close pages (of fifty lines each) suited him very well; they gave him enough 'elbow-room' (to use one of his own favourite expressions), but not too much. Third, Dickens was in need of constant and almost physical contact with an audience. This requirement of his nature was to lead him to his theatrical activities (including, of course, his public readings of extracts from his works). Publication of a three-decker at one blow could not have satisfied his needs; when a novel was spread out over nineteen months, a number of reactions made the mode of the 'audience' perceptible to him. There were reviews of the separate parts, a few letters, the talk of the town, something in the atmosphere perhaps, and – most measurable of all – the sales figures supplied by the publishers. This had its dangers, for the reactions could be disappointing or even depressing, but Dickens was a man of real courage, he was a born fighter, he would strive hard to remedy his mistakes; in any case, he seems to have been unable to write in a vacuum. Finally, Dickens was also a man of habit and to a certain extent of superstition. One of his reasons for doing things the way he did them was simply that he did them that way, that he had fallen into the habit of doing them that way, and no other. Just as he had to have a certain size and thickness of paper, or ink of a certain colour, or certain statuettes on his desk while he worked, he needed a regular schedule of writing. And so the form of publication that had raised him to the pinnacle of fame in a few weeks of 1836 had earned his grateful affection for ever. He felt safe with it. He remained faithful to it.

For *Pickwick* had been almost immediately taken to the hearts of the general public. Among the professional critics, the situation was less clear-cut. While no one could deny that a new genius had made his appearance on the literary scene, reservations and doubts could be, and were, voiced about the nature, profundity and permanence of Boz's genius. Because he wrote so fast in his early years, the notorious prophecy was made that, as he had risen like a rocket, he would come down like the stick.[4]

Signs of a rapid decline, however, failed to become visible. As novel followed novel in quick succession, it was open to anyone to decide that Boz was overwriting himself, and thus inevitably riding for a fall. Meanwhile, he did something genuinely new in each new novel. If *Barnaby Rudge* showed less gusto than *Pickwick* or *Nickleby*, it was a novel of such a different nature that comparison in those terms was inadequate, almost irrelevant. It would have been just as true to claim that *Barnaby Rudge* evinced more power (dramatic and historical) than *Pickwick*, or even than *Oliver Twist* which it resembled rather more. But that could not have proved that Dickens had made progress from 1836 to 1841. What was obvious was that he had been exploring his potentialities in various directions, and on the whole with remarkable success.

This diversity of the early batch of fast-produced novels is shown by the case of *Nicholas Nickleby*, in that it is the only one of the five that has anything to do with the most traditional form of the English novel, that belongs to the tradition of *Tom Jones* or *Roderick Random*, that is, the tradition of the loose sequence of adventures with a good-natured impetuous young man for its central (and eponymous) figure, leading to his love-marriage after many difficulties. By the same token, *Nickleby* is the only novel of Boz's early years that is in the least a forerunner of *Martin Chuzzlewit*.

After the two years of *Master Humphrey's Clock* (1840–1) and the intensive drudgery connected with it, Dickens treated himself to a half-year's holiday, which he spent energetically visiting the United States of America. It was after his return to England that he resumed novel-writing and thought of *Martin Chuzzlewit*. It was after he had let off some of the steam accumulated during his journey by writing and publishing his *American Notes for General Circulation* that he felt ready to go into harness once again.

Because of this longer interval than usual between the new novel and its immediate predecessor, because of the way the intervening time had been spent, there was a real break, and *Martin Chuzzlewit* marks a turning-point in Dickens's career.

This can be shown on the evidence of the cover designs of the works published by Dickens up to and including *Dombey and Son*. *Sketches* had 'BOZ' in the title in gigantic letters. *Pickwick* and *Nickleby* advertised themselves as 'Edited by "Boz" '; *Master Humphrey's Clock* (paradoxically, since it had been intended to be a weekly publication including contributions by various hands, genuinely 'edited' by Dickens) was announced as 'By "Boz" '! *Chuzzlewit* reverted to the thin conventional disguise of editorship, but dropped the inverted commas around the name of Boz in 'Edited by Boz'. And that was Boz's last appearance on a title-page. *Chuzzlewit*'s successor, *Dombey and Son*, was to be simply 'by Charles Dickens', and so would all the later novels. *Chuzzlewit* is thus either the last novel of the first period or the earliest of the later novels.

## NOTES: CHAPTER 1

1  See T. P. Cooper, 'Dickens's crest', *Dickensian*, vol. 27, no. 219 (1931), pp. 236–7.
2  The Crewes, that is, the family of John Crewe (later Lord Crewe) at Crewe Hall, Cheshire.
3  Mrs Dickens's father, Charles Barrow, was the culprit and absconded to escape imprisonment in 1810, a few months after the Dickenses' marriage. See Edgar Johnson, *Charles Dickens: His Tragedy and Triumph* (London, 1953), Vol. 1, pp. 7–8.
4  Abraham Hayward in the *Quarterly Review*, October 1837. The reviewer had shrewdly observed a falling-off in the later numbers of *Pickwick*, in which he discerned that 'the particular vein of humour which has hitherto yielded so much attractive metal is worked out'; yet he was modest enough to claim no personal merit for his rocket-and-stick prophecy, for 'it requires no gift of prophecy to foretell [Boz's] fate'.

# CHAPTER 2

# The Text and its Variations

The textual history of a Dickens novel is not always particularly lively and interesting. It cannot compare, for instance, with the field offered by the works of Proust or, before him, of Balzac. On the other hand, the student of Dickens's text enjoys certain advantages: the materials required for that kind of examination are plentiful and accessible. And, because it was only after the Second World War that Dickens's work came to be regarded as real literature, these materials have, so to speak, just begun to be exploited. They had lain untapped for several decades after the novelist's death.

*Martin Chuzzlewit* first appeared in nineteen monthly instalments from January 1843 to July 1844. Nineteen may seem, and is, an odd number. But the reason is simple enough: the July 1844 part was, as in the case of the other 'monthly' novels written by Dickens, called by courtesy a 'double number'; it carried the superscription 'Numbers XIX and XX' and, as far as the text proper was concerned, was exactly 50 per cent longer than an ordinary instalment: forty-eight pages instead of the usual thirty-two. But it sold for double the usual price, two shillings instead of one; and, with half-title and verso, title-page and verso, dedication and verso, preface, contents, and even errata-slip and verso, the other sixteen pages were actually there, numbered in roman numerals. And the author must have received, if not earned, a double fee. The purchaser of a Victorian novel in nineteen/twenty monthly parts would thus have paid twenty shillings in all, or one pound.[1] This made his purchase easier than in the case of the more respectable three-decker, the novel in three volumes which dominated the book market during some seventy years, that is, throughout Queen Victoria's reign, with the support of the circulating libraries and of the magazine editors. The total price of the nineteen/twenty monthly parts was substantially lower than that of a novel in three volumes (which would be sold at half a guinea per volume, or a guinea and a half – that is 31s 6d – for the set, so that the novel in parts was more than a third cheaper). Besides, the buyer of the novel in parts was more assured of getting his full money's worth of printed matter. Publishers of three-deckers would invariably sell you three volumes, but the size and typography varied considerably. And, above all, the fact that the twenty shillings would be staggered over a period of a year and a half made a real difference.

The documents available for the textual study of a Dickens novel published under such circumstances usually comprise: the complete manuscript, one or more sets of galley-proofs, the text as printed in nineteen monthly parts, and the parts later bound into one volume (in which form the text is normally identical with that of the separate parts); three other editions published in Dickens's lifetime – the Cheap, the Library and the Charles Dickens editions – described below.

For novels of later date than *Chuzzlewit*, there exists in addition one earlier stage, Dickens's working notes or number-plans or, as he came to call them himself, 'mems' (that is, memoranda, what he must bear in mind while writing his successive chapters). These 'mems' have been described and discussed.[2] Most of them have by now been published in their entirety as part of the apparatus of critical editions.[3]

No such helps to writing seem to have been used, or felt by Dickens to be necessary, in the early years of his career. None, at any rate, have been preserved. And it appears that his method originally consisted of spending some time in mental effort before he put pen to paper. What he called 'imaging forth' or 'thinking out' was thus a preliminary stage to be gone through.[4] After which Dickens could at once proceed to the actual writing of his novel in a form which was as a rule very nearly definitive; he did not allow himself much time for revision and improvement of his manuscript, which he never treated as a rough draft and of which he never made a fair copy.

The first appearance in a Dickens manuscript of anything resembling the systematic 'mems' of later years dates back to *The Old Curiosity Shop* (1840). The novelist's notes in preparation for that story do not cover anything earlier than chapter LXV and consist only of a belated effort to disentangle the family history of Little Nell's grandfather, and of lists of characters and incidents jotted down in pre-paration for the end of the book.[5] Nothing of the kind subsists with the manuscript of *Barnaby Rudge* (1841), and there is little reason to suspect that in that single case 'mems' were used and then destroyed.

The first novel for which a complete set of 'mems' have been preserved is *Chuzzlewit*'s immediate successor, *Dombey and Son* (and from that point of view, again, *Martin Chuzzlewit* marks a transition or the end of a phase, the more or less happy-go-lucky phase of easy writing and flowing inspiration). The manuscript of *Chuzzlewit* itself contains only two sheets of crude 'mems' concerning numbers IV and V (chapters IX–XV).[6] There is no evidence that other sheets of 'mems' for *Chuzzlewit* ever existed, though it is not impossible, or even improbable, that they did. However, a letter Dickens wrote to his friend John Forster (10 November 1843), when he was at work on chapters XXX–XXXII, shows that his approach to the problems of literary composition still varied. To Forster he said on that occasion: 'I have been all day in *Chuzzlewit* agonies – conceiving only. I hope to bring forth to-morrow.'[7] *Martin Chuzzlewit* thus appears to have been prepared in part by the old method of hard thinking, in part by the new method of writing guidelines.[8]

The *Chuzzlewit* manuscript has one unusual characteristic: it contains a sizeable rejected fragment of chapter VI; nearly ten pages, close to the beginning of that chapter, were devoted to a quarrel between Charity Pecksniff and her sister, and their reconcilement through the good offices of their father and at the expense of Tom Pinch.[9] This passage was not salvaged for future use – as might have been done easily. It was sacrificed bodily and finally.

After the first edition in one volume, brought out by Chapman & Hall in 1844, with a short preface dated 25 June 1844 and a respectful dedication to Miss Burdett-Coutts, *Martin Chuzzlewit* was of course reprinted many times during its author's lifetime.

As will appear later, the novel had met with disappointing sales in monthly numbers, averaging 20,000 and never exceeding 23,000 parts per month, instead of the 40,000 to 70,000 for some of the previous works. Even such relatively low figures placed Dickens far ahead of all his serious competitors, but they created severe financial problems as well as friction between him and his publishers.[10] These disappointments were to exert considerable influence over Dickens's career. For instance, they encouraged him to write his 'Christmas Books', beginning with *A Christmas Carol* in 1843. That, in its turn, though remarkably popular, fast-selling, critically acclaimed and taken to the nation's heart, had failed to restore Dickens's solvency or to relieve him from the burden of his debts. This led him to move away from the friendly and accommodating publishers of his first books,

Chapman & Hall. His characteristically bold notion was, not to shift from one existing firm to another, but to create his own publisher or, more precisely, to set up Chapman & Hall's printers, Bradbury & Evans, as independent publishers. Because they were inexperienced and ill-equipped, Bradbury & Evans were understandably reluctant and they needed much goading. But goading was something that Dickens could and did provide, being himself urged by a mixture of business flair and emotional excitement. In the event, Bradbury & Evans did become publishers of books and journals, and were to be the publishers of Dickens's novels and magazines for some fifteen years, until another quarrel, in the late 1850s, though not connected with commercial interests, made the pendulum swing back and caused Dickens to return to Chapman & Hall for the remainder of his life.

The first edition of *Martin Chuzzlewit* in book form, brought out in 1844 under Chapman & Hall's imprint, eventually sold at least as well as Dickens's other novels.[11] It was kept constantly in print. The novel was included in the Cheap Edition in 1849, with a new preface dated November 1849. The Cheap Edition sold in three forms: as thirty-two weekly parts, as eight monthly parts, and as one volume. In 1858, *Chuzzlewit* appeared in two volumes in the Library Edition (which never quite took off) and finally, in 1867, in one volume again, as part of the Charles Dickens Edition, with a revised, undated preface by the author.[12] Besides, all post-1868 editions of both *American Notes* and *Martin Chuzzlewit* include a 'Postscript' dated May 1868 and paying a tribute to the improvements the novelist had observed in America in the course of his second visit there.[13]

It is out of the question to go into the complete and detailed textual history of *Martin Chuzzlewit* here. That is the proper business of textual editors. The work has been done by Margaret Cardwell for the Clarendon Dickens, under the general editorship of Kathleen Tillotson and James Kinsley. The volume came out at the very end of 1982, just in time to become our edition of reference and to allow me to print in this place a summary of its characteristics.

Earlier and more amateurish sampling of the two most textually relevant versions of the novel – the first edition of 1844 and the Charles Dickens Edition of 1867 – had yielded unsensational but valuable results. The two editions had been compared with each other and with later reprints such as the Oxford Illustrated Dickens *Chuzzlewit* of 1951 (edited by Geoffrey Russell) and the Penguin English Library volume of 1968 (edited by P. N. Furbank). Writing his introduction in 1951, Russell did not even mention the existence of any textual problems; the only earlier edition referred to on the verso of the title-page is the first edition of 1844, but the copy-text used was in fact that of the Charles Dickens Edition of 1867 (no other preface is printed or alluded to than the undated one of 1867). By 1968 complete textual innocence was no longer permissible or conceivable, and Furbank reprinted all three of the prefaces, as well as the cancelled fragment of manuscript. And he has a 'Note on the text', in which he states what his policies have been: 'I have used the "Charles Dickens Edition" as my copy-text, correcting some obvious errors revealed by collation with the 1844 edition and borrowing a few other readings from this latter.' These claims are both intrinsically reasonable and truthfully made.

The sampling referred to above was carried out on the basis of thirty complete separate pages selected at regular intervals throughout the novel. It was thus found that, out of some seventy-six changes between 1844 and 1867, more than two-thirds affect punctuation alone: in the sample-packet of pages hyphenation is altered in five cases; eight commas are cancelled, but fourteen new ones are inserted; one dash becomes a comma, and four become colons; seven semicolons and one colon become commas; one semicolon becomes a colon and one colon a semicolon; one comma becomes a period; one period and one comma become exclamation marks, and one exclamation mark becomes a comma. These changes are too bewilderingly irregular to suggest any kind of conclusion.

The 1844 edition appeared with an errata-list of ten items. Eight of the corrections were made in the Charles Dickens Edition; two were not, but at least two original misprints not listed in the errata were repaired. The Charles Dickens Edition also introduced a few substantive alterations, two of which are clearly mistakes and found themselves eliminated from later editions (*effected* for *affected* in chapter I; *of* substituted for *than* in chapter XXI). Two or three changes are indifferent (one *upon* altered to *on* in chapter XI, a repeated *who* introduced in chapter XVI without being either indispensable or harmful). One alteration weakens the text, but may well result from accident (in chapter XVI, 'and in great numbers too; and too often' becomes 'and in great numbers, and too often'). In another case, accident results in the omission of one *do* from a sentence where it is needed; this Charles Dickens Edition error has unfortunately been perpetuated in at least the Penguin version of the text, but not in the Clarendon edition. A few changes, like those in the punctuation, seem to be connected with house style only (*Sir* is decapitalized to *sir*; *leaped* becomes *leapt*, and *had n't* becomes *hadn't*). Finally, in seven or eight cases, the text seems to have been authorially modified for the 1867 edition; and that, in comparison with *Bleak House*, for instance, is a high percentage and evidence of genuine revision work.[14] Among these changes (occurring mostly in the later sections of the novel) are *Insurance/Assurance* (the Anglo-Bengalee), *a deep one/a deep file, standing up in one/going into a*. There is at least one probable mistake in the text of the first edition that has never been emended in any later publication.[15]

All this makes the Charles Dickens Edition of *Martin Chuzzlewit* an indispensable complement to the first edition of 1844, though it is clearly not superior to it. That is why it was not adopted as copy-text by the Clarendon editor, but of course systematically examined and exploited.[16] Margaret Cardwell's introduction contains by far the best and most complete account of the history of the text and its publication. Her textual annotations are conveniently located at the foot of the page, and they enable readers to see for themselves what Dickens was trying to achieve and to form their own conclusions as to whether changes made after the manuscript was completed were always for the better. It is particularly valuable to have several passages restored, not into the text, but as footnotes, when they had been cancelled by the author for various reasons that are a matter for conjecture.

Various characters have benefited or suffered from alterations of that kind. Mark Tapley, for instance, who is sometimes felt to be underemployed and underdeveloped in the course of the story, is found, on close examination of Margaret Cardwell's edition, to have endured losses. That of a too explicit compliment paid him by the narrator on his generous and helpful behaviour to a family of fellow-travellers to America (XVII, 283; Penguin 366) one can bear with fortitude, but it remains a sign that Dickens did not do with Mark all he had intended to do; he tended to sacrifice Mark when he had to cut out a portion of what he called an 'overwritten' number, that is, an instalment with 'overmatter', in excess of his strictly calculated monthly allowance of space. Another passage of comment about Mark's attitude to the same people as in the previous case, but this time issued by Mark himself, also went by the board, without too much damage to the book. Mark's character is not complex and had already been clearly established (XXXIII, 518; Penguin 589). But there is at least one set of brief cancellations involving Mark which are to be deplored, because the passage as originally written lent to his personality a touch of good-humoured yet telling banter about his American experiences that one may miss from the published version of the story (XXXV, 548–9; Penguin 622–3).

Jonas Chuzzlewit also finds his speech shorn of at least one picturesque expression and his description of one epithet, for no other obvious reason than a fear of excessive or premature explicitness. The cancelled part of Jonas's speech occurs in conversation with his father, whom he reproaches with talking of want at his time of life. What the reader finds is simply: 'You're a nice old man to be talking of want at this time of day.' But in the original manuscript the sentence went on thus: 'when you ought to be keeping your mind on Worms' (XVIII, 299: Penguin 362). The epithet is applied to Jonas's expression when looking at Tom Pinch; in the published version mention is made only of 'an expression in his features', whereas in the manuscript it had been called a 'diabolical expression' (XXIV, 391; Penguin 459).

The case of Mrs Gamp is more disconcerting in that she must have been felt by Dickens, from her earliest appearance, to be an outstandingly successful creation and seems to the reader to be created with triumphant ease. It is now seen that a good deal of tentative work went into that creation. Even her name was a matter of some uncertainty at first: the manuscript shows that Dickens had thought of calling her Gample or Gimple before settling for the superb, and superbly exploited, name of Gamp (XIX, 311; Penguin 374). One of the most felicitous retrievals from Dickens's manuscript is the pronunciation 'proformed' for 'performed' (XIX, 319; Penguin 382); it had been missed by the compositor at Bradbury & Evans's, and his having missed it was unobserved by Dickens when he read the proofs. The case is not unusual in Dickens's career, but it is good to have the accidental error repaired, even at this late date. It is interesting to find that the phonetic peculiarities of Gampese caused difficulties to the author himself and that the one word *goldian* (in 'goldian guineas': XXV, 406; Penguin 474) was adopted only after several attempts including *gold, golgian, goulgian* or *goalgian*, and *gouljian* or *goaljian*! The Clarendon edition also supplies a whole new paragraph of first-rate Gampiousness (XXIX, 464; Penguin 535) which was to be found in the manuscript but had appeared in no printed form of the novel.

Now and again it is Dickens's own phrasing that is altered, as when, while working on the manuscript, he substituted the more pointed 'a wiry-faced old damsel' for 'a grim old virgin' (XVI, 273; Penguin 336).

Finally, among the useful appendixes at the end of the Clarendon volume will be found the interesting variations which preceded Dickens's choice of the name of Chuzzlewit and a few others.[17]

Thus does Margaret Cardwell's edition of *Martin Chuzzlewit* provide both the best text of the novel and the most complete documentation on its development.

## NOTES: CHAPTER 2

1 The monthly parts were called in the publishers' account-books '20 parts as 19'. See Robert L. Patten, *Dickens and His Publishers* (Oxford, 1978), e.g. p. 393. Additional information was obligingly supplied by Professor Patten in private correspondence.

2 By John Butt and Kathleen Tillotson, *Dickens at Work* (London, 1957), and by Sylvère Monod, *Dickens romancier* (Paris, 1953), and *Dickens the Novelist* (Norman, Okla, 1968).

3 See, e.g. the Clarendon editions of *Dombey and Son*, *David Copperfield*, *Little Dorrit* and *Edwin Drood*, and the Norton Critical editions of *Hard Times* and *Bleak House*. See also H. P. Sucksmith, *The Narrative Art of Charles Dickens* (London, 1970).

4 See Monod, *Dickens the Novelist*, p. 238.

5 ibid., pp. 203–4.

6 They may be called crude by Dickens's own later standards of refinement and sophistication.

7 *The Pilgrim Edition of the Letters of Charles Dickens*, Vol. 3 (Oxford, 1974), p. 595. This is an extract quoted by Forster himself in his *Life of Dickens* and of which the original and the rest of the text have disappeared. Forster is not completely reliable when he prints Dickens's correspondence, but the present sentences contain nothing improbable.

8 The nature of Dickens's work at that stage is analysed and illustrated by Sucksmith, op. cit., pp. 88–9 and 96–8.

9 Printed as 'Appendix A' in the Penguin English Library edition by P. N. Furbank (Harmondsworth, 1968), pp. 921–5. Also in Clarendon edition, as Appendix B, pp. 837–42. Further discussion of this item is to be found below in Chapter 11.

10 See Patten, op. cit., ch. 7 ('Trouble in Eden') and ch. 8 ('The Break'), pp. 119–56.

11 See John Forster, *The Life of Dickens* (1872–4), Everyman's Library (London, 1927), Vol. 1, p. 285: 'Its sale . . . has ranked next after *Pickwick* and *Copperfield*'. Forster's assertion is borne out by the figures supplied in John A. Sutherland's *Victorian Novelists and Publishers* (London, 1976), p. 36; these figures concern the printing of the Charles Dickens Edition between 1867 and 1870. *Pickwick* has an easy lead with 76,000 copies, but *Chuzzlewit* shares the second place on the list with *Copperfield* (with 45,000 copies each); all the other novels lag far behind.

12 *The New Cambridge Bibliography of English Literature*, ed. George Watson, Vol. 3, in an entry compiled by Philip Collins, says that the Charles Dickens Edition of *Chuzzlewit* has a frontispiece by F. Stone. The copies I have seen, however, have only eight of the thirty-eight original illustrations by 'Phiz'. The various prefaces are examined below in Chapter 11.

13 See below, Chapter 11.
14 See Norton edition, ed. G. H. Ford and S. Monod (New York, 1977), 'A note on the text', pp. 808–10.
15 See chapter X: 'the love they would have diffused over their whole existence', where *their* does not make sense, while *his* cries out to be substituted for this unfortunate possessive.
16 See *Martin Chuzzlewit*, ed. Margaret Cardwell, the Clarendon Dickens (Oxford, 1982). References in this section are to the Clarendon text and given parenthetically in the form 'XVII, 283'. (The corresponding references from the Penguin edition are added for convenience' sake; e.g. 'Penguin 366').
17 Clarendon edition, p. 834.

# CHAPTER 3

# Starting the Machinery
# (Chapters I–XIV)

A Dickens novel in nineteen/twenty monthly instalments is a huge and complex machinery. In order to determine by what means the machinery is set in motion, the beginning of the novel is here subjected to close separate analysis. The first fourteen chapters of *Martin Chuzzlewit* are treated – perhaps arbitrarily – as constituting the initial phase; but chapter XV, which completes the sixth monthly instalment, takes Martin junior across the Atlantic, and thus clearly opens another phase of the story.

The first chapter is entirely separate from the rest and is more in the nature of a prologue than a preliminary part of the story. It does not present any of the characters who will appear in the novel, and does not tell of any action or incident of any relevance to what is to follow. Dickens here seems to be following the tradition created by his admired predecessor Fielding in *Jonathan Wild*. If chapter I of *Martin Chuzzlewit* can be connected with anything else in the novel, it is with its complete original title. With this, and with this only, it shares a tone and a mood of ponderous facetiousness. This complete title is seldom printed anywhere these days. It does not appear at all in the Penguin English Library or the Oxford Illustrated editions; quite correctly, since they are reproducing earlier editions in volume form, and these carry only the words *The Life and Adventures of Martin Chuzzlewit* on the title-page. The first edition of 1844 even has, in addition, opposite the frontispiece, a still shorter version, the *Martin Chuzzlewit* by which the book came to be most currently known and referred to, even by Dickens himself (when he did not abbreviate it further, to plain *Chuzzlewit*). But for the wrappers of the monthly numbers Dickens had concocted the following rigmarole: 'The Life and Adventures of Martin Chuzzlewit, his relatives, friends and enemies: comprising all his wills and his ways, with an historical record of what he did, and what he didn't: showing, moreover, who inherited the family plate, who came in for the silver spoons, and who for the wooden ladles. The whole forming a complete key to the House of Chuzzlewit. – Edited by Boz. With illustrations by "PHIZ".'[1] No less; no more. It remains puzzling that a man of Dickens's intelligence and talent should have, however fleetingly, and even in a spirit of good-humoured parody, thought it worth his while to spend his creative energy on such mediocre stuff.

Readers who consider this original title as a feeble joke may derive comfort from the thought that it was ephemeral, and that the jocularity and expansiveness of Dickens's titles for his later works were to be kept within reasonable bounds in the case of *David Copperfield* (1849–50) and to disappear for good with the next book (printed versions of *Bleak House*, 1852–3, were never called anything more, or less, than that). The most curious aspect of the complete title coined for *Chuzzlewit* is that it has no relevance whatsoever to a single line of the novel beyond the end of the fourth chapter. Neither of the two Martins dies and leaves (or receives) an inheritance. The joke is gratuitous as well as, on the whole, somewhat feeble. It was soon, fortunately and mercifully, forgotten.

Yet what one comes across on beginning to read the novel itself, the notorious first chapter of *Martin Chuzzlewit*, is hardly less disconcerting and offputting. As George Gissing wrote:

Originally the book had a long cumbrous title, in a strain of facetiousness which now strikes us as unworthy of it and of the author; it is in keeping, however, with the first chapter, an utterly mistaken bit of sub-acid jocosity, which might well have been omitted from later editions, and certainly would never have been missed.[2]

The first chapter of *Martin Chuzzlewit* raises a critical problem of some magnitude. It is devoted to the pseudo-genealogy of the eponymous family. It contains raillery which may seem levelled at people who support the aristocracy and worship the past, writers like Disraeli, but also Carlyle (and, later, Ruskin). The onslaught on absurd pretensions is in itself more than acceptable, but the tone is leaden, and the generalizations are too vague to be telling. The attack on 'the great' looks back to Fielding's example once more – Jonathan Wild had been termed 'the great' from the very title-page of the book ironically recording his life – but the attack also foreshadows the most vulgarly (and incompetently) polemical parts of Dickens's *A Child's History of England* (1851–3). A great part of the chapter is based on a series of puns, the words and phrases thus exploited being: *come over, Match-Maker, Duke Humphrey, the Lord No-Zoo, my uncle, interest* and *Golden Balls*. Dickens may appear to be amusing himself. Whether he can still amuse (or ever *did* amuse) many of his readers by such means is more doubtful. The element of parody – of genealogists, historians, editors and commentators – is not contemptible, and belongs to a traditional genre. But the tradition is not lightly followed.

The feebleness of the chapter was almost unanimously agreed upon until a fairly recent date. It is only too easy to collect unfavourable, often withering, opinions about it. From Sir Arthur Quiller-Couch in 1925 ('sorrier stuff could scarcely be written')[3] to Geoffrey Thurley in 1976 ('a disastrous relapse to the facetiousness of *Pickwick*'),[4] via Harvey Peter Sucksmith ('a ghastly failure')[5] or Garrett Stewart ('blustering absurdities'),[6] there hardly seems to be room for diverging opinions. Even Albert J. Guerard, who treats *Martin Chuzzlewit* with serious attention, says that the book 'begins as badly as any important English novel, with a chapter of random and juvenile garrulity on the forbears of the Chuzzlewits'.[7]

Any attempt to define the meaning of the first chapter is bound to go one step further, in that it implies that the chapter does mean something. Thus such statements amount to an incipient defence of that performance. Angus Wilson, for instance, writes: 'The whole of the first chapter . . . is given up to a mockery of concern with ancestors and family trees. A man, for Dickens, is himself, and himself alone.'[8] V. S. Pritchett is much more favourably impressed by the chapter, and much more ready to take it seriously: 'His comic genealogy of the Chuzzlewit family is not all of a piece. It satirizes many kinds of believers in genealogy. Beginning in the spacious manner of Fielding, in order to set a grave tone, it proceeds to irony about William the Conqueror.'[9] Pritchett is one of the few twentieth-century readers to express hearty enjoyment of chapter I.

But the first chapter of *Chuzzlewit* has found supporters on other grounds. Steven Marcus, whose analysis of Dickens's early novels has proved particularly stimulating, includes the 'sardonic genealogy' of the first chapter among the illustrations of his statement that 'of all Dickens's novels, *Martin Chuzzlewit* is in one sense the most Joycean, for language itself is one of its subjects'.[10] Alexander Welsh ingeniously selects the opening paragraph for grave attention;

according to him, it 'ironically balances a common motif in English fiction, family snobbery, against the Christian exegesis of the Old Testament, originated by St Paul'.[11] Mary Rosner sees the first chapter as written 'about fiction making and fiction makers'.[12] But the main argument in favour of the chapter is the recent delighted insistence on the truly astonishing fact that it provides evidence of Dickens's early awareness of the ur-Darwinian theories of Blumenbach and Monboddo. This was referred to by Fred Kaplan in 1975,[13] before being finally illuminated by Mary Rosner in 'A note on two allusions: *Martin Chuzzlewit*, chapter I'.[14] She shows that Lord Monboddo's argument for a connection between men and the orang-utan was a well-known butt for ridicule, while the allusion to J.F. Blumenbach and an analogy between swine and men is more difficult to trace to any specific statement issued by the German scientist.

However interesting it may be to find that Dickens had heard of such people and even had some (more or less distorted) notions about their work, his intention seems to have been derisive and facetious on this point as in the rest of the chapter, which should not perhaps be taken with too much gravity.

Chapters II and III have jocular headings, which seem to derive from Fielding. They introduce the reader to a country scene, elaborately described, and then to the Pecksniff household: Mr Seth Pecksniff, widower and architect, who takes in pupils, and his two unmarried daughters, Charity (or Cherry) and Mercy (or Merry).[15] He is sanctimonious, and makes a great show of his humility. A permanent inmate of the household is an old-looking though youngish man named Thomas Pinch. Meanwhile an old man and a young lady have arrived at the nearby inn, the Blue Dragon; they are Martin Chuzzlewit the elder, an aged, rich, distant relative of Pecksniff's, and his lady companion Mary Graham. The old man is ill; when he gets a little better, he is visited by Pecksniff, who tries, not unskilfully, to ingratiate himself with him, even pleading for the old man's grandson, Martin Chuzzlewit the younger, who has behaved rebelliously (in the matter of love and marriage). With the end of chapter III closes the first monthly instalment of the novel.

The next one opens with the arrival of other Chuzzlewit relatives, all drawn by news of the old man's illness and eager to get their share of his inheritance. The most entertaining of these – as will be seen more completely in chapter 7 below – is Montague Tigg, not a relative himself, but a companion and supporter of Chevy Slyme, who is one

of Pecksniff's cousins, and a complete (though pretentious) nonentity
in his own right. There is an *omnium gatherum* of the prospective heirs,
who fail to agree about precedence or about their respective rights and
wrongs; but the inconclusive meeting is brought to an abrupt end by
the announcement that old Chuzzlewit is better and has gone away. At
that point (at the end of chapter IV), one large chunk of the
introduction or exposition has been completed. Chapter V, which ekes
out the second instalment, ushers in Martin Chuzzlewit the younger,
whom Tom Pinch goes to meet in Salisbury. Tom and Martin get on
well enough together, although it appears that they admire the same
girl. Mary Graham had been the occasion of the rift between the two
Martins. She had also, involuntarily and unconsciously, produced a
great impression on Tom's heart while old Martin was laid up and she
heard Tom play the organ in the village church.

No very sensational events occur in the course of the third monthly
instalment (chapters VI, VII and VIII). Pecksniff welcomes the new
pupil, then shows a propensity for exploiting that young man's inborn
talent and leaving him alone while Charity, Mercy and himself repair
to London. The contrast between Tom's meekness and Martin's
flagrant selfishness is insisted upon. While the two prentice architects
are left to their own devices and see some more of Tigg and Slyme,
the Pecksniffs travel to London and settle down in Mrs Todgers's
boarding-house.

The fourth monthly part is again composed of two chapters rather
than the more usual three, and is entirely devoted to London and
Todgers's. In chapter IX, after a wild extravaganza about the location
of the boarding-house, the character of Mrs Todgers and the life of
the lodgers, with the welcome addition of the three Pecksniffs, are
evoked in detail, culminating in an elaborate Sunday dinner. Mr
Pecksniff and his daughters, accompanied by Mrs Todgers, pay a visit
to Miss Ruth Pinch, Tom's younger sister, who is employed as a
governess by arrogant people living near London. In chapter X the
real reason for this metropolitan holiday transpires: an interview takes
place between Old Martin Chuzzlewit and the Pecksniffs, at the old
man's request; he wishes to become better acquainted with them and
he contemplates making his home as a paying guest in their house.
Another scene at Todgers's completes the chapter and the number.

The next instalment (V) is the third two-chapter part (there will be
only one more after that, two months later). Chapter XI is the last to
be devoted to the 'Town and Todgers's' episode. It is an important

chapter because it introduces another branch of the Chuzzlewit family: Anthony (Old Martin's brother, also a widower, as though widowhood, or widowerhood, ran in families, like a kind of hereditary disease), his son Jonas and his old clerk Chuffey. Jonas flirts with his cousins Charity and Mercy, and Anthony discusses with Pecksniff the prospects opened by that incipient courtship. Chapter XII reverts to the country and to Young Martin, who practises architecture (on his own) and patronizes Tom Pinch; the two young men are invited to have dinner in Salisbury by a former pupil of Pecksniff's. When the latter returns from London, he sends Young Martin out of his house after a scene of rather obscure mutual vehemence. Martin announces that he will go to America. In the first two chapters of number VI, Young Martin's mishaps on the road and in London are related; he has to pawn his watch and meets Tigg (who has parted from Slyme), fails to get employment, but receives an anonymous gift of money and is helped by Mark Tapley, who forces himself upon Martin as his unpaid servant and companion. Before sailing away to America, Martin has a brief encounter with Mary Graham. He does not appear much to his advantage, but she loves him. They part sadly enough. In the next chapter, and before the end of that number, the American episodes have begun.

In addition to the disappointment connected with the first chapter, this opening section of *Martin Chuzzlewit* suffers from other weaknesses, but it has its strengths as well and it presents a number of interesting characteristics.

The existence of two persons bearing the same name is an unusual feature. In its earlier version, as was made apparent above, the title did seem to concern the older rather than the younger Martin, since it alluded to questions of inheritance. The definitive version or shorter form, however, is equally applicable to the one as to the other. Yet, as will soon appear, it is the younger Martin's story that the novel tells, and that is in accordance with the most typical pattern. In most novels, where boy meets girl, falls in love, courts her, surmounts obstacles, so that eventually boy marries girl, and they live happily ever after, a young man – say, a Nicholas Nickleby or a David Copperfield – is the central figure.

Both grandfather and grandson have been adversely criticized as at least partial failures of Dickens's unique power of lively and forceful characterization. Of the older Martin, whom we meet first, there is not really very much to remark, partly because through the greater part of the book he appears under a disguise, and partly because when the disguise is finally dropped what is revealed is that there had never been very much interesting depth beneath it.

In chapter II, however, we may note that the relationship existing between him and Mary Graham, the young woman who acts as his paid companion, is original. In spite of the gap between their respective ages and social situations, she calls him 'Martin', explicitly with his full concurrence;[16] and that must be taken as an early sign that Old Martin, wayward and arbitrary as he is meant to appear, has some better qualities and a certain perception of the intrinsic dignity of all human beings, which may go far to account for his seemingly perverse actions later on. Unfortunately, it must be admitted that on his first appearance Martin, for so old and ill a man, is surprisingly long-winded and holds forth at excessive and even boring length. Probably the rereader of the novel, who sees better what this protracted conversation with Pecksniff tends towards, can derive more enjoyment from such a scene, but one's first contact with it is unlikely to elicit much enthusiasm. Later Old Martin will sink into apparent apathy and thus become a man of fewer words. Even then, however, he remains addicted to a quaint, stilted, archaic way of speaking, illustrated for instance in his commentary on his brother and nephew, Anthony and Jonas Chuzzlewit:

My brother had in his wealth the usual doom of wealth, and root of misery. He carried his corrupting influence with him, go where he would; and shed it round him, even on his hearth. It made of his own child a greedy expectant, who measured every day and hour by the lessening distance between his father and the grave, and cursed his tardy progress on that dismal road. (XXIV, 452/385–6)

Living human beings do not express themselves thus in ordinary conversation, or even at any time, except on the stage. And this may be in part responsible for Gissing's curt dismissal: 'In Old Martin we have not the slightest belief'[17] or 'the mask known as Old Martin, a thing of sawdust';[18] or James R. Kincaid's more recent outburst: 'the most unsatisfactory character in all of Dickens'.[19]

Old Martin's elaborate plot has aroused even more irritation than his speech. For a considerable length of time, he pretends to be taken in by Pecksniff, to rely on him, to be influenced by him. This protracted deception can hardly have been a pleasure to himself, for he had to place an iron constraint upon his every word and attitude in order not to give himself away. Nor is his purpose in so doing entirely clear. He plans in part to punish, in part to reform, his grandson, but since the immediate consequence of Old Martin's attitude is Young Martin's departure for America, where he very nearly dies, out of reach of sympathy and advice, it is clear that the grandfather's plot was fraught with dangers and that the cure might have been effected in a far more disastrous way than he had expected. In so far as Pecksniff is also a target of Old Martin's strategy, he may have wasted his efforts, for he can only laboriously bring to light what had been glaringly obvious from the beginning: that Pecksniff was hypocritical and mercenary. There are moments when not much is to be said in defence of Old Martin's elaborate and disagreeable deception. This is particularly the case in chapter XLIII, when Young Martin returns from the United States. Then nothing *is* said to explain why the moment of truth and revelation is further delayed. In other words, Old Martin may appear to have been playing, with uncharacteristic talent, a thoroughly unworthy game, for which he has been duly blamed (or Dickens taken to task) by numerous critics: H. M. Daleski ('singularly masochistic . . . from the start an implausible Boffin')[20] and H. P. Sucksmith ('improbable motivation . . . melodramatic posturing')[21] among others. Even the few who have admired, and the fewer who claim that they have enjoyed, the scheme must rest their case on moderately convincing arguments. This is the case of Geoffrey Thurley, who sees Old Martin's plot as the moral centre of the novel, as providing 'the morally controlled structure of *Martin Chuzzlewit*'.[22] As to Alexander Welsh, he insists that in order to punish the guilty in *Chuzzlewit* 'Dickens has Martin Chuzzlewit senior play the role of God'[23] and it is true that, in chapter LXII in particular, Old Martin helps Dickens considerably by displaying absolute power, ordering people about and gathering all the characters together, thus demonstrating that he possesses the omnipotence usually regarded as an attribute of God alone.

It would be unfair to insist exclusively on the inartistic aspects of Dicken's characterization and contrivance. One might lose sight of the fact that Dickens knew what he was doing, and handled characters and readers with some skill and subtlety even at this point. For instance, in the somewhat tedious passage of chapter III, already referred to, in the course of which Old Martin holds forth to Pecksniff about the disappointments in store for the rich man in touch with mankind, the old man is made to exclaim, 'I recognise the true unworldly ring of *your* metal' (III, 91/39), and the reader may believe that Martin is taken in by Pecksniff; but a little later Martin looks at Pecksniff 'with a keenness which the other seemed to feel' and, a little later again, 'the old man cast an angry glance towards the candlestick, as if he were possessed by a strong inclination to launch it at his cousin's head' (III, 93/40–1). These are clear enough indications of Old Martin's real attitude and of the care with which the novelist, while exhibiting the old man's acting as good enough to mislead Pecksniff, gives more than one hint to readers that *they* should not let themselves be misled so easily. This may unfortunately suggest the sad reflection that hypocrisy can only be vanquished by superior hypocrisy, that Pecksniff, the perfect, ideal, accomplished, professional hypocrite, is hoist with an improved version of his own petard; he fails to take in his intended victim and is taken in by him. Pecksniff is thus, so to speak, the naïve, though not the innocent, hypocrite, deceptively secure in the devices that have so long and so often ensured his success.

As for Young Martin, he might be regarded as the hero of the novel, in the sense that he is the young man whose adventures, and whose love-story, occupy the centre of the stage most frequently. He is not, however, like Nicholas Nickleby or David Copperfield before and after him, a likeable or admirable character, so that he must be said to fill the place destined for the hero rather than to *be* that hero. Of course, this is in accordance with Dickens's purpose; there is no failure on the author's part to make the reader share his own favourable evaluation of his young man's character. Undoubtedly the novelist attempted to analyse the character ruthlessly rather than to exalt him. Dickens was even somewhat heavy-handed in his treatment of Martin; in chapter XIV, for instance, at the end of the initial section, when Martin takes leave of his unfortunate inamorata, there is a ponderous paragraph (XIV, 304/243), the core of which comments on Mary's lack of recognition of Martin's deficiencies: 'The heart where self has found no place and raised no throne, is slow to recognise its ugly presence when it looks upon it.' The same kind of tone will be heard later, when Martin's attitude to Mark Tapley is examined: 'Poor Martin! For ever building castles in the air. For ever, in his very selfishness, forgetful of all but his own teeming hopes and sanguine plans' (XXI, 416/350–1). For the heart of the matter lies precisely in Martin's selfishness; that is what is profoundly wrong with him. His selfishness and self-centredness are illustrated graphically, and even typographically, in the course of Martin's parting conversation with Mary Graham, when he tells her that she must confide in Pinch: 'it will be a great consolation to you to have anybody, no matter how simple, to whom you can speak about ME' (XIV, 303/241). As if such devices were not clear enough, Dickens has placed by Martin's side companions – Tom Pinch at first and later Mark Tapley – whose altruistic leanings and forgetfulness of self help to emphasize the ugliness of Martin's conduct and personality. Chapters VI and XVII, in that respect, are particularly illuminating. But perhaps the worst – that is, the clearest – denunciation of Martin's selfishness is contained in the commentary on his reactions to Tom Pinch's gift to him ('He found a curious gratification, too, in thinking what a winning fellow he must be to have made such an impression on Tom; and in reflecting how superior he was to Tom': XIII, 275/214). There is also the crushingly ironical heading of chapter XIV: 'In which Martin bids adieu to the lady of his love; and honours an obscure individual whose fortune he intends to make, by commending her to his protection.'[24] In short, Martin is more like Roderick Random or Peregrine Pickle than he is like Tom Jones. The type of charming egoism in a young hero is very Smollettian.

Of course, the real trouble with Young Martin is not that the reader does not like or admire him as a person; it is that so little interest can be taken in him as an artefact that he fails to come fully alive, as well as to signify very much.

It takes all the innocence of the French critic Alain – who read all Dickens's fiction in the old Hachette translations and thus could hardly have a very accurate notion of what the books were like in the original – to feel admiration for Martin: 'C'est ce qu'on nomme un caractère; il tient de son oncle Martin un égoïsme bienveillant.'[25] It would be difficult to be wider of the mark or to utter so many questionable statements in so few words: Young Martin is almost emphatically *not* what is called a character; Old Martin is not his uncle but his grandfather; and the selfishness which the young man is supposed to have inherited from the latter relative can hardly be termed benevolent. Critics who have had access to the English text of *Martin Chuzzlewit* are less tender, like Albert J. Guerard, who diagnoses the deficiency as 'an extreme example of conceptual as well as dramatic failure'.[26]

And that is a test of Dickens's genius and intriguing evidence of its mystery. A failure on that scale, when it touches the 'hero' of a book, might be expected to make that book unreadable. It obviously does nothing of the kind. This may well be linked with the fact that, as hinted above, Dickens himself is on our side; according to John Lucas, 'in *Chuzzlewit* Dickens sees through the sort of hero he celebrates in *Nicholas Nickleby*'.[27]

In the early chapters the opposition between the two Martins, as one of the mainsprings of action, is very much in evidence without being made powerfully interesting. It is indeed destined to be a central element in the book and its moral scheme: each of the Martins contributes in the enlightenment and conversion of the other. It would be more effective if both of the Martins had been made more memorably credible, their enmity less superficial, their reactions and plans less absurd. Dickens probably intended the reconciliation of the end (in chapter LII) to arouse the reader's emotion; but, unlike other more or less similar episodes in the English novel, in which a deplorable misunderstanding is dispelled (Elizabeth and Darcy in *Pride and Prejudice*, or David and Agnes in *Copperfield*), the end of *Chuzzlewit* and the changed tone of the grandfather–grandson relationship is likely to leave the reader cold. It is possible to be in addition disconcerted, at the thought that the whole story is geared towards making the younger Martin very rich, and presumably for that reason very idle. He is in one important sense back at square one and recovers what had been his original prospect for life, that of being a gentleman, and thus losing the moral benefit he might have derived from his hard experiences. He does work, though desultorily, at Pecksniff's, he does not work at all in London or in the United States. He has always subsisted on money given by others – Tom, Mark, Mary, Old Martin either in disguise or by proxy (for the kind American Mr Bevan will be refunded by Martin's grandfather, much against Pecksniff's advice). After which . . . there is nothing else. That is the end of Young Martin's career, of his usefulness in life. Perhaps he thus simply illustrates the survival of the gentlemanly ideal. But that is unlike Dickens's usual attitude, which is more modern.

It is difficult to share Earle Davis's generous enthusiasm: 'the reader feels pleased when Martin's grandfather finally gives him the money he wanted all the time'.[28] Having wanted the money all the time is not the same thing as having earned it, or deserved it in any way. It is covetousness, not effort, that is thus rewarded. And it is hard to conceive of a way of life suitable for Young Martin beyond the end of the novel. He seems doomed to do nothing real, to be reduced to the kind of confused intriguing with which Martin the elder kills time until time is finally ready to kill *him*.

But Earle Davis is one of the few critics who are fully convinced that Young Martin's story is that of a progress, in other words, that he has undergone a genuine conversion by the end of the novel. H. M. Daleski complains that Dickens's way of presenting the young man's spiritual progress 'emphasises the utter triviality of his experience'.[29] True, Geoffrey Thurley defends at some length, and not entirely through paradox, the treatment of Martin's moral crisis at Eden;[30] and there are some valid remarks in his analysis, but they cannot completely overcome the objection (propounded by Alexander Welsh, among others)[31] that Martin's conversion hardly improves him and that he is not sufficiently meaningful for the reader to mind very much what happens to him, one way or another.

Thus, in the first quarter of the novel, the reader encounters difficulties of belief and assent. There are in fact other feeble points and further signs of the author's hesitancy. What is meant is aspects that are likely to appear feeble to twentieth-century readers but may well have been relished and admired by Dickens's contemporaries. The success of a book like *Martin Chuzzlewit* can be measured in more than one way – for example, by its impact on its first readers, by its posthumous reputation, by the reaction of critics and readers of the present day. It is probably the case that Dickens, at least in that comparatively early phase of his career, wrote mainly for his contemporaries and was legitimately pleased with himself when they were pleased with him. But the presumably higher aim of educating his public, which certainly formed part of Dickens's overall purpose at least from the early 1850s on, may not have been completely foreign to him even in 1843.

Of course, there are also many attractive and promising aspects in the first fourteen chapters of *Martin Chuzzlewit* which can abundantly justify interest and admiration. For one thing, Dickens has succeeded in producing a novel, or the beginnings of a novel, in which there is an alternation of genuinely rural, genuinely provincial, and intensely metropolitan scenes. Mr Pecksniff's Wiltshire village, Salisbury and London are all placed before the eyes of the reader. Perhaps there is less reality, less felt life, more artifice (as may appear from the number of elaborate purple patches) in the country scenes and landscapes;

perhaps it is mainly on arriving in London and at Todgers's that Dickens seems to come into his own. This is understandable enough, considering that one of the places described in the London of *Martin Chuzzlewit* happens to be Furnival's Inn, where Dickens had lived since 1834 when he had his first independent establishment, before his marriage. And that is more than could be said of Salisbury or of any village in England. But the interesting fact is that Dickens thought this alternation between the various areas of English life important enough to give it a place in his fiction, considered himself as able to bring it off, and on the whole did so.

And it is obvious that, from the second chapter on, Dickens has excellent and forceful material at his disposal. The Pecksniffs have been created, and it would be difficult to conceive of a family holding out better promise of amusement and of telling satire.

The narrative itself has not perhaps been set going very forcefully. It might be contended that there has been through the first fourteen chapters no action, properly speaking: the most decisive step taken is Young Martin's departure for the United States. Even that, however, is rather negative; Martin takes himself off, and he does that after having made one false start in life – arriving in Mr Pecksniff's house, then leaving it, with nothing to show for it in any direction. That is a state of things which is reminiscent of the iterative circularity of events in *Nicholas Nickleby* (1838–9), and thus, as far as narrative technique is concerned, looks backwards rather than forwards in Dickens's career. But, if the narrative has not made any spectacular move so far, it is at any rate under way.

The main hesitation under which Dickens may seem to have laboured in the early phase of *Martin Chuzzlewit* concerns the tone of the novel. The question may be asked – and he may even have asked himself the question – is the writer going to return to an atmosphere reminiscent of *Sketches by Boz*? The scenes at Todgers's contribute to that impression, since the first of the 'Tales' in *Sketches by Boz* had been called 'The Boarding-House'. On the other hand, isn't Dickens going to take advantage of the experience accumulated through writing *Oliver Twist*, *Nicholas Nickleby*, *The Old Curiosity Shop* and *Barnaby Rudge*? Had he learnt nothing between *Sketches* and *Chuzzlewit*, in seven very busy years? And hadn't he also read and reread a number of works by his predecessors and contemporaries?

Careful examination of various aspects of the rest of the novel ought to provide answers to some of the above questions. Meanwhile, by the end of chapter XIV, the machinery has been constructed, and is ready to work, if not actually working. In this novel which is in part about architecture and about architects, the foundations are laid elaborately and they look solid enough.

## NOTES: CHAPTER 3

1  This is cut out into seventeen lines, treated with great typographical whimsicality. See the reproduction given as the frontispiece to the Clarendon edition.
2  George Gissing, *The Immortal Dickens* (London, 1925), p. 114.
3  Sir Arthur Quiller-Couch, *Charles Dickens and Other Victorians* (Cambridge, 1925), p. 21.
4  Geoffrey Thurley, *The Dickens Myth: Its Genesis and Structure* (London, 1976), p. 86.
5  H. P. Sucksmith, *The Narrative Art of Charles Dickens* (London, 1970), p. 85.
6  Garrett Stewart, *Dickens and the Trials of Imagination* (Cambridge, Mass., 1974), p. 117.
7  Albert J. Guerard, *The Triumph of the Novel: Dickens, Dostoevsky, Faulkner* (New York, 1976), p. 239.
8  Angus Wilson, *The World of Charles Dickens* (New York, 1970), p. 16.
9  V. S. Pritchett, 'The comic world of Charles Dickens', in Ian Watt (ed.), *The Victorian Novel: Modern Essays in Criticism* (London, 1971), p. 39.
10  Steven Marcus, *Dickens from Pickwick to Dombey* (New York, 1965), p. 217.
11  Alexander Welsh, *The City of Dickens* (London, 1971), p. 124.
12  Mary Rosner, 'The Siren-like delusions of art', *Dickens Studies Newsletter*, vol. 10, nos 2–3 (1979), pp. 47–8.
13  See his *Dickens and Mesmerism: The Hidden Springs of Fiction* (Princeton, NJ, 1975), p. 21.
14  *Dickens Studies Newsletter*, vol. 12, no. 1 (1981), pp. 12–13.
15  One is once more reminded of Jonathan Wild, whose three aunts were christened Grace, Charity and Honour.
16  See III, 93/40: 'There is a compact between us . . . that she call me always by my Christian name, I her, by hers.' References to the text are given, as explained in the Foreword, with chapter-numbers in roman numerals, and page-numbers in both Penguin and Clarendon editions (in that order) separated by an oblique line.
17  Gissing, op. cit., p. 119.
18  Quoted in Stephen Wall (ed.), *Charles Dickens: A Critical Anthology* (Harmondsworth, 1970), p. 230.
19  James R. Kincaid, *Dickens and the Rhetoric of Laughter* (London, 1971), p. 133.
20  H. M. Daleski, *Dickens and the Art of Analogy* (London, 1970), p. 108. Mr Boffin is a character in *Our Mutual Friend* (1864–5), who also implausibly acts a repellent part.
21  Sucksmith, op cit., p. 226.
22  Thurley, op. cit., pp. 82–3.
23  Welsh, op. cit., p. 122.
24  Chapter-headings in the first edition, and in the Clarendon edition, are printed in capitals throughout.
25  Alain, *En lisant Dickens* (Paris, 1945), p. 71.
26  Guerard, op. cit., p. 243.
27  John Lucas, *The Melancholy Man: A Study of Dickens's Novels* (London, 1970), p. 58.

28  Earle Davis, *The Flint and the Flame: The Artistry of Charles Dickens* (Columbia, Mo., 1963), p. 144.
29  Daleski, op. cit., p. 110.
30  See Thurley, op. cit., pp. 91–5.
31  See Welsh, op. cit., p. 122.

# CHAPTER 4

# The American Episodes

When Mr Pickwick is a prisoner in the Fleet because he has refused to pay the costs of the case won against him by Mrs Bardell and Dodson & Fogg, Tony Weller suggests that he should be smuggled out of the prison in a 'pianner' in which 'there ain't no works'. After which, Tony adds, 'Have a passage ready taken for 'Merriker. The 'Merrikin gov'ment will never give him up, ven they find as he's got money to spend, Sammy,' and later, when his opponents have disappeared, 'let him come back and write a book about the 'Merrikins as'll pay all his expenses and more, if he blows 'em up enough'.[1] In which Tony Weller does not show practical sense equal to that of his more famous son; Mr Pickwick is incapable of accepting such a crude subterfuge and he is probably even more incapable of writing a book of any kind. But the implied criticism of America, and the gibe against the British travellers who made money out of their visits to the United States, may well have been remembered by Dickens when he decided to send Young Martin across the Atlantic. In the meantime, of course, Boz had himself visited America, and he had already written and published one book about his travels there. He was now going to increase the vigour and harshness of his criticism, and it has been claimed that his doing so, and his sending Martin abroad at all, was due to motives similar to those suggested to Mr Pickwick by Tony Weller – a need and a desire to retrieve his finances.

Apart from the preliminary announcement in chapter XIII, and subsequent brief references in chapter XLVIII, the American episodes are to be found in eight chapters (or a little under one-seventh of the total number). These chapters follow the opening section examined above, but do not come all together. They are contained in a first batch of three consecutive chapters: XV–XVII (spanning the end of the sixth instalment and the beginning of the seventh); in another triplet (XXI–XXIII, coinciding this time with the whole of the ninth monthly portion); and two more chapters (XXXIII–XXXIV) placed at the beginning of the thirteenth number. A brief outline of the

American adventures of Martin Chuzzlewit the Younger and his travelling companion, partner, friend and servant Mark Tapley is easily supplied; the two young men cross the Atlantic aboard the *Screw* line-of-packet ship, and they reach New York, where they make a number of acquaintances and one real friend. After leaving the coast to go west, they purchase a house and some land in a place called Eden, where Martin intends to settle and make his fortune as an architect. They eventually travel to Eden by steamboat, and find that it is only a desolate swamp; Martin soon falls ill, and is tended by Mark, whose kindness he will be able – and willing – to repay in part when Mark falls ill in his turn. When they are both sufficiently recovered to contemplate travelling again, they decide to borrow money from their single American friend, write to him, receive his loan, get back to New York, and finally return to Liverpool.

The incidents of this brief and unsatisfactory American career of Martin Chuzzlewit are unimportant; what counts, what makes the interest of that section of the novel, is in part the satire of the United States and in part the technique of alternating irregular sequences of chapters about the characters left in England with chapters about American events. That device faintly and indirectly foreshadows the bolder experimental procedures employed later by Dickens in *Bleak House*.

The problems created by the decision to alternate, and yet link together, these foreign episodes and the main plot or plots centred in England are serious and difficult ones. They include, not only for the later critic but also for the creative artist at work on his novel, the question of determining *what* is central and what secondary at a given moment. Is young Martin the centre of the story and does the centre therefore travel with him? Or is the centre where Old Martin and Pecksniff are? It cannot be claimed in any case that Dickens triumphantly surmounted all the difficulties and solved all the problems of this double narrative thread; but he certainly gave himself excellent training for his more sophisticated future work. If he failed to produce in *Martin Chuzzlewit* a wholly harmonized and integrated narrative, or to fuse the American episodes completely into the bulk of his English story, it is probably due in great measure to the relative extemporization, to the suddenness of Martin's announcement that he would go to the States and, in the last resort, to the nature of periodical publication and especially of periodical writing. When it appeared that circumstances made it opportune for Martin to leave

England, four complete numbers, or nearly one-quarter of the novel, had already seen the light of print and could no longer be altered or tampered with. What did not lead to Martin's expedition was there all the same, and still is.

And, indeed, what are the circumstances that cause Martin's departure and his choice of the United States as his goal? There is nothing improbable either in the departure or in the choice, under the circumstances of the story: a more or less gifted and less or more energetic young man who found himself at the end of his tether could hope to improve his finances by a spell of hard work in a country that must be recognized as developing, enterprising, resourceful, promising, and that had the further advantage of being, though remote, English-speaking. Australia and New Zealand no doubt offered similar prospects, but they were more distant, less advanced, less well known, and probably less attractive to readers of fiction as well as less easy to deal with for writers of fiction.[2] This was true at the time when *Chuzzlewit* was published. It must have been almost equally true at the time of the events narrated in the book. That time is never openly specified in the text of the novel, but there are signs that it does not go back in time beyond the 1830s. The characters still travel across England by coach and across the ocean aboard sailing ships, but steamers are to be seen in harbours and on rivers, and railway trains are used at least in the American episodes. The earliest railways had begun to run in England and in the United States in the late 1820s and early 1830s.

However, it is quite certain that Martin would not have gone to America – perhaps he would never have left Britain at all – if Dickens himself had not been through certain recent experiences memorable both in themselves and in their bitter aftermath. What happened is familiarly known. Charles Dickens had spent the first six months of the year 1842 in the United States. In the later part of 1841, while completing *Barnaby Rudge* and then beginning to recover from the protracted, almost uninterrupted, entirely colossal creative labours of the past five years, he had become possessed by a desire to see America and a conviction that he would be happy there, that he would find there a country in accordance with his wishes and ideals. He had had some flattering correspondence with distinguished American admirers, and he had received many expressions of a wish that he should go to the States and assurances that he would be received as a person of the first importance. Once he had made up his mind that he

must go, his iron will came into operation and stormed through
preparations. Dickens overcame, or ignored, all objections and
obstacles, including his wife Kate's tearful reluctance to leave four
very young children behind. It was out of the question that *she* should
be left behind to look after them; so they would be looked after by
Mrs. W. C. Macready, with some help from Dickens's younger
brother and other relatives. The question of money was solved just as
imperiously, and in a way which was characteristic of the position to
which Dickens had hoisted himself in the English publishing world.
His American correspondents invited him on Pickwickian terms, that
is, to travel at his own expense,[3] which was in any case the only status
he could think of accepting. But Dickens did not have large savings,
and he depended on his continued literary production. So he entered
into an original agreement with the firm of Chapman & Hall; while he
was travelling and for several months after his return, they would pay
him a substantial monthly allowance, to be deducted from later
earnings, produced by as yet unwritten and even unplanned books.
This meant that Dickens and his growing family would live on
anticipated earnings, and that Chapman & Hall felt they had better
run the risk of losing fairly large sums (should Dickens die suddenly,
or become incapacitated, or lazy, or otherwise reluctant or unable to
supply further popular masterpieces) than the risk of his moving to a
rival firm.

The mutual expectations of Dickens and America were high; the
eagerness to achieve an encounter was great on both sides. They may
not have been entirely clear-sighted or reasoned out. Michael Slater
has shown that there was an element of illusion and delusion in the
great expectations fostered on both sides.[4] Dickens believed himself to
be a democrat, possibly even a republican, for whom America must
indeed be the land of freedom, and thus politically and morally
exhilarating. America, or a number of literate Americans, shared that
view and could hope that they would at long last find in Dickens an
admiring and appreciative British visitor.

The interest aroused by the United States was not restricted to
England. Alexis de Tocqueville was sent by the French government in
1831–2 to investigate the American penitentiary system. His book, *De
la démocratie en Amérique* (1835–40), was widely read and influential.
Though Dickens does not anywhere mention Tocqueville by name, it
is not unlikely that he had come across his work and derived from it
some of his sanguine expectations.

It was more or less understood from the first that Dickens would take notes and publish an account of his visit when he returned home, in the form of a travel book rather than a novel. The early stages of Dickens's first American visit in 1842 could only encourage the mutual illusion, for there was euphoria and enthusiasm during the few days in Boston. From the start, certainly, Dickens entertained minor reservations about the American way of life and especially about American manners; but he proved remarkably, unexpectedly, uncharacteristically patient, as though he had been determined to be pleased. It must be admitted that, though profoundly and representatively English in many respects, Dickens was not on the whole chauvinistic or xenophobic. Very few of his remarks about the States, whether in *American Notes* or in *Chuzzlewit* or in his private correspondence, amount to a denial of the right of a foreign nation to be foreign, that is, to be different from the English. There are a few exceptions. *Chuzzlewit* includes some hostile generalizations about Americans. In chapter XXI, for instance, the narrator writes: 'within the house and without, wherever half a dozen people were collected together . . . They[5] did the same things; said the same things; judged all subjects by, and reduced all subjects to, the same standard' (XXI, 415/349). Such a charge of uniformity can only be proffered against a nation by an external observer who has been unwilling or unable to take note of the more subtle differences within that nation. But simplifications of that kind remain rare in the novel.

In any case, Dickens's somewhat negative attitude was fostered by his rapid disillusionment, his personal problems and a number of specific objections by which he let his mind become clouded. The first shock that significantly altered his basic attitude seems to have occurred in New York, when Dickens took advantage of three days' illness to read the American press. He was appalled by the nature and tone of its comments about himself and his wife, and by its almost unanimous disapproval of what he had said about the need for an international copyright. Dickens expressed extraordinarily vivid indignation in a letter to one of the friends he had made in Boston: 'I vow to Heaven that the scorn and indignation I have felt under this unmanly and ungenerous treatment has been to me an amount of agony such as I never experienced since by birth.'[6] In this excessive but characteristic outburst he seemed to be forgetting such episodes as the death of his young sister-in-law Mary Hogarth five years before.

Once his disillusionment had made itself felt, it grew apace. It fed on a number of specific objections. The most respectable was his disapproval of slavery, still in existence in the southern States. Later he would undergo the influence of Carlyle's pamphlet *Occasional Discourse on the Nigger Question* (November 1849). He would even, again following Carlyle, rise in defence of Governor Eyre's ruthless repression of a Jamaican mutiny in 1865.[7] But in the early 1840s Dickens was still an uninhibited supporter of emancipation. His other objections to America appear less serious, but some of them may have rankled more, possibly because they concerned the background of his daily life and thus weighed on him, personally, to a greater extent. He was, for instance, disgusted by the Americans' table manners, by their habit of spitting in public places (including confined spaces like railway carriages and small steamers), by their general lack of cleanliness,[8] and by what he regarded as a lack of proper respect for his privacy, amounting to rudeness and indiscretion. The American press, in its chauvinistic pride, irritated him by supporting every American habit, every single element of the American way of life, and by its intolerance of even the slightest criticism or reservation about America. With regard to the inadequacies and the crudeness of the American press, or a large part of it, in the early 1840s, Dickens had a point, and much reason to grumble. Noel C. Peyrouton, in an article devoted to the reports of the 'Boz Dinner' in Boston, unearthed specimens showing that it was almost impossible to caricature the lower kind of American journalist of the time.[9]

On one point, however, while possibly minimizing the reality of his own experiences, Dickens went beyond what was probable in the case of his hero: the way in which Boz had been treated with extreme and indiscreet curiosity was accounted for by his being a celebrity; when Martin, a poor immigrant and hardly budding architect, is made to hold a levee and shake hundreds of hands, it really appears that the novelist is determined to exploit his own misadventures and take his revenge, with little regard for verisimilitude.

Finally, there is one item which may have influenced Dickens's unfavourable reactions, though it is not mentioned either in *American Notes* or in *Chuzzlewit*, and does not play any great part even in the letters to his friends, and that is the intense weariness of constant travelling. Anyone who has been on even a short lecturing tour knows how much it takes out of you to meet new people in new places every day, to have to watch yourself permanently, to be as it were on tap as well as on display at every stop. Multiplying such impressions by twenty would give some idea of what must have been Dickens's case. Besides, it should be remembered that the young author who travelled in the United States in 1842 had been working inordinately hard for years already. Members of his family and of his inner circle of friends would later complain that Dickens exhausted them as well as himself by his lack of ability to give himself any rest, by his inability to rest and relax. He always tended to take his holidays strenuously and frantically.[10] Certainly, in 1842, weariness reinforced his discontent and accounted in part for his ill-humour and moments of misanthropy (in the form of anti-Americanism).[11]

Dickens's impressions of America are available in three forms. There are his letters to his friends at home, mainly to John Forster, who was under strict injunction to circulate the letters judiciously, but also to preserve them, for the novelist had every intention to use them, sometimes verbatim, in his forthcoming travel-book. Then there is the travel-book, entitled *American Notes for General Circulation*, brought out a few months after Dickens's return to England. Lastly, there are the American episodes of *Martin Chuzzlewit*. There is a gradation from letters to *Notes* to novel, and the whole history is illuminating to the reader of *Chuzzlewit*.

The most striking aspect of the letters is probably their change of tone, from initial exhilaration to the depths of disenchantment, then to frantic and somewhat childish excitement at the thought of going home. Dickens, who had had to deploy a great deal of imperious energy in order to satisfy his vivid desire to see America, seemed long before the end of his trip to regard himself as an unfortunate exile, a transported convict, who had been wrenched away from his native land and made to wander and labour abroad. At any rate, the thought of seeing home once again sent him into a state of agitation and expectancy such that he could not contain himself. On 26 May 1842, for instance, he wrote to Forster: 'We shall soon meet, please God, and be happier and merrier than ever we were, in all our lives. . . . Oh home – home – home – home – home – home – HOME!!!!!!!!!!!!'[12]

Then came the publication of *American Notes* on 19 October 1842. It showed a sharp deterioration in Dickens's view of America, due in great part to the appearance in August in a New York paper of a forged letter purporting to have been written by Dickens, but with which he had had nothing to do, even if the sentiments expressed in it were not very different from his real opinions at the time.[13] This incident, and the bad faith of some American editors, had again rubbed Dickens in a sore spot and incensed him against the whole of the American press. This had a regrettable influence on the writing of *American Notes*. It took all of Forster's persuasiveness to prevent Dickens from printing a motto which made the reference of the title more explicit. It would have been given as a quotation from some *Old Bailey Report*, and ran thus: 'In reply to a question from the Bench, the Solicitor for the Bank observed, that this kind of notes circulated the most extensively, in those parts of the world where they were stolen or forged.'[14] Forster was also influential, less felicitously, in cancelling a preface which he later reproduced in his biography of his friend, and in which Boz explained why he did not mention in the book the reception given to him in America: 'not because I am, or ever was, insensible to that spontaneous effusion of affection and generosity of heart in a most affectionate and generous-hearted people; but because I conceive that it would ill become me to flourish matter necessarily involving so much of my own praises, in the eyes of my unhappy readers'.[15] Those lines were more dignified and friendly than anything to be found in the book itself. One can only surmise that Forster was, however incompetently, more anti-American than his friend.

*American Notes* is not one of Dickens's major works. It is unexciting, not to say dull. Dickens had hoped that it contained a lesson which might be taken to heart by American readers, and thus contribute in changing America for the better. He harboured illusions about the strength of the book; so did his American critics in the New York press and elsewhere, who attached more importance to a minor performance than circumstances justified. The Oxford Illustrated edition of *American Notes* (in which the work is coupled with Dickens's only other travelogue, *Pictures from Italy*) has an introduction by Sacheverell Sitwell, written in a tone of pleasant innocence. Sitwell was struck, significantly, by the only characteristic that *American Notes* does not possess, its great length. It is in fact, mercifully, one of the shortest of Dickens's works. But it may be thought still too long for what it has to say.

Apart from the narrative of the crossing, which does not particularly concern Americans, the real overture to the visit is the chapter about Boston, which begins in a very good-humoured as well as humorous tone, though on the very second page there is a brief angry outburst about 'that most hideous blot and foul disgrace – Slavery'.[16] Dickens finds a great deal to praise, though he begins early to deride American English, and his comments on Emerson and Transcendentalism are slightly condescending: 'This gentleman has written a volume of Essays, in which, among much that is dreamy and fanciful . . . there is much more that is true and manly, honest and bold. Transcendentalism has its occasional vagaries (what school has not?)' (III, 57). In these early stages, Dickens seems happy, for instance when meeting enlightened working girls in Lowell. He speaks mostly of places, landscapes, buildings, objects, and there is perhaps a conscious avoidance of people. The tone undergoes a spectacular change with the New York section, especially after Dickens has paid a visit to the terrible prison ominously called The Tombs. Yet, even after that, there is an expression of strong attachment to the United States and to the author's American friends:

> I never thought that going back to England, returning to all who are dear to me, and to pursuits that have insensibly grown to be a part of my nature, I could have felt so much sorrow as I endured, when I parted at last, on board this ship, with the friends who had accompanied me from this city. (VI, 96)

Then the protests against spitting – that is, against the constant expectoration of tobacco juice by tobacco-chewers – become obtrusive, but they are overshadowed by Dickens's powerful indignation aroused by the Philadelphia Prison. The system practised there was the 'separate system', also known as the solitary or the cellular system. It was based on having the prisoners occupy individual cells day and night, never seeing their fellow-prisoners, or even their warders.[17] By the time Dickens reaches Washington, DC, his patience wears thin, and spitting (and other forms of uncleanliness) makes his blood boil: 'those two odious practices of chewing and expectorating began about this time to be anything but agreeable, and soon became most offensive and sickening' (VIII, 112). Slavery comes into the picture, and Dickens grows satirical at the expense of Congress. Here and there in the later chapters can be found a few remarks that one might term ethno-psychological, some of which are harmless rather than offensive, and perhaps justified: 'whenever an Englishman would cry "All right!" an American cries "Go ahead!" which is somewhat expressive of the national character of the two countries' (IX, 131). Dickens then goes on denouncing personal uncleanliness among Americans, to an extent which may appear amusing and paradoxical to a late-twentieth-century European traveller, but he also takes every opportunity of paying compliments, like this about Cincinnati: 'The society with which I mingled, was intelligent, courteous, and agreeable. The inhabitants of Cincinnati are proud of their city as one of the most interesting in America: and with good reason' (XI, 164). Unfortunately, Dickens did a great deal of travelling by river-steamer, and he hated it. There is a perceptible resumption of good spirits when the Prairie is reached, obviously because it is the furthest point to be visited, the point from which begins the journey back. He shows great interest in Indians and their fate. He writes a special chapter on slavery, as a kind of appendix after narrating the passage home; he has acquired no manifest expertise in the field of slavery, though he has collected, and now prints, a few original documents. Then come his concluding remarks, some of which are favourable: Americans, he says, 'are, by nature, frank, brave, cordial, hospitable, and affectionate. Cultivation and refinement seem but to enhance their warmth of heart and ardent enthusiasm', so that an American can be 'one of the most endearing and most generous of friends'. But there are reservations also, because their qualities are 'sadly sapped and blighted in their growth among the mass; and that there are influences at work which endanger them still more, and give but little present promise of their healthy restoration; is a truth that ought to be told' (XVIII, 244). Dickens then proceeds to attack the dishonesty of Americans, their commercial habits, their press, their lack of humour ('They certainly are not a humorous people, and their temperament always impressed me as being of a dull and gloomy character': XVIII, 248), and their dirt.

Every late edition of *American Notes*, as of *Martin Chuzzlewit*, carries the postscript written after Dickens's second visit to the United States, in 1867–8, and destined to make amends for his former strictures by admitting that there have been spectacular improvements in many directions.[18]

Dickens was undoubtedly sincere, and he may even have been right, in claiming that he never was anti-American; but this amounted to asserting that what he disliked about Americans was only what was dislikeable in them, that when he grew angry against them it was because they made him angry. None of which was likely to soothe their hurt pride or prove acceptable to them. While it is true, as was seen above, that Dickens had very little chauvinism in him,[19] yet his reactions to the United States were conditioned by his own profound

Englishness. He did not praise England to the skies; on the contrary, he was ready enough to criticize English habits and institutions or the English character. *Chuzzlewit*, particularly, was written in great part as a protest against hypocrisy as the British national vice. But whether he liked it or not, whether he was conscious of it or not, many of the American traits that he disapproved of were consequences of the fact that Americans were different, were, as Mr Podsnap would have said (twenty-two years later, in *Our Mutual Friend*), 'Not English'.

In any case, there is no doubt that *American Notes* displeased Dickens's American friends and was rejected indignantly by a fair proportion of the American press. Its publication was the occasion of a lively controversy. Some impression of it can be gained by consulting Fred G. Kitton's *Dickensiana* (1886), a forerunner of Philip Collins's volume in the 'Critical Heritage' series. It is significant that in a collection of early reviews of Dickens's works Kitton should devote seventeen pages to *American Notes*, referring to and/or quoting from fourteen reviews of that work, while only one page is given to a single review of *Chuzzlewit*. Extracts from American articles on the travel-book can show how much ill-humour Dickens's comments on the United States had aroused. For instance, J. P. Thomson, writing in the *New Englander* (Boston and New York, January 1843), said:

We should hardly have thought it possible for so many pages of Notes on America to be written, and so little to be said in them which is of the least importance to the reader. The experiment, however, has been successfully made, and Mr Dickens has proved himself to be utterly incompetent to write anything which does not savour strongly of his former occupation . . . We regret that Mr Dickens has published these volumes; for they bear the mark of hasty compositon, evince no genius, add nothing to the author's reputation as a writer, and exhibit his moral character in a most undesirable light.

And an anonymous contributor to the *Southern Literary Messenger* (of Richmond, Virginia, January 1843) called *American Notes* 'utterly weak, frivolous, and inconclusive throughout' before asserting:

Although the greater part of this book should only call forth a pitying smile at the vanity and folly of its author, his bitter assaults and foul calumnies in relation to an institution which he has not really troubled himself to understand in any of its bearings deserve the indignant scorn of an insulted and slandered people.[20]

The slandered institution which Dickens has failed to understand was of course Negro slavery.

There was therefore, subsequently to the publication of *American Notes*, a great deal of mutual ill-humour between Dickens and his American critics. In his defence, to a certain extent, may be quoted the British reaction, voiced by James Spedding in the *Edinburgh Review* of January 1843: 'To us it appears that Mr Dickens deserves great praise for the care with which he has avoided all offensive topics, and abstained from amusing his readers at the expense of his entertainers.'[21] Unfortunately, by writing *American Notes*, Dickens had also signally failed to entertain his entertainers.

In addition to the disagreeable phases of this controversy, there was, as has been mentioned before, disappointment over the sales of the early numbers of *Chuzzlewit*, and the imminent financial danger which the general public's apparent reluctance to take the new novel to their hearts represented for the author. This unsatisfactory situation created an urgent need to do something, to introduce some major change that would make *Chuzzlewit* popularly attractive. By sending Martin across the Atlantic, at a time when it was generally known that Dickens had a grudge against America, it could be hoped that the Weller effect might be repeated. Might not America turn out to be the Sam Weller of *Chuzzlewit*, the novelty that would force the story out of the rut of moderate success into the empyrean of wild and remunerative popularity? The same role might have been played by a character whose originality was comparable to Sam's, Mrs Gamp, but it seems that the urge to say more about America carried the day. That was the card played by Dickens for all it was worth. Judging by the plethora of books devoted to the United States and by the success of many, high hopes could indeed be entertained.[22]

In order to exploit his recent American experiences in his current novel, Dickens reworked portions of his letters, as he had already done in *American Notes*. But he did so with what Harry Stone calls 'increasing artistic sophistication'[23] and, in a process of further deterioration of his feelings about America, deliberately omitted the aspects he had liked and admired, like Niagara.

Martin Chuzzlewit's career in the United States is not in itself a fascinating subject for study. What does he do and see in America?

The answer is he does not do very much, except go from one place to another, fall ill, get cured and return home. But he sees and undergoes a great deal, and this has such an effect on him that his American experiences may be regarded as opening his eyes to some moral realities, to some unpalatable truths about himself, so that, if he does not act, he changes, he matures. The two climactic elements of his experience are his repeated exposure to the American character (as interpreted by Dickens) and his prolonged exposure to the deleterious climate of Eden, a settlement where he lets himself be swindled into purchasing property. It is based on a place called Cairo (in Illinois), which Dickens had seen and taken a dislike to. There is a lugubrious description of it in *American Notes*:

We arrived at a spot so much more desolate than any we had beheld, that the forlornest places we have passed, were, in comparison with it, full of interest. At the junction of the two rivers [Mississippi and Ohio], on ground so flat and low and marshy, that at certain seasons of the year it is inundated to the house-tops, lies a breeding-place of fever, ague, and death; vaunted in England as a mine of Golden Hope, and speculated in, on the faith of monstrous representations, to many people's ruin. A dismal swamp, on which the half-built houses rot away: cleared, here and there, for the space of a few yards; and teeming, then, with rank unwholesome vegetation, in whose baleful shade the wretched wanderers who are tempted hither, drop, and die, and lay their bones; the hateful Mississippi circling and eddying before it, and turning off upon its southern course a slimy monster hideous to behold; a hotbed of disease, an ugly sepulchre, a grave uncheered by any gleam of promise; a place without a single quality, in earth or air or water, to commend it: such is the dismal Cairo. (XII, 171)[24]

This obviously overwritten paragraph, a purple patch of a kind, conveys a strange animosity. It has not been proved, and it is indeed improbable, that Dickens himself had bought land in Cairo and lost heavily in the speculation; but perhaps he knew people who had gone through such an experience, or perhaps he was simply shocked by the contrast between advertisements seen back in England and the unpleasant reality of the place. In any case, the accumulation of disparaging epithets is striking: *desolate, forlornest, flat, low, monstrous, dismal, rank unwholesome, baleful, wretched, hateful, slimy, hideous, ugly, dismal*; Dickens's dislike extends to the Mississippi in general, thus contradicting much literary celebration of the same river. There is something personal in this animus, which remains intriguing. The episode in *Chuzzlewit* which is based on it is not without force, however. It has been claimed that in the Eden scenes there was something of the spirit later to be found in Conrad's *Heart of Darkness*.[25]

If Dickens's attack against America culminates in this episode or sequence of episodes, it is because 'Eden' combines natural disadvantages (those of a wild country) and the ruthless exploitation of the gullibility of immigrants. One cannot blame America for being made up in part of insalubrious areas and as yet unclaimed land. One can, and in Dickens's opinion one must, protest against the dishonesty of people who sell that land, make a profit on it and doom the excessively trustful English to disease and death. One also has to blame the press, or public opinion, who do not disapprove of such malpractices.

For there is in *Martin Chuzzlewit* much violent satire of the United States. One of the most famous sections, in the American part of *Chuzzlewit*, is the 'Watertoast' incident. Watertoast is a place where Martin and Mark, travelling away from New York by rail, arrive on the first evening of their journey. They spend the night in the 'National Hotel', call at a land agent's the next morning and purchase an allotment in Eden, then leave to reach their property by river-steamer. In Watertoast, they are given a chance of attending a meeting of the Watertoast Association of United Sympathizers, and Martin is compelled (under threat of violence) to hold a levee, to shake hands with hundreds of Watertoasters. The meeting of the Association is held in order to give support to 'a certain public man in Ireland' (XXI, 425/360) who is fighting for the good cause of Freedom against British oppression. The meeting goes very well, or at least very vociferously, until a letter arrives in the course of the proceedings, by which it is revealed that the Irishman is in reality a traitor to the cause of Freedom. In fact, he favours the emancipation of Negro slaves. The Watertoast Association is therefore immediately dissolved. This incident was of course criticized as totally improbable when *Chuzzlewit* was first published; Dickens defended himself in the prefaces of 1849 (Cheap Edition) and 1867 (Charles Dickens Edition). K. J. Fielding has shown that the Irishman referred to was Daniel O'Connell, and quotes a letter written by him in March 1843 to

protest against the publication by an American paper of a supposed
letter by himself. There was thus a limited amount of sympathy
between O'Connell and Dickens, as far as their respective attitudes to
the United States and complaints about the American press were
concerned. But of course the novelist had not gone into all the
political implications of either the Irish question or the problem of
Negro emancipation.[26] Dickens himself had mentioned that the real
name of his model for the Watertoast Association had been a certain
'Brandywine Association', whose proceedings he had almost literally
transcribed.

George Gissing considers that 'Dickens in America was Dickens the
satirist without counterpoise of his native tenderness',[27] and it is true
that the attack is at times unmitigated. The central objection at the
core of Dickens's enmity is excellently summed up by J. Hillis Miller
when he writes that 'Dickens' America is an entire society which lives
as pure surface, a surface which hides a profound void'.[28] Of course,
such a fundamental condemnation of a whole as complex and vast as a
large country is unfair and simplifying. Dickens did attempt to restore
the balance by showing his readers at least one good American, in the
person of Mr Bevan, from Massachusetts, whom Martin meets in New
York and who befriends and helps him in a variety of generous ways.
Theoretically, even one Bevan should be enough to redeem America; a
country which can beget a just man, clear-sighted enough to see the
defects of his compatriots though not ready to desert them, is not lost.
However, the uses to which Dickens put his good American prevent
him from offering a balanced view of American realities, for he throws
his weight almost wholly on the side of the author's harshest
criticisms. Mr Bevan appears mainly in chapters XVI and XVII.
Instead of countering Martin's strictures, he reinforces them by saying
things like: 'You are right. So very right, that I believe no satirist
could breathe this air. If another Juvenal or Swift could rise up among
us to-morrow, he would be hunted down' (XVI, 339/276). Or:

I do not find and cannot believe, and therefore will not allow that
we are a model of wisdom, and an example to the world, and the
perfection of human reason; and a great deal more to the same
purpose, which you may hear any hour in the day. (XVII, 342/279)

Admittedly, Mr Bevan is not denied the right to aim a few shafts at
England, as when he says that in the field of education 'We shine out

brightly in comparison with England, certainly, but hers is a very extreme case' (XVII, 342/279). Yet such fleeting admissions seem to be there partly in order to reassure the reader that Bevan is a trustworthy witness and that his most severe reproaches levelled at America must be accepted at their face value. Enlisting one, so to speak, schismatic American in the anti-American crusade of Martin Chuzzlewit and Charles Dickens was at any rate unlikely to reconcile transatlantic critics and readers angered by what they saw as systematic enmity and constant unfairness. It is difficult to question the rightness of Harry Stone's conclusion on this point when he says that 'Mr Bevan is so wooden and Anglicized a Dickensian mouthpiece that he serves as an additional indictment of America rather than as a believable symbol of America's basic soundness'.[29]

A final sample of Dickens's treatment of American realities can be provided by an examination of the speech of his American characters. Even in his early and on the whole benevolent private letters about his American visit, Dickens shows amusement at the variety of English spoken by the citizens of the United States. He obviously prided himself on his own ability to observe and render the differences between British and American English. He was convinced that British English was superior or, simply, was right, and American English wrong and on the whole ridiculous. There exists thus, on this particular point of language, that refusal of otherness, of the right to be different, which is so rarely observable in Dickens. His treatment of American English in *Martin Chuzzlewit* seems to have attracted rather less critical attention than other aspects of that novel or even of its American episodes. Ralph Waldo Emerson, one of Dickens's American friends for a time, wrote in his journal, after reading *American Notes*: 'He has picked up and noted with eagerness each odd local phrase that he met with, and, when he had a story to relate, he joined them together, so that the result is the broadest caricature.'[30] Emerson saw that the speech, like the manners, of Dickens's American characters was a thing of shreds and patches, concentrating peculiarities from diverse origins, and thus artificial and unlike reality. And Randolph Quirk comments on 'the alleged American liking for periphrasis' which, he claims, is 'taken as a sign, not only of genteelness but of an allied pomposity and ponderousness with which Dickens does not hesitate to link aspects of pronunciation in the unkinder chapters of *Chuzzlewit*'.[31]

It may be of interest to observe that Dickens makes fun, for instance, of the emphatic pronunciation of *to* as *toe* in American (for example, XXII, 433/367), but that this peculiarity will later be found ascribed in *Bleak House* (1852–3) to Mr Chadband, a loud and inane preacher; so that seems to imply that it is the kind of affectation which Dickens instinctively connects with the speech of a hypocritical windbag. In chapter XXXIII one comes across the name 'Illi*noy*', thus spelt and emphasized as if to show that Americans have funny ways of pronouncing even the words that belong solely to their country. Dickens does not tell us how they should pronounce the name of Illinois, but it is clear that he does not approve of their way of doing it, nor perhaps recognize their right to decide in such matters (XXXIII, 592/521). Mostly, however, American speech and its tendency to excessive emphasis are ridiculed by means of a complex system of capital letters and hyphens, a system which is neither entirely clear nor entirely coherent (not everybody knows, for instance, how to make a capital initial *sound* different from a lower-case letter). Here is a typical example (XXXIV, 612/538): 'The name Of Pogram will be proud Toe jine you. And may it, My friends, be written on My Tomb, "He was a member of the Con-gress of our common country, and was act-Tive in his trust".' It would thus seem that American rhetoric consists partly in emphasizing the less important words, and making pauses in odd places inside long words.

While correcting the proofs, Dickens clearly gave great attention to his American episodes. It is thus interesting to note that he decided to omit one of the few compliments he was ready to pay America, though it concerned its landscape only. It was at proof stage that Mark and Martin's first view of the United States from the deck of their steamer ceased to be one of 'noble heights, and lovely islands' as on first proof, to become simply one of 'some heights, and islands'. On the other hand, the novelist gave up his intention of printing at the end of the fourth paragraph of chapter XXI this further taunt about America: 'Great Republics flaunting a Lie before the world, make their sons false to their professed Institutions; false to themselves; false to each other; false to all mankind' (XXI, 406/341) – though it is doubtful whether this omission was intended to soften the satire. A little later, irony replaces plain statement without decreasing the force of the attack. The narrator has been speaking of American gentlemen in general and their way of life as observed by Martin Chuzzlewit. In the text as printed we read that 'Martin even began to comprehend their being the social, cheerful, winning, airy men they were', while in manuscript what he comprehended was their being 'the listless, weary, apathetic clods they were' (XXI, 349; Penguin 415).

The hostile attitude of the novelist understandably antagonized his American critics. The notorious article in *Brother Jonathan* (July 1843) is typical of the indignation aroused, though not of the highest critical abilities called into play: 'Scarcely were eyes ever laid upon anything in which the spirit of malignity and thorough hatred were more conspicuous'; the writer then denounces 'the utter impotency of infuriate malice' and hits on the curiously effective device of speaking henceforth of Dickens as 'the Dickens'; he accuses 'the Dickens' of having been out to make money during his trip, of having been disappointed at the indifference to his person among the American population, when he 'departed on a short tour of espionage to the West, a sadder and a madder man' and concluded that the citizens of a much maligned country could 'despise his narrow and bitter spirit of prejudice'.[32]

By 1861 criticism had become more discriminating, and an anonymous reviewer of the Library edition of *Chuzzlewit* wrote as follows about the question of satire and exaggeration: 'the whole representation of America may be more ludicrous than America is in reality; but the separate facts are not exaggerated, farther than the skill of the artist, which brings out forcibly every point he takes, makes a certain degree of exaggeration inevitable'.[33]

So, it was only in the late 1860s, after Dickens's second visit to the States, that reconcilement would be effected. The 'Postscript' bears eloquent witness to a complete change of mood.[34]

Reactions to these episodes have been varied. Norman and Jeanne MacKenzie quote in their biography of Dickens two persons who expressed intense amusement. One was no less than the author in person, writing in July 1843: 'I have nearly killed myself with laughing at what I have done of the American No. – though how much comicality may be in my knowledge of its Truth, I can't say'; the other was Thomas Carlyle, who confided in a letter to John Forster: 'The last *Chuzzlewit* on Yankee-doodledum is capital. We read it with loud assent, loud cachinnatory approval!'[35] Of course most Americans failed to kill themselves with laughing or to indulge in 'loud cachinnatory approval'. Yet it has also been felt that, even if the satire could be condoned, artistic reservations should be voiced as to the value of the American sections of the novel. It is difficult to claim that they are entirely successful. Edward J. Evans, in one of the

studies devoted specifically to that part of the book, protests against
the view that it is an excrescence.[36] Yet his feeling that he has to
refute the opposite view is evidence of the persistence and force of that
view. The very words 'unaccountable excrescence', to which Evans
takes exception, are quoted from an early British review of the novel.

The 'excrescence' theory tends to be successfully contradicted
nowadays. It was all very well to put forward such an objection in the
days when Dickens was admired for being in the main an inspired
extemporizer of ungainly and exuberant comic masterpieces. Now that
he is given greater credit for artistic organization and intent, the
connection between American and English scenes in *Chuzzlewit* is
more readily accepted. As we have seen, the worst that can be alleged
against Dickens's American characters in the novel is that they are no
better than their British counterparts, whereas they ought to be
better, given their form of government and their shorter history. Of
course there is less variety among the American characters, and not
one of them is examined in depth, and that may be a deficiency of the
overall picture, because it makes it appear more unfavourable than it
basically is, even in comparison with England. But Scadder is not
worse than Tigg, or Chollop than Jonas. John Holloway has brilliantly
demonstrated the similarities between, for instance, Mr Norris and
Mr Pecksniff.[37] One presumably unprejudiced commentator, however,
points to what he regards as Dickens's perception of a significant
difference between British and American dishonesty. Northrop Frye
writes:

> American shysters are no better and no worse than their British
> counterparts, but there is a more theoretical element in their lying,
> and bluster about their enlightened political institutions is much
> more used as a cover for swindling. In America, in other words, the
> complacent Podsnap and the rascally Lammle are more likely to be
> associated in the same person.[38]

There may be a great deal of truth in this, though in 1843 Dickens
had probably not yet sorted out his views as to the Podsnappishness
and Lammleity of the English people, whereas in the 1860s he must
have been more impressed by the deplorable fallibility of human
beings in general than by the generic or genetic deficiencies of
individual ethnic communities. Even in 1843, according to C. A.
Bodelsen,

If Dickens's American critics had read *Martin Chuzzlewit* with a lower blood-pressure they would have discovered that the American and the English scenes are used as parallel examples of two societies that have both, though in different ways, erected acquisitiveness into a principle.[39]

But a low blood-pressure was by no means what Dickens had aimed at, either in himself or in his American readers.

To sum up, there is not very much in the American scenes of *Chuzzlewit* which can be proved untruthful,[40] but they are marked by a definite lack of sympathetic acceptance, in spite of Michael Slater's overall impression that Dickens was a 'natural American'.[41] It is not to be denied that comic effects are often achieved, and many critics and readers have continued to enjoy them.[42] No one need deny that there are occasional moments of superb comedy in what might be called the American notes of *Martin Chuzzlewit*, what Albert J. Guerard terms 'a pure creative joy in grotesque invention'.[43] The unevenness of the American chapters seems to have been caught in Angus Wilson's terse conclusion: 'good, often inspired journalism, although somewhat repetitious'.[44] In other words, the chapters did a little, but not perhaps anything decisive, to enliven the pages of *Chuzzlewit* and ensure its emergence from relative unpopularity. The sales figures which Dickens found disappointing and alarming were so only in comparison with his own former triumph. They were alarming only because he had accustomed himself to living on a scale justified by exceptional popularity, and overoptimistically anticipated the earnings from his new work. Hence his disenchantment and anxiety, certainly not justified by any failure in his power of entertaining and delighting the reader.

## NOTES: CHAPTER 4

1  *Pickwick Papers*, Oxford Illustrated edition (1948), ch. XLV, p. 638.
2  Dickens does send a bunch of characters to Australia at the end of *David Copperfield*, but he does not go with them.
3  See *Pickwick Papers*, Oxford Illustrated edition, ch. I, p. 2: 'That this Association cordially recognises the principle of every member . . . defraying his own travelling expenses.'
4  See his *Dickens on America and the Americans* (Brighton, 1979), an excellent book to which the present chapter obviously owes a great deal; see in particular pp. 3, 8 and 9.
5  In the original manuscript Dickens had used the ironical form *These choice spirits* instead of *They*.

6  *The Pilgrim Edition of the Letters of Charles Dickens*, Vol. 3 (Oxford, 1974), p. 77.

7  See Michael Goldberg, *Carlyle and Dickens* (Athens, Ga, 1972), and Fred Kaplan, *Thomas Carlyle: A Biography* (Ithaca, NY, 1983).

8  On these points – table manners, spitting and cleanliness – a recent article by Dean Hughes ('Great expectorations: Dickens on America', *Dickensian*, vol. 79, no. 400 (1983), pp. 66–76) shows that Dickens's criticism was on the whole justified.

9  See 'Bozmania vs. Bozphobia: a Yankee pot-pourri', *Dickens Studies*, vol. 4, no. 1 (1968), pp. 78–94. Noel Peyrouton, who died prematurely in 1968, was himself an American and a Bostonian, and cannot be suspected of anti-American prejudice. See also Paul P. Davis, 'Dickens and the American press, 1842', *Dickens Studies*, vol. 4, no. 1 (1968), pp. 32–77, and K. J. Fielding, '*Martin Chuzzlewit* and "The Liberator" ', *Notes and Queries*, vol. 198, no. 6 (1953), pp. 254–6. This is confirmed by another American scholar, Harry Stone, in 'Dickens' use of his American experiences in *Martin Chuzzlewit*', *PMLA*, vol. 72, no. 3 (1957), p. 472.

10 See Philip Collins (ed.), *Dickens: Interviews and Recollections*, 2 vols (London, 1981), e.g. Vol. 1, p. 133.

11 Jerome Meckier sees Dickens as having experienced more profound personal, social and political disillusionment with America. See his valuable article 'Dickens discovers America, Dickens discovers Dickens: the first visit reconsidered', *Modern Language Review*, Vol. 79 (1984), pp. 266–77.

12 *Letters*, Vol. 3, p. 248.

13 See Slater, op. cit., p. 21, and *Letters*, Vol. 3, pp. 625–7.

14 See Slater, op. cit., p. 22.

15 ibid.

16 *American Notes*, Oxford Illustrated edition (1957), ch. III, p. 26. Further references to the text of *American Notes* will be to the same edition, and given in the form of chapter- and page-numbers in parenthesis (thus, here, III, 26).

17 See Philip Collins, *Dickens and Crime* (London, 1962), pp. 57–60. Collins points to the distinction between that system and the 'silent system' practised by Dickens's friend George Laval Chesterton, governor and reformer of the Coldbath Fields prison. Under the silent system the prisoners would sleep in dormitories and work in association, though they were forbidden ever to speak with one another.

18 See below, Chapter 11.

19 See Edgar Johnson, 'Dickens's anti-chauvinism', in Clyde de L. Ryals (ed.), *Nineteenth-Century Literary Perspectives* (Durham, NC, 1974), pp. 201–10, and Steven Marcus, *Dickens from Pickwick to Dombey* (New York, 1965), pp. 248 and 250–1.

20 *Dickensiana* (London, 1886), pp. 238–40.

21 See ibid., p. 236.

22 Frances Trollope had certainly made money with her *Domestic Manners of the Americans* (1832). See M. Pachter and F. Wein (eds), *Abroad in America: Visitors to the New Nation, 1776–1914* (New York, 1976), and Michael Slater (ed.), *Dickens on America and the Americans* (Brighton, 1979).

23 Stone, op. cit., p. 466.

24 On his return to Cincinnati, Dickens was to come once more in sight 'of the detestable morass called Cairo' (XIV, 187).

25 See Marcus, op. cit., p. 254.

26 See Fielding, op. cit., and Lowell L. Blaisdell, 'The origins of the satire of the Watertoast episode of *Martin Chuzzlewit*', *Dickensian*, vol. 77 no. 2 (1981), pp. 92–101.

27 George Gissing, *The Immortal Dickens* (London, 1925), p. 117.

28 J. Hillis Miller, *Charles Dickens: The World of His Novels* (Cambridge, Mass., 1958), p. 130.

29  Stone, op. cit., p. 469.
30  25 November 1842; quoted in Stephen Wall (ed.), *Charles Dickens: A Critical Anthology* (Harmondsworth, 1970), p. 62.
31  Randolph Quirk, *The Linguist and the English Language* (London, 1974), p. 27, n. 25.
32  Reprinted in *Dickensian*, vol. 10, no. 4 (1914), pp. 97–8. Only one-third of *Chuzzlewit* had appeared before *Brother Jonathan* reviewed it.
33  Philip Collins (ed.), *Dickens: The Critical Heritage* (London, 1971), p. 195.
34  See below, Chapter 11.
35  *Dickens: A Life* (Oxford, 1979), pp. 142–3.
36  See Edward J. Evans, 'The established self: the American episodes of *Martin Chuzzlewit*', *Dickens Studies Annual 5*, ed. Robert B. Partlow, Jr (1976), pp. 59–73.
37  See John Holloway's 'Dickens and the symbol' in Michael Slater (ed.), *Dickens 1970* (London, 1970), pp. 68–72.
38  Northrop Frye, 'Dickens and the comedy of humors' (from R. H. Pearce (ed.), *Experience in the Novel*, New York, 1968), in Ian Watt (ed.), *The Victorian Novel: Modern Essays in Criticism* (London, 1971), p. 56. Podsnap and Lammle are well-known characters in *Our Mututal Friend* (1864–5).
39  *Essays and Papers* (Copenhagen, 1964), p. 42.
40  Harry Stone, op. cit., p. 477, even asserts that they are 'too real, too factual', and that it is paradoxically one of their great faults.
41  Slater, *Dickens on America*, p. 67.
42  Not only G. K. Chesterton and Sir Arthur Quiller-Couch, but also a recent commentator like John Lucas (*The Melancholy Man: A Study of Dickens's Novels* (London, 1970), see p. 125) is shaken out of his predominant gloom to find the American scenes very funny.
43  Albert J. Guerard, *The Triumph of the Novel: Dickens, Dostoevsky, Faulkner* (New York, 1976), p. 246.
44  Angus Wilson, *The World of Charles Dickens* (New York, 1970), p. 160.

# CHAPTER 5

# Mrs Gamp and Mrs Harris

The enormous importance and the lasting fame of Mrs Gamp are not to be accounted for on statistical ground. Mrs Gamp appears in only eight of the novel's fifty-four chapters: XIX, XXV, XXVI, XXIX, XL, XLVI, XLIX and LI, with one brief mention in chapter LII. If chapter-headings are what we go by, investigation proves still more disconcerting: Mrs Gamp's name is encountered only once, in the heading of chapter XLVI (where, the reader is told, 'Mrs. Gamp makes tea', while three other characters make other things). Mrs Gamp's close friend Mrs Harris does put in an appearance in one chapter-heading – that to chapter XLIX, which reads: 'In which Mrs. Harris, assisted by a teapot, is the cause of a division between friends' – and, as Mrs Harris has no existence independently of Mrs Gamp, that chapter-heading may be regarded as containing a reference to the latter person. Finally, there are three chapter-headings which seem to allude to Mrs Gamp with typical Victorian prudery, in the form of the adjective 'professional': 'some professional persons' in chapter XIX (glorified by Mrs Gamp's first appearance), 'in part professional' in chapter XXV and 'In which some people are . . . professional' in chapter XXIX. As Mrs Gamp's profession is that of nurse and midwife, it is not to be openly mentioned in so prominent a place as a chapter-heading. On the other hand, the allusion may give the Victorian reader a delightful sense of complicity and initiation into a slightly indecent mystery. But that is only the slightest, least enduring and least interesting of the mysteries connected with Mrs Gamp and her two friends, Mrs Harris and Betsey Prig. The most fascinating of these problems is no less than that of literary creation and art.

Mrs Gamp's case is not unlike that of Sam Weller, whose appearance in *Pickwick Papers* did more than anything else to turn the early trickle of sales into a flood. Mrs Gamp also had some influence on the reception of *Martin Chuzzlewit*: not as much as Dickens probably hoped and had every right to expect, for he knew what he was doing when he created her. She did not prove capable of turning the tide or of making *Chuzzlewit* as overwhelmingly popular as its predecessors had been, but in the long run she made a name for herself. She was at once talked about and enjoyed, and she has remained one of the best-remembered characters in *Martin Chuzzlewit* – better remembered, it has been claimed, than the book in which she figures so strikingly: 'Today', E. W. F. Tomlin writes, 'many more know of Mr Pickwick and Mrs Gamp than have read through *Pickwick Papers* and *Martin Chuzzlewit.*'[1] Among the conscientious readers of the novel, only Mr Pecksniff can rival Mrs Gamp in sheer memorability. Perhaps Jonas Chuzzlewit is also likely to stay in the reader's recollection; but all the other characters are either too easily forgettable, or at best fairly honourable defeats like Tom Pinch or Mark Tapley.

But it is not only among her colleagues in *Chuzzlewit* itself that Mrs Gamp shines supreme. She is, in her own right, one of the most stupendous characters ever created by Dickens. A sampling of critical opinion about Mrs Gamp is revealing. G. K. Chesterton is one of her enthusiastic admirers and invokes the most distinguished shades in his praise of Dickens's achievement when he created her: 'Mrs Gamp is, indeed, a sumptuous study, laid on in those rich, oily, almost greasy colours that go to make the English comic characters, that make the very diction of Falstaff fat, and quaking with jolly degradation.'[2] And George Gissing had been no less warm in his commendation:

> Among all the names immortalized by Dickens none is more widely familiar than that of Mrs Gamp. It is universally admitted that in Mrs Gamp we have a creation such as can be met with only in the greatest writers; a figure at once universal and typical; a marvel of humorous presentment; vital in the highest degree attainable by this art of fiction.[3]

Recent critics have been just as enthusiastic. Steven Marcus devotes to Mrs Gamp an inspired section of his book on Dickens's early fiction, too long to be quoted in full, but from which the following phrases may be selected:

> that rare phenomenon, the character as creative artist, an imaginary person endowed with the same kind of vitality that imagined her . . . She represents what might be called the Schizophrenia of Election, just as Pecksniff sometimes represents the paranoia of

it . . . a creature of ritual, or immemorial formulae and conventions for dealing with the life of adversity and pain . . . a female Old Mortality, one of the guardians of human destiny . . . a kind of pagan, cockney goddess, beyond – like the Immortals – human suffering, but privileged to be a spectator and caretaker of it.[4]

Angus Wilson's analysis of Mrs Gamp's connection with death, birth and sex is also masterly.[5]

It will already have appeared from the above quotations that Mrs Gamp is not an easy character to discuss in precise terms. Dickens's achievement in her creation is bound to remain in part mysterious, and literary analysis seems to be powerless to determine exactly what the achievement consists of and how it has been arrived at. So that Gampian criticism comprises more tributes than analyses. The difficulties of critical commentary about her are similar to the embarrassment experienced over Mr Micawber (in *Copperfield*), whose greatness as literary creation is unanimously recognized, but about whom little has been written profitably or illuminatingly. Mrs Gamp shares at least one characteristic with Mr Micawber: both would be repellent in real life, and most people would go out of their way to avoid them; yet, though they are the kind of people Gissing characterizes as 'personally ignoble',[6] we can't have too much of them in their respective novels. Was it some sublime instinct that prevented Dickens from giving us too much of Mrs Gamp? In any case, it is clear that we are left under the impression that we could have taken more of her in the book.

Perhaps the reader's keen enjoyment in fiction of what would be detestable in real life is in its way analogous to what Charles Lamb discussed in his essay 'On the Artificial Comedy of the Last Century', and perhaps in Mrs Gamp's company we are, like Elia, 'glad for a season to take an airing beyond the diocese of the strict conscience'[7] or beyond the diocese of strict decency, honesty and cleanliness, beyond the diocese of the genteel and the tolerable.

Like Mr Micawber, then, Mrs Gamp is analysable only in part, but there are aspects of Dickens's achievement that can be isolated and examined under the microscope. Meanwhile Dickens himself provides minute descriptions of the character and her surroundings in the text of the novel.

This is, for instance, how the narrator fondly lingers over the details of Mrs Gamp's night attire:

she took out of her bundle a yellow night-cap, of prodigious size, in shape resembling a cabbage; which article of dress she fixed and tied on with the utmost care, previously divesting herself of a row of bald old curls that could scarcely be called false, they were so very innocent of anything approaching to deception . . . Finally, she produced a watchman's coat, which she tied round her neck by the sleeves, so that she became two people; and looked, behind, as if she were in the act of being embraced by one of the old patrol. (XXV, 481/412)

In such passages, Dickens is obviously enjoying himself, and he preserves the same high spirits whenever he has occasion to provide further particulars about Mrs Gamp's physical existence. It is only near the end of the novel, when she is about to entertain her friend and frequent 'pardner' Betsey Prig, with whom there will occur a memorable and Homeric battle, that the narrator takes the reader inside Mrs Gamp's apartment. He then supplies a full description of its furniture, including an enormous bedstead,

the sacking whereof, was low and bulging insomuch that Mrs. Gamp's box would not go under it, but stopped half-way, in a manner which, while it did violence to the reason, likewise endangered the legs, of a stranger . . . The bed itself was decorated with a patchwork quilt of great antiquity; and at the upper end, upon the side nearest to the door, hung a scanty curtain of blue check, which prevented the Zephyrs that were abroad in Kingsgate Street from visiting Mrs. Gamp's head too roughly. (XLIX, 824–5/742–3)

After the bed come the chairs, then the bandboxes, then the chest of drawers, all endowed with exuberant comicality. And the description leads to a cupboard, and to the teapot in which, 'from motives of delicacy', Mrs Gamp kept her spirits.

The physical presence of the character is thus ensured and made striking in itself, even if she were to remain silent. But of course silent is what Mrs Gamp can never remain for more than a few seconds, and her extraordinarily idiosyncratic speech is what has given most delight to generations of readers of *Chuzzlewit*. It has also puzzled literary critics, because its case presents in a more limited form the kind of difficulty that the character as a whole offers to understanding and appreciation. While it is impossible not to see it as a keen and constant source of amusement, it is by no means easy to determine precisely where the amusement comes from, or even to list all the peculiarities of Mrs Gamp's way of expressing herself in English. There has been no dearth of critical rhapsodies about what we may call 'Gampese', but few detailed and specific discussions. George Gissing refers to 'this thick, gurgling flux of talk'[8] which he regards as perfect of its kind, though unlike anything ever heard in real life, and he finds it recognizably distinct from her friend Betsey Prig's speech. It takes a linguist of Randolph Quirk's calibre and literary sensibility to venture into direct and minute examination. Quirk writes:

comparison of Mrs Gamp's speeches throughout *Chuzzlewit* shows an increasing density of identifying features, indicating an increased interest in this aspect of the lady on the part of author and public alike, and preparing us for her eventual abstraction from the novel to become the central figure of one of his best-known 'Readings'.[9]

It is indeed fascinating to think that, when he wrote *Chuzzlewit* Dickens could not have foreseen that he would one day give public readings of passages from his works, and yet he was already providing himself with splendid materials for them; which draws attention to the oral/aural nature of his achievement in the creation of Mrs Gamp.

Finally, Garrett Stewart writes: 'Sairey Gamp is one of the most stubbornly escapist personalities in Dickens, and her unrelieved, spasmodic language is not expressive so much as defensive.'[10] It is interesting to note that Stewart here, like many other critics, succumbs to the temptation of writing about 'Sairey' Gamp, whose real name, of course, is Sarah. Does it not amount to discussing Mrs Gamp on her own terms, to accepting her own image of herself? Surely that would be a dangerous procedure. Yet Garrett Stewart's notion of the defensive nature of Mrs Gamp's speech is stimulating. A character whose language serves as a barrier against communication, instead of fulfilling the normal and natural function of speech for the purposes of communication, is indeed intensely original. It is true that Gampese is phonetically and grammatically unique, though not entirely coherent. In the first place, Mrs Gamp's English comprises a number of what might be called ordinary peculiarities, by which are meant features common in lower-class English or specifically cockney forms. Examples of the former category are *chimley* or *chimbley*; the shortening and de-diphthongization of the *-ow* ending (so that Mrs Gamp speaks of *feller, piller, widder, winders, narrer* and *follerin'*); mispronunciations like *nothink, aperiently* ('apparently'), *skelinton* ('skeleton'), *t'other*,[11] *imperent* ('impertinent'), *airy* ('area'), *agen* ('against'), *arterwards, ast* ('ask'), *pardner, farden* ('farthing'), *darter* ('daughter'), *likeways* ('likewise'), *wunst* ('once'), *fust* ('first'), *heerd* ('heard'); the loss of *n* from *an*;[12] and the omission or addition of an initial aspirate *h* – Mrs Gamp thus speaks of *art* ('heart'), *andsome, ouse* (and even *custom-us* for 'custom-house'), and of *owls* for 'howls', while, conversely, she pronounces the *h* in 'honourable' and says *hus* when she means 'us'. As to the *o* which is used to represent the vowel sound used by her in words like *wos* ('was') and *wot* ('what'), it is a less striking characteristic, both because it is not regularly represented thus, and because it is after all not different from the normal pronunciation of such words; while Mrs Gamp's tendency to use *that . . . that . . .* in the sense of *so . . . that . . .* is also found in Dickens's own English, at least when he is at his most journalistically jocular. The major cockney features of Gampese are the *v/w* shifts and the substitution of an *ai* sound (as in 'eye') for an *oi* sound (as in 'joy'); thus she says *pint* ('point'), *biling, jines* ('joins'), *nisy, lamp-iling, pizon* (for 'poison'), *disapintin'*, or *jints*.[13]

The specimens given above have already made it appear that neither Gampese nor its transliteration is beyond criticism. The two weaknesses that close analysis renders apparent are the unsystematic nature of some phenomena and the use of little devices which are of such doubtful relevance that they amount to cheating in order to produce amusement. Among the unstable mispronunciations included in Gampese may be quoted: *calcilation* (for 'calculation', but that word is sometimes given *as* 'calculation'); *such*, given alternately as *sich, sech* (and Mrs Gamp does occasionally say *set* for 'sit'), and *such* (and she also says once or twice *jest* for 'just' and *shetters* for 'shutters'). She seems to waver between *an't* and *ain't* (both for 'haven't' and for 'am not'/'is not'). She is very uncertain about her *-ing* ending, which she tends to reduce to *in* or *in'*, but occasionally pronounces in full. And she is erratic in her distribution of *wery* and *very*; a pinch of *werys* are sprinkled among a fairly steady flow of *verys*.

This supposed cockney characteristic, illustrated in full force by Sam Weller and more especially by his father Tony in *Pickwick Papers*, is one of the linguistic features that give delight to the reader of Mrs Gamp's scenes, but it may have given some trouble to her creator. Mrs Gamp says things like *inwallable* ('invaluable'), *this walley of the shadder*, *wale of grief*, *in a wale* ('valley of the shadow', 'vale'), *wictim*, *wexagious* ('vexatious'), *obserwation*, *perwisin'* ('providing'), *wentersome*, *efferwescence*, *wessel*, *sitiwation* and *rewive*. The reverse phenomenon is less frequent, but will be found in operation in *vich* (for 'which') and *elsevere*. Both the likelihood and the picturesqueness vary from sample to sample. Fortunately they do not vary in inverse ratio – or, at least, not regularly. For instance, *inwallable* and *perwisin'* are amusing without being in the least improbable; but *wexagious* is a superb invention and loses nothing of its appeal by its remoteness from most people's experience of spoken English heard in real life anywhere. Mrs Gamp's idiosyncratic *g*, however, deserves, and will receive, separate treatment. Meanwhile, a brief list has to be given of words in which it is not clear which mispronunciation, if any, is denounced or signalled by the spelling adopted in the text.

When we come across a word spelt *creetur*, for instance, it is difficult to determine what difference from the standard pronunciation is suggested in the first syllable (is *feat* phonetically distinguishable from *feet*?); as to the second syllable, the omission of the final *e* may be intended to imply that Mrs Gamp makes *creature* rhyme with *Creator* rather than with *thatcher* or with *nature*; but that is by no means self-evident, and her rendering of *nature*, in any case, is alternatively *natur* and *nater*, while for *tortures* she says *torters*! In some similar cases like *misfortun*, the reader's puzzlement is identical; in others, the pronunciation palmed off upon Mrs Gamp by the narrator as reporter – and one cannot forget that Dickens's attention to phonetics must have been cultivated when he practised stenography – is not noticeably different from current speech or, at least, is intrinsically acceptable. *Ev'ry*, or *p'raps*, or *wen* or *wile* (for 'when' or 'while') and even *constitooshun* are at worst mild departures from usage; finally, the rendering of 'police' as *pelisse*, 'conquer' as *conker*, 'business' as *bis'ness*, 'requires' as *rekwires* and 'burying' as *berryin'* is good fun, but it is fun that the author is having on his own, with the vagaries of language, rather than with his good lady's eccentricities. Dickens may also be suggesting a comic idea of how Mrs Gamp might have spelt certain words, or imagined their spelling – if she could spell at all.

Of course, there are genuine idiosyncrasies in Mrs Gamp's speech, and she owes part of her reputation to them, mainly to her highly individual use of *which*, her substitution of *g* for a variety of other consonants, a few devices like interruptions of her speech in order to address everyone present in turn or biblical misquotations, and general exuberant inventiveness.

Mrs Gamp's grammar, like her pronunciation, is shaky in more ways than one. She is very generous with the third-person singular form in verbs, transferred by her to every other person (*I bears, you knows, we tries, my duties is*). She is not particular about the forms of past tenses: *knowd, throw'd, grow'd* are good enough for her, and she uses phrases like *to have wrote* or *he was took*. She is addicted to double negations and her pronouns are as shaky as her verbs; but while most of her errors in that direction are colloquially common her *which* is made to do duty for an astonishing variety of other pronouns or conjunctions, in order to link clauses that may not have much connection with each other. She begins by substituting *which* for *who*, as in 'Mr. Mould, which has undertook the highest families'; but later, speaking of daughters, Mrs Gamp will add 'which, if we had had one', thus turning *which* into a mere equivalent of 'and' or 'and, in this respect' or 'and, talking of that'. In that respect, Joe Gargery, in *Great Expectations*, may be regarded as her pupil, with his 'which I meantersay' and 'which her name, Pip, ain't Estavisham'.[14] The weakness of the relative function of her own *which* can also be illustrated by the following examples: 'I do require it [drink]; which I makes confession' or, again, near the end of the Gampian career, 'If she had abuged me, bein in liquor, which I thought I smelt her wen she come, but could not so believe'. The phenomenon has been splendidly analysed by Garrett Stewart, who speaks of 'her use of "which" as a sort of vague, all-purpose coordinator' and adds:

This abuse is a grammatical liberty which sets Sairey free from the normal rules and responsibilities of subordination; she uses the relative pronoun as a conjunction, often just as an empty filler, as if to imply syntactical rigor without the necessary expenditure of effort.[15]

Perhaps it is Mrs Gamp's extravagant use of *g*, however, that is most clearly remembered about her speech. By listing the main examples of this phenomenon some conclusions can be drawn about the intended equivalents. In a considerable number of cases, the letter *g* stands instead of a *z* sound, as in *suppoge*, and the reader is encouraged to suppose that Mrs Gamp pronounces such words with the sound of *s* in 'pleasure'; thus for her: *suppoge, suppoging* (though there is at least one early *suppose*), *impoged*, *dispoged*. In the corresponding nouns, *impogician* and *dispogician*, the *-cian* ending is a little puzzling (for it is hard to represent to oneself in what way the pronunciation of that ending can differ from what would have been conveyed, less picturesquely, by the more usual *-tion* ending). There are also *excuge*, *surprige*, *roge* and *rouge* ('rose' and 'rouse'), *abuged*, *repoge*, *nige* (with double effect, for this is Mrs Gamp's rendering of 'noise') and *rager* (for 'razor'). Almost equally straightforward, though perhaps a trifle less probable, is the substitution of the same letter and sound for an *s* (as in 'simple') of ordinary speech. Gampese thus has: *satigefaction*, *promige*, *experienge*, *poultige*, *releage*, *sacrifige*, *furnage*, *bage* ('base'). *Satigefaction* is an interesting example of the complications Mrs Gamp exposes herself, and her transliterator, to; *\*satigfaction* would have run the risk of being misread with a hard *g*; but *satigefaction* runs the other risk of being given either undue diphthongization or an additional syllable. Both with *z* and *s* sounds we come across examples of great ingenuity in the transliteration. When Mrs Gamp wishes to speak of Saint Paul's Fountain, that becomes 'Saint Polge's Fontin', and her Jonas's belly is 'Jonadge's belly' (in which the *d* is clearly inconsistent). Nor are those the only problems Dickens encountered in the course of his exhilarating exercise in exploratory phonetics: 'brazen' could not be *\*bragan*, so it had to be *Bragian*, where the *i* is almost certainly not intended to be pronounced, but only to serve as a diacritic, like the *e* in *satigefaction* and *Saint Polge's*. The same is probably valid also in the case of 'reason'/*reagion*, and again, though not quite for the same reason, in *confugion* ('confusion'); and in the last-named example, of course, the pronunciation suggested is not different from that of ordinary speakers, who do say *confugion*, though they do write 'confusion' (and there is also one *occagion*/'occasion', which is precisely similar). There are still more puzzling phenomena. While it is understandable that, in accordance with the basic principles of Gampese, 'denies' should become *\*denige*, it is less satisfactory to find that word in the form of *deniges* (whether in two or three syllables, it seems that the final *z* sound of ordinary English is rendered twice); and does Mrs Gamp really reconstruct a whole conjugation on the basis of the idiosyncratic infinitive *denige*? In any case, she does use both *deniged* and *deniging*. In her beautiful word *indiwidgle*, it is the vowel sounds of the ending '-dual' that cohere into a hyper-Gampian *g*. And the basic principle is completely lost sight (or hearing) of, or overextends itself, when it comes to words like 'packet'/*package*, or 'impeaches'/*impeaged*. And, finally, how can the worthy locutress reconcile her sense of duty to herself with the sudden appearance in her speech, during the very end of her career, of the letter *j* instead of, or perhaps in addition to, her by now classical and chaste *g*? *Propojals*, *perfeejus*, may be acceptable, but *topjey-turjey* is pure delirium. On one occasion at least, in chapter XLIX, the delirium may be induced by a drunken state.

At times there is method in Mrs Gamp's verbal madness, and one of her methodical devices is to interrupt her speech as many times as she needs in order to include as many addresses to individual people as there are people in the room whom she must propitiate. The best-known example of this procedure is to be found in chapter XLVI, where Mrs Gamp begins a speech with an exclamatory apostrophe to Merry – 'Why, goodness me! Mrs. Chuzzlewit!' – then goes on her rambling way, with no fewer than six later pauses introduced so as to adapt her remarks, more or less incongruously, to Cherry, Chuffey, Tom Pinch, Merry once more, Augustus Moddle and Mrs Todgers (XLVI, 780/700–1.)

The use of malapropisms and related devices has already been illustrated by the example of *pelisse*/'police'; there are a few others, like 'if I was led a Martha to the stakes' (meaning a martyr, of course) or, more than once, *my mortar* for 'my motto'. That comic device, which has for the author the advantage of apparently palming off on his character one of his own worst puns, is not overexploited in *Martin Chuzzlewit*. Mrs Gamp's treatment of biblical quotations and phrases is more individual and may be compared with the achievement of *Bleak House*'s Mr Chadband in the same holy field. Mr Chadband is a preacher of a kind, and fills his sentences with biblical vocabulary, thus inbuing them with a religious tone rather than precise reference to Scripture or to moral teaching. Mrs Gamp's desire to be edifying is one of her constant characteristics, but her attitude to the Bible is inevitably less professional than Chadband's. Dickens no doubt felt that he could derive amusement from Mrs Gamp's incompetence and confusion without running the risk of being charged with irreverence (the same risk is avoided in Chadband's case by the vagueness of the allusions, though Chadband was in fact resented by some Evangelical critics).[16] Mrs Gamp's fondness for the phrase 'wale' or 'walley' may derive from Scripture either via Bunyan or directly, but a more characteristic and amusing example is provided by a section of the speech already referred to above, when she speaks of '*your* good lady's too, sir, Mr. Moddle, if I may make so bold as speak so plain of what is plain enough to them as needn't look through mill-stones, Mrs Todgers, to find out wot is wrote upon the wall behind' (XLVI, 780/701).

But once a number of specific devices and peculiarities have thus been described, and to a certain extent analysed, there remains the central aspect of Mrs Gamp's charm, which lies in her inexhaustible verbal creativity, in her exuberant inventiveness, manifested either in the form of separate words and phrases or in whole sentences, paragraphs and speeches.

Among her isolated achievements may be quoted the following: *inwalieges* ('invalids'), *owldacious* ('*audacious*'), *half-dudgeon* ('half-dozen'), *serpient* ('serpent'), *goldian* ('golden'), *cowcumber* ('cucumber'), *guardian* ('garden'), *raly* ('really') and *rayal* ('real'), *Ankworks* ('Antwerp'), *parapidge* ('parapet') and *disregardlessness*.

The longer specimens often combine several devices and many forms of eccentricity: 'the last Monday evening fortnight as ever dawned upon this Piljian's Projiss of a mortal wale'; 'whether I sicks or monthlies' (this, out of context, may need translation into more ordinary English: Mrs Gamp means 'whether I act as sick-nurse or as monthly nurse'); 'Rich folks may ride on camels, but it ain't so easy for them to see out of a needle's eye'; 'Gamp is my name, and Gamp my nater' (the superb gratuitousness of the assertion is no doubt a fruitful source of the reader's enjoyment here: Gamp is her married name, and can only have been an acquired characteristic, if it means anything; but the assertiveness of the assertion, and the beautiful balance of the sentence, do more than compensate for the lack of significance; in fact they provide an insight into the possibility of using language in order to express mood and character rather than meaning); 'I feels the sufferins of other people more than I feels my own, though no one mayn't suppoge it' (here the grammar has run riot, and the play with negation may have more involuntary relevance than she herself *mayn't suppoge*); 'beneath this blessed ouse which well I know it, wishin' it ware not so, which then this tearful walley would be changed into a flowerin' guardian'; 'he was born into a wale . . . and he lived in a wale; and he must take the consequences of sech a sitiwation' (a striking example of Mrs Gamp's pseudo-stoicism, at the expense of others, for that is her only comment on being told that Young Bailey, a brilliantly precocious boy for whom she professed friendship, has died suddenly).

That Dickens's achievement is the creation of Gampese is unique has been recognized. In so far as any truly creative handling, or even manipulation, of language is poetical, the nature of the achievement is akin to poetry. That is how it has been appraised, for instance, by Walter Allen: 'Mrs Gamp; with whom, dirty gin-sodden old midwife and layer-out of corpses as she is, Dickens soars into great poetry, for if her characteristic flights of fantasy are not great poetry one doesn't know what else to call them'[17] – though Angus Wilson uses another analogy when he writes that 'Mrs Gamp's dialogue is a triumph, perhaps the greatest triumph in literature of verbal collage'.[18]

Her speech is not, of course, Mrs Gamp's single title to fame. Nor does it function in a vacuum. Mrs Gamp's professionalism, her double profession, is what her conversation feeds on. It connects her with both ends of human life and, because birth is not unfairly associated in many minds with procreation, thus does the heavyweight matron skate over the thinnest of ice. On the other hand, her serving as sick-nurse by the bedside of people suffering what may well turn out to be terminal diseases appeals in Dickens (and his readers) to a certain fondness for the gruesome and the macabre. On two consecutive pages of the novel, allusions are made which are not of the lightest, but may be regarded as not unfair specimens of the kind of effect to be looked for from such a source; and that is on the occasion of Mrs Gamp's first appearance in the story. 'It chanced on this particular occasion that Mrs. Gamp had been up all the previous night, in attendance upon a ceremony to which the usage of gossips has given the name which expresses, in two syllables, the curse pronounced on Adam.' Soon after this laboured allusion to 'labour' comes this: 'It gave Mr Pecksniff much uneasiness to find from these remarks that he was supposed to have come to Mrs. Gamp upon an errand touching – not the close of life, but the other end' (XIX, 374–5/311–12). Such coyness Dickens did not regard as unworthy of himself as a serious novelist, but as almost inexhaustibly amusing, and thus legitimately to be aimed at.

In her funereal capacity Mrs Gamp is in touch with the undertaker Mr Mould (Dickens indulged in no excess of subtlety when he chose that name) and his family. Mould is not Dickens's first or last undertaker figure. There had been Mr Sowerberry in *Oliver Twist*, and there would be Mr Omer (and the whole firm of Omer & Joram) in *David Copperfield*; all three are comic figures, and even a post-

Copperfieldian burial scene, such as the funeral of Mrs Gargery in *Great Expectations*, is treated as predominantly – indeed, as overwhelmingly – comic. This is not untraditional, and later writers (like H. G. Wells in the excellent funeral chapter of his *The History of Mr Polly*) will follow in Dickens's tracks. But there is full justification for V. S. Pritchett's remark that 'The fact is that to Dickens as to all primitive natures, there was something comic in death. Especially there was something funny in dead wives.'[19] Not that this is an eccentric attitude on Dickens's part. He stands well within an age-old tradition in this respect. The best part of chapter XXV is devoted to the Mould establishment and family, and it abounds in examples of funereal humour. The reader is told, for instance, that 'from the distant shop a pleasant sound arose of coffin-making with a low melodious hammer, rat, tat, tat, tat, alike promoting slumber and digestion' (XXV, 469/401–2), or finds that Mr Mould expresses his regard for Mrs Gamp in highly professional terms: 'She's the sort of woman now . . . one would almost feel disposed to bury for nothing: and do it neatly, too!' (XXV, 475/407). Mrs Gamp herself, in the course of the same chapter, presents a grimmer image of the same sinister warping of her thoughts and feelings by professional habits; she is supposed to be watching by the bedside of a sick young man, and before going to sleep herself she examines her patient:

> By degrees, a horrible remembrance of one branch of her calling took possession of the woman; and stooping down, she pinned his wandering arms against his sides, to see how he would look if laid out as a dead man. Hideous as it may appear, her fingers itched to compose his limbs in that last marble attitude.
> 'Ah! said Mrs Gamp, walking away from the bed, 'he'd make a lovely corpse.' (XXV 479/410)

There is considerable force in the passage, but words like *horrible* and *hideous* are examples of overemphasis; perhaps *marble* is also a little indiscreet, as evidence of narratorial interference in order to infuse solemnity into the macabre farce of the scene. As to the whole phrase 'Hideous as it may appear',[20] it raises huge problems, which concern the relationship between author, narrator, character and reader, as well as the questions of mimesis and credibility. If the phrase means anything, it is that the scene may well appear too hideous to be true, though we as readers must accept the narrator's assertion that it is true to life. But is it life as observed in reality or the life – no less true in its way – created by the novelist's imagination? We are left in doubt on this point. Mrs Gamp, in any case, has thus contributed her mite to the ugly side of the funereal humour in the chapter. To its sunny side she also has a contribution to make, and she does so when she recalls the young Mould girls playing in the undertaker's shop: 'ah, the sweet creeturs! – playing at berryins down in the shop, and follerin' the orderbook to its long home in the iron safe!' (XXV, 472/404). A charming picture of the innocent pleasures of childhood, almost of the *vert paradis*, though, as it happens, the paradise in that case is *pervers* as well as *vert*, for the little girls, in whose veins flows true undertaking blood, are literally making a game (a *jeu interdit*), making fun, of the saddest ceremony known to man, and enacting a symbolical performance which associates burying with mercantile value (the iron safe).

Mrs Gamp is said to have had an original in real life. It was while he was already at work on *Martin Chuzzlewit* that Dickens heard, through his rich friend, Angela Burdett-Coutts, of a nurse who took care of her companion Hannah Meredith. The nurse was eccentric in several respects, and things like her yellow nightcap, her fondness for snuff and for spirits were immediately transferred to Mrs Gamp.[21] But, as usual, these merely external details do not do very much to enlighten the processes of literary creation or the workings of genius. What Miss Meredith's illness may have done for the novelist was to draw his attention to the unsatisfactory organization of nursing in England at the time, where dirty and dishonest women like Mrs Gamp could set up shop as nurses and ruthlessly exploit their patients. There is indeed a strong element of social satire, or denunciation, presented through Mrs Gamp and her 'pardner' or accomplice Betsey Prig. 'Accomplice' is certainly not too strong a word, for Mrs Gamp may be said to be plotting with Betsey for their mutual comfort, at the expense of, and in fact against, the patients they so callously share. They are always ready to compassionate themselves or each other, but never their victims. Mrs Gamp is further characterized by her fondness for alcoholic drinks. The gin she keeps discreetly in a teapot, so that she can put her lips to it when she feels 'so dispoged', must disappear rather fast, and it leaves unsavoury after-effects both on her breath and on her temper; indeed, it is responsible for the momentous quarrel between the two ladies and leads to their final separation in chapter XLIX.

No list of Mrs Gamp's prominent characteristics would be complete without mention of her umbrella, since that item of her equipment has caused her entrance into dictionaries of the English language as a common noun. Presumably no one, nowadays, mentions an umbrella as a gamp, except as an esoteric joke. But the allusion is still faintly recognizable, and the fact is a tribute to Mrs Gamp's enduring reputation. It is all the more remarkable as her umbrella, though striking enough in every sense of the word, is not the most astonishing specimen of that instrument to be found in Dickens's work. Kind Mrs Bagnet, in *Bleak House*, has one which serves a larger variety of uses.[22]

Mrs Gamp has a noticeable tendency to flirtatiousness. At least she good-humouredly submits to Young Bailey's affectation of flirting with her. This extraordinary little piece of sexual grotesquerie has not been much discussed by Dickens's critics. That may be because it is not insisted on in the novel itself, but simply thrown off by the way, like so many other things which are both shrewd and amusing.

But the core of Mrs Gamp's personality is far from tender. She is a hard-hearted and obdurate woman. That is why, by the end of the story, she cannot be converted to the same extent as another grasping and ageing woman, the famous Mrs Todgers who keeps a boarding-house in London. It is possible that Dickens changed his mind about Mrs Todgers and that he had originally intended her to remain unpleasant to the end. In the event, however, he made it appear that a superficial glance at her could alone condemn her, and that when you knew her better, or when she had been mellowed by trials, the true qualities of her being shone; he even went out of his way to point it out (as he was to do later in the case of Miss Mowcher in *Copperfield*). Mrs Gamp, on the contrary, is firmly admonished by Old Martin at the end of the novel, when he advises her of 'the expediency of a little less liquor, and a little more humanity, and a little less regard for herself, and a little more regard for her patients, and perhaps a trifle of additional honesty' (LII, 894/810).

It is still necessary to mention the, so to speak, third and fourth halves of Mrs Gamp's fictional existence. What I call the third half is the significant though abortive desire felt by Dickens to resurrect Mrs Gamp in connection with his charitable efforts conducted by means of private theatricals. John Forster, who was himself a member of Dickens's company when they went on tour in 1847, records (under the heading of 'Splendid Strolling' of which Dickens was very fond) that after performances in Manchester and Liverpool the financial takings had fallen short of Dickens's expectations by about one hundred pounds. He wanted five hundred guineas to be given to Leigh Hunt in order to help him pay his debts. In order to make up for the deficiency, the novelist proposed to publish and put on sale 'a little *jeu d'esprit* in the form of a history of the trip, to be published with illustrations from the artists' (Frank Stone, Augustus Egg, John Leech and George Cruikshank had been among the strolling amateurs); 'and his notion was to write it in the character of Mrs. Gamp'. Dickens explained to Forster:

> The argument would be, that Mrs. Gamp, being on the eve of an excursion to Margate as a relief from her professional fatigues, comes to the knowledge of the intended excursion of our party; hears that several of the ladies concerned are in an interesting situation; and decides to accompany the party unbeknown, in a second-class carriage – "in case"![23]

Forster says that the joke perished because the artists failed to provide illustrations; but he reprints the beginning that Dickens had written; there are five or six pages of it. They are not immoderately amusing. As in the case of the attempted reappearance of the Wellers in *Master Humphrey's Clock*, the remake is greatly inferior to the original production; the jokes tend to be both mechanical (and repetitive) and so private as to be almost dull. The 'argument' in itself, as described by Dickens, was unexciting and faintly indelicate, if he proposed, among other things, to make fun of his friends' wives' pregnancies. The episode is interesting mainly because the idea occurred to Dickens in connection with Mrs Gamp, as it had in connection with Sam and Tony Weller, but with no others of his hundreds of characters, if we except Mrs Lirriper, who was the central figure of two 'Christmas Stories' and who is also a felicitous creation; the implication is that Dickens knew when he had been brilliant, and he sanctioned the outstanding brilliancy of his own achievement in Mrs Gamp's case by this unequivocal though inefficient gesture.

The last aspect of Gampism that clamours for mention at this stage is the last half of her personality, which happens to be in fact her double, namely Mrs Harris, who may well be the most original and inspired element of this admirable creation. Much amusement is produced, whenever Mrs Gamp appears, by having her record conversations held between herself and one Mrs Harris, who seems to be always at hand to pay warm tributes of loving and admiring friendship to Mrs Gamp's many virtues, such as her abstemiousness, her conscientiousness, her honesty, her low charges. Mrs Harris, for reasons which are made obvious in the course of the novel, never appears in person on its stage; but she seems to be perpetually fluttering in the wings; and her portrait, though never completely accurate, receives little touches concerning her children, her husband, even her brother-in-law, and little snatches of her past and present history; her evidence is always reported by Mrs Gamp as having been delivered to herself. She is so admirably convenient and irrefutable that suspicions soon arise in the reader's mind that she may be no more than a figment of Mrs Gamp's heated brain, no more than what Garrett Stewart felicitously calls 'her imaginary idolatress'.[24] This happy contrivance shows Mrs Gamp to be resourceful, imaginative and brazen. Part of the advantages derived from Mrs Harris's availability lies in the duplication effect. Mrs Gamp, when she is reporting a conversation with her friend, becomes for all practical purposes and temporarily two persons. She is thus both divided and multiplied. This invention has of course been admired by many critics, and the way Mrs Harris comes to be caught in the quarrel between Mrs Gamp and Betsey Prig and bandied between the two tipsy ladies is another splendid inspiration. The title of chapter XLIX does not do full justice to Mrs Harris, when it says that she, 'assisted by a teapot, is the cause of a division between friends'. She is not so much the cause as the dramatic consequence, or visible sign, of the breach. On the other hand, the etching by 'Phiz' which illustrates that chapter and is called 'Mrs. Gamp propoges a Toast' is one of the best in the book; it is symbolical of Mrs Harris's role in the story; for she is not a concrete presence, but the conscious reader can without difficulty imagine or almost visualize her, hovering above the two tipplers. And surely the dresses hanging from the top of the bed-frame are in sufficient number and of sufficient amplitude to clothe her; admittedly, they are Mrs Gamp's own spare dresses, but Mrs Harris herself also belongs to Mrs Gamp and is clothed only by Mrs Gamp's spare imaginary flights. Geoffrey Thurley is no doubt right when he suggests that the fun of the scene is quite out of the ordinary: 'That a scene between two gin-soaking old nurses can have power to move, as this scene undoubtedly does, argues roots deeper than simple comedy.'[25] Betsey Prig's flat denial of Mrs Harris's existence ('I don't believe there's no sich a person!') may be the most unkindest cut of all, since it is tantamount to a denunciation of a fraud, a fraud which had been hitherto implicitly accepted, though not believed in, by the whole Gamp circle. Mrs Gamp is temporarily put out by what appears to her as the finality of such a denial ('to be told at last' or 'to come at last to sech a end as this'); her mental world, so elaborately and lovingly created by herself, is brutally shattered. But by the end of the chapter, two pages later, she will have recovered her fertile Harrisogenic creativity, and will be holding forth about Mrs Harris 'with little Tommy Harris in her arms, as calls me his own Gammy' (XLIX, 834–7/752–5). But she has had a narrow escape; she has indeed suffered a loss, that of Betsey's friendship, barely avoiding the greater loss that the destruction of Mrs Harris could have inflicted.

In the superb mastery with which Dickens created the character of Mrs Gamp and enriched her with the ectoplasm of Mrs Harris, there is only one weakness or blemish, and that is the early and indiscreet analysis of the whole phenomenon by the narrator, in a passage called by Guerard 'one of those Dickensian redundancies the reader itches to cut off'.[26] But the reader cannot cut it off, he can only forget about its existence, forget that he had been told in chapter XXV:

> a fearful mystery surrounded this lady of the name of Harris, whom no one in the circle of Mrs. Gamp's acquaintance had ever seen . . . There were conflicting rumours on the subject; but the prevalent opinion was that she was a phantom of Mrs. Gamp's brain . . . created for the express purpose of holding visionary dialogues with her on all manner of subjects, and invariably winding up with a compliment to the excellence of her nature. (XXV, 471–2/403–4)

This is not only unnecessary and indiscreet, but humiliating, as a sign of Dickens's distrust of the reader's intelligence.

Yet what remains in the reader's mind concerning Mrs Gamp is the remembrance of several admirable scenes (with the Moulds and with Betsey Prig particularly), of felicitous phrases, of a great artistic achievement in the field of eccentric, linguistic and humorous characterization, which is enough to ensure, even if Dickens had done nothing more in his novel, that *Martin Chuzzlewit* gives delight.

## NOTES: CHAPTER 5

1  See 'Dickens's reputation: a reassessment', in E. W. F.Tomlin (ed.), *Charles Dickens 1812–1870: A Centenary Volume* (London, 1969), p. 288.
2  G. K. Chesterton, *Charles Dickens* (London, 1906), pp. 147–8.
3  George Gissing, *Charles Dickens: A Critical Study* (London, 1898), pp. 100–1.
4  Steven Marcus, *Dickens from Pickwick to Dombey* (New York, 1965), pp. 261–4.
5  See Angus Wilson, *The World of Charles Dickens* (New York, 1970), pp. 177–8. As to Veronica M. S. Kennedy's article, 'Mrs Gamp as the Great Mother: a Dickensian use of the archetype', *Victorian Newsletter*, no. 41 (1972), pp. 1–5, a Jungian 'reading', I must confess that, unless it is intended as a parody, I fail to see what purpose it serves.
6  See Gissing, op. cit., pp. 121–5.
7  See *Essays of Elia* (1823), Everyman's Library (London, 1906), p. 166.
8  Gissing, op. cit., pp. 126–8.
9  Randolph Quirk, 'Charles Dickens, linguist' in his *The Linguist and the Language* (London, 1974), p. 7.
10  Garrett Stewart, *Dickens and the Trials of Imagination* (Cambridge, Mass., 1974), p. 171.
11  A variant of 'the other' made more famous by Rogue Riderhood in *Our Mutual Friend*, who plays such inspired variations on it as *t'other t'other* and *t'otherest*.
12  In *a easy*, for instance, which is reminiscent of Mr Bumble's 'The Law is a Ass' in *Oliver Twist*.
13  *Jines* for 'joins' is an interesting case, in that the final *e* appears necessary to suggest the sound intended in *jines* whereas the existence of a real word *pint* enables the writer to dispense with that device for Mrs Gamp's rendering of 'point'. *Pizon* is also interesting because the *z* spelling shows that the ending in *-son* would have suggested an unvoiced consonant – as in 'bison' or 'unison' – and made the word unrecognizable. And in *disapintin'* the cancellation of one *p* seems gratuitous, as it can reflect no phonetic peculiarity.
14  See *Great Expectations*, ed. Angus Calder, Penguin English Library (Harmondsworth, 1965), e.g. ch. VII, p. 79, and ch. XV, p. 139.
15  Stewart, op. cit., p. 171.
16  See Dennis Walder, *Dickens and Religion* (London, 1981), pp. 5 and 168.
17  Walter Allen, 'The comedy of Dickens', in Michael Slater (ed.), *Dickens 1970* (London, 1970), p. 26.
18  Wilson, op. cit., p. 177. His discussion of Mrs Gamp (see pp. 177–8) is among the most stimulating analyses of that character and its various functions.
19  V. S. Pritchett, 'The comic world of Dickens', in Ian Watt (ed.), *The Victorian Novel: Modern Essays in Criticism* (London, 1971), p. 34.
20  Omitted from the Library Edition of 1858, but present everywhere else, from the original manuscript to the Charles Dickens Edition.
21  See Edgar Johnson, *Charles Dickens: His Tragedy and Triumph*, 2 vols (London, 1953), Vol. 1, p. 453.
22  See *Bleak House*, ch. XXXIV (Norton Critical Edition, ed. George H. Ford and Sylvère Monod (New York, 1977), pp. 418–19).
23  John Forster, *The Life of Charles Dickens* (1872–4), Everyman's Library (London, 1927), Vol. 2, pp. 5–6.
24  Stewart, op. cit., p. 172.
25  Geoffrey Thurley, *The Dickens Myth: Its Genesis and Structure* (London, 1976), p. 103.
26  Guerard, op. cit., p. 258.

# CHAPTER 6

# Pecksniffery

The heading of this chapter is based on Dickens's own example. Chapter XI in the first book of *Our Mutual Friend* is entitled 'Podsnappery', a felicitous coinage for a delightful chapter. Of course, by 1864 the novelist had become bolder, and knew more clearly what he was doing, what he was aiming at, when he was achieving a particularly triumphant success.

The part played by Pecksniffery in the overall structure of the novel is at least as important as that of the American episodes and considerably greater than that of Sarah Gamp; it has just been seen that, however splendid and admirable she is, she is marginal to the action. A resemblance between the Pecksniff case and the American episodes is that there is a kind of structural alternation within *Chuzzlewit*, not only between England and the United States, but also, on the English side, between various groups of characters, such as those living mainly in London and those based mainly in the vicinity of Salisbury.

The character of Mr Pecksniff has been praised as much as that of Mrs Gamp, as one of the most successful inventions in the book. But the two worthies are not in the same class.

For one thing, Pecksniff has a definite literary source; instead of, like 'Sairey', a real-life origin. Admittedly, according to K. J. Fielding, Samuel Carter Hall, a minor writer and journalist disliked by Dickens, had unwittingly sat for the portrait of Pecksniff.[1] Yet the connection with Molière's famous Tartuffe seems more important, and even decisive. And it points to a purpose on Dickens's part which is even more systematic and abstract than in Mrs Gamp's case. The comparison between Pecksniff and Tartuffe was openly invited by one of Phiz's illustrations for the original edition in monthly parts. In chapter LII the scene of Seth Pecksniff's chastisement at Old Martin's vigorous hands is represented graphically: he falls to the ground while Martin stands and towers over him with his raised stick, and three of the books laid on the table fall with him; they may have been put down on the table originally by Tom Pinch, who oddly chooses that moment to investigate or reorganize Old Martin's library – clumsily enough, since he is also dropping books to the floor on his own account and in his own corner. Pinch's victims are anonymous; so is one of the books dragged down by Pecksniff's fall, as the one that remains for ever in the air has only a small circle on the cover, or perhaps the initials 'C D'; the book already on the floor is *Paradise Lost*; and the one falling *to* the floor is called 'TARTUFFE/PAR/ MOLIERE'. It is evidence of Phiz's emblematic tendencies, ably analysed by Michael Steig.[2] Since the etching was sanctioned by Dickens, it suggests the inevitable connection between Molière's character and Pecksniff. The comparison was made at an early date – for instance, by the French critic Hippolyte Taine, in one of the least odd sections of his essay on Dickens.[3] There he claims that, hypocrisy being the national vice of England, Pecksniff would be impossible, unbearably repellent in France. Tartuffe has become unthinkable since Voltaire, he asserts, and the French prefer the affectation of vice to that of virtue; he then analyses some of the distinctions between Tartuffe and Pecksniff. Indeed, the comparison between the two characters is one of the compulsory rhetorical exercises expected of a would-be critic of *Martin Chuzzlewit*, especially if he is French.

Almost every writer on *Chuzzlewit* has discussed some aspect or other of Pecksniff or of the Pecksniffs. On the specific point of Pecksniff's *tartufferie* (a word used by Taine and very current in French), perhaps the clearest statement, paradoxically, is that of Q. D. Leavis. Paradoxically, because the Leavises' book on Dickens does not deal with *Martin Chuzzlewit* specifically. But in her chapter on *Copperfield* Mrs Leavis wrote: 'His ambition to write an English *Tartuffe* which has produced an English Pecksniff, the exponent of national hypocrisy in its early Victorian forms, gave him also the scene of Tartuffe's exposure, a scene inevitable with a dominant evil character of this type'.[4]

In fact there is no very close resemblance between Molière's Tartuffe and Dickens's Pecksniff, apart from the original design of both authors to denounce and expose hypocrisy; and even that is not identical. Tartuffe is basically a *faux dévot*, ruthlessly exploiting religion or the religiosity of his misguided victims for his own ends, whether financial or amorous, whereas Pecksniff is on the whole a lay moralist preacher, whose allusions to theology are few and far between; he is a philanthropist (or poses as one) rather than a *dévot*.

Besides, Molière, when he was charged with having ridiculed religious belief and saintly conduct, insisted that it was only spurious faith and conduct that he had attacked, the exception rather than the rule, whereas Dickens was openly denouncing hypocrisy as the national vice of Victorian England. Pecksniff's hypocrisy has attracted a good deal of attention and has been diversely appraised. It may have demanded some courage of John Forster to plead guilty of Pecksniffery as a national characteristic; he did so while rejoicing that it was still better than what Taine regarded as the French attitude to vice and virtue, but he did so openly and unambiguously, starting from the idea that the anti-American satire in *Chuzzlewit* was more than compensated by the denunciation of Pecksniffery in Britain:

They [Americans] had no Pecksniff at any rate. Bred in a more poisonous swamp than their Eden, of greatly older standing and much harder to be drained, Pecksniff was all our own. The confession is not encouraging to national pride, but this character is so far English, that though our countrymen as a rule are by no means Pecksniffs the ruling weakness is to countenance and encourage the race. When people call the character exaggerated, and protest that the lines are too broad to deceive anyone, they only refuse, naturally enough, to sanction in a book what half their lives is passed in tolerating if not worshipping . . . They agree to be deceived in a reality, and reward themselves by refusing to be deceived in a fiction.[5]

Another bold-faced attempt at annexation of Pecksniff to a community was recently made on behalf of the Evangelicals by Norris Pope; in his book *Dickens and Charity* Pope makes similar claims in the case of every disagreeable exploiter of popular and ignorant piety, from Stiggins in *Pickwick* to Chadband in *Bleak House*. Of Pecksniff himself, this is what Norris Pope has to say (in his chapter called 'Dickens and Evangelicalism'):

[in] the unctuous Pecksniff, the suspiciously Low Church Tartuffe of the novel *Martin Chuzzlewit* . . . there is little solid ground for proving that Dickens was deliberately ridiculing any religious party or sect, although there were surely more than enough hints to make evangelicals uncomfortable.[6]

I find this comment interesting. Norris Pope is saying in effect that Dickens attacked the Evangelicals without naming them, but by depicting them in such a way that they could not fail to recognize themselves.

Hypocrisy is not the sum total of Pecksniff's personality. He is also a shining example of the vice that Dickens was even more spectacularly exposing in the novel as a whole and in the person of his young 'Hero' in particular: selfishness. Indeed, hypocrisy is an attitude in life adopted by Pecksniff and his kind in order to serve their own interests, exclusively, under a disguise of morality and altruism; but selfishness is at the core of every step taken by Seth Pecksniff. Walter Allen calls him 'the absolutely selfish man . . . a monster of self-regard' and sees him as disturbing rather than merely absurd.[7] And Kathleen Tillotson shows that the central theme of *Chuzzlewit*, whether selfishness or hypocrisy, has not been made sufficiently clear or evident, and that in Pecksniff himself 'Dickens's comic inventiveness is still overflowing, neither subordinated to the general purpose nor fully contained by moral and social criticism'.[8]

Unlike Mrs Gamp, his rival for the crown of Dickens's supreme achievement of characterization in *Chuzzlewit*, Pecksniff is indeed, it must be emphasized, involved in the plot, or plots, of the novel. His career in the course of the events narrated by Dickens is worth watching with some care, even if there is much truth in Chesterton's comment that he is at his best when he has least to do, or that 'While Pecksniff is the best thing in the story, the story is the worst thing in Pecksniff'.[9] The novel begins with him and he occupies a good deal of space in many chapters (at least fourteen, plus seven others in which he is represented by his offspring).

The first portrait of Pecksniff is given in chapter II: 'Mr. Pecksniff was a moral man: a grave man, a man of noble sentiments, and speech' (II, 62/11) and much more to the same effect. In this early example the irony is perhaps exceptionally fine, in that the word *sentiments* could be taken to imply a modicum of sincerity if it had not been coupled with *speech*; coupled with *speech* as they in fact are, Pecksniff's *sentiments* can only be phrases or formulas. The irony to which he is constantly exposed will soon enough be understood by the reader, and expressions like 'worthy man' or 'ample benevolence' (IV, 95/42–3) are not intended to take us in. Things become even clearer when praise of the man and his intentions is closely associated with his unsavoury actions – he was, we are told, 'purposing, in the fervor of his affectionate zeal, to apply his ear once more to the keyhole' (IV, 96/43) – and this goes on through many scenes. Other ironical devices are the references to Mr Pecksniff's enemies, who were always denouncing him behind his back, but who are themselves denounced by the narrator as 'calumniators' (X, 217/158); the anonymous enemies belong to the mock-heroic style, to which Dickens has recourse on many occasions and in several ways – for instance, by pretending that there is harmony between the placidity of Pecksniff and the tranquil breast of Nature herself (XXX, 550/479).

Pecksniff is far from being all of a piece, and he is often not only diverting but truly admirable in his own right, and in his own way. His pleading with Old Martin in Young Martin's favour is of course insincere, special pleading, but it is done with skill (III); his dealing with cadgers, like Slyme and Tigg, is masterly (IV, 104/50-1) and much more virile than Young Martin's or Tom Pinch's reaction of easy acquiescence to similar requests. One of his sentences, when showing Martin round his house, will be recognized with delight by many readers who have encountered other humbugs in real life: 'Various books you observe . . . connected with our pursuit. I have scribbled myself, but have not yet published' (V, 136/81). It is this 'not yet published' which strikes me as the infallible sign of unjustified pretensions. Mr Pecksniff will later, more surprisingly, reveal his alcoholic leanings, and even be seen in a splendid comic scene of drunkenness. When he is on his way to London we are told:

> That he might the better feed and cherish that sacred flame of gratitude in his breast, Mr. Pecksniff remarked that he would trouble his eldest daughter, even in this early stage of their journey, for the brandy-bottle. And from the narrow neck of that stone vessel, he imbibed a copious refreshment. (VIII, 174/119)

As to the episode at Todgers's (IX, 208 ff./150 ff.), it is almost too well known to need detailed allusion here. But mention must be made of the fact that under the influence Mr Pecksniff discloses his amorous and even libidinous nature, which will be abundantly confirmed in his disagreeable scene with Mary Graham (XXX, 546/475 and 553–4/482–3). Dickens, who has often been charged with excessive reticence in sexual matters, seems to have shrewdly observed and denounced in Pecksniff's case the repellent desires of a man past his youth, constantly wearing a saintly mask, but whose virility, or simply his pruriency, still troubles him, and erupts when he is off his guard and believes himself to be safe. In all this, of course, Pecksniff resembles Tartuffe once more, and Dickens is clearly indebted to Molière.

Among his other characteristics the most striking is his toadying (manifest, for instance, during his visit to Ruth Pinch's employer, when he enthuses over the disagreeable and spoilt girl whom Ruth is supposed to be teaching: IX, 197/140–1). That, combined with his thick skin and the contrast between his preaching and his example, will eventually ruin him with Old Martin. The scene in which the latter tells him of the slanderous imputations from which they are likely to suffer if they join forces as they prepare to do is not particularly convincing in terms of ordinary verisimilitude, but it serves a purpose in the plot and the development of Pecksniff's role. Martin begins to tell him: 'the tale, as I clearly foresee, will run thus: That to mark my contempt for the rabble whom I despised, I chose from among them the very worst, and made him do my will'. And the conclusion of the longish tirade is: 'Lay your account with having it to bear, and put no trust in being set right by me.' At which Pecksniff expresses his delighted admiration for the old man and assures him that for such a patron he 'would bear anything whatever!' (X, 223/164–5). From which it can be inferred that Old Martin sees through Pecksniff and takes him in, rather than the other way round.

On the other hand, Pecksniff pleases the reader by his resourcefulness; he is very seldom disconcerted or taken aback. There is one occasion, at the end of chapter XX, when events are momentarily too much for him: Old Martin knocks at his door just when Jonas has proposed to Mercy Pecksniff and thereby angered her elder sister Charity, who had counted on receiving the offer herself. Everything is at sixes and sevens in the house, and Pecksniff knows very well that Old Martin is unlikely to approve of his boorish nephew, or of the contemplated match. Dickens cleverly keeps the reader waiting for three whole chapters (they are American chapters) before showing him how Pecksniff recovers his imperturbable self-possession and extricates himself from the difficulty. He will do so again, under more exacting circumstances, when he has overheard Mary Graham's disclosures to Tom Pinch about Pecksniff's importunities (XXXI).

The true nature of Pecksniff is exhibited whenever he appears on the stage of the novel, as well as – less felicitously perhaps – analysed and denounced both by the other characters and by the narrator. For instance, Old Martin's brother Anthony apostrophizes Pecksniff in the course of a very early scene: 'Pecksniff . . . don't you be a hypocrite' (IV, 110/56). And chapter XLIV begins thus: 'It was a special quality, among the many admirable qualities possessed by Mr. Pecksniff, that the more he was found out, the more hypocrisy he practised' (XLIV, 753/675). All of which may appear to be at best unnecessary, at worst indiscreet.

Yet Pecksniffery at its height is often truly diverting. Pecksniff telling his daughter 'Mr. Pinch is a fellow-creature, my dear . . . and we have a right, it is our duty, to expect in Mr. Pinch some development of those better qualities, the possession of which in our own persons inspires our humble self-respect' (II, 68/15–16) is achieving a masterpiece of hypocrisy, and incidentally reveals his tendency to use words without much regard for their precise meaning or sequence as long as they can create an overall impression of virtue. He cannot perhaps be called right-thinking, because he does not think half as much as he talks, but he aims at uttering a vague continuous noise evocative of received ideas, of ideas received uncritically by right-thinking persons.

Once Pecksniff has been thus observed, enjoyed and analysed by the critical reader, a few questions may well present themselves to his mind. For instance, does Pecksniff see through himself, or does he take himself in? In other words, is he a sincere or even an honest hypocrite, or does he practise hypocrisy deliberately all the time? An early passage like the following might seem to lend itself to being read either way. Mr Pecksniff is addressing his daughters:

'There is disinterestedness in the world, I hope? We are not all arrayed in two opposite ranks: the *off*ensive and the *def*ensive. Some few there are who walk between; who help the needy as they go; and take no part with either side. Umph!'

There was something in these morsels of philanthropy which reassured the sisters. They exchanged glances, and brightened very much. (II, 66–7/14)

In that case, what lies behind the speech delivered by Pecksniff is in fact unequivocal; he has just announced that he would take a new pupil (no other than Martin junior) without the usual premium. His 'Umph!' is intended to give the lie to the literal meaning of his words and to imply that he will find financial advantage in the transaction he contemplates. That is perfectly understood by the daughters, and the glance they exchange registers that understanding. Thus there seems to be double-dealing, if not within Pecksniff's breast, certainly within his family circle. One pleasant feature of a detestable character like Tigg is that he does *not* take himself in, or affect to do so; though emphatically a swindler, he is not what Dickens was to call in *Great Expectations* a self-swindler,[10] and there is a form of honesty in his profound dishonesty. The contrast is striking.

The other queries are more factual and point rather to loose ends in the plot than to mysteries in the character's build-up. Why does Pecksniff, when he comes to London, put up at Mrs Todgers's mediocre boarding-house (VIII)? Why does Anthony Chuzzlewit summon Pecksniff, whom he dislikes and knows to be a hypocrite, to his deathbed, and why does he insist on having his son Jonas marry Pecksniff's daughter (XVIII)? Or, how can Pecksniff hope to intimidate Mary Graham and to make her yield to his importunities by threatening to harm Young Martin if she does not acquiesce? For at that moment Martin is lying, desperately ill, out of reach, in the settlement of Eden; and Pecksniff, who does not know where he is, can do nothing against him (XXX). Finally, at the end of the book, the reader is given to understand that Pecksniff has lost all his money in the fraudulent failure of Tigg's insurance company. It is true that, with Jonas's help, Tigg had lured Pecksniff's money from him. But Pecksniff is unlikely to have handed over to him a large sum in cash. Tigg is murdered on his way back to London, and there is no way in which Pecksniff's fortune could have been conveyed to Tigg's accomplices, for them to abscond with it.

A less obvious trait of Pecksniff's personality is his gullibility, which plays such an important part in the story; this man who devotes his life to taking others in is easily taken in by such a vulgar crook as Tigg, simply because the latter invites him to join in the exploitation of the gullibility of other victims and thus speaks a language wholly accessible to Pecksniff. Pecksniff's own language is a masterly achievement on Dickens's part and is second only to Mrs Gamp's as a source of delight for the reader. In addition to the examples already given above other gems can be quoted, like the following announcement of his and his daughters' forthcoming visit to London, an announcement made to the new pupil Martin Chuzzlewit:

We shall go forth to-night by the heavy coach – like the dove of old, my dear Martin – and it will be a week before we again deposit our olive-branches in the passage. When I say olive branches . . . I mean, our unpretending luggage.

To which he adds this comment on the illusions of youth:

> I remember thinking once myself, in the days of my childhood, that pickled onions grew on trees, and that every elephant was born with an impregnable castle on his back. I have not found the fact to be so; far from it; and yet those visions have comforted me under circumstances of trial. (VI, 141–2/86)

Among many other instances of the Pecksniffian style at its best, the way in which the saintly man reacts to Charity's announcement of Jonas Chuzzlewit's proposal to her sister Merry, and to Charity's attitude under these trying circumstances, is possibly the most exemplary. He is as surprised as the Misses Pecksniff are, for Jonas had given all to understand that he was interested in the elder sister; but Pecksniff adapts himself to the new situation beautifully, chiding Charity ('Oh, for shame! Can the triumph of a sister move you to this terrible display, my child? I am sorry; I am surprised and hurt to see you so. Mercy, my girl, bless you! See to her. Ah, envy, envy, what a passion you are!') before greeting his future son-in-law with empty or deceptive warmth: 'Jonas! . . . Jonas! the dearest wish of my heart is now fulfilled!' (XX, 402/337–8).

Pecksniff has given so much pleasure throughout the book that his final public appearance makes the reader somewhat uneasy. Old Martin's revenge and punishment, his recourse even to physical violence in chapter LII, seem excessive, out of proportion as well as out of character on both sides. The reader may even feel that Pecksniff's protest against Old Martin's hypocrisy deserves to be taken into consideration:

> Whether it was worthy of you to partake of my hospitality, and to act the part you did act in my house, that, sir, is a question which I leave to your own conscience. And your conscience does not acquit you. No, sir, no! (LII, 891/807).

While there can be little doubt that Dickens invites us to sympathize with Old Martin, and does not ask himself Pecksniff's question,

which, according to him, is only part of the hypocrite's display of
offended virtue, the question remains in the air. It is not properly
answered, and perhaps it cannot be; perhaps Pecksniff has here
accidentally hit upon a moral truth of some magnitude. Whatever we
may make of the scene in chapter LII, I suppose few readers are
satisfied with the single later reference to Pecksniff, which occurs in
chapter LIV, in the course of an impassioned address to Tom Pinch,
and runs thus: 'For a drunken, begging, squalid-letter-writing man,
called Pecksniff: with a shrewish daughter: haunts thee, Tom' (LIV,
916/832). The reader must accept that Pecksniff has a shrewish
daughter left on his hands; and there is no unlikelihood in his being
addicted to writing begging letters; but it is difficult to visualize him
as 'squalid', to conceive of him in that state for ever. He had real
talents, and all Old Martin's righteous indignation is unlikely to have
altered him so drastically, to have deprived Pecksniff of all his
resources. This point has been perceived by more than one critic; it is
indeed fairly obvious, and is often regarded as one of the weaknesses
of *Martin Chuzzlewit*.

Like Mrs Gamp, Pecksniff is a character whose power is prolonged
and multiplied because he does not appear in isolation. Mrs Gamp has
her Prig and her Harris. Pecksniff has his two daughters. One point,
which I do not remember having seen noticed before, is that a certain
change of attitude to the Pecksniff girls on the author's part is made
apparent by the illustrator's altered treatment of the same characters;
in the early plates (69/17) they are shown as plain, or even ugly; by the
end, the younger girl has become quite presentable, and the elder has at
least become far less repellent. There is even one plate in which they
are both pretty (243/183). Miss Charity Pecksniff is the occasion of a
felicitous phrase when her voice is said to be such that it 'might have
belonged to a wind in its teens' (II, 60/9), and she is the object of
much ironic commentary throughout. For example, in the first
paragraph of chapter VI we read that

the sweet girl's countenance, was always very red at breakfast-time.
For the most part, indeed, it wore, at that season of the day, a
scraped and frosty look, as if it had been rasped; while a similar
phenomenon developed itself in her humour, which was then
observed to be of a sharp and acid quality, as though an extra lemon
(figuratively speaking) had been squeezed into the nectar of her
disposition, and rather damaged its flavour' (VI, 140/83).

Here, the words *scraped*, *frosty*, *rasped*, *sharp* and *acid* contrast with *sweet girl* and *nectar of her disposition*, between which they are sandwiched. Charity Pecksniff, in that respect, and by virtue of that analysis, is a forerunner of one of Dickens's most acid characters, Mrs Snagsby of *Bleak House*. Mrs Snagsby evinces a greater mastery of the arts of shrewishness, but the very same words are to be found in her first portrait as here: *sharp*, *frosty*, *acid* and *lemon-juice*, to which, for good measure, are added *pints of vinegar*.[11] Charity Pecksniff is involved in two love-stories or courtships, or apparent courtships. Jonas Chuzzlewit pretends to be interested in Charity, as has been seen already, but at the last moment shifts his proposal to the younger sister, and thus hurls Cherry into the depths of vindictive disappointment. Once she has returned to London on her own, and settled at Todgers's, she captures by main force 'the youngest gentleman in company', Mr Augustus Moddle, who had earlier been reduced to despair by his hopeless attachment to Mercy, and the certainty that she 'was 'Another's'', not his. The comedy involved in the scenes between Cherry and her Augustus is not at a very high level, and lacks lightness of touch; Dickens never quite outlived Boz's cheap journalistic belief that the enforced celibacy of a girl so plain as to be unmarriageable is uproariously funny. It is also a pity, and it also detracts from the success of the end of the novel, that the bulk of the last chapter should be devoted to Cherry's second disappointment, when she finds herself jilted and deserted on what was to have been her wedding day; instead of which Moddle is on his way to Van Diemen's Land (LIV, 912–15/826–31). Her humiliation, besides, which I am afraid we are meant to find amusing, has to occur in full view of a large circle of guests, acquaintances and relatives. Once more, a comparison with a similar incident in a work of Dickens's later days imposes itself. What happens to Cherry Pecksniff here is what was to happen to Miss Havisham in *Great Expectations*; but with what different effect, and in the hope of arousing what different feelings and interests in the reader's mind and heart!

The younger Miss Pecksniff, Mercy or Merry, undergoes other ordeals. Between the two sisters, though they can occasionally indulge in quarrels, there is at the beginning a certain amount of mutual understanding, as also between them and their father. But there are differences in character, and Dickens may have been aware, like more modern psychologists and sociologists, that the differences resulted in great part from the roles into which the family cast each of the children. Charity being the elder must be reasonable, staid, prim and proper. Mercy being the younger must remain girlish or, as her father likes to term it, 'playful' or 'ardent'; although she has been for many years out of her teens, she is still displayed with a doll on her lap when a visitor arrives, for it is part of the Pecksniffian strategy that Mercy should appear so young that Charity is not to be thought as old as she looks and, besides, Mercy should not be seen in the light of a rival to her sister, who has to go first. The strategy is analysed by the narrator: 'What a pleasant sight was that, the contrast they presented: to see each loved and loving one sympathizing with, and devoted to, and leaning on, and yet correcting and counterchecking, and, as it were, antidoting the other!' (II, 62/11). That the strategy is intended to be perceived as deliberate and to exert influence on the girls' behaviour, and eventually on their characters, seems probable, and much to Dickens's credit.

Jonas Chuzzlewit courts Mercy eccentrically, across, or through, the elder sister, until he proposes to the younger one. Mercy deliberately blinds herself to the real nature of her betrothed. In chapter XI, for instance, Jonas's speech, aspect and conduct, especially his brutal and contemptuous treatment of poor old Chuffey, fail to disguise his personality, and are not intended to do so; there is no excuse for Mercy's obstinacy, apart from the old maid's fear of never finding a husband and thus thinking *any* husband better than none at all. No other reason is seriously given for her acceptance of Jonas, in a spirit of foolish assurance that she can tame him. Old Martin's clear warning to her (XXIV, 463/396–8) remains unheeded, almost unheard by Merry in her giddy mood and spoilt-child attitude, which the family influence has prevented her from outgrowing. One of the most astonishing moments in the whole story is the conversation in which, having long since found out her mistake and the true blackness of her husband's personality, she actually forgives Old Martin for his failure to dissuade her (XXXVII, 657/582; and, again, LIV, 907/822). In all fairness to Dickens, it must be admitted that an early note in Merry's favour had been heard when the reader was told that she 'really had her share of good humour' (XI, 244/185). In any case, as a newlywed, Mercy soon ceases to be Merry, and she sinks to some of the dreariest pathos, or even bathos, in the whole book, when she is discovered as 'the merry one herself. But sadly, strangely altered! So careworn and dejected, so faultering [sic] and full of fear; so fallen, humbled, broken; that to have seen her, quiet in her coffin, would have been a less surprise' (XXVIII, 525/454). As to the end of the chapter in which that description occurs, it is difficult for a Dickens-lover to quote its tearful, prayerful, preachifying sentences. Suffice it to say that by the end of the novel, when Jonas has died, and she appears to take this blessed deliverance as a further cause for sorrow, one can only conclude, regretfully, that the widow Merry turns out to be one of the least merry widows ever.

The novel begins with Seth Pecksniff, and seems to concentrate the reader's attention on his character and actions deliberately both then and later. Pecksniff occupies two or three times as much space as Mrs Gamp. His hypocrisy gains him a local position; he is looked up to and respected in and around his village. As Andor Gomme has noted, his hypocrisy is not all of a piece:

> while Pecksniff remains a bland and pretentious hypocrite through the book, the nature and consequences of his hypocrisy *are* progressively revealed . . . Only gradually does the viciousness which is Pecksniff's real nature show itself: he does not simply want to appear better than he is; he uses his cloak of meekness as a cover for the ugliness of his schemes and intentions.[12]

Yet neither his hypocrisy in general nor his specific schemes gain much else than regard and position for him. He is more than once defeated, and taken in, much to his detriment. His not being taken in by himself renders his gullibility all the more surprising; trained as he is in devious speech and attitudes to others, he ought to be prepared for unmasking the deviousness *of* others. But there it is. What does he achieve by the end? He has constructed one building, a school, for which, much against probability, he has been able to exploit the labours of Young Martin, whereas neither Martin nor himself has the minimal expertise required to conceive, alter or carry out plans of any complexity or value. He has extorted from his few students small sums of money in the form of premiums and board; no doubt he made them pay exorbitant prices for very little given in return, but even that was hardly likely to make him rich. And, finally, he has long enjoyed the blind veneration of the adorable and adoring Tom Pinch, as well as having, Macbeth-like, 'bought/Golden opinions from all sorts of people'; but he has enough fineness or at least percipience in his nature to care less for the golden opinions of all sorts of people than for the devotion of a truly good man like Tom. That, and that alone,

can give him comfort and the modicum of self-approval most human
beings need in order to live at peace with themselves. Now, at every
other turn of the novel, Pecksniff fails dismally; he fails in his plot
against the two Martins, fails to deceive the older man and to ruin the
younger one; he fails in his hope of getting rid of his daughters by
marrying them off to the first taker. He fails to marry Mary Graham
and thus satisfy both his greed and his lust. John Carey, discussing
the scene of Pecksniff's proposal to her[13] in terms of cannibalistic
appetite, accuses Dickens of denying his own sympathy with such
appetites.[14] Pecksniff's sexuality is vivid and repellently convincing;
yet it is doomed to remain frustrated. Pecksniff fails further to make
big money by speculation. And finally he fails even to preserve Tom
Pinch's good opinion and to continue to be highly regarded by most
people around him. As has been seen already, he is duped both by
Tigg and by that most improbable of actors, Old Martin Chuzzlewit.

From a worldly and sentimental point of view, therefore,
Pecksniff's failure is complete and spectacular. But at least, as an
artistic creation rather than as a person, he does achieve immortality
and stature. If it is still possible nowadays, nearly a century and a half
after his first appearance in print, to discuss him at great length, it is
because he is substantial and even disturbing. As Michael Steig has
pointed out, comparing Pecksniff with early Dickensian grotesques
like Jingle, Squeers or Quilp:

> A Pecksniff is much more profoundly disturbing because he exists
> within 'respectable' society, and mirrors some of its pervasive
> ethical confusions. He is a figure with a mask but we never know
> which is self and which is mask (as Phiz's frontispiece will so
> beautifully bring out); and from one standpoint he is the
> quintessence of bourgeois respectability.[15]

In the Pecksniff family, it is without surprise that we find George
Gissing fanatically admiring the two daughters, as he does all the
disagreeable and shrewish female characters in Dickens; Gissing, in
both his books on Dickens, enthuses about Charity and Mercy,
asserting that 'for insight and careful workmanship [they] perhaps
take precedence of all Dickens's underbred young women' and that
there is no excess in their portraiture, so that 'they are bits of
admirable "realism" '.[16] Chesterton, no less predictably, did not agree
with Gissing and, on the contrary, thought that, whether Dickens

'knew it or not, the only two really touching figures in "Martin Chuzzlewit" are the Misses Pecksniff'.[17] With few exceptions,[18] modern readers are likely to experience difficulty in taking the pathos of either sister quite seriously. They will probably agree with John Lucas's balanced analysis of the lack of promising material for evolution in depth about Mercy:

> wonderfully though Dickens convinces us that Mercy is a silly, frivolous, but humanly interesting girl, there is very little room for him to develop his interest in her. As Jonas's wife she lapses into a stock figure of suffering who at best provides further evidence of her husband's brutality – evidence which is hardly needed.[19]

As for Miss Pecksniff, as the elder girl is properly to be called, she may have been intended for a study in frustration, and even as 'a first sketch for Rosa' (Rosa Dartle in *Copperfield*),[20] but she is far more rudimentary in that respect; Augustus Moddle is very far from being an ur-Steerforth, and not everyone shares James R. Kincaid's view of the

> really dark and bitter romance of Charity Pecksniff and Augustus Moddle. We laugh at Moddle, first of all, to economize pathos, I think, and to protect ourselves from the pain of those committed to trying for human contact and failing.[21]

Do we laugh at Moddle? Only if we receive some sense of his existence as a coherent and credible potential human being. It may not be the case.

Pecksniff himself has sometimes been discussed in terms of high – and possibly excessive – seriousness, in so far as Dickens probably intended him as in the main a figure of fun, through whom he would castigate manners by means of laughter. But possibly the best and most complete discussion of Pecksniff is to be found in Steven Marcus's *Dickens from Pickwick to Dombey*, where five packed pages are devoted to him; they are rich in fine and suggestive phrases, such as 'a totalitarian of the moral life' or 'Mr Pickwick turned inside out'.[22]

One point remains controversial; how does the late-twentieth-century reader react to the end of Pecksniff's career, that is, to his punishment at Old Martin's hands and to his final degradation? There has been, as late as the 1950s, at least one distinguished 'whole-hogger', a critic who went all the way with Dickens and asserted that 'The reader looks forward with tickled anticipation to the hilarious denouement of Pecksniff's discomfiture'.[23] But with expressions like 'looks forward', 'tickled' and 'hilarious' he is in a minority. Not that that is a way of settling literary disputes. Alain did ask the question in those very terms:

> Je ne sais si ces scènes d'expiation, où je sens un abus de force et une sorte de vengeance, plaisent autant qu'on est porté à le croire; ici il faudrait des témoignages de lecteurs.[24]

But some eminent readers' testimonies are available, like Chesterton's, who said the Pecksniff's 'fall at the end is one of the rare falls in Dickens'.[25] And Bernard Darwin speaks of 'an artistic mistake'.[26] More recent critics are less addicted to issuing trenchant opinions, dealing out praise or blame – or, at least, they do not do it so openly. Even Edgar Johnson, however, admits that Pecksniff is superb in his last scene, and perhaps most people remember him thus and not as the 'begging, squalid-letter-writing man' of the final chapter; for, in his confrontation with Old Martin, Pecksniff, though not likeable, behaves with admirable aplomb, and even has, as has been seen before, a valid point against his opponent, who has vanquished him only by borrowing from him his least honourable weapons of disguise and hypocrisy. In that scene, Pecksniff goes out, not of course in a blaze of glory, but with his own despicable brand of dignity, and in perfect fidelity to his own unpleasant self. It is thus that he is likely to remain branded in the reader's memory, as one of the unquestionable masterpieces of Dickensian characterization.

## NOTES: CHAPTER 6

1  See K. J. Fielding, *Charles Dickens: A Critical Introduction* (London, 1958). p. 77. Margaret Cardwell, in her introduction to the Clarendon *Chuzzlewit* (p. xxxviii), accepts this identification.
2  See Michael Steig, *Dickens and Phiz* (Bloomington, Ind./London, 1978).
3  Which eventually became chapter I of book V of his *Histoire de la littérature anglaise* (Paris, 1863). See Vol. 5, pp. 45–6.
4  F. R. and Q. D. Leavis, *Dickens the Novelist* (London, 1970), pp. 112–13.
5  John Forster, *The Life of Charles Dickens* (1872–4), Everyman's Library (London, 1927), Vol. 1, pp. 293–4.
6  Norris Pope, *Dickens and Charity* (London, 1978), pp. 15 and 25–6.

7   See Walter Allen, in Michael Slater (ed.), *Dickens 1970* (London, 1970), pp. 15–17.
8   Kathleen Tillotson, *Novels of the Eighteen-Forties* (London, 1954), pp. 161–2.
9   See G. K. Chesterton, *Charles Dickens* (London, 1906), p. 148.
10  See *Great Expectations*, ch. XXVIII (Oxford Illustrated Dickens (1953), p. 213).
11  See *Bleak House*, ch. X (Norton Critical Edition, ed. G. H. Ford and S. Monod (New York, 1977), p. 116).
12  See A. H. Gomme, *Dickens* (London, 1971), pp. 68–9.
13  Though he speaks of Mary *Grant*, he must mean Graham.
14  John Carey, *The Violent Effigy: A Study of Dickens' Imagination* (London, 1973), p. 23. For the opposite view (that there is nothing sexual in Pecksniff's pursuit of Mary), see George J. Worth, *Dickensian Melodrama: A Reading of the Novels* (Lawrence, Kan., 1978), p. 73.
15  Steig, op. cit., pp. 60–1.
16  George Gissing, *The Immortal Dickens* (London, 1925), p. 135. See also his *Charles Dickens: A Critical Study* (London, 1898), p. 184.
17  Chesterton, op. cit., p. 189.
18  Like Robert Garis, a lucid critic. See *The Dickens Theatre: A Reassessment of the Novels* (London, 1965), p. 240.
19  *The Melancholy Man: A Study of Dickens's Novels* (London, 1970), p. 120.
20  Fielding, op. cit., p. 79.
21  James R. Kincaid, *Dickens and the Rhetoric of Laughter* (London, 1971), p. 142. Although Moddle in his farewell letter (LIV, 915/831) mentions the Talmud, he is unlikely to have been intended as a Jewish character. When closely investigated by experts, however, the letter may seem to bristle with clues. Moddle is not a characteristically Jewish name, but a *Model* was the first editor of the Talmud in the eighteenth century, and Karl Marx's mother belonged to that Model family. Van Diemen's Land is of course the old name of Tasmania, but also the title of an anti-Semitic play by W. T. Moncrief, staging a Jew called Barney Fence and renamed Ikey Solomons in a later version. But *no* English translation of the Talmud had appeared before 1856; the Greek notion of Fate is foreign to the Talmud. If there is some verbal reference in Moddle's words to a religious text, it is to the Bible (Jonah), not the Talmud. And, in any case, neither Augustus Moddle in the 1830s nor Charles Dickens in the early 1840s could have read a single line of the Talmud. So the allusion remains mysterious, in so far as it is not merely farcical or evasive.
22  Steven Marcus, *Dickens from Pickwick to Dombey* (New York, 1965), pp. 235–40.
23  Edgar Johnson, *Charles Dickens: His Tragedy and Triumph*, (London, 1953), Vol. 1, p. 479.
24  Alain, *En lisant Dickens* (Paris, 1945), p. 75 ('I do not know whether these scenes, in which I feel an abuse of force and a kind of revenge, please as much as one tends to believe; here one would need some readers' testimonies').
25  Chesterton, op. cit., p. 148.
26  Bernard Darwin, *Dickens* (London, 1933), p. 75.

# CHAPTER 7

# Crime and Punishment

Dickens's interest in crime and its punishment was lifelong and passionate. It has been studied in depth by Philip Collins.[1] Yet its contribution to the conception and working-out of an individual novel like *Chuzzlewit* may still be found worth exploring.

Before *Chuzzlewit* had come first of all *Sketches by Boz*, in which many pieces had been devoted to criminals and to the workings of justice. The last two items in the 'Scenes' section are called 'Criminal Courts' and 'A Visit to Newgate'. The last piece in the series of 'Characters' is entitled, more surprisingly, 'The Prisoner's Van', and one of the most famous of the 'Tales' is 'The Black Veil', in which a mother calls upon a doctor to attend to the body of her son, just after he has been hanged. *The Posthumous Papers of the Pickwick Club* did not lend themselves to so lush a display of Dickens's fondness for criminal themes and characters. Mr Pickwick becomes an inmate of a prison and thus makes the acquaintance of 'a new and not uninteresting Scene in the great Drama of Life',[2] but it is a debtors' prison, and the author's purpose is largely to show that insolvent debtors are *not* criminals, though they are treated as such. However, among the nine 'interpolated tales' to be found in *Pickwick*, one is called 'The Convict's Return'. *Oliver Twist* was much more preoccupied with crimes of all kinds (burglary, prostitution, and receiving of stolen goods, and eventually murder) as well as with their proper punishment by imprisonment and death. *Nicholas Nickleby*, though written in a merrier and more varied mood than *Oliver Twist*, treats of the sombre and criminal machinations of Ralph Nickleby and his accomplices. Ralph's punishment is not dealt to him by legal forces, but by his own hand, which does not make it less decisive and gloomy. In *The Old Curiosity Shop*, the first of the two novels published as serials in *Master Humphrey's Clock*, the criminal note is again more subdued (though it has not disappeared, and Quilp is indeed one of the most powerfully drawn of Dickens's unscrupulous brutes). But in the second, *Barnaby Rudge*, crime runs riot: Barnaby's father is a murderer, the Anti-Popery rioters perpetrate all manner of criminal actions, and one of the most striking and convincing figures in the story, presented with loving care by the author, is no less a character than Dennis the hangman.

Between the conclusion of *Barnaby Rudge* and the inception of *Chuzzlewit*, the main event in Dickens's life had been, as we know, his visit to America, related in his book *American Notes*. Contemporary reviewers of that idiosyncratic travelogue had been struck, as modern readers are bound to be in their turn, by the considerable amount of space occupied in it by prisons. As a traveller, Dickens was in those days remarkably interested in the penal system of the countries he visited. Certainly one of the most powerful passages in the otherwise unsensational *American Notes* is that devoted to the description and discussion of the Tombs prison in New York, or to the Philadelphia gaol run on what was known as the solitary system. This fascination, which amounted at times to an additional, near-professional, speciality, may have had its origins in Dickens's childhood experiences. Not every novelist has at the age of 12 seen his father taken to prison (again, it was to a debtors' prison that John Dickens went, but it was still a prison), then seen the rest of the family join him there. Not every novelist has had to call upon his parents in prison, to share meals with them there – in short, to regard a prison as the temporary family centre, and as his home. For a novelist who was to become the apostle of the home and its values, this early experience must have been intensely traumatic.

In *Martin Chuzzlewit*, then, though no prisons are explored, it comes as no surprise to find crime, criminals, the police and even (in Nadgett) a kind of private detective occupying a fairly central place. George Gissing writes that 'an impression of scoundreldom was never better conveyed than in the group surrounding Montague Tigg, and of all Dickens's murders the most effective from every point of view is that wrought by the sullen, brutal Jonas'.[3] Indeed, *Martin Chuzzlewit* is one of the best illustrations of Dickens's curious and on the whole intelligent treatment of the theme.

Crime tends to be connected with secrecy, a connection which has led to the flourishing development of detective fiction and the mystery-story. Archibald C. Coolidge sees the omnipresence of secrets as the hallmark of *Chuzzlewit*, and writes that Dickens in that novel 'said that all men were secrets, an idea which relates his curiosity to his attempt by humorous and romantic oddity and contrast to make

his reader interested in apparently commonplace people and things'.[4]
Around the character of Mr Nadgett, Dickens has built up an
elaborate and perhaps overexplicit atmosphere of secrecy. The first
introduction of that character (at the end of chapter XXVII,
516–17/446–7) insistently strikes that keynote. The reader is told that
Nadgett 'was a man at a pound a week who made the inquiries. It was
not virtue or merit in Nadgett that he transacted all his Anglo-
Bengalee business secretly and in the closest confidence; for he was
born to be a secret.' In that single paragraph the word *secret* (or
*secretly*, or *secrets*, or *secreted*, for Nadgett 'seemed to have secreted his
very blood') is found no fewer than thirteen times. And Dickens
seems to have derived much pleasure from this display of his verbal
agility, since he returns to the charge at the beginning of chapter
XXXVIII, called 'Secret Service'. Mr Nadgett is there designated as
'man of mystery' (XXXVIII, 661/586), and the next two pages or so
(XXXVIII, 662–4/586–7) are full of expressions like 'quite a secret',
'secret manner', 'his own mystery', 'a mysterious change . . . in his
mysterious life', 'his own mysterious way', 'his slow and secret way',
and a total of nine uses of 'mystery' and 'mysterious', plus five of
'secret' and 'secretly'.

As to Jonas Chuzzlewit, he is one of Dickens's most interesting
criminal figures. He is shown in an unpleasant light from his earliest
appearance in the story. His most perceptible trait at first sight is a
kind of coarse brutality. The narrator shows that this is ascribable
both to heredity and to education; and another aspect of the character
is the demonstration that brutality and bullying are by no means
incompatible with cowardice and weakness.

It is in chapter IV that the reader makes the acquaintance of Jonas
and his father Anthony:

the face of the old man so sharpened by the wariness and cunning of
his life, that it seemed to cut him a passage through the crowded
room, as he edged away behind the remotest chairs; while the son
had so well profited by the precept and example of the father that
he looked a year or two the elder of the twain, as they stood
winking their red eyes, side by side. (IV, 107/53)

More details as to his bringing up are provided in chapter VIII:

it had been conducted from his cradle on the strictest principles of the main chance. The very first word he learned to spell was 'gain', and the second (when he got into two syllables) 'money'

– the two least pleasant consequences of the system being that Jonas 'imperceptibly acquired a love of over-reaching' his own father and a habit of looking on the latter, impatiently,

> as a certain amount of personal estate, which had no right whatever to be going at large, but ought to be secured in that particular description of iron safe which is commonly called a coffin, and banked in the grave. (VIII, 177/121)

Next comes the demonstration of Jonas's miserliness, for even when he is trying to ingratiate himself with his cousins, the Pecksniff girls, he endeavours to do so as cheaply as he can (for instance showing them 'as many sights, in the way of bridges, churches, streets, outsides of theatres, and other free spectacles, in that one forenoon, as most people see in a twelvemonth': XI, 234–5/175).

There is some disagreement as to Dickens's success in the creation of Jonas. Gissing is distinctly unenthusiastic:

> Neither at a black-hearted villain was [Dickens] really good, though he prided himself on his achievements in this kind. Jonas Chuzzlewit is the earliest worth mention; and what can be said of Jonas, save that he is a surly ruffian of whom one knows very little? The 'setting' of his part is very strong, much powerful writing goes to narrate his history; but he remains mechanical.[5]

Swinburne, by contrast, thought that

> Jonas Chuzzlewit has his place of eminence for ever among the most memorable types of living and breathing wickedness that ever were stamped and branded with immortality by the indignant genius of a great and unrelenting master. Neither Vautrin nor Thenardier has more of evil and of deathless life in him.[6]

Late-twentieth-century commentators do not often pass such wholesale judgements. Ross H. Dabney, for instance, analyses the character of Jonas as follows:

Dickens gets more inside him, gives him origins and connects him explicitly to values and principles in society. He represents an extreme development in the operation of the acquisitive principle, but he is also convincingly sullen, cunning, frightened, belligerent, and desperate . . . Finally, Dickens thrusts Jonas into a complex of apprehension, murder, terror, the chase, and final annihilation which he has already presented in Sikes's last days, and which comes up repeatedly in later books.[7]

Albert J. Guerard also finds much interest in Jonas, whom he connects, not with the earlier Sikes but with the much later Bradley Headstone of *Our Mutual Friend*:

The portrait of Jonas is richer, in a number of ways, than the pendant one of Bradley . . . Jonas's personality undergoes real change. The earlier Jonas . . . had the sympathetic attraction of a rough humor as well as great vitality, and a cynical honesty that broke through the hypocrisies of Pecksniff.[8]

As to Geoffrey Thurley, his view is that Jonas

is Dickens's first significant essay in the portraiture of Victorian commercialism. It is hard to agree with Edmund Wilson in bracketing him with Arthur Gride . . . as a 'conventional curmudgeon'. Jonas has a horrible life of his own and a vein of mocking humour.[9]

The 'rough humor' mentioned by Guerard, or the 'mocking humour' referred to by Thurley, is indeed an interesting trait of Jonas's personality. He is wholly detestable from the first, but he also provides entertainment of a kind. When Pecksniff hears of his having applied for, and been granted, Mercy's hand instead of Charity's as had been expected by all, and tells him that thus the dearest wish of his heart is fulfilled, Jonas reacts with a form of coarse wit which is evidence of his verbal, if not mental, resourcefulness, and places him in the category of Quilp (*The Old Curiosity Shop*) rather than of Sikes (*Oliver Twist*) or of Ralph Nickleby:

Very well; I'm glad to hear it . . . That'll do. I say! As it an't the one you're so fond of, you must come down with another thousand,

Pecksniff. You must make it up five. It's worth that to keep your treasure to yourself, you know. You get off very cheap that way, and haven't a sacrifice to make. (XX, 403/338)

As regards the way in which Jonas and Jonas's personality are put across to the reader, there are a few difficulties. The narrator occasionally indulges in psychological analysis, and that is not invariably of a high order. At the beginning of chapter XXVIII, for instance, occurs a fairly laborious paragraph, beginning thus:

> There were many powerful reasons for Jonas Chuzzlewit being strongly prepossessed in favor of the scheme which its great originator had so boldly laid open to him; but three among them stood prominently forward. Firstly, there was money to be made by it. Secondly, the money had the peculiar charm of being sagaciously obtained at other people's cost. Thirdly, it involved much outward show of homage and distinction . . . The latter considerations were only second to his avarice; for, conscious that there was nothing in his person, conduct, character, or accomplishment, to command respect, he was greedy of power . . . he determined to proceed with cunning and caution, and to be very keen in his observation of the gentility of Mr. Montague's private establishment. For it no more occurred to this shallow knave that Montague wanted him to be so, or he wouldn't have invited him while his decision was yet in abeyance, than the possibility of that genius being able to over-reach him in any way, pierced through his self-conceit by the inlet of a needle's point. (XXVIII, 518–19/447–8)

This passage does not show Dickens at his best. The analysis is heavy-going in its very style. Besides, the second reason adduced for Jonas's prepossession in favour of Montague's scheme is somewhat feeble. And phrases like 'this shallow knave' and 'his self-conceit' leave the field of analysis altogether for that of invective, and betray a kind of angry detestation of Jonas by the narrator which is harmful to the tone of the narrative. And this goes on; similar phrases recur throughout the rest of the chapter and of the book. Thus Jonas is designated as 'the blundering cheat' (XXVIII, 524/453), 'The ill-favored brute' (XXVIII, 527/455), 'the base-souled villain' (XXVIII, 528/457), 'humbled, abject, cowardly, and mean' and 'Not prepossessing in appearance at the best of times' (XLI, 708/633), or the reader is told that 'the whole mean, abject, sordid, pitiful soul of the man, looked at her, for the moment, through his wicked eyes' (XLVI, 792/713). Not that any of the terms used in these passages is undeserved or excessive, but the feeling may arise that it is the novelist's business to let the reader see that a character is mean, abject, etc., not to tell him so. The reader of *Martin Chuzzlewit* is shown how repellent Jonas is, and has no need of this extraordinary degree of insistence on the author's part.

Another possible reservation concerning the characterization of Jonas Chuzzlewit has to do with his language. In the specimens given above it has appeared natural enough, that is, as coarse and limited as his personality. But there are one or two episodes where Jonas is credited with rhetorical powers which may seem surprising and out of character (as well as incompatible with the situation of the moment). For it is when he comes home drunk in the night that he makes his most elaborate speeches to his unhappy wife Mercy:

> Griffins have claws, my girl. There's not a pretty slight you ever put upon me, nor a pretty trick you ever played me, nor a pretty insolence you ever showed me, that I won't pay back a hundredfold. (XXVIII, 527/456)

The elegant ternary structure of that sentence is no mean achievement for a man who had been 'stumbling out of the coach in a heap', and then had had to be pushed into the house, before he 'staggered into a seat', where he 'sat blinking and drooping, and rolling his idiotic eyes about', a moment before he delivered that speech (XXVIII, 526–7/455). Equally curious and noteworthy are the archaic phrases which he is addicted to, such as 'Hark ye!' or 'ecod' used in the course of the same conversation; a trend which Jonas has in common with his uncle Old Martin, for some obscure reason. They are not provincials. They are living at the earliest in the second quarter of the nineteenth century. But perhaps Old Martin and Jonas have simply inherited such phrases from the tradition of the stage; at any rate, it is in moments of melodramatic intensity that the old-fashioned turns of speech crop up with the most striking abundance.

Dickens's interest in Jonas Chuzzlewit is focused on his actions even more than on his personality. There is first of all an obscure plot surrounding the death of Jonas's father, Anthony Chuzzlewit. It involves the attempt to murder his father by giving him poison. The plot is so involved that after many readings it is still not clear to me what exactly happened in it. How was it that Jonas himself and his repentant accomplice Lewsome could believe he had succeeded in that criminal attempt, but had been mistaken or deceived? Perhaps few readers will care to remember, or turn back to, the scene (LI) in which old Chuffey, speaking 'like a man inspired', undeceives Jonas and the rest by explaining that Anthony had accidentally found out his son's intention, had burnt the poison instead of taking it, but had pretended to take it, and had eventually died of a broken heart, killed with unkindness though not murdered.

Before these events come to light, however, there is a period during which Jonas, though already surly and frightened, haunted or haunted-looking, takes part in scenes of lighter comedy, such as his courtship of Merry Pecksniff, across or through her sister Charity. The eccentric nature of the proceedings provides genuine entertainment, as in chapter XI, when Jonas seems to be flirting with the elder Miss Pecksniff, but keeps asking her questions about 'the other one', as he calls Merry (XI, 232/172–3). Even in those early days, there are hints of something sinister in Jonas's character. Near the end of chapter XXIV, for instance, when Merry protests against a brutal squeeze her fiancé has inflicted upon her in a fit of ill-humour, the reader is told that 'Mr. Jonas withdrew his arm; and for a moment looked at her more like a murderer than a lover' (XXIV, 467/399). At this point, Dickens undoubtedly knew what he was going to make of Jonas, and took pleasure in throwing out such a veiled foreshadowing of his intentions. The rapid deterioration of the relationship is not meant to come as a surprise; on the contrary, Mercy, like the reader, has had explicit warnings which she has chosen to disregard; and she can only blame herself for what happens to her. As appeared in the preceding chapter, critical opinion, and perhaps readerly reaction, varies as to the degree of sympathy Mercy henceforth enlists. A modicum of agreement can perhaps be reached as to the relative seriousness of Dickens's treatment of an unfortunate marriage-relationship, especially in comparison with the tone found earlier, in the days of *Sketches by Boz*, *Pickwick Papers*, *Oliver Twist* (the Bumbles), etc. Ross H. Dabney says:

> The match between them is of high importance. Aside from that of the Bumbles, it is the first evil marriage actually to take place in a Dickens novel . . . It is not, strictly speaking, mercenary, it is not

forced, in a literal sense . . . Dickens handles Merry's approach to marriage extremely well. She accepts Jonas out of sheer emptiness and frivolity.[10]

And J. Hillis Miller shows similar interest in Jonas's side of the bargain:

there are many sadists in Dickens's novels, but no character in Dickens, except, perhaps, Quilp, is more purely and undilutedly a sadist than Jonas Chuzzlewit. Jonas marries Mercy Pecksniff entirely for revenge.[11]

The next step in Jonas's ugly career comes inexorably. Jonas, who had intended to commit parricide and thought he had done so, who had later become a brutally sadistic husband, is only too ready to fall into the clutches of a swindler like Montague Tigg. When the latter, through his detective employee Nadgett, has unearthed the most compromising facts, or supposed facts, of Jonas's shady past, Jonas characteristically attempts to flee the country. On finding that flight is impossible, he at once decides that he has no other chance of escaping punishment than murder. Murder begets murder. It is as a direct and inescapable consequence of his putative parricide that Jonas is cornered into murdering Tigg. The profound irony of the situation lies in the fact that Tigg is murdered as the possessor of damnatory information about Jonas which turns out to be false. Murder was thus unnecessary; it has been, so to speak, gratuitous, but the point made by Dickens, and I think brilliantly made in *Martin Chuzzlewit*, is that crime has its own psychological laws which have relatively little to do with ordinary logic.

The most interesting and original aspect of the episode is Dickens's detailed analysis of the way in which Jonas works himself deliberately into a murderous mood and keeps it up within himself. The French critic Hippolyte Taine was much struck by the presentment of an obsession and its development, which he saw as verging on madness.[12]

Other criticisms of the episode object to its use and abuse of melodrama, and thus point to its connection with the stage in its inferior forms.

Philip Collins draws attention to a more distinguished connection between the murder in *Chuzzlewit* and the theatre by showing that it is full of echoes of *Macbeth* (especially the stormy weather and the knocking at the door).[13]

Less attention, as usual, seems to have been paid to the actual writing and to its lavish employment of rhetoric, not always of the highest order. In chapter XLIV there is much emphasis on Tigg's assertion 'I shall travel home alone' (XLIV, 762/683); he has been alarmed by Jonas's ominous presence by his side, and he is relieved and reassured to find that Jonas is returning to London on his own before him. But there is definite dramatic irony in the statement, for the reader may already guess that, if it may be true that Tigg will travel alone, he will probably never get home. At the same moment in the story, there is what might be termed an indiscreet capitalization in Jonas's announcement 'I have Something to do'. There was surely no need to lay stress on Jonas's ominous obsessiveness at this stage: it was already very much to the fore throughout the last twenty pages or so. Other examples of rhetorical capitalization will be found in chapter XLVI ('Guilty Deed': 791/712). And there is a veritable orgy of it in a brief paragraph of chapter XLVII, with Day, Night, Night, Glory, down to 'Glory's blood-relation, bastard Murder!' (XLVII, 799/719). Chapter LI contains several examples of melodrama and grandiloquence. Here is a paragraph purporting to express Jonas's emotions when he hears himself denounced by Lewsome:

> he heard the voice of his accomplice . . . openly proclaiming with no reserve, suppression, passion, or concealment, all the truth. The truth, which nothing would keep down; which blood would not smother, and earth would not hide; the truth, whose terrible inspiration seemed to change dotards into strong men; and on whose avenging wings, one whom he had supposed to be at the extremest corner of the earth came swooping down upon him. (LI, 861/779)

Then comes the description of Chuffey, the doting old clerk, whose mind is suddenly restored to him in order to enable him to serve justice, punishment and vengeance:

> The trembling figure of the old man shook with the strong emotions that possessed him. But, with the same light in his eye, and with his arm outstretched, and with his grey hair stirring on his head, he seemed to grow in size, and was like a man inspired. (LI, 863/780)

And finally, out of a whole series of rhapsodic comments on the denunciation and arrest of Jonas for the murder of Montague Tigg, and on the way in which these revelations seem to affect the very atmosphere and reverberate in wider and wider waves of horror around the house, may be quoted this culminating instance:

> 'Murder', said Nadgett, looking round on the astonished group. 'Let no one interfere.'
> The sounding street repeated Murder. Barbarous and dreadful Murder; Murder, Murder, Murder. Rolling on from house to house, and echoing from stone to stone, until the voices died away into the distant hum, which seemed to mutter the same word. (LI, 866/783)

The novelist who wrote these lines was certainly at a high pitch of excitement, and expending enormous energy.

Yet what is more interesting, more original and more genuine than these outpourings is the analysis that goes on behind the creation of character and incidents. Dickens is indeed at his best when he describes the murderer's mind both before and immediately after the commission of his 'Guilty Deed':

> His watchfulness of every avenue by which the discovery of his guilt might be approached, sharpened with his sense of the danger by which he was encompassed. With murder on his soul, and its innumerable alarms and terrors dragging at him night and day, he would have repeated the crime, if he had seen a path of safety stretching out beyond. It was in his punishment; it was in his guilty condition. The very deed which his fears rendered insupportable, his fears would have impelled him to commit again. (LI, 852/770)

> He tried – he had never left off trying – not to forget it was there, for that was impossible, but to forget to weary himself by drawing vivid pictures of him in his fancy . . . His mind was fixed and fastened on the discovery, for intelligence of which he listened intently to every cry and shout . . . Still he was not sorry. It was no contrition or remorse for what he had done that moved him; it was nothing but alarm for his own security. The vague consciousness he possessed of having wrecked his fortune in the murderous venture, intensified his hatred and revenge, and made him set the greater

store by what he had gained. The man was dead; nothing could undo that. He felt a triumph yet, in the reflection. (LI, 853/771)

It is difficult to believe, when reading such forceful evocations, that there is no authorial identification with the criminal. The exploration that is undertaken as soon as the murder has been accomplished, at the end of chapter XLVII (803–5/723–5) is indeed impressive and seems in a way sympathetic. Perhaps this justifies the note of boastfulness that occurs a little later, in another of the overexcited rhetorical paragraphs about Jonas's post-crime condition:

> The raging throat, the fire that burned within him, as he lay beneath the clothes; the augmented horror of the room when they shut it out from his view . . . the starts with which he left his couch,[14] and looking in the glass, imagined that his deed was broadly written on his face; and lying down and burying himself once more beneath the blankets, heard his own heart beating Murder, Murder, Murder, in the bed. What words can paint tremendous truths like these! (XLVII, 805/725)

It might have been better for the book if Dickens had left the reader to decide that these *were* truths, and that they were *tremendous*, instead of stunning him with such massive assertions. But no doubt he was aware of the strength and penetration of his imaginative reconstruction. The line between assurance and cocksureness is hard to draw. The spirit in which the sentence was penned is the same that had inspired, two years before, the preface to the third edition of *Oliver Twist*, in which Dickens attempted to reply to some criticisms levelled by reviewers at the character of Nancy: 'It is useless to discuss whether the conduct and character of the girl seems natural or unnatural, probable or improbable, right or wrong. IT IS TRUE.'[15] Here the vividness of the assertion is placed at the service of a less worthy cause, probably, but in the more proper context of a preface. In Jonas's case, however, one need not disagree with Philip Collins's view that the treatment of Jonas in the relevant chapters is 'a striking flight of imagination' because 'At this point Dickens shows real interest and inwardness'[16] or with the same critic's comment that

> By convention, blackmailers are fair game for murderers, so that Dickens can afford to enter more sympathetically into Jonas's

consciousness – which is, besides, more complicated, intelligent, and sensitive than his predecessors'.[17]

About Jonas's intelligence there can be doubts, but it is true that he is less stupid than Sikes or Rudge, and that he thinks and feels more and, yes, more finely.

To the murder and the murderer, then, it appears that Dickens devoted the very best of his mental and emotive powers. What about the victim, Montague Tigg or Tigg Montague? He has also found some favour with reviewers and students of *Martin Chuzzlewit*. There is of course no unanimous agreement about his merits as a character. John Lucas complains that he

> embodies an abstract moral concept rather than illuminating any considered social criticism on Dickens's part . . . Tigg the comic trickster suddenly changes into Tigg the frightened victim . . . This switch seems to me utterly implausible.[18]

But is it certain that a comic trickster, when threatened with murder, would not change into a frightened victim? At any rate, one finds an admirer and defender of Tigg in the person of Steven Marcus, who writes of him as 'one of Dickens's most seductive and amiable scoundrels' and asserts that 'beneath Tigg's rascality exists a germ of truth: in order to become a person of extraordinary importance and privilege in the modern world, one must *will* it, must be able to posture that importance and seize that privilege'.[19]

From his very first appearance in chapter IV, Tigg shows extraordinary verve and verbal gusto, almost to the point of appearing as a minor Dick Swiveller (of *The Old Curiosity Shop*). Also, Tigg's first name is suggestive of Shakespeare, and his treatment of Shakespeare is splendidly glib and offhand. When he attempts to convey his opinion of Slyme he says: 'he is, without an exception, the highest-minded, the most independent-spirited; most original, spiritual, classical, talented, the most thoroughly Shakespearian, if not Miltonic; and at the same time the most disgustingly-unappreciated dog I know'. And to refer to the event of his own death: 'if I am gone to that what's-his-name from which no thingumbob comes back' (IV, 99/46). Tigg always remains genuinely amusing and preserves his likeable glibness and aplomb (IV, 104/50–1). His speech about Slyme's position brings to the reader's mind echoes of at least three famous Dickens characters, Mr Micawber (in *Copperfield*) on the one hand, and a cross between Sir Leicester Dedlock and Skimpole (in *Bleak House*) on the other. The last-named are not so inconceivable a combination as might be thought at first sight, for there was mutual sympathy between the two men, who, on the one occasion when they met, got on swimmingly.[20] Tigg, in fact, says this:

> when such a man as my friend Slyme is detained for a score – a thing in itself essentially mean; a low performance on a slate, or possibly chalked upon the back of a door – I do feel that there is a screw of such magnitude loose somewhere, that the whole framework of society is shaken, and the very first principles of things can no longer be trusted. (VII, 159/103)

Nor is he less lively when he sounds like Mr Jingle in *Pickwick* while throwing off personal reminiscences:

> If you could have seen me, Mr. Pinch, at the head of my regiment on the coast of Africa, charging in the form of a hollow square with the women and children and the regimental plate-chest in the centre, you would not have known me for the same man. (VII, 166/110)

And, indeed, what makes him rise superior to all the other characters he brings to mind is that, in the midst of all this clowning, he never takes himself in or intends to deceive others as to what he is saying; he is never so solemn as Sir Leicester, so artfully innocent as Skimpole, so verbose for verbosity's sake as Micawber.

When next encountered, in a pawnshop in London, Montague Tigg has dropped Slyme in despair of ever extracting from him any substantial advantage, but he has not lost his capacity for making amusing speeches and striking comic attitudes, or his verbal inventiveness (see XIII, 281–4/219–24). It is true that when he reappears in the novel as a successful swindler on a large scale he is hardly to be known as the same man. But the very principle of the episodes connected with the Anglo-Bengalee Disinterested Loan and Life Assurance Company is that superficial alterations may be enough to deceive gullible people, though they should not be trusted by honest observers. The heading of chapter XXVII in which the Company is introduced to the reader for the first time, says as much:

'Showing that old friends may not only appear with new faces, but in false colours.' And the text of the same chapter harps upon the theme:

> Though turned and twisted upside down, and inside out, as great men have been sometimes known to be; though no longer Montague Tigg, but Tigg Montague; still it was Tigg: the same Satanic, gallant, military Tigg. The brass was burnished, lacquered, newly stamped; yet it was the true Tigg metal notwithstanding. (XXVII, 497/427)

It may seem odd that, having reversed rather than changed his name, and being now seen in good clothes and luxurious accommodation, Tigg should not be identified as Tigg by Jonas or by Pecksniff. But the point made by Dickens is still that people see what they want to see, and nothing else, and that when they hope to take advantage of an investment they are unlikely to pay much attention to details like names and physical features. One need not contend that all this is artistically satisfactory or faultless; merely that it is deliberate and coherent, even though there are moments when Dickens goes too far into melodrama and sombre machinations.

Thus, in *Martin Chuzzlewit*, the victim of crime is himself a criminal, who has moved from mere makeshifts, unrepaid loans and other petty devices for keeping alive to a large-scale swindle, which can only result in making a hugh amount of money in a very short time, and then absconding with it. He can promise and for a few months pay high interest on the sums entrusted to him, by receiving more sums of the same kind. As no real gain or profit is made, the company cannot last very long; it is bound to be found out, exposed, and to end with a resounding crash. Tigg, or Montague, is murdered.

That, then, is Tigg's punishment, and it is final enough to satisfy any appetite for retribution. In Jonas's case, the legal punishment works rather obscurely through the agency of Nadgett, who is a kind of private detective, and yet can engineer Jonas's arrest and enlist the help of the official police, including a now repentant Chevy Slyme, ironically involved in wreaking the vengeance of society on his own cousin Jonas Chuzzlewit. The work of justice, punishment by law, is something in which Dickens always took fascinated interest. His interest was also – at least, in those days – intelligent and generous; he was one of those who fought for the abolition of the death penalty, though he was soon to withdraw from the bold abolitionist position into the plea for a mere cessation of public executions.[21] In any case, the revenge of society, in the form of legal chastisement, is frustrated as far as Jonas is concerned, since he kills himself shortly after being arrested and before being committed for trial.

*Martin Chuzzlewit* is an early example of Dickens's fascination with police activities and with detection. Of Nadgett, Philip Collins writes that he is 'like Bucket, a "character"'. He moves in the melodramatic atmosphere of mystery, diligence, and uncanny perceptiveness' and that the passages concerning him 'display a delight in a professional mystery'.[22] There can be no doubt that Nadgett possesses qualities which Dickens admires and perhaps envies very much: a kind of supernatural clear-sightedness, and the ability not to betray emotion under any circumstances. No doubt Nadgett also has some of the actor's capabilities which were no less dear to Dickens; he could assume various functions and personalities. But he was the very reverse of the Crummleses (in *Nickleby*) or Mr Wopsle (in *Great Expectations*) or any other ham actor, in that, instead of verbal, vocal and gestural overemphasis, he constantly resorted to underemphasis. He was, if such a category is conceivable, a perfectly unreadable actor, supremely gifted for inexpressiveness, for the suppression of expression. Dickens once defines him as 'Mr. Nadgett, man of mystery to the Anglo-Bengalee Disinterested Loan and Life Assurance Company' (XXXVIII, 661/586), as though 'man of mystery' could be an official title or a position in life; in any case, being a 'man of mystery' is the essence of the man. A puzzling point about the characterization of Nadgett is the extent to which, while admiring him enthusiastically, Dickens may have wished to present him at the same time as somewhat ridiculous: after all, Nadgett is forever making appointments with the man who never comes, and, even worse, he is writing letters to himself which it surprises him to find in his own pockets and which he then destroys by putting them in the fire. He thus appears as a strange combination of pertinacious professional efficiency with absentmindedness and the other harmless eccentricities of a mild crank. This lack of coherence in the portrait and perhaps of unity in the creation of the character, or in the intention of the author, may account for some unfavourable criticism levelled at Nadgett and a certain failure of readers in general to perceive the interest of the character and its important place in the development of Dickens's work.

Nadgett's elaborate police machinery fails in two ways: by charging

Jonas with a crime he has not committed, and by not securing his legal punishment for the murder of Tigg. It may thus seem that Dickens was more interested in crime than in punishment after all, more interested in psychological and moral states than in actions. Perhaps he was out to show that the true punishment of crime consists in remorse, or rather, since it is far from clear that Jonas experiences remorse (indeed, the narrator states the reverse openly, as has been seen above), in other forms of mental torture for the criminal. One might even say that Dickens goes beyond the conventional view of crime and punishment, or crime and remorse, by showing that because of its psychological consequences crime *is* punishment. What need is there, either of the workings of justice of or conscience, since crime destroys the criminal as a human being?

Augustus Moddle, who had fallen in love with Mercy Pecksniff, and later became engaged to, and jilted, her elder sister, repeatedly gave it as the reason for his gloom that Mercy had become 'Another's'. This reference to Jonas Chuzzlewit as 'Another' is not without some subtle reverberations. For we may ask ourselves, using the terminology that has become familiar to readers of Joseph Conrad, whether Jonas Chuzzlewit is truly 'Another', or whether he is not rather, more alarmingly, 'One of us', or at least a 'secret sharer'. In other words, did Dickens intend, more or less consciously, to depict Jonas Chuzzlewit as a representative of ordinary mankind, as an *homme moyen* not particularly *sensuel* but with few exceptional traits? Mediocre, Jonas undoubtedly is, but the original, etymological meaning of 'mediocre' is precisely that: of middle degree, in between two extremes. Isn't Jonas, after all, a banal type of human being, warped by education, misled by circumstances, and thus turned into a hideous criminal by opportunity, the kind of person before whom the reader should exclaim: 'There, but for the grace of God, go I'?

There is also a line with what has sometimes been called the sensation, or sensational, novel. Dickens was to become a close friend of Wilkie Collins, one of the most gifted authors of sensational novels of the 1850s and 1860s. So far, Dickens himself had already published one truly sensational novel, *Barnaby Rudge*, in which there was a criminal riddle to be solved before the end of the story. In *Oliver Twist*, on the other hand, while there had been more than enough mysteries, they had nothing to do with the most criminal act (the murder of Nancy by Bill Sikes) which had been perpetrated before the reader's eyes. And *Martin Chuzzlewit* resembles *Oliver Twist* much more than *Barnaby Rudge* in that respect. Because the reader again sees Jonas preparing for and committing his 'Guilty Deed', *Martin Chuzzlewit* is neither a *roman policier* nor even a mere sensation novel. In the field of crime and punishment, it is a fascinating psychological and moral case-study.

# NOTES: CHAPTER 7

1 *Dickens and Crime* (London, 1962).
2 According to the heading of chapter XL.
3 George Gissing, *The Immortal Dickens* (London, 1925), p. 135.
4 See Archibald C. Coolidge, Jr, *Charles Dickens as Serial Novelist* (Ames, Ia, 1967), p. 108. Coolidge's reference seems to be to the end of chapter XXVII. If so, it concerns Nadgett and his class rather than mankind at large; but the general idea was also expressed elsewhere, unoriginally, by Dickens.
5 George Gissing, *Charles Dickens* (London, 1898), p. 112.
6 A. C. Swinburne, *Charles Dickens* (London, 1913), pp. 29–30.
7 Ross L. Dabney, *Love and Property in the Novels of Dickens*, (London, 1967), pp. 41–2.
8 Albert J. Guerard, *The Triumph of the Novel: Dickens, Dostoevsky, Faulkner* (New York, 1976), pp. 252–3.
9 Geoffrey Thurley, *The Dickens Myth: Its Genesis and Structure* (London, 1976), p. 95. Arthur Gride is a repellent old man in *Nicholas Nickleby*.
10 Dabney, op. cit., p. 43.
11 J. Hillis Miller, *Charles Dickens: The World of His Novels* (Cambridge, Mass., 1958), pp. 127–8.
12 See Stephen Wall (ed.), *Charles Dickens: A Critical Anthology* (Harmondsworth, 1970), p. 102.
13 Collins, op. cit., p. 299.
14 Dickens had originally used the ordinary word *bed* in his manuscript; but he must have substituted *couch* in order to avoid too many repetitions.
15 *Oliver Twist*, ed. Kathleen Tillotson, \Clarendon Dickens (Oxford, 1966), p. lxv.
16 Collins, op. cit., p. 278.
17 ibid., p. 279.
18 John Lucas, *The Melancholy Man: A Study of Dickens's Novels* (London, 1970), pp. 122–3.
19 Steven Marcus, *Dickens from Pickwick to Dombey* (New York, 1965), pp. 227–9.
20 See *Bleak House*, ch. XLIII.
21 See Philip Collins, op. cit., or my 'Dickens et la peine de mort', in A. Zviguilsky (ed.), *Actes du colloque sur la peine de mort dans la pensée philosophique et littéraire* (Paris, 1980).
22 Collins, op. cit., p. 215.

# CHAPTER 8

# The 'Stock of the Soup' Thickens

In his study of *The Metaphysical Novel in England and America*,[1] Edwin M. Eigner expresses his belief that the plot and meaning of *Martin Chuzzlewit* were preconceived by Dickens, and that the novel has a centre. But, even if there *is* a preconceived centre in the plot and in the meaning of *Martin Chuzzlewit*, that novel contains much else besides.

Hence the expression used in the heading of the present chapter, an expression supplied by Dickens himself, who used it in a letter to John Forster, written while he was working on, or making plans for, *Dombey and Son*. The long letter was written, according to Forster, on 25 July 1846, and sent to him with the first four chapters of *Dombey*. Dickens explained what he proposed to do with the main characters of his new novel, and added: 'So I mean to carry the story on, through all the branches and off-shoots and meanderings that come up', and also, a little later, 'This is what cooks call "the stock of the soup". All kinds of things will be added to it, of course.'[2] Nearly every word in those two sentences seems illuminating. At that stage of his career, once he had defined to himself and to his friend the 'preconceived centre' of his novel in progress, he foresaw that there would be much else in the book: branches, off-shoots, meanderings, all kinds of things. And these will come 'of course'. Thus one realizes that Dickens's own impression is that there are two kinds of elements in the novel he is preparing to write: the elements he has determined on, and the rest. His materials, he knows, will proliferate spontaneously, not perhaps uncontrollably, but without needing much guidance from him.

Because the revealing letter of July 1846 concerns *Dombey* and not *Chuzzlewit*, because we have no similar document available for the earlier novel, it is impossible to tell with absolute certainty what Dickens regarded as his central preconception in it, and what were in that case the 'branches, off-shoots, and meanderings'. It is, however, more than probable that the love-story or -stories must have been seen by the author as of central interest, especially in their relationship with the moral theme of selfishness: Young Martin at first loves selfishly, and has to be cured by harsh trials before he becomes worthy of marrying his girl. Most of the episodes, characters and incidents examined in the previous chapters are of sufficient importance to Dickens's purpose to have made part, if not of the preconceived centre (it is far from certain, for instance, that the American experiences of Martin and Mark had indeed been preconceived), at least of what came to be the 'stock of the soup'. But some aspects have not yet been touched upon, and in an attempt to provide a fairly comprehensive survey of the critical problems posed by *Chuzzlewit* it is necessary to examine as many of them now as can be compressed within one chapter.

*Chuzzlewit* has in fact an enormous cast, and one of the consequences is that Dickens ran into various difficulties in the matter of names for so many men and women. His attitude to characters' names has not been much studied.[3] It is obvious that he took an interest in the problem. In his early works, he varied between the farcically meaningful (Verisopht) and the merely picturesque (Pickwick, Nickleby, Chuzzlewit). He did not exclude ordinary names like Weller, Allen or Bevan. He was particularly fond of certain sounds or syllables, like *-ick* or *-le*. And he had the knack of coining some remarkably forceful monosyllables like Quilp or Gamp. An example of his search for adequate names is provided by Chuzzlewit itself. When he began his mental quest for a suitable titular name, Dickens followed his usual procedure of proliferation, approximation and elimination; his working-list gropes around Sweezleden, Sweezlewag, Chuzzletoe, Chuzzleboy, Chubblewig, Chuzzlewig.[4] Dickens seems to be rejecting *Sweedle-* as the first and major part of the name he is trying to create, but he will salvage it in a slightly modified form for Sweedlepipe; considering that there had already been a Nickleby, the preference for that kind of name appears marked indeed. Then, once he has decided to leave aside Sweedle, he toys with *Chuzzle-* and *Chubble-*. Perhaps *Chubble* would have been more clearly farcical than his final choice. But it is with his last syllable that he jotted down some really astonishing ideas; the *-wit* he was to adopt in the end is certainly better than such jocular syllables as *-wag*, *-boy*, *-wig*, and especially the rather flat-footed *-toe* (salvaged, none the less, for the

Spottletoes of chapters IV and LIV). No doubt, the final choice is not better justified in the sense that nobody in the Chuzzlewit family is a wit, but it is less farcical than any of the others. Another curious circumstance about the name is that it is criticized within the novel itself, and by its bearer, Young Martin, who explains to Tom Pinch on first meeting him that Martin *is* his Christian name: 'I wish it was my surname, for my own is not a very pretty one, and it takes a long time to sign. Chuzzlewit is my name' (V, 129/74). This is curious because Martin is criticizing Dickens for giving him and even for coining such a name.

Dickens sometimes appears like the stage-manager with too few performers at his disposal. Some of his actors must play more than one part. Thus, through one of those quirks of fate of which he was inordinately fond, Chevy Slyme reappears before the end of the novel in a policeman's uniform and takes part in the arrest of his cousin Jonas Chuzzlewit. That is again no mere economizing of invention. In fact it takes gigantic powers of invention to achieve both the coincidence and the metamorphosis from ne'er-do-well to guardian of the law and order. But it is not without some subtle irony, in the sense that Slyme who was a fraud has become the protector of law-abiding citizens (even if he is mediocre in his new role and not above temptation). Meanwhile his former associate, henchman and extoller, Montague Tigg, has crossed the border in the opposite direction, by becoming the founder of a fraudulent company and a blackmailer on a large scale; in fact, by the time Slyme turns up again as a policeman, Tigg has already been murdered as a consequence of his dishonest practices and it is for this crime that Slyme has to arrest Jonas. The name of Tigg's swindle or bubble is the Anglo-Bengalee Disinterested Loan and Life Assurance Company, a name which Dickens seems to have coined after some hesitation between the forms Insurance and Assurance. He must have been particularly delighted with the word 'Disinterested' in that title, which runs so spectacularly away from the truth. As to the connection between loans and life assurance, it is to a certain extent explained in chapter XXVII (see 514–15/444–5), but the financial mechanism through which the company could be created and do its 'work' for some months is not really accounted for; nor is it intended to be made wholly clear. What Dickens wanted to point out was that unscrupulous people could without too much trouble tap the inexhaustible resources of human gullibility and greed; on being offered huge profits, investors with available funds would be only too ready to lay them down, almost unquestioningly, eager to get the better of others. That had been the principle on which Ralph Nickleby had conducted part of his business, with his 'United Metropolitan Improved Hot Muffin and Crumpet Baking and Punctual Delivery Company'. No doubt the later fraudulent financiers of *Dorrit* (Mr Merdle) and *Our Mutual Friend* (Mr Veneering) were similarly exploiting the mania for supposedly advantageous investment, for making money quickly and painlessly; that is a historical feature of nineteenth-century England. A still later example in literature is Joseph Conrad's 'the great de Barral' (in *Chance*), who does not admit even to himself his dishonesty, though he, like all the others, has nothing to give, does not create or increase value in any way, and can only rob thousands of Pauls to pay a few Peters. The historical accuracy of Dickens's picture is demonstrated, in the *Nickleby* case at least, by Norman N. Russell in an article entitled '*Nicholas Nickleby* and the commercial crisis of 1825'.[5] That crisis involved the simultaneous failure of about eighty country banks and hundreds of newly launched joint-stock companies. Thus did massive but imprudent investments result in panic and ruin. Dickens had already satirized the 'bubble' companies and the gullible investors in his *Mudfog Papers* of 1837. When *Nickleby* was published, there had been another crisis, in the mid-1830s, known as the 'little Railway Mania'. The greater Railway Mania was to take place in 1848, after the end of *Martin Chuzzlewit*. In three successive decades, covetousness and gullibility, ruthlessly exploited by dishonest speculators, had caused disasters in Britain. Yet the legislation concerning joint-stock companies had been altered twice. In 1825, incorporation of companies by Act of Parliament had been made compulsory. While *Chuzzlewit* was being written, however, a new law was under discussion, which was enacted in 1844 and endeavoured to ensure both the greater freedom and the greater responsibility of the joint-stock companies. Registration with the Board of Trade was substituted for parliamentary incorporation. This did not of course prevent the crisis of 1848, but it was a step towards a more reliable system. Dickens himself was not involved in any of the wild schemes and resounding disasters. But he was a keen observer of human follies and distresses.

The other aspect of the Anglo-Bengalee which has intrigued readers and critics is the mystery of its beginnings in the few months between Tigg's appearance as a down-at-heel borrower from the pawnshop and his emergence as a very elegant and high-living company director. Once the company is afloat, established in expensive accommodation, everything must go smoothly, of course, for a time; money draws money. And the description of the richly decorated offices is one of the set-pieces in the novel, and with the elaborate repetition of the adverb *newly* (XXVII, 500/430) foreshadows the famous introduction of the Veneerings in *Our Mutual Friend* and the equally lavish use of *bran-new* in chapter II (book I) of the later novel. In *Chuzzlewit* the analysis of the external show and the side-effects of those garish company offices is done in a masterly way, while revealing a very pessimistic view of human nature (XXVII, 505–10/437–40).

Among the truly minor characters, Jobling the medical man who comes to be employed by Tigg's Anglo-Bengalee Company is interesting in at least two ways. First, because of his earlier presence at the time of Anthony's death, this method of having only one physician in the whole of the novel being characteristic of Dickens; it makes his fictional universe shrink. It would have done so even more perceptibly if he had not given up the intention revealed in the original manuscript of making Jobling the medical accomplice of Lewsome; the intention may have been abandoned because it would have been in bad taste for Jobling to gloat over Anthony's death if he had supplied his son with poison in order to dispose of the old man. The name Jobling, in any case, is given to the doctor only in his later appearances and in connection with the Anglo-Bengalee; it says what it means; it was to be used again, in *Bleak House*, for Guppy's feckless friend Tony.

Chuffey, the old retired clerk of Anthony Chuzzlewit, is a more puzzling case. It would be difficult to imagine a more unappetizing character than this dotard, who is a slow and messy eater, and whose function in life, at least in fictional life, seems to be to express admiration and affection for the repellent old Anthony and, to a certain extent, also for the even more repellent Jonas, while he knows that Jonas had intended to murder Anthony. Certainly, in that miserly family, an exception has been made in favour of Chuffey, who is provided with a home and sufficient resources in his old age, for no very good reason apart from vague sentimentality, which seems odd on Anthony's part; and Chuffey's gratefulness is so far understandable. In a way, one might say that Dickens's interest in such a 'senior citizen' anticipates the thinking and the feeling of the twentieth century about this difficult and worrying problem. It is, however, as a

Victorian and in order to work – successfully – on the emotions of
other Victorians that Dickens made so much of the pathos of
Chuffey's decrepitude. He was, we are told, delighted to find that of
all the characters in *Chuzzlewit* Chuffey happened to be the favourite
of Sydney Smith. And Sydney Smith had the deserved reputation of
being a great wit. Tastes do not merely differ. They evolve. One is
tempted to add: Thank God they do.[6] One can readily agree,
however, that Chuffey is among the least insignificant of the hangers-
on of the Chuzzlewit family.

Augustus Moddle is in a class by himself. Though he finds himself
unhappily involved with the two Pecksniff girls in succession, and
they are members of the Chuzzlewit tribe, he is by no means a mere
hanger-on of the family. No very subtle effect is achieved in
connection with this unfortunate person, who first appears as the
'youngest gentleman' among the boarders at Todgers's and gets
browbeaten by the older members of the group, led by the
insufferable Jinkins. Moddle is shy, and there is some psychological
verisimilitude in the way his shyness makes him regard himself as
romantic and almost pride himself on his deficiencies, whereas he
never gives evidence of distinction in any field. He falls in love – or
thinks he falls in love – with Mercy Pecksniff, but sorrowfully resigns
himself to loving in vain. Once Mercy has married Jonas and thus
become, as Moddle puts it, 'Another's', he can luxuriate in perpetual
gloom and despair, until the more robust Charity comes along and
takes him by storm, practically compelling him to declare himself. His
unexpected, unbelievable success in this unpremeditated conquest
does not cure him of his gloom. Cherry drags him along with her
wherever she goes; eventually, on the day chosen for their nuptials
Augustus Moddle absconds to the Antipodes, and lacks courage to
break with his bride otherwise than by letter. Moddle (whose name
seems intended to be ironically suggestive of the model young man he
is) is but a faint and feeble character, as he is intended to be, of course.

The same consonants as in Moddle's name, in a different order,
appear in the patronym of Mr Mould the transparently named
undertaker, with whom Dickens indulges his fondness for making fun
of the funeral trade. This was not to everybody's taste, and one
contemporary reviewer, writing in the *North British Review* in March
1845, was distinctly unamused and took Dickens to task for

a very uncalled for and, we will say, unfeeling attack on a

respectable class of tradesmen, in the person of Mr Mould the undertaker. He is satirized, not for any individual vices, but for the unavoidable peculiarities of his indispensable craft.[7]

This pious reviewer may have had undertakers among his relatives or friends, or money invested in the trade; in any case, he failed to recognize that the association between the 'indispensable craft' and private profit-making was (and is) distasteful and in a way scandalous, and made (and makes) hypocrisy one of its 'unavoidable peculiarities'.

But, indeed, through the Mould episodes Dickens manages to explore not only the humour of funerals but also something like the philosophy of undertaking. In chapter XIX, in fact, Mr Mould endeavours to explain why people spend more money on a death than on a birth, and comes up with the following comment: 'It's because the laying out of money with a well-conducted establishment, where the thing is performed upon the very best scale, binds the broken heart, and sheds balm upon the wounded spirit. Hearts want binding, and spirits want balming when people die.' There may be excessive insistence on the contrast between professional mourning and genuine grief, and excessive irony at the expense of 'the funeral, pious, and truthful ceremony that it was' (XIX, 385–6/322–3), but there is also an attempt, and a largely successful one, to present the undertaker's trade from the undertaker's standpoint. In that respect, *Martin Chuzzlewit* is in part a forerunner of Aldous Huxley's *After Many a Summer* and Evelyn Waugh's *The Loved One* and other criticisms of the funeral parlours of America.

Mark Tapley is also an original creation and a character in whom Dickens took much interest. That he is not totally convincing and engaging is shown, for instance, by J. B. Priestley's comment that 'we could do without Mark Tapley'.[8] Mark's early appearance at and around the Blue Dragon may not seem very promising, but as soon as he turns up in London and forces himself upon Martin as his unpaid servant he reveals himself as the third character in *Chuzzlewit* (after Tigg and Bailey Junior) possessed of ebullient verve. He is also a formidable ironist and gives evidence of his ability in that direction when he approaches Young Martin and describes himself as one 'as wants a gentleman of your strength of mind to look up to' or goes on to ask: 'will you, in climbing the ladder as you're certain to get to the top of, take me along with you at a respectful distance?' (XIII, 293/231). This is well expressed, shrewdly calculated, and efficiently though indirectly accusatory. On the whole Mark Tapley is a satisfactory and reassuring embodiment of moral health in a world – or in two worlds, the Old and the New – where corruption and vices like selfishness and pride are rampant.

Dickens may have partly changed his mind about the role to be played by Mark Tapley in the story as a whole. Mark's language may have been originally intended to be a more prominent aspect of his character than it eventually turns out to be. His speech could be described as a kind of semi-cockney; semi- only, because he is not a Londoner, but he does tend at times to use cockneyisms. He seems to have received a more or less perfunctory sprinkling of such forms as *sitiwation*, *wentersome*, *wessel* (XIII, 291/230), or the picturesque 'popilated by lots of wampires' (XIII, 295/234). Patrick J. McCarthy has studied Mark's language in greater detail than other critics and does not regard the cockney element as of paramount importance, whereas the essential phrases about 'credit in being jolly' seem to him overworked.[9]

When Mark is entrusted with a ferocious part of the anti-American satire it seems out of character; that is undoubtedly the case when he is made to launch into a protracted rhetorical tirade (with such sentences as 'Take notice of my words, sir. If ever the defaulting part of this here country pays its debts': XXIII, 439/372).[10] He is then voicing the grievances of Dickens and many other Englishmen at the time; he can do no harm to the cause, but the cause certainly harms him as a character. His real strength consists perhaps most of all in that he contrives, nearly throughout, to be saintly without becoming boring.

That is why the disappointment expressed by Barbara Hardy seems excessive or unfair. She complains of comedy and simplification in Mark Tapley's 'attempts to find situations where it will be hard and so creditable to be virtuous'.[11] However, Dickens does not show Mark as trying to be *virtuous* but *jolly*. The involuntary substitution of *virtue* for *jollity* is significant. A self-respecting modern critic has no use for the characters' virtue, which is so often tedious; jollity is more acceptable. Unfortunately, Mark Tapley does eventually succumb to the temptations of virtue and saintliness and starts preachifying in the final chapters.

In the post-fictitious world beyond the end of the novel, Mark Tapley will at any rate derive no credit from being jolly as Mrs Lupin's second husband, for his former employer, the comely, comfortable, easy-going widow, is described by Dickens with greedy fascination. Thus does *Chuzzlewit* contain examples of the two types of females that the novelist clearly found sexually appealing. There is, as will be seen later, the child-like, doll-like, presumably innocent, *petite* woman or girl (exemplified here by Ruth Pinch). And there is the matured, promisingly experienced, filled-in, plentiful, what French calls *plantureuse* (and really English should have such a word as 'planturous', for that is what Mrs Lupin is), adult woman. Dickens obviously found both types irresistible; at any rate, when he describes either, he appears to be in a state of sexual arousal. But Mrs Lupin is not an important character in *Chuzzlewit*; her true significance is as part of Mark Tapley's future – as his reward, in fact; and his reward is unmistakably sexual: *le repos du guerrier*.

Poll Sweedlepipe and Bailey junior come almost in one breath. Poll in the first place offers an intriguing illustration of Dickens's eccentric choice of names, of his quaint delight in strikingly inadequate names. Undoubtedly he rejoices in having a man called Poll, just as in *Bleak House* he will rejoice in having a girl called Charley. That is one of the forms taken by his inordinate and freely indulged fondness for incongruities. As regards Sweedlepipe, there is a very elaborate portrait of him, beginning with 'He was a little elderly man, with a clammy cold right hand, from which even rabbits and birds could not remove the smell of shaving soap' (for Sweedlepipe, like Mrs Gamp, combines two trades, being both a barber and a 'bird-fancier'; he is also, of course, Mrs Gamp's landlord). The portrait extends over nearly two full pages (XXVI, 485–6/416–17). The care lavished by Dickens on this description is remarkably generous, considering the meagreness of Sweedlepipe's part in the novel. But perhaps this lavishness can be accounted for by the existence of an original model for Poll in real life, according to one expert historian.[12]

Critical tributes to Dickens's success in the portraiture of Poll Sweedlepipe wax particularly eloquent when they couple him with his youthful friend and counterpart Bailey junior. Such is the case with James R. Kincaid's analysis of what he calls 'perhaps the gayest and sweetest comic pair in Dickens'.[13]

In the book itself, as soon as Bailey appears, when he is only an underling among the servants at Todgers's boarding-house, it is clear that Dickens is curiously impressed by the boy; he enjoys and even admires Bailey's vivaciousness, for instance, when he keeps the Pecksniff girls informed of the preparations going on for the dinner-

party in their honour (IX, 200/143). The novelist enjoys and admires
Bailey's most vulgar characteristics, such as his use of cheap
conventional pantomimic gestures; phrases like 'favoring them . . .
with many nods and winks and other tokens of recognition, and
occasionally touching his nose with a corkscrew' are followed by an
intrusive but dazzled authorial or narratorial comment; 'the proceedings of this remarkable boy, whom nothing disconcerted or put out of
his way' (IX, 204–5/147). Later, Bailey is described as indulging in
'action expressive of a faithful couple walking arm-in-arm towards a
parochial church, mutually exchanging looks of love', or demonstrating
'the bitterness of his contrition by affecting to wipe away his scalding
tears with his apron, and afterwards feigning to wring a vast amount
of water from that garment' (XI, 230–1/171–2). What seems to have
happened is that Dickens only gradually discovered the Weller-like
resources of Bailey junior, and gave vent to the delight the discovery
caused him; he comments on Bailey's language (XI, 230/171), displays
his sometimes mediocre jocularity (see, for instance, XI, 247–8/188–9)
which seems to the author not merely acceptable but truly enjoyable,
as evidence of verve, liveliness and ebullience of spirits. And it is true
that Bailey has great verbal resources and is ready to pounce on ready-
made phrases to show their inadequacy; when Poll, after seeing, and
being impressed by, Lewsome's face, 'informed Mr. Bailey, in
confidence, that he wouldn't have missed seeing him for a pound. Mr.
Bailey, who was of a different constitution, remarked that he would
have staid away for five shillings' (XXIX, 538/467). In a sense, Bailey,
by virtue of these very characteristics, is the fittest possible page-boy
or groom for Mr Montague of the Anglo-Bengalee; his showy,
demonstrative, verbal side is admirably suited to impart and receive
brilliancy to and from the bubble company. Like Poll's name, the
immense experience of life flaunted by Bailey at his tender age is one
of the incongruities that Dickens almost specialized in. When Bailey
recalls, as Montague's employee, an incident of his earlier career, he
'spoke as if he already had a leg and three-quarters in the grave, and
this had happened twenty or thirty years ago'. Nor does Dickens leave
well alone. The paragraph goes on, reaching its climax, perhaps, with
'He walked along the tangible and real stones of Holborn Hill, an
undersized boy; and yet he winked the winks, and thought the
thoughts, and did the deeds, and said the sayings, of an ancient man'
(XXVI, 489–90/419–20). All of which makes of Bailey junior a close
forerunner of Young Smallweed in *Bleak House*; but this ur-

Smallweed is much less disagreeable than his successor. His ebullience, his zest for life, his gift for gaining friends and providing entertainment make him a pleasant companion indeed, instead of, like 'Small', a prematurely desiccated morsel of mankind. Kincaid, once more, has a fruitful comment to make:

> Young Bailey, first of all, has a gift of parody which is reminiscent of Sam Weller, but is without Sam's cynicism. He is, perhaps, a slightly freer, lighter version of the Artful Dodger, borrowing his predecessor's use of endlessly happy irony.[14]

It is a pleasure to concur in this analysis, with the reservation that one who is not bent on privileging the rhetoric of laughter in Dickens's works will probably find that no irony in the world, indeed no comic attitude whatsoever, can be endlessly happy. And that is why the most enthusiastic critical comments on Dickens's achievement in the characterization of Bailey junior tend to appear strained. That is the case of P. N. Furbank's claim for the centrality of Bailey's character in the novel.[15] And also of B. B. Pratt's *rapprochement* between Bailey and Puck. But Pratt has some valid and original remarks to make as well, when she writes that 'His self-assured naïveté supersedes [for Bailey] the opinion of others', that 'to himself he is a vital, unlimited, masculine, entirely competent personage of considerable consequence', or, again, when she demonstrates that Bailey enables Dickens to enact vicariously some of his repressed aspirations to release from conventions.[16] Dickens's enjoyment of Bailey's performances may well express his nostalgia of a less distinguished, but also less inhibited life. For that very reason, on the other hand, it may appear that Bailey looks back, rather than to *A Midsummer Night's Dream*, not much farther than *Sketches by Boz*.

There remain Mrs Todgers and her boarding-house. Todgers's occupies a prominent place in the history of Dickens criticism, since Dorothy Van Ghent's 'The Dickens world: a view from Todgers's', originally published in the *Sewanee Review* in 1950, proved to be almost as epoch-making and seminal as Edmund Wilson's earlier article or J. Hillis Miller's later book; it inaugurated a new and more serious way of looking at Dickens. It conferred upon him a new status as a writer worthy of that kind of modern and philosophical approach. Not that Van Ghent's interpretation of Dickens's art as based on hallucination was a novelty, since that had been the view of both

Hippolyte Taine and George Henry Lewes, among the novelist's own contemporaries. But Dorothy Van Ghent had the advantage of being able to establish an impressive *rapprochement* with another writer of the twentieth century when she drew attention to

> the relatively innocent prospect from the roof of Todgers's boarding-house, in *Martin Chuzzlewit*, a description which bears a curious resemblance to passages in M. Sartre's *La Nausée* and other writings, where non-human existences rage with an indiscriminate life of their own . . . the observer on Todgers's roof is seized with suicidal nausea at the momentary vision of a world in which significance has been replaced by naked and aggressive existence.[17]

This is a splendid perception of the real importance and significance of *La Nausée*, and a fine tribute to Dickens's visionary quality. Perhaps it goes a little too far in making Dickens an existentialist *avant la lettre*, but the passage Dorothy Van Ghent discussed comes as a shock to the reader who has been enjoying the mild and traditional comedy of life at Todgers's.

Several recent critics have clearly been influenced by Van Ghent's views about the view from Todgers's. The influence is not always openly admitted, but that may be because it is self-evident that anyone discussing the view knows about her article. J. Hillis Miller does mention Van Ghent's 'excellent article' in a footnote to his own elaborate comment on the same passage from *Chuzzlewit* which, he points out, he interprets differently. For him:

> The observer of this scene knows that there is a spiritual life other than his own present somewhere, but he does not know exactly where it is, and is forced to attribute life indiscriminately to everything he sees . . . more astonishingly, he discovers that to this constant metamorphosis of things there corresponds a metamorphosis of himself . . . The climax of this experience is a double disintegration of the self.[18]

F. S. Schwarzbach sees in Todgers's 'an example of the possibility of a positive human in the very midst of a modern human environment'.[19] James R. Kincaid is attracted to the comic potentialities of Mrs Todgers's character, since she 'shows how one can face a black reality and live with it without the necessity of violence or madness'.[20] As for Albert J. Guerard, he sees Todgers's as in the main 'a place of communion and good-nature', and Mrs Todgers as 'one of the hundreds of Dickensian minor figures whose dialogue brings scenes to light'.[21] Guerard thus seems almost to echo the reactions expressed by Gissing eighty years before.

A glance at the *corpus delicti* itself reveals an aspect of the Todgers case which has not been much in evidence in the critical discussions concerning it.

The early descriptions of both the boarding-house and its mistress are far from appetizing. Todgers's is first seen as 'a very dingy edifice, even among the choice collection of dingy edifices at hand' (VIII, 180/125), then as 'a house of that sort which is likely to be dark at any time' with 'an odd smell in the passage' and a back-parlour commanding 'a perspective of two feet, a brown wall with a black cistern on top' (VIII, 181–4/126–8). The gloom is partly relieved by the narrator's infectious gusto and by his use of picturesque comparisons, as when he speaks of 'a gruff old giant of a clock' (VIII, 182/126). As to Mrs Todgers, though dignified with the title of 'the presiding deity of the establishment', she is then said to be 'a lady, rather a bony and hard-featured lady – with a row of curls in front of her head, shaped like little barrels of beer' and is soon seen looking at the Misses Pecksniff 'with affection beaming in one eye, and calculation shining out of the other' (VIII, 182–3/126–7). On the very next page, chapter IX opens with a fanfare of assertion: 'Surely, there never was, in any other borough, city, or hamlet in the world, such a singular sort of place as Todgers's' (IX, 185/128). And this is followed by the wildest extravaganza about the difficulties and impossibilities of finding one's way to Todgers's. So that deliberate exaggeration, pure fantasy rub shoulders with humorous descriptive realism worthy of the days of *Sketches by Boz*.

But by the end of the novel Mrs Todgers is greatly altered, like Mercy Pecksniff, possibly for the same moralizing purpose. Even if calculation had been shining out of one of her eyes only, the reader had better not remember it when coming across the following comments or sermon:

> in some odd nook of Mrs Todgers's breast, up a great many steps, and in a corner easy to be overlooked, there was a secret door, with 'Woman' written on the spring, which, at a touch from Mercy's hand had flown wide open, and admitted her for shelter.

When boarding-house accounts are balanced with all other ledgers, and the books of the Recording Angel are made up for ever, perhaps there may be seen an entry to thy credit, lean Mrs. Todgers, which shall make thee beautiful! (XXXVII, 658/583)

And the same religious spirit is responsible for three brief sentences in the last chapter: 'She had a lean lank body, Mrs. Todgers, but a well-conditioned soul within. Perhaps the Good Samaritan was lean and lank, and found it hard to live. Who knows!' (LIV, 910/824–5) Who knows? The narrator, apparently, knows a great deal, he can read souls, he has access to the ledgers of the Recording Angel, he is half-angel, half-God himself. What has happened is that Mrs Todgers has been *Mowcherized*. Like Miss Mowcher later, in *David Copperfield*, Mrs Todgers had been intended to be an unpleasant character and to play an unpleasant part. Partly, no doubt, because of the needs of his plot, but partly also out of a feeling not unlike remorse, Dickens changed his mind in mid-course. The phrase 'a corner easy to be overlooked' is particularly revealing, and prefigures the dreary preachifyings of Miss Mowcher to David. The theme is even pretty much the same: do not trust appearances. The truth of human beings is hidden or latent, and the true side of a personality is more often than not its brighter side. It is himself that Dickens may be taking to task, when he reproaches the early part of the narrative for having so facilely ignored 'a corner easy to be overlooked'. André Gide liked to claim that it is with edifying feeling that one produces bad literature ('C'est avec de bons sentiments qu'on fait de la mauvaise littérature'); both Mrs Todgers and Miss Mowcher, when manipulated by Dickens for excellently edifying purposes, lend support to this pessimistic view; for the literary result is deplorable. Recording Angels and Good Samaritans have very little in common with the usual inmates of a low but comfortable boarding-house like Todgers's; Mr Jinkins is not a Good Samaritan, nor is the youngest gentleman a Recording Angel; Dickens's effusions do not ring true. It was while writing *Chuzzlewit* that Dickens told Forster of the way in which his characters had 'opened out'; it was to him, he said,

one of the most surprising processes of the mind in this sort of invention. Given what one knows, what one does not know springs up; and I am as absolutely certain of its being true, as I am of the law of gravitation – if such a thing be possible, more so.[22]

So Dickens could be surprised by the development of his own creations. In the case of Mrs Todgers, he was not alone.

Finally, it may be interesting to note, as Michael Steig points out, that Dickens did not give his illustrator 'a chance to interpret "Town and Todgers's", this novelist's first great attempt at a surrealistic rendering of the city's alienation'.[23] Phiz, who was good at rendering aspects of London, was never called upon to try his hand at the mysterious, fantastic region in which Todgers's was located. Perhaps it had to remain fantastic and to exercise the reader's imagination rather than appear before his bodily eyes.

This survey of the minor characters in *Martin Chuzzlewit* has shown that the soup is thick and tasteful. This, probably, more than anything else, may account for the enduring success of the novel.

## NOTES: CHAPTER 8

1   (Berkeley, Calif., 1978), see pp. 34–8. The 'metaphysical' novelists studied by Eigner are Dickens, Bulwer, Melville and Hawthorne.
2   Quoted by John Forster in his *Life of Charles Dickens*, Everyman's Library (London, 1927), Vol. 2, p. 20. Reprinted, without other authority than Forster's, in *The Pilgrim Edition of the Letters of Charles Dickens*, Vol. 4 (Oxford, 1977), p. 590.
3   See, however, Fred Kaplan (ed.), *Charles Dickens' Book of Memoranda* (New York, 1981); and my *Dickens the Novelist* (Norman, Okla, 1968).
4   See Edgar Johnson, *Charles Dickens: His Tragedy and Triumph*, (London, 1953), vol. 1, p. 439, and Clarendon edition, p. 834.
5   *Dickensian*, vol. 77, no. 3 (1981), pp. 144–50. See also, e.g., R. K. Webb, *Modern England* (London, 1969), pp. 266–72.
6   For Sydney Smith's reaction to Chuffey, see Margaret Cardwell's introduction to the Clarendon *Chuzzlewit*, p. xxx.
7   See Philip Collins (ed.), *Dickens: The Critical Heritage* (London, 1971), p. 187.
8   J. B. Priestley, 'The Great Inimitable', in E. W. F. Tomlin (ed.), *Charles Dickens, 1812–1870: A Centenary Volume* (London, 1969), p. 21.
9   Patrick J. McCarthy, 'The language of *Martin Chuzzlewit*' in *Studies in English Literature, 1500–1900* vol. 20, no. 4 (1980), p. 644.
10  The awkwardness of this sentence may be due to the late insertion of the words 'the defaulting part of' by a presumably penitent author.
11  Barbara Hardy, *The Moral Art of Dickens* (London, 1970), p. 12. My italics.
12  See W. J. Carlton, 'The barber of Dean Street', *Dickensian*, vol. 48, no. 301 (1952), pp. 8–12.
13  James R. Kincaid, *Dickens and the Rhetoric of Laughter* (London, 1971), p. 143.
14  ibid., p. 160.
15  P. N. Furbank, introduction to the Penguin English Library edition of *Chuzzlewit* (Harmondsworth, 1968), pp. 16–17.
16  B. B. Pratt, in *Nineteenth-Century Fiction*, vol. 30, no. 2 (1975), pp. 185–99. Quotations from pp. 190, 194 and 189. The late Branwen Bailey Pratt's keen interest in and insight into that character may have been stimulated by the coincidence with her own middle name.

17  Dorothy Van Ghent, in *Sewanee Review*, vol. 58, no. 3 (1950), pp. 425–6.
18  J. Hillis Miller, *Charles Dickens: The World of His Novels* (Cambridge, Mass., 1958), pp. 116–17.
19  F. S. Schwarzbach, *Dickens and the City* (London, 1979), p. 92.
20  Kincaid, op. cit., pp. 150–1.
21  Albert J. Guerard, *The Triumph of the Novel: Dickens, Dostoevsky, Faulkner* (New York, 1976), pp. 240–1.
22  *Letters*, Vol. 3 (Oxford, 1974), p. 441.
23  Michael Steig, *Dickens and Phiz* (Bloomington, Ind./London, 1978), p. 85.

# CHAPTER 9

# The Salt of Pinch

The Pinches stand above the rest of the minor characters, and in several ways above some of the major figures in the novel. The difficult question facing a late-twentieth-century critic of *Martin Chuzzlewit* is to decide whether Tom and Ruth bring into the book the salt of Pinch or whether they are themselves so insipid as to make large sections of the story tasteless. As one who has read and studied Dickens for several decades, I may say that my own attitude to the Pinches has varied over the years, and each successive attitude has left traces in print; the truth is that I used to like Tom and Ruth Pinch, to admire Tom, to be charmed by Ruth, to be moved by the brother's selflessness and enchanted by the sister's pretty innocence. My latest rereadings have produced such an opposite impression that I am afraid of falling into the other excess. Dickens's own basic attitude never varied: he was in love with Tom and Ruth; he adored Ruth and revered Tom, and thus worshipped them both, more than was good for either of them as characters in fiction.

Edgar Johnson has suggested that Ruth is one of the figures who owed much to Dickens's fond remembrance of his deceased sister-in-law Mary Hogarth. She had died in 1837 at the age of 15 and Dickens, who had been very fond of her admiring and stimulating companionship, proved to be inconsolable for several years: 'Mary's gaiety and tenderness', Johnson writes, 'certainly animate loving, laughing Ruth Pinch in *Martin Chuzzlewit*.'[1] But there is another candidate for the dubious honour of having inspired the creation of Ruth Pinch; and that is Mary's younger sister Georgina, who entered the Dickens household in 1842, and had come to stay, even after Mrs Dickens went out of it, dismissed by her husband in 1858.[2] Georgina's claims are supported by Angus Wilson in his persuasive study of the relationship between Ruth, Georgina and what he calls the housekeeper ideal:

Georgy's effect upon the *dramatis personae* of his fiction was less happy . . . There appears in *Martin Chuzzlewit* Ruth Pinch, the first of the little housekeeper heroines, whose existence as human beings (let alone as physical, sexual beings) is all subordinated or, indeed, forgotten in admiration for their qualities as man's helpmeet. As Georgina was still only a visitor of sixteen years when *Martin Chuzzlewit* was written, it seems likely that Ruth Pinch was Dickens's ideal into which Georgy trained herself to grow, rather than the other way round.[3]

In fact the two theories are not contradictory; the two sisters were very much alike, and Dickens said that when Georgina came to stay with them he seemed to see Mary alive again.

The test of the reader's reaction to Ruth Pinch comes when she is living in London with her brother in a kind of semi-conjugal double celibacy. She then develops the little childish mannerisms which make many hearts melt, but make some minds regard her as a kind of idiot girl. When she reproaches Tom with having too high an opinion of her, she stresses her protest by 'pinching him upon the cheek' (XLVI, 772/692), and that is the sort of passage I now find it difficult to read without malaise. The (unhappily punning) phrase also has an element of embarrassing lubricity, often present when Dickens writes about Ruth: 'Pleasant little Ruth!' he calls her, 'Cheerful, tidy, quiet little Ruth!' and goes on with expressions like *doll's house*, *delight*, *glorious*, *blessed little pocket*, *laughing musically*, *merry pride*, *coyness*, and of course a lavish sprinkling of the favourite epithet *little* (XXXIX, 672/597). Part of the difficulty is that the narrator has seriously maligned Ruth by accusing her of being, among other wonders deliriously listed above, a 'quiet little Ruth'. She is never that; either she is laughing without the slightest provocation or she is 'chatting away the whole time' or, as likely as not, doing both simultaneously. She is, in fact, a terribly imperious, coquettish and demanding companion. No one could do a stroke of work, or read one page, in a room where she stood or sat; not without excuse did Tom's attention wander from his writing when she was by (XXXIX, 675/600). That is her whole purpose in life. There are moments when she seems to be unmitigatedly silly; when she is indulging in her notorious cookery, she keeps coming back for items she has hare-brainedly forgotten, and 'making a separate journey for everything, and laughing every time she started off afresh'; and there is the episode of the apron, which 'took an immense time to arrange; having to be carefully smoothed down beneath – Oh, Heaven, what a wicked little stomacher!' and so on, until the narrator says that he won't go on because 'this is a sober chronicle' (XXXIX, 676/600–1). But it is nothing of the kind; Dickens sounds wildly excited, nor does his coyness disguise the excitement. He seems to be libidinously doting over this description of a kind of inverted striptease turn.

Dickens's attitude to Ruth Pinch continues to be gushing and melting; when he says that 'the fragrant air was kissing Ruth' (XLVIII, 807/727), the suggestion that he would love to do the same is unmistakable. The overemphasized prettiness of the scenes of courtship and love in the Temple Garden near the fountain, is – to many readers – intolerable: 'that tiny precious, blessed little foot . . . the lightest, easiest, neatest thing you ever saw' (LIII, 896/812). The coyness with which reference is made to a kiss that isn't the wind's is absurd: ' "Do you think I would ask you?" he returned, with a – well! Never mind with what' (LIII, 898/814) and, again, 'It is of no use saying how that preposterous John answered her, because he answered her in a manner which is untranslatable on paper, though highly satisfactory in itself' (LIII, 899/814–15). Yet there can be no doubt that Dickens enjoyed himself when he wrote in that style, and rather prided himself on his achievement in that line of humorous delicacy. The reader may meanwhile forget that Ruth Pinch is supposed to be a governess, and thus an educator. Philip Collins has a few words to say on this aspect in his *Dickens and Education*: 'Ruth Pinch is a cypher . . . as a governess.'[4] Philip Collins had reminded his readers that there are only two governesses in Dickens's fiction, the other being *Little Dorrit*'s more picturesque Mrs General, of 'prunes and prisms' fame. Dickens's interest in governesses, he adds, had been inspired by the fact that his own sister Laetitia had recently become one, and the appearance of Ruth Pinch in *Chuzzlewit* led to the novelist being invited to address the Governesses' Benevolent Institution in 1844. This has historical interest, but is not convincing as an explanation. The choice of a governess's job may have owed something to Laetitia's employment, but what else could Ruth have done? And what else did females who were ladies in reduced circumstances do in the fiction of the time, or in real life?

Besides, Dickens did not pay too much attention to Ruth's profession; in fact, he really begins to rave about her after he has freed her from the repellent constraints of her employment and left her at liberty to behave all day long like an absurd doll-like creature. That attitude reaches its climax when Ruth's freshness and charm are played consciously and systematically against the playing of the Temple Fountain. Dickens advertises her as 'the brightest and purest-hearted little woman in the world', 'the spring of hopeful maidenhood', 'so fresh a little creature', and twenty other expressions in which the insistence on purity and maidenhood has something almost languorous and nostalgic about it (XLV, 763/684). When he takes to apostrophizing Ruth's 'foolish, panting, frightened little heart' repeatedly (XLV, 764/685), he is utterly losing control over his feelings and urges. This is criticized with extreme severity by Andor Gomme, who calls it 'a coy and simpering game'.[5] The other scene that arouses the displeasure of anti-Ruth readers and critics is the making of the beef-pudding, called 'rather tiresome' by Edwin B. Benjamin.[6] Very much depends on how the individual reader is affected by Ruth's laughter and love; they are part of the charm of a certain type of woman in the eyes of a certain type of man (which undoubtedly included Dickens).

Ruth's brother is a much more important figure. He is not, like her, mainly ornamental. He is intended to have thematic significance, by providing a bright contrast with the almost universal selfishness that Dickens was out to denounce in *Chuzzlewit*. J. Hillis Miller considers that the case of Tom Pinch expresses, contrary to Dickens's intention, 'the impasse to which total unselfishness leads' and also that the novelist

> wants to present Tom as an attractive figure, but he cannot help betraying by his patronizing tone the fact that he would rather sympathize at some distance from such a character than actually be such a person. Indeed, Tom is shown throughout the novel as something of a fool.[7]

Which is partly true. Of course, Dickens could not hope to identify himself fully with a selfless character; he was by no means selfless himself, and could not have written one line of fiction if he had been. One shudders at the thought of having to read a tale told by Tom Pinch. It would not even be full of sound and fury, and Tom is not an idiot; but it would certainly be empty of force and intellectual wealth, and thus would be signifying nothing. Even if Tom Pinch is, as Ross H. Dabney has it, 'morally . . . much finer than Young Martin',[8] Dickens has not been completely successful in his attempt with him. Perhaps he could not succeed entirely. Complete selflessness, in the world of men, is a crippling disability. On the whole, it would appear that Dickens hoped the reader, like all the worthwhile characters within the story itself, would come to respect and love Tom Pinch. Eventually so much respect and love surrounding him would be Tom's reward and compensate for his failure to gain the more usual forms of happiness, such as wealth, a love-marriage, parenthood, etc. But Dickens's attempt to surround Tom with love is overdone and fails at least in great part for that very reason.

It is true that from Tom's very first appearance Dickens has spared no effort to bring out his excessive humility and gullibility. His praise of Pecksniff and belittling of himself (II, 73–4/21–2) are characteristic. It is interesting that Tom's grandmother is said to have been a gentleman's housekeeper, like Dickens's own paternal grandmother (and, of course, like the more glamorous Mrs Rouncewell in *Bleak House*). The detail may have been introduced in order to account for Tom's low position in life, but this could have been achieved in a number of other ways, and it is tempting to think that the novelist is in fact unconsciously creating a link between himself and a favourite character. The contrast between Tom Pinch's selflessness and Young Martin's self-centredness is certainly not understated (VI, 146/90–3) and 155/99–100) and in fact Martin's patronizing attitude to Tom is, though less interested, not unlike Pecksniff's. Martin, who is much given to building castles in the air – he seems to regard this as part of his training as an architect, and really builds little else that we know of – is kind enough to welcome Tom in one of them. This is how he puts it:

> If I took it in my head to say, 'Pinch is a clever fellow; I approve of Pinch'; I should like to know the man who would venture to put himself in opposition to me. Besides, confound it Tom, you could be useful to me in a hundred ways . . . it would be devilish creditable, Tom (I'm quite in earnest, I give you my word), to have a man of your information about one, instead of some ordinary blockhead. Oh, I'd take care of you. You'd be useful, rely upon it! (XII, 252–3/192–3)

Dickens's preference for Tom is shown in other ways than this gross caricature. It is shown by having the narrator identify himself with, and adopt the naïve viewpoint of, Tom during his walk through the streets of Salisbury in chapter V, which transfigures everything there, even the meal he gets at the inn, and eats 'with a strong appreciation of [its] excellence, and a very keen sense of enjoyment' (V, 125–7/70–2).

Altogether, the treatment of Tom Pinch by Dickens soon becomes sentimental, In chapter XII, Martin has been describing his own prospective connubial bliss and the way in which he would tolerantly associate Tom, in his proper place and at a proper distance, with it:

> It may have required a stronger effort on Tom Pinch's part to . . . shake his friend by both hands, with nothing but serenity and grateful feeling painted on his face . . . than to achieve many and many a deed to which the doubtful trumpet blown by Fame has lustily resounded. Doubtful, because from its long hovering over scenes of violence, the smoke and steam of death have clogged the keys of that brave instrument; and it is not always that its notes are either true or tuneful. (XII, 254/194)

Mary Graham, Martin's betrothed, with whom Tom has fallen hopelessly in love, is much more considerate than the young man, but there is one occasion when he nearly confesses his feelings to her and exclaims:

> I shall live contentedly here long after you and Martin have forgotten me. I am a poor, shy, awkward creature: not at all a man of the world: and you should think no more of me, bless you, than if I were an old friar!

Dickens is so melted by Tom's goodness and by his supernatural self-denial that his narrator comments at once: 'If friars bear such hearts as thine, Tom, let friars multiply; though they have no such rule in all their stern arithmetic' (XXXI, 559/487–8). Nor has Tom in his, if this gushing sentence make any discernible sense.

Later, when Tom's eyes have been opened to the villainousness of Pecksniff, when he has been given a job by an anonymous *deus ex machina*, as though he were one of the sorry heroes of the so-called Angry Young Man novels of our time, a job with little enough to do and good payment for it, he has to show his blindness and unhappiness in new forms. He fails to see what is going on between his sister and John Westlock; and this is pointed out with a kind of pathetic humour that is not without charm. When John has given evidence of his desire to spare Ruth any uneasiness, Tom reacts as follows: 'Really John was uncommonly kind, extraordinarily kind. If he had been her father, Tom said, he could not have taken a greater interest in her' (L, 840/758). But this leads, in conjunction with Ruth's discovery of the state of her brother's heart, to one of the most elaborate and most ponderous stretches of moralizing about him: the long edifying speech to his sister, which begins – perilously, and unpardonably, it seems to me – with the words, 'You think of me, Ruth, and it is very natural that you should, as if I were a character in a book' (L, 845/763).

There is undoubtedly a certain kind of beauty in Tom's character. When he presents his departing friend Martin with the only money he owns, a half-sovereign hidden in a book, he has scrawled on the paper in which it is wrapped up, 'I don't want it, indeed. I should not know what to do with it if I had it', thus providing a superb example of his genuine and thoughtful generosity. The real beauty that lies in the simplicity and dignity of Tom's character comes out even better in his words (uncommented, for once) to John Westlock when he has been disabused about Pecksniff: 'I grieve to say that you were right in your estimate of his character. It may be a ridiculous weakness, John, but it has been very painful and bitter to me to find this out, I do assure you' (XXXVI, 639/566).

Is Tom's simplicity of the heart, as some have thought, or of the soul, as Joseph Gold claims?[9] The distinction is not perhaps so clear-cut as to assume great importance.

The narrator's numerous apostrophes to Tom are highly intrusive and very hard to take. Nor are they made less artificial by Dickens's use of the second person singular. They will be found time and again, beginning with chapter XII: 'The air was cold, Tom', or 'The loveliest things in life, Tom, are but shadows' (XII, 256–7/196–7). One sees here that Tom is to be made the privileged recipient of occasional platitudes, worthier of Mr Sapsea (in *Edwin Drood*, 1870) than of Charles Dickens. It goes on to the final paragraph of the novel, which, at the close of a largely farcical chapter, is another of those worshippingly pious addresses to Saint Pinch: 'Ah Tom, dear Tom, old friend! Thy head is prematurely gray . . . As it resounds within thee and without, the noble music, rolling round ye both, shuts out the grosser prospect of an earthly parting, and uplifts ye both to Heaven!' (LIV, 916–18/831–2).[10] That final sentence of the novel concerns Tom and Ruth, his sister, not Mary Graham-Chuzzlewit, with whom Tom had been in love. In this concluding section, the author seems to be both eating his cake and yet having it, vicariously; he has married and enjoyed little Ruth, as John Westlock, and he can have her company in perfect purity and sexlessness, as Tom. The final section is in great part a hymn to Tom's supernatural virtues, as a kind of implicit compensation for his celibacy.

Pinch has sometimes been seen as a descendant of earlier Dickens characters; such is the view of Barbara Hardy, who writes that 'Tom is a mixture of child and clown, a descendant of Pickwick, and his loss of innocence is not new, though perhaps more conspicuous than Pickwick's. But it is quickly healed and rewarded.'[11] Similarly, Garrett Stewart thinks that 'Tom Pinch is not a comic character at all, but merely a "funny" man. It is Dick Swiveller, in *The Old Curiosity Shop*, who is the last comic hero in the works of our foremost comic writer.'[12]

Revaluations of Tom's character have occasionally been attempted. C. A. Bodelsen's analysis (collected in 1964) was particularly detailed.[13] Jerry C. Beasley's appeared as recently as 1974 and presented Pinch as the 'moral and structural center' and therefore 'in a certain respect the most important character'[14] in the novel. What emerges from the spectrum of opinions expressed by the critics is that admiration for and enjoyment of the character of Tom Pinch nowadays tend to be asserted in a militant and querulous tone. This shows that Pinchophiles expect to meet stiff resistance to their views (and this tends in turn to make them fall into excess), but also that the torch of Pinchophilia is still being proudly carried from time to time by enthusiastic volunteers.

From the Pinches as persons to the question of love and even eroticism in *Martin Chuzzlewit* is an easy progress. The love-story of Martin and his Mary is so refrigeratingly sexless that the only promises of enjoyment are to be looked for elsewhere – in the marriages of John Westlock with Ruth Pinch and Mark Tapley with the widow Lupin. It takes the ingeniousness of very modern readers indeed to find out a crudely sexual motive in the relationship between Tom and Mary. Several critics base their comments on an unfortunate sentence in chapter XXIV, concerning the interest in music shared by Mary and Tom:

> When she spoke, Tom held his breath, so eagerly he listened; when she sang, he sat like one entranced. She touched his organ, and from that bright epoch even it, the old companion of his happiest

hours, incapable as he had thought of elevation, began a new and deified existence.

God's love upon thy patience, Tom! (XXIV, 462/395)

I have deliberately quoted the first words of the paragraph following the much exploited sentence about the organ. It is not of obvious relevance to the commentaries about to be evoked; but, precisely, such commentaries can only be made if one deliberately disregards the context and the piously admiring tone of what follows. One would like to know, for instance, exactly what Robert M. McCarron means when he calls the phrase 'she touched his organ' a 'sexual pun'.[15] McCarron's analysis is otherwise acceptable, but if the implication is that Dickens was having sly fun on his own by playing on the possible ambiguity of the word *organ*, this is so irreconcilable with the novelist's obvious and avowed Pinch-worship as to remain unconvincing. If, on the other hand, what is meant is that this ambiguity, which unquestionably exists in the word itself, enables some readers and critics whose minds work that way to pounce on its latent potentialities, well and good. But that is unlikely to be the kind of credit claimed by McCarron. There remains at least one other possible reading, which is more genuinely tentative and questioning, like Jerry C. Beasley's in the above-quoted essay. He refers to the 'almost embarrassing picture of Tom playing his organ – that instrument once elevated by Mary Graham's touch . . . for the rest of his days might be used . . . although it is difficult to believe that Dickens was at all aware of the auto-erotic suggestion of this picture'.[16] Of course, the word *is* there and carries with it implications beyond those of which the writer himself was conscious.

Not that Dickens is guiltless of Victorian mini-eroticism. In the course of one evening in New York, Young Martin lets his glance turn to two young ladies who attract him, 'not only from being, as aforesaid, very pretty, but by reason of their wearing miraculously small shoes, and the thinnest possible silk stockings; the which their rocking-chairs developed to a distracting extent' (XVII, 349/286). Needless to say, the very fact that the novelist, by thus displaying his obsession with tiny feet and thin stockings, must have felt that he was indulging in a daring game rules out any intentionality in the case of the organ.

Reverting to Ruth, who is clearly treated as a source of erotic emotions, Alexander Welsh writes: 'If anyone, it is really Tom who has discovered the sexual attraction of his sister./ The novel is designed so that the love of brother and sister appears to outlast that of husband and wife.'[17] This has beyond question a great deal of truth in it. If Dickens was not much given to sexual puns in print (nor, it would seem, in private conversation), he had a highly idiosyncratic and very complex notion of relations between siblings and their potential interference with conjugality.[18] Margaret Lane, on the other hand, lays stress on two further points; she comments on the feat accomplished by Dickens when he introduced an erotic element into an 'everyday practical' task like the making of Ruth's first beef-steak pudding, and comments:

> This is the way little women behave, and it can be very fetching. A marked insistence, however, on the little-woman image, though it endeared Dickens to his contemporaries, is one of the barriers, an accident of time, taste, fashion, between him and the modern reader.[19]

The connection between eroticism and food is not new. It may not come as a surprise to our post-Freudian century, but its intuitive recognition by a writer of the preceding era is worth stressing. The eating scene with Mrs Waters in *Tom Jones* and several passages in *Jonathan Wild* show the existence of a tradition of that kind, but the originality of Dickens lies in the sexual innocence of at least the female character involved. The change of tastes and ideals is an important factor in the making and unmaking of reputations, for authors, books, episodes and characters alike. John Carey's reaction, for instance, which appears so wittily reasonable nowadays, would have been unthinkable in the 1840s. Carey is irritated by the forms of eroticism in *Chuzzlewit*; thus, he writes that when John Westlock

> makes advances towards Ruth Pinch, Dickens's genial chuckles increase in volume, along with his coy professions of ignorance about what's going on. Oh! foolish little heart . . . Dickens positively hugs himself at the deliciousness of it all, and what he finds so delicious, we should note, is female alarm . . . The male appetite needs to be whetted by the fearfulness of its prey.[20]

Coyness is certainly something that has become unpalatable to readers of the present day, though one may wonder whether a change of mood is not already in the offing, now that many readers of fiction have supp'd full with accurate descriptions of sexual organs and what they can do.

By the end of the novel, Tom participates in a *ménage à trois* with John and Ruth, so that his chastity and his falling back upon his organ are induced by the double taboo prohibiting both adultery and incest. The last paragraph of the novel tells Tom that it is his little sister who comes in from the garden and sits beside him (LIV, 918/832). She had indeed made clear stipulations before agreeing to marry John: 'I am never to leave him, *am* I, dear? I could never leave Tom. I am sure you know that.' Which had elicited the following reaction from the young man: ' "Do you think I would ask you?" he returned, with a – well! Never mind with what' (LIII, 898/814). But we do mind that, in the course of an intolerably coy and arch scene, where the actual words of love exchanged by the young people are the only unemotional items, Ruth and John should kiss each other, so to speak, in Tom's honour, should commune or communicate in the species of a kiss in their worship of Tom.

Again, it has already appeared that Dickens is treating himself to various kinds of vicarious erotic enjoyment. He is Mark to Mrs Lupin; to Mary Graham he is Pecksniff rather than Young Martin, because Pecksniff is sexually aroused by her; and to Ruth he is both Tom and John.

There have been noticeable critical variations. Floris Delattre, a serious French Dickensian of the early decades of the present century, sees *Chuzzlewit* as 'une œuvre grave et forte, qui, avec les personnages de Tom et de Ruth Pinch, le couple exquis du frère et de la sœur . . . renferme quelques-unes des créations les plus vivantes de son œuvre'.[21] The phrase 'le couple exquis du frère et de la sœur' sounds exquisitely guileless. Dickens himself had referred to Tom and Ruth, in a letter to Lady Holland, as 'two of the greatest favorites I have ever had'[22] and gone on to call them 'little sparklers' whose influence 'is intended to refine and improve the rest' of the characters. R. C. Churchill, however, expressed widely different views; in an impressive analysis of *Chuzzlewit* as a comic masterpiece, he included an intelligently argued condemnation of the sentimentality surrounding the Pinches and the courting of Ruth by John Westlock.[23] It would be wrong to give the impression that there had been unanimous approbation of Tom and Ruth Pinch for about a century, succeeded by unanimous dislike since the 1950s. On the contrary, George

Gissing, by the end of the nineteenth century, had already called Tom 'a mere walking virtue'.[24] And even now one might do well not to dismiss too summarily John Forster's serious discussion of Tom's character and his arguments in Tom's favour:

> there is nothing so common as the mistake of Tom Pinch [his implicit belief in Pecksniff's goodness]; and nothing so rare as his excuses.
>
> The art with which this delightful character is placed at Mr. Pecksniff's elbow in the opening of the story and the help he gives to set fairly afloat the falsehood he so innocently believes; contribute to a management of the design more skilful in this than in any former work by Mr. Dickens.[25]

It thus appears that Tom and Ruth Pinch, as characters, are antagonistic to the dominant mood of the present moment. But further reversals of taste and opinion may well be in store; they may even have already begun. Dickens himself provides an early example of a change, if not in mood, at least in emphasis. The last sentence of the novel, in all editions since the Cheap Edition of 1850, reads:

> As it resounds within thee and without, the noble music, rolling round ye both, shuts out the grosser prospect of an earthly parting, and uplifts ye both to Heaven! (LIV, 918)

In the original manuscript and in the first printed edition of 1844, the same ending was given as follows:

> The noble music, rolling round her in a cloud of melody, shuts out the grosser prospect of an earthly parting, and uplifts her, Tom, to Heaven! (Clarendon, p. 832)

P. N. Furbank, who drew attention to this change in the 'Note on the text' of his Penguin edition of the novel,[26] locates it in the Charles Dickens Edition of 1868 (in fact, 1867). The change was in reality made, we now know, as early as 1850.[27] It had taken no more than six years, then, for Dickens to become less exclusively Ruthophile. For this is what the twice-made substitution of 'ye both' for 'her' amounts to. Unless it is a final tribute to the brother-and-sister love. Tom and Ruth must go to Heaven together, not separately.

## NOTES: CHAPTER 9

1 Edgar Johnson, *Charles Dickens: His Tragedy and Triumph* (London, 1953), vol. 1, p. 203.

2 There is a third candidate – Maria Beadnell, Dickens's one-time fiancée of the early 1830s – if one accepts Michael Slater's categories. Ruth is more a 'Maria' type than a 'Mary' type of heroine. See his *Dickens and Women* (London, 1983).

3 Angus Wilson, *The World of Charles Dickens* (New York, 1970), pp. 173–4.

4 (London, 1963), see pp. 131–4.

5 A. H. Gomme, *Dickens* (London, 1971), p. 99.

6 In 'The structure of *Martin Chuzzlewit*', *Philological Quarterly*, vol. 34, no. 1 (1955), p. 43.

7 J. Hillis Miller, *Charles Dickens: The World of His Novels* (Cambridge, Mass., 1958), pp. 121–2.

8 Ross L. Dabney, *Love and Property in the Novels of Dickens* (London, 1967), p. 47.

9 See *Dickens Studies Annual 2*, ed. Robert B. Partlow, Jr (1972), where Gold writes: 'Sylvère Monod calls Tom "simple-minded" but simple-souled is nearer to the truth', p. 159.

10 The Clarendon reading is different at this point. It is not adopted here, for reasons that will soon be made apparent.

11 *The Moral Art of Dickens* (London, 1970), p. 12.

12 *Dickens and the Trials of Imagination* (Cambridge, Mass., 1974), p. 173.

13 (Copenhagen, 1964), pp. 34 and 43.

14 See Jerry C. Beasley, 'The role of Tom Pinch in "Martin Chuzzlewit"', *Ariel*, vol. 5, no. 2 (1974), pp. 77, 79, 84.

15 Robert M. McCarron, 'Folly and wisdom: three Dickensian wise fools', in *Dickens Studies Annual 6*, ed. Robert B. Partlow, Jr (1977), p. 54 (the other two wise fools are Barnaby Rudge and, more surprisingly, Dick Swiveller).

16 Beasley, op. cit., p. 87, n. 14.

17 Alexander Welsh, *The City of Dickens* (London, 1971), pp. 150–1.

18 This has often been perceived, but the definitive treatment of the theme is probably Michael Slater's in his *Dickens and Women*.

19 Margaret Lane, 'Dickens on the hearth', in Michael Slater (ed.), *Dickens 1970*, (London, 1970), p. 158.

20 John Carey, *The Violent Effigy: A Study of Dickens' Imagination* (London, 1973), pp. 166–7.

21 Floris Delattre, *Dickens* (Paris, n.d. [1929?]), p. 5 ('A grave and strong work, which, with the characters of Tom and Ruth Pinch, the exquisite couple of brother and sister . . . contains some of the liveliest creations in his work').

22 *The Pilgrim Edition of the Letters of Charles Dickens*, Vol. 4 (Oxford, 1977), p. 145 (10 June 1844).

23 See Boris Ford (ed.), *The Pelican Guide to English Literature*, Vol. 6, *From Dickens to Hardy* (Harmondsworth, 1958), pp. 120–1.

24 George Gissing, *The Immortal Dickens* (London, 1925), p. 119.

25 Anonymous review of *Chuzzlewit* in the *Examiner*, 8 October 1844. Reprinted in Philip Collins (ed.), *Dickens: The Critical Heritage* (London, 1971), p. 185. Also used by Forster in his *Life of Charles Dickens* (1872–4), Everyman's Library (London, 1927), vol. 1, p. 296.

26 (Harmondsworth, 1968), p. 29.

27 See Clarendon edition, p. 832. The Clarendon editor, Margaret Cardwell, rather questionably restores the earlier version of this passage, where the change was deliberate and the later form represents Dickens's final 'intention'.

# CHAPTER 10

# The Evolution of Dickens's Style and Method within *Martin Chuzzlewit*

In this chapter the word 'style' is taken in its broadest possible sense, as not only the way of writing, but also the way of being a literary artist, that is, including composition and the handling of the narrative, as well as the various forms and levels of the comic in the novel under consideration.

Before launching *Martin Chuzzlewit*, Charles Dickens had tried his hand in several distinct ways and struck out in several different styles of fiction-writing. *Sketches by Boz*, being his first work, very much a juvenile production and quite unpremeditated as a book, offers a splendid, almost dazzling, display of unusual, and unusually diverse, talents, mainly of the descriptive, sentimental and humorous kinds, but certainly no basis for analysing a distinctive stylistic personality. *Pickwick Papers* was also in part born from accident, the accident of a commission to illustrate with a definite amount of letterpress the etchings of a well-known artist. It thus confirmed the author's ability to write well and his humorist's genius, but it also provided evidence of a gift for characterization that the book, instalment after instalment, lavishly exhibited, together with a modicum of control over a large-scale, more or less continuous narrative. *Oliver Twist*, though begun while *Pickwick* was still in progress, tried to do something sharply different: a more concentrated story, of tragic adventure. Dickens did not give up the most rewarding strings his bow had already been shown to be equipped with (such as humorous characterization), but he ventured into a totally new social milieu and constrained himself to give prominence to facts and incidents, and especially to their concatenation. *Nicholas Nickleby* was begun before *Oliver Twist* had been completed, and seemed to show that Dickens wanted relaxation from the strain of writing about malefactors and their plottings and counterplottings. In a way, by returning to the format of *Pickwick*, though with a conventional young man as the new novel's hero or central figure, Dickens appeared to come into his own, to make his final choice of the kind of novelist he wanted, and was going, to be. But he must have found that the strain had not been sufficiently relaxed and his ill-advised, almost naïve belief that he could make as much money by publishing less demanding works (by enlisting collaborators, for instance) resulted in the accidental birth of the two *Humphrey* novels. *The Old Curiosity Shop* was indeed a cross between the *Oliver Twist* formula of the persecuted child's story and the broad picaresque of *Nicholas Nickleby*; but it was also a novel written in weekly instalments, eventually shorter than the full twenty-month product of the *Nickleby* or *Pickwick* plan. *The Old Curiosity Shop* was followed by *Barnaby Rudge*, Dickens's first attempt to tinker with the historical tableau, a novel planned and promised (in fact, contracted for) several years before, and somewhat reluctantly begun in order to keep *Master Humphrey's Clock* going for a further year. *Barnaby Rudge*, owing something to Scott's influence, is in a way more literary than its predecessors in Dickens's work, and branches off from the author's line of development rather than being a stage within it (not that it is free from humorous characterization, or from sentimentality and melodrama). *Chuzzlewit*, after an interval of partial rest, shows a desire to revert once more to the *Pickwick* style of novel: the leisurely, twenty-instalment plan, the central figure announced in the title, the wide variety of characters and incidents, and perhaps also the shadowy outline eked out by the author's trust in his own powers of improvization.

On the whole, then, it may be said that by the time he wrote *Martin Chuzzlewit* Dickens had given abundant evidence of his stylistic idiosyncrasies and of his ability to reach a wide audience by his writings. But he had not yet absolutely and definitively found himself, stylistically speaking.

## (i)  NARRATIVE METHOD

To begin with the methods of composition, which have always, justifiably, been regarded as the weaker side of Dickens's art as a novelist in its earlier phases, *Martin Chuzzlewit* has met with some critical disfavour, though that attitude is no more unanimous than any other set of judgements about Dickens.

George Gissing expresses himself bluntly on this point: 'a novel more shapeless, a story less coherent than *Martin Chuzzlewit*, will not easily be found in any literature'.[1] Yet he must have felt that this high-and-mighty dismissal raised more questions than it solved, for he wrote in a later essay: 'But for this imperfection, the book would perhaps rank as his finest';[2] in other words, *Chuzzlewit* would be a very good novel if it were not such a bad one. Barbara Hardy, protesting against what she regarded as the misplaced ingeniosity of the efforts made by recent critics (recent in 1962) to exonerate Dickens from the Gissing kind of charge, roundly asserted that *Chuzzlewit* was 'a badly organized novel'.[3]

It is true that the novel itself is made up of more than one plot. This is recognized, for instance, by Archibald C. Coolidge, who says that '*Martin Chuzzlewit*, when examined chapter by chapter, proves to be a mixture of at least three stories, young Martin's reform, Pecksniff's hypocrisy and exposure, Jonas Chuzzlewit's murder and capture'.[4] It thus appears that an attempt to list the plots of the novel is bound to leave out large sections of the book. Coolidge's enumeration does not include the American episodes at all. Or, if they come under the heading of 'young Martin's reform', it seems somewhat out of proportion to enlist the whole of the United States, harsh climate, brutal mode of life, commercial malpractices and all, in the service of such a trifling cause as the conversion of one rather uninteresting young Briton!

It is also true, and indeed obvious, that the sudden decision to send Martin across the Atlantic involved the novelist in technical difficulties. As it was out of the question either to have the whole complicated cast join him in America, or to leave the other major characters and plots dormant while Martin's American experiences lasted, some kind of division or alternation of British and American scenes had to be worked out. Because the novel was called *Martin Chuzzlewit* and Young Martin would naturally seem better qualified for the hero of the story than his grandfather, Dickens had moved, so to speak, the centre of action, or at least the central actor, away from the main centre of his novel. In that respect, he may have been helped by his early decision that there would be two Martins; as long as one of them was on stage, or concerned with what went on there, the author was still keeping the promises of the title. Yet, on the whole, he cannot be said to have moved with ease and smoothness among the obstacles he had created for himself.

The eighth monthly instalment ended with chapter XX, when a knocking had been heard at Mr Pecksniff's door in the midst of an acute crisis. Number IX and chapter XXI open with a violent wrench away from the English countryside, and the jocular emphasis on this movement does little to make it appear more natural: 'The knocking at Mr. Pecksniff's door, though loud enough, bore no resemblance whatever to the noise of an American railway train at full speed. It may be well to begin the present chapter with this frank admission' (XXI, 405/340–1).

Yet this was only one additional factor among the organizational problems with which Dickens was faced. The alternation of Salisbury and London scenes had already introduced, and went on introducing, similar complexities. These are apparent, for instance, in the transition between chapter XXXI and chapter XXXII; we go to sleep, as it were, with Tom Pinch in Salisbury, who is on his way to London, and we arrive in London in the morning with another traveller from Salisbury, and on another day (575–6/503–4). Also, the distribution of narrative elements between the various chapters and between the successive monthly parts demanded skill which Dickens was only gradually acquiring. The principle was no doubt that each of the batches of two or three chapters that formed one monthly number must have some kind of unity, mark some phase in the progress of the story as a whole, and also that the break between numbers must be more marked than that between mere chapters. However, the principle could not always be adhered to, and one finds, for instance, that chapter XLI and chapter XLII, placed respectively at the end of number XV and at the beginning of number XVI, are entitled 'Mr. Jonas and his Friend, arriving at a Pleasant Understanding, set forth upon an Enterprise' and 'Continuation of the Enterprise of Mr. Jonas and his Friend' (708–18/632–41). This makes it appear, not only that the same episode can overlap the division between monthly numbers, but also that the division between chapters is itself occasionally artificial, unconvincing, more a matter of length than anything more organic.

That may be part of the reason why those critics who recognize unity in *Martin Chuzzlewit* find it in the themes rather than in the narrative. Thus, Kathleen Tillotson discusses some expressions used by Dickens in a preface to the novel, saying that he had endeavoured 'to resist the temptation of the current Monthly Number' and to adhere to a central 'purpose and design'; this, Kathleen Tillotson says, had not been completely achieved, far from it:

What was new was little more than the endeavour; the temptations were not always resisted nor the constraint effective; [there was only] a very general 'purpose and design', leaving much room for improvisation and modification. There was no narrative plan, no dynamic view of the interaction of the characters.[5]

There is much unquestionable truth in such reservations.

One aspect of the narrative organization that lends itself to direct analysis is the treatment of the chapter-headings, and the way in which they reflect, or attempt to disguise, the author's occasional perplexities. *Martin Chuzzlewit* is interestingly characteristic in that respect. I mean that it does not show much progress since the days of *Oliver Twist* (1837–9). Not that this should come as a surprise, for Dickens had not given himself much additional training in the meantime, since neither *The Old Curiosity Shop* in 1840 nor *Barnaby Rudge* in 1841 (the two *Humphrey* novels) had carried any chapter-headings. *Oliver Twist* had begun with heavily jocular headings and moved on to brisker and crisper ones when the action took on speed and violence. In *Chuzzlewit*, chapters II and III, for instance, have headings in pure Fieldingese ('Wherein certain Persons are presented to the Reader, with whom he may, if he please, become better acquainted' and 'In which certain other Persons are introduced; on the same Terms as in the last Chapter');[6] the next chapter-headings tend to become slower, longer, more ponderous, often ironical; and, apart from two or three exceptions (IX, 'Town and Todgers's'; XX, 'Is a Chapter of Love',[7] and XXXVIII, 'Secret Service'), they will remain elaborate and often sententious (at least in the sense of being made up of one or more sentences) to the end of the novel. A characteristic example of slow and detailed chapter-heading is provided by chapter XIII ('Showing, what became of Martin and his desperate Resolve after he left Mr. Pecksniff's House; what Persons he Encountered; what Anxieties he Suffered; and what News he Heard'). Another, in the American section, is even more strikingly enumerative and makes use of periods instead of semicolons, even appearing to refuel itself with two introductions of 'also' when it seems to have died out:

More American Experiences. Martin takes a Partner, and makes a Purchase. Some Account of Eden, as it appeared on Paper. Also of the British Lion. Also of the kind of Sympathy professed and entertained by the Watertoast Association of United Sympathisers. (XXI)

This is almost like a miniature table of contents and rather obviously cannot have been written before the chapter was complete, since it recapitulates what has been put into it rather than defines the author's purpose in advance.

Irony is rampant in the headings to chapter IV (about 'family affection' among the Chuzzlewits), XIV (at Young Martin's expense, on account of his patronizing attitude to Tom Pinch), XIX ('the Filial Piety of good Mr. Jonas'), XXIII (the arrival at Eden is called 'The Joyful Occasion'), XXXVIII (with regard to saintly Tom Pinch, a kind of inverted irony is practised, when it is said that 'He Retaliates upon a fallen Foe'), XLVIII (referring back to Jonas's 'Filial Piety'). Other headings are too allusive to tell the reader anything about what is going to happen in the chapter, and they may be sententious, like that to chapter XXVII: 'Showing that Old Friends may not only appear with New Faces, but in False Colours. That People are prone to Bite; and that Biters may sometimes be Bitten.' An element of symmetry is more than once introduced; such is the case in two chapters in succession: XXVIII, 'Mr. Montague at Home. And Mr. Jonas Chuzzlewit at Home'; XXIX, 'In which some People are Precocious, others Professional, and others Mysterious; all in their several Ways'. Several headings, as has been seen already, underline the artificiality of some divisions between chapters; thus in the headings to chapters XLI, XLII, XLIV, XLVII and LI a story within the novel is advertised in its various phases: 'Mr. Jonas and his Friend . . . set forth upon an Enterprise', 'Continuation of the Enterprise . . . ', 'Further Continuation of the Enterprise . . . ', 'Conclusion of the Enterprise . . . ', ' . . . contains the Sequel of the Enterprise'. More ingenuity is displayed in the heading to chapter XLVI: 'In which Miss Pecksniff makes Love, Mr. Jonas makes Wrath, Mrs. Gamp makes Tea, and Mr. Chuffey makes Business.'

The ending of the novel is an aspect that has been more than once adversely criticized. Not by Edgar Johnson, though, who writes dispassionately and rather sympathetically of 'the overtones of symbolism and allegory' which 'glimmer in the Christmas-pantomime transformation-scenes that end *Martin Chuzzlewit*, with Old Martin as the beneficent Prospero bringing the pageant to a close'.[8] And Geoffrey Thurley even has a few words of praise: 'the *dénouement* of *Martin Chuzzlewit* is a watershed in Dickens's creative life. It marks his recognition of the seriousness of the task that confronted him.'[9] It is difficult, however, to perceive much seriousness in this ending, whether one regards it from the point of view of stagecraft or of thematic significance.

There is in fact a discrepancy between the growing seriousness of Dickens's thoughts and perceptions, and the broad comedy and reassuring if rough-handed distribution of rewards at the end of his novel.

In the step-by-step workings of his narrative machinery, some creakings are also heard. The narrator does his job somewhat noisily. References to the reader have appeared in the chapter-headings. Others occur in the text of the novel itself. Most of the passages about to be examined may be due to the influence of Sterne or, again, of Fielding. The great eighteenth-century novelists, admired and to a certain extent emulated by Dickens, already tended to turn their 'implied reader' into a sort of collaborative figure. Recent critics and literary theorists have explored this complicated game at great length and with extreme refinement.[10] Dickens was probably less intellectually ambitious than his masters. And in a straightforward narrative like *Martin Chuzzlewit* no confessional attitude à la *Tristram Shandy* is expected from the narrator. The latter's interference is bound to be felt as more intrusive in consequence.

When Jonas's motives are analysed, we are told that 'His ignorance, which was stupendous, may be taken into account, *if the reader pleases*, separately' (XI, 242/182; my italics). Wouldn't the sentence be smoother without the words 'if the reader pleases'? What do these words amount to? They must be a kind of pseudo-consultation of the reader's wishes (pseudo- only, for the reader is powerless to object), that is, of apology to the reader for some narratorial decision or procedure. Now, an apology implies that one isn't doing the right thing. Pointing out one's faults of method, even jocularly, is bad policy. Apparently the narrator enjoys himself and his part in the triangular relationship with characters and readers. He is not sparing of his narratorial comments on the progress of his task. A revealing example appears at the close of chapter VIII and part III: 'Whether Mr. Pecksniff's business in London was as strictly professional as he had given his new pupil to understand, we shall see, to adopt that worthy man's phraseology, "all in good time!" ' (VIII, 184/128). Perhaps the inverted commas around the last words are wholly justified by their being a quotation of Pecksniffese which the narrator is reluctant to make quite his own; but perhaps also the inverted commas are revealing of a half-hearted stance: the narrator is at the same time using and disavowing the words. In any case, the whole paragraph is centred on the phrase 'we shall see' and that smacks suspiciously of narratorial comment on narrative manipulation. That is not, of course, intrinsically unacceptable, but it may legitimately be asked why it has been introduced and what good it does to the book.

Likewise, the narrator of *Martin Chuzzlewit* will more than once be found playing with the limitations of his own omniscience – writing, for instance: 'Of all that passed in this period, only the following words of Mr. Pecksniff's utterance are known' (X, 213/155). Or he will personify the narrative, calling it either 'this chronicle' or 'this history' and ascribing to it certain functions and initiatives. 'Leaving them [Martin and Mark] to blend and mingle in their sleep the shadows of objects afar off . . . be it the part of this slight chronicle . . . to change the scene, and cross the ocean to the English shore' (XVII, 361/297). Thus at the end of chapter XVII. And the game, such as it is, goes on through the first two paragraphs of chapter XVIII, with the help of hollow generalizations: 'Change begets change. Nothing propagates so fast . . . Most men at one time or another have proved this in some degree.' It takes fifteen lines for the point to be reached, and the point is the extent to which 'that limited sphere of action which Martin had deserted' illustrates the universality of change; this, the reader is told, 'shall be faithfully set down in these pages' (XVIII, 361/298). Elsewhere, mention is made of 'this history's ears' (XXI, 405/341), or of 'the duty of this history' (XXX, 540/469), or a reservation is appended to some assertion, 'for anything this history knows to the contrary' (XLVIII, 807/728). Perhaps the facetiousness of the first sentence of chapter XXXI will not appear particularly light-handed in its attempt to achieve Shandian style: 'The closing words of the last chapter, lead naturally to the commencement of this, its successor' (XXXI, 556/485). In short, for various reasons, which must remain largely conjectural, but some of which at least may have to do with his youthfulness, lack of experience and high spirits, combined with the influence of the eighteenth-century tradition, Dickens still seems to be often playing with his narrative, or around it, rather than soberly constructing and writing it.

It has often been felt that publication in instalments created special temptations for the writer, temptations to introduce an element of sensation, something impressive, at the end of each monthly part, something that would keep the reader on tenterhooks and make sure that he would buy the next issue. A close examination of Dickens's practices over the years fails to confirm that he was ever much influenced by such temptations. It has been seen above that, on the contrary, one instalment sometimes happened to be a mere continuation of the previous one, with nothing sensational in between, with no effort at exploiting suspense in the least. There are, however, two exceptions in *Chuzzlewit*. In chapter XLI, that is, at the end of the fifteenth monthly instalment, the last words are: ' "It will be a stormy night!" exclaimed the doctor, as they started' (XLI, 717/641). And indeed, as the reader has witnessed Jonas's mounting and dangerous excitement, the doctor's exclamation reverberates more like a dark omen than a mere weather forecast. More striking still is the separation between chapters XLVII and XLVIII (that is, between numbers XVII and XVIII). Jonas has 'done the Deed' and is awaiting discovery: 'For he knew it must come; and his present punishment, and torture, and distraction, was, to listen for its coming./Hush!' (XLVII, 806/727). That may not be truly great art. But to close a large section of a long novel with 'Hush!' is an original decision; no doubt it mainly echoes Jonas's own attitude of expectancy, which makes him breathlessly silent. But isn't it at the same time an invitation to readers to hold their breath, to listen intensely, in similar expectancy, and if, so, to hold their breath for four weeks?

Another element of the *feuilletonesque* technique, as it is called in French, that is, the technique of the sensational serial leaning towards melodrama, is the use of coincidence. Dickens was very fond of coincidences and believed that they occurred all the time in real life, at least in his own life, much more strikingly than in any of his works of fiction. It is none the less true that his large-scale employment of coincidence may appear excessive, and intended to make things easier for him when he has to give new twists to his complicated plots. When Pecksniff arrives in Anthony Chuzzlewit's London house at the very moment when Jonas is stealthily reading his father's will (XVIII, 364/301), that is a typical example of what Dickens regarded as legitimate. When Lewsome, Jonas's former accomplice, has fallen ill, he is nursed by Mrs Gamp. Thus, when he utters the name of Chuzzlewit in his delirium, that will draw the attention of his nurse (who works in Jonas's house during the day and with Lewsome during the night: XXV). The chance meeting between Martin and Mark, on their return from America and when they have just landed at Liverpool, and Mr Pecksniff inaugurating the construction of a grammar school (XXXV, 622/548) taxes the reader's credulity and is perhaps the most impudent example of Dickens's attitude to coincidences. As to the presence in London of Martin and Mark's former neighbours in Eden in America, it is called, with extravagant cynicism (on Dickens's part, though the words are spoken by Tapley), 'A concidence as never was equalled!' (LIV, 911/825). That Dickens did all this with a clear conscience, however, is shown by some narratorial comments which act as a kind of justification for the use of coincidence, in connection with the relationship between Nadgett and Pinch:

> As there are a vast number of people in the huge metropolis of England who rise up every morning, not knowing where their heads will rest at night, so there are a multitude who shooting arrows over houses as their daily business, never know on whom they fall. Mr. Nadgett might have passed Tom Pinch ten thousand times . . . yet never once have dreamed that Tom had any interest in any act or mystery of his. Tom might have done the like by him, of course. But the same private man out of all the men alive, was in the mind of each at the same moment. (XXXVIII, 661/586)

This is tantamount to saying that innumerable coincidences exist in the world and that the writer who picks up one of them occasionally, for his own purposes, is within his rights.

The rights of novelists, in any case, cannot be restricted or defined. If the story works, carries readers along with it, whatever artifice has been used to construct it is thereby justified. Otherwise readers of *Martin Chuzzlewit* might complain that there is something too violently unnatural in the circumstances that accidentally prevent Tom Pinch from uttering Nadgett's name in Jonas's presence (XLVI, 790/711). That is not a mere detail; as the narrator himself points out at once, had Jonas known that Nadgett was spying upon him, he would have realized the utter futility of murdering Tigg, and would thus 'have been saved from the commission of a Guilty Deed' (XLVI, 790–1/712). Yet there is even more artificiality in Montague Tigg's soliloquy:

> 'I would rather have lost', he said, 'a thousand pounds than lost the boy just now. But I'll return home alone. I am resolved upon that. Chuzzlewit shall go forward first, and I will follow in my own time.

I'll have no more of this', he added, wiping his damp forehead. 'Twenty-four hours of this would turn my hair grey!' (XLII, 727/651)

It is only on the stage that people address speeches to themselves aloud and feel the need to articulate and marshall their thoughts in such a way. An already experienced novelist like Dickens might have dispensed with that speech, and reported Tigg's resolve in his third-person narrative. But where he adds insult to injury is in the final sentence about Tigg's hair running the risk of turning grey. A little earlier, Jonas had shown Tigg that he was not taken in by this black hair, and saw very well that it was both false and dyed (see XLI, 713/737)! If Jonas knows that, Tigg cannot be ignorant of it; false hair or dyed hair does not turn grey in twenty-four hours. So Tigg is not merely addressing himself, he is lying to himself and, it would seem, taking himself in.

It would be unfair to close this enumeration of various technical minutiae in *Chuzzlewit* on a note of disappointment. Dickens was to give evidence a little later in his career of some interest in craftsmanship and even in experiment. *Bleak House*, parts of *Little Dorrit* and, from another point of view, *Hard Times* and *A Tale of Two Cities* are examples of his ambitions and, to varying degrees, of his achievement in that respect. The last section of *Chuzzlewit* already shows similar aspirations to rise above mere humdrum chronologically treated sequences of events. At the end of chapter XL there is a gathering of various characters on the wharf from which the Antwerp packet is about to depart: Tom Pinch and Ruth, but also Mrs Gamp, are there; Nadgett has put in a brief and secretive appearance; Montague Tigg arrives on the scene in time to welcome Jonas when he disembarks (with his wife Merry). The end of chapter XL then serves as a point of reference for a series of subsequent chapters. Chapters XLI and XLII are spent by narrator and reader in the company of Jonas and Montague, who organize, and accomplish, their journey to Salisbury (the separation between monthly numbers XV and XVI occurring between those two chapters). Chapter XLIII reverts to the night before the journey and to Martin and Mark, who had been lost sight of since their arrival at Liverpool (chapter XXXV, end of number XIII). They are now at the Blue Dragon, near Pecksniff's dwelling, which they will visit in the morning. On leaving the house, they encounter Jonas, and the two strands of the plot thus meet, or cross. Chapter XLIV brings together Pecksniff (present in XLIII), Jonas (glimpsed at the very end of XLIII, but central to XL–XLII) and Montague Tigg (an important presence in XLI–XLII). In chapter XLV, with which number XVII opens, there is a fresh return to the end of chapter XL, this time to pick up Tom and Ruth, with whom we stay through chapter XLVI (but Jonas appears again, this time in London, and leaving his own house in disguise). Jonas is practically alone in chapter XLVII (the murder chapter, which closes number XVII). And in chapter XLVIII, reverting to Tom and Ruth, the reader sees them welcoming Martin and Mark (not heard of since the end of XLIII) and making contact with John Westlock, thus neatly locking two pieces of the puzzle, for John had shown unexpected interest in the mystery of the wharf and in Jonas's affairs (chapter XLV, with a reference back to chapter XL) and now produces a secret visitor (Lewsome) who has disclosures to make about Jonas.

This is skilful and even subtle. Thus Dickens's attitude to technical problems in *Martin Chuzzlewit* combines the use of all kinds of conventions with an intelligent effort to construct an original and elegant narrative edifice.

## (ii)  MODES OF WRITING

Similar unevenness will appear from an examination of the writing proper, of what usually goes by the name of style. *Martin Chuzzlewit*, as a work of immense length and little unity of inspiration and purpose, can be shown to contain specimens of most of the early varieties of Dickens's style. The absence of stylistic unity was denounced by R. C. Churchill in severe terms: he speaks of 'the bad writing in *Chuzzlewit*, the vulgar pathetic touches . . . the absolute lack of any critical discrimination in a writer who could produce such things'.[11] George Gissing, on the other hand, had found the writing almost entirely admirable. In his view, 'For the most part, the prose of *Chuzzlewit* is excellent, much riper than that of *The Old Curiosity Shop*, and more varied than that of *Barnaby Rudge* . . . This is Dickens in full command of his resources.'[12]

Dickens's ambitions are perceptible in various parts of his novel. He certainly wanted to write well, and to be recognized as writing well. His ambition to be regarded as a serious writer may be seen also in his use of literary quotation and reference. When the persistent smell in Mrs Todgers's house is described as 'the concentrated essence of all the dinners that had been cooked in the kitchen', and it is said that this smell, 'like the Black Friar in Don Juan, "wouldn't be driven away" ' (VIII, 181–2/126), the reference appears to imply some real familiarity with the text of Byron's poem, or at least with Adeline's song, between stanzas XL and XLI of canto XVI.[13] The allusions to Shakespeare, which are frequent in Dickens, are as often as not to stage performances, that is, to visual effects (and especially, of course, to poor performances) rather than to the text, the words, the poetry; thus, when Mr Norris the son, in New York, wishes to dismiss the subject of Negro slavery 'he made a wry face, and dusted his fingers as Hamlet might after getting rid of Yorick's skull' (XVII, 351/288).

In the writing itself, there is a certain amount of archaism, affectation and, one might almost say, pedantry, though the author's humorous intention usually saves his sentences from falling into that vice. His purpose is not to display his learning, but to ridicule those who yield to that kind of temptation. Even so, when Dickens describes the coachman who is taking Tom Pinch away from Salisbury and who is apt to form wrong impressions about Tom's relationship with Mrs Lupin, and calls him 'this lax rover', he is making use of a fantastically unnatural and recherché phrase (XXXVI, 635/562). Other archaic words and forms occur here and there in *Martin Chuzzlewit*. 'Other the like results' (VI, 140/85), 'place of espial' (IX, 189/132), 'the hardy wight' (XII, 256/196), and 'as they turned them [in the sense of themselves] round, what time the stronger gusts came sweeping up' (XII, 257/196), or 'laved the wound' (XXIV, 459/392) – all these are evidence either of Dickens's high spirits in humorous passages or of an intention of writing more poetically than usual, or of both at once.

At the opposite end of the scale of language, Dickens can be found guilty of another affectation, that of using vulgar turns of phrase. Thus, in the first description of the Pecksniff girls, the emphatic resumption of 'was the youngest Miss Pecksniff' at the end of a sentence beginning with 'She was' occurs no less than three times in one paragraph (II, 61–2/10–11). Likewise, when the author revels in the vulgarities of Todgers's, he writes things like 'It had not been papered or painted, hadn't Todgers's' (VIII, 182/126). And at the end the exuberant mood induced by the imminent relief of having completed his task leads him to write 'he sang songs, did Fips, and made speeches, did Fips' (LIII, 903/818). The word *aggravation* in the sense of irritation or provocation is used four times (mostly near the beginning of the book (in chapters IV and VII). The construction with the double *that* (as an equivalent of *such . . .* or *so . . . that*) had always been a favourite mannerism of Dickens's (or a favourite vulgarism, but the line is not easy to draw between the two categories of affectation). It is to be found in *Chuzzlewit* as early as chapter IV, where George Chuzzlewit is said to overfeed himself, 'to that extent, indeed, that his eyes were strained in their sockets' (IV, 108/54); and there are ten other examples of the same phrase. The use of *vast* (XI, 231/172) or *vastly* (XVII, 348/286 and XXVIII, 522/351) in the sense of *great* or *very*, like that of *monstrous comfortable* (twice in XVII, 349/286), and perhaps that of *a deal of* rather than *a great deal of* (IX, 200/143),[14] smacks of eighteenth-century usage (if not of still earlier days), and forms of expression which have become obsolete may be retained for jocular purposes or go down as well as up the social scale. All these are in the main proofs of the former journalist's still youthful ebullience, little tricks and pranks, little linguistic capers that he indulges in and perhaps prides himself on, in the same way as he always discloses his admiring enjoyment of any piece of mimicry or pantomine (for instance, in IV, 98/45 and 101/47), never seeming to consider that they are very inferior forms of art or of self-expression.

Much of the novel has been written with extreme attention to detail, with real stylistic ambition, and some of it must in fact be described as overwritten.

The author devoted considerable energy, for instance, to the formal introductory portraits of several characters. That is the case for Mrs Lupin (III, 79–80/27), whose portraiture is particularly elaborate, entirely methodical, and reinforced by manipulatory comments. These serve, among other things, as evidence of the narrator/author's consciousness of what he is doing, and conscientiousness in doing it: 'though she was not exactly what the world calls young, you may make an affidavit, on trust, before any mayor or magistrate in Christendom, that there are a great many young ladies in the world . . . whom you wouldn't like half as well'. In the case of the picture given in chapter XXVII (505–6/437) of Mr Jobling, the effect is considerably heightened:

He has a portentously sagacious chin, and a pompous voice, with a rich huskiness in some of its tones that went directly to the heart, like a ray of light shining through the ruddy medium of choice old burgundy. His neckerchief and shirt-frill were ever of the whitest, his clothes of the blackest and sleekest, his gold watch-chain of the heaviest, and his seals of the largest.

While the sentences are harmoniously built, while picturesque images (like that of old burgundy) are employed to liven up the period, the main purpose is never lost sight of, and it is of course to suggest psychological and social traits through details of physique and clothing. Jobling, thanks to this procedure, is placed before the reader's eye, both as an individual, and as *the* rising and already prosperous physician. The mention of his voice in particular is effective: that voice has the precise quality that a doctor's voice must have in order to inspire confidence; it is what might be called a medical voice; but, while every reader will more or less identify that quality as something long vaguely familiar, Dickens has been able to put it recognizably in a few well-chosen and forcibly evocative words.

When he strains his talent, the result is inevitably quite different. And there are unfortunately in *Martin Chuzzlewit* many passages which produce the impression that Dickens wrote, not as he liked to write, but as he thought it his duty to write. I am referring mainly to the pages which aim at the poetical style. And this is usually connected with the description of landscapes or nature. Not that Dickens has completely failed to enlist critical support in that quarter. Coral Lansbury writes that 'in *Martin Chuzzlewit* there is a new note in Dickens' description of landscape' and explains that 'the language describing autumn in Chapter II is no longer confined to a few formal phrases. Rather it summons up Wordsworth and Shelley in brilliant rhetoric.'[15] Admittedly, Lansbury sees Dickens as parodying rather than straightforwardly emulating both Wordsworth and Shelley, but even that seems excessive.

It is true that, in the evocation of the Temple Fountain near which Ruth Pinch and John Westlock meet, Dickens achieves certain effects:

Merrily the tiny fountain played, and merrily the dimples sparkled on its sunny surface . . . Merrily the fountain plashed and plashed until the dimples, merging into one another, swelled into a general smile . . . Merrily the fountain leaped and danced, and merrily the smiling dimples twinkled and expanded more and more, until they broke into a laugh against the basin's rim, and vanished. (XLV, 764–5/685–6)

The three paragraphs just quoted are placed apart from each other, at three separate points of a scene and dialogue which they punctuate and frame. The combination of repetition and variation from each to the next is not without adroitness and the rhythm of the sentences is rather winning. Yet that is one of the passages that may pall, and even become almost embarrassing, when one rereads the book again and again. It is perhaps too palpably artificial, contrived. J. Hillis Miller said: 'One theme of *Martin Chuzzlewit* is a condemnation of poetry as a lie.'[16] That may be so, but only at the deepest level. On the surface, poetry may be condemned once or twice in a jocular tone, but a tribute is paid to it again and again, the tribute of attempting to produce it in narrative and evocative prose. Hence a long series of purple patches.

One of the most striking is the one which has become famous as the 'Yoho' passage. It is an impressionistic evocation of Tom Pinch's stagecoach journey from Salisbury to London, punctuated by twenty-one occurrences of the interjection 'Yoho!' or, for good measure, 'Yoho! Yoho! (XXXVI, 631–6/558–64). Again, one's attitude to such rhetoric may vary. I used to enjoy it and have praised it in print, but nowadays my heart sinks at the first appearance of the word 'Yoho'. John Forster uninhibitedly expressed his delight with the 'Yoho' passage; another contemporary, writing anonymously in 1861, seemed to voice both reactions at once:

> we lose all notion of a coach and of scenery, and of everything else, in the wealth of fine writing. We feel more and more anxious that Tom Pinch should get to London, and that this Yohoing would stop. But the story probably gains in our eyes by the interlude. We like our author to enjoy himself.[17]

Most of the poetical or pseudo-poetical paragraphs in *Chuzzlewit* are likewise devoted to the description of nature. When coming across an opening sentence like 'What better time for driving, riding, walking, moving through the air by any means, than a fresh, frosty morning' (V, 118/64), an experienced Dickens-reader must realize that he is in for a protracted piece of meteorological nature-worship. Again, when Martin and Tom are going to meet John Westlock in Salisbury and it turns out that Mr Pecksniff's horse and gig are not available, the two young men set out on foot. The 'Better than the gig!' sequence is hardly inferior to the 'Yoho' passage as an illustration of Dickens at his purple-patchiest; in a page and a half, the gig is mentioned fifteen times, *better than the gig* serves as a refrain or burden, and exclamatoriness is rampant. Elsewhere, there is a piece of fine writing about the wind at sea and the progress of a ship:

> Whither go the clouds and wind, so eagerly? If like guilty spirits they repair to some dread conference with powers like themselves, in what wild region do the elements hold council, or where unbend in terrible disport?
>
> Here! Free from that cramped prison called the earth, and out upon the waste of waters. Here, roaring, raging, shrieking, howling, all night long. (XV, 308/246)

And this goes on drearily. It does not appear to be the kind of thing that Dickens, who could do so many other things triumphantly, could succeed in doing even moderately well. He is unlike himself at such moments, which sound artificial, perhaps conventional, probably uninspired and insincere.

The last of the set-pieces connected with climate and travelling concerns the night-journey undertaken by Tigg and Jonas from London to Salisbury in stormy weather (XLII, 718–20/641–3). This is rather more successful than in the previous cases, because a thunderstorm lends itself to impressionistic treatment, combining as it does vivid effects of light and sound, which are efficiently exploited by Dickens. His vocabulary is lush, there are repetitions, symmetries, variations; there is a certain amount of stilted writing and occasionally a perceptible straining after effect and sensation; but the circumstances of a spectacular thunderstorm are sufficiently exceptional and violent in themselves to make exceptional and violent treatment of the language in which it is presented acceptable to the reader.

Finally, there are three or four other passages in *Chuzzlewit* which are more in line with Dickens's spontaneous artistry, for various reasons. The satirical element in the description of the Anglo-Bengalee offices, for instance, makes it powerful in spite of its use of rhetorical repetition (XXVII, 500/430–1). Also the description of Covent Garden (which takes up nearly one page: XL, 696–7/621–2) has a certain genuine flavour. It is as though Boz, finding himself once more on his own ground, recovered his full powers of picturesque and imaginative evocation. In 'scents as of veal-stuffing yet uncooked, dreamily mixed up with capsicums, brown-paper, seeds' the Inimitable, as Dickens

liked to dub himself, is truly inimitable because he imitates no one but
himself, thus doing something, stylistically, that no one else could do.

On the other hand, when he knows what he is doing but obeys an
intellectual rather than an emotional impulse, he may lapse into
overwriting. Not that genuine emotion is an infallible guide to good
writing; the reverse has more than once proved to be the case (for
instance, where Tom and Ruth Pinch are concerned). But a modicum
of personal involvement, over and beyond the urge to produce a
supposedly artistic effect, is indispensable. It may be lacking in a
passage like the following, elaborately, too elaborately it may seem,
connecting and contrasting murder and nature:

> The last rays of the sun were shining in, aslant, making a path of
> golden light along the stems and branches in its range, which even
> as he looked, began to die away: yielding gently to the twilight that
> came creeping on (XLVII, 801–2/722)

– and so on, for ten more lines, which serve as preparation for Jonas's
gory deed; so gory, in fact, that when 'the doer of this deed' emerges
from the thicket he leaves in it 'a dark, dark stain that dyed and
scented the whole summer night from earth to Heaven'. That is not, I
think, Dickens at his best. Not much progress has been accomplished
since the days of *Oliver Twist*, the end of which had been written four
or five years before, with Nancy's murdered body left in its 'pool of
gore that quivered and danced in the sunlight on the ceiling', that
body which is 'mere flesh and blood, no more – but such flesh, and so
much blood'.[18]

Grandiloquence also occurs in the speech of several characters. The
artificial quarrel between Martin and Tom is essentially a quarrel
about nothing at all, being based on a misunderstanding; so, many
words are arrayed on both sides, and they sound as hollow as they are
(L, 841–3/758–61). And of course, in the highly melodramatic scene
of Jonas's unmasking after the murder, the language of both the
narrator and the characters becomes intensely grandiloquent: 'The
truth, which nothing would keep down; which blood would not
smother, and earth would not hide . . . ' is what we read (LI,
861/779); then, a few pages later: 'Another of the phantom forms of
this terrific Truth! Another of the many shapes in which it started up
about him, out of vacancy . . . The dead man might have come out of
his grave, and not confounded and appalled him so' (LI, 867/783). As

has been observed before, the capitalization of initials (*Truth* here) is one of the signs that rhetoric momentarily takes over.

Naturally, though reservations have to be introduced about the success, the efficiency or the genuineness of a few passages in *Chuzzlewit*, the enduring admiration aroused by that novel also rests in part on the quality of the author's writing in it, a quality that assumes many forms.

Dickens's style had always been, and was to remain, powerfully imaginative. Taine was to complain that Dickens's imagery was morbid; he says, referring to Tom Pinch's disappointment over Pecksniff, once he has found out the true worth of his former idol: 'On pense aux fantaisies d'Hoffmann; on est pris d'une idée fixe et l'on a mal à la tête. Ces excentricités sont le signe de la maladie plutôt que de la santé'.[19] Fortunately, George Henry Lewes, while also identifying Dickens's imagination as hallucinatory, gave him an unsolicited and posthumous certificate of perfect mental sanity.[20] There can be no doubt that Dickens saw things in his own way, and imposed on observable realities the distortions in shape and colour due to his imaginative processes; which were of great vividness. But this usually resulted in revealing to his readers aspects of the real world that they had failed to perceive, but could recognize. Thus, the frequent reification of a human being, that is, the treatment of such a being as an inanimate object it is thought to resemble, is both a humorous procedure and a way of disclosing something fundamental about him: 'Mr. Pecksniff continued to keep his mouth and eyes very wide open, and to drop his lower jaw, somewhat after the manner of a toy-nutcracker' (II, 61/10). The reverse process, that is, the anthropomorphic treatment of inanimate objects, in reality emphasizes the same kind of perception of a kinship between temporarily or permanently mechanized men or women and things. Quite a string of illustrations can be found within one short passage of the novel:

> vagabond race of trucks . . . the throats and maws of dark no-thoroughfares . . . the monument with every hair erect upon his golden head . . . chimney-pots . . . whispering . . . an oval minia-ture, like a little blister . . . a door with two great glass eyes in its forehead (IX, 186–9/130–2 and 202/145).

The reader will have recognized the splendid description of the outside and inside of Todgers's, which is true Dickens, truer Dickens than the author of the tableaux mentioned earlier. Old Chuffey is referred to as being 'like the rest of the furniture' (XI, 237/178), but that hardly counts as an image, since he is so old and decrepit that he *has* become to all practical intents and purposes a thing.[21] He is not treated to a reifying image, he is shown as actually reified. A more remarkable case is that of the American general, a visitor at the Norrises', who has fallen to the floor on entering their drawing-room, and is helped to rise to his feet: 'But his uniform was so fearfully and wonderfully made that he came up stiff and without a bend in him, like a dead Clown' (XVII, 352/289). I call this case remarkable, because the comparison is both effective and yet gruesomely incongruous. Most people have seen a clown shamming death, but it is here suggested that the resemblance is with a genuinely dead clown, preserving in death his clown-like attribute of stiffness. The sentence gives food for thought as well as material for inner vision, or visualization of the scene. Another American, Elijah Pogram, 'shook hands with Martin, like a clockwork figure that was just running down' (XXXIV, 605/532). That is again very interesting, for we have here a more or less human being (more or less only, for the Americans in *Martin Chuzzlewit* have by this time ceased to be fully human) compared to an object made by man and intended to simulate human attitudes. Like the dead clown, the automaton stands halfway between full independent humanity and full inanimate essence.

Another tone characteristic of *Chuzzlewit*, another stylistic experiment or at least attempt made by Dickens in that novel, is the tautly tragic. Though the tragedy is never wholly liberated from melodrama and still in part derives from it, there is evidence of greater ambition than in, say, *Oliver Twist* or *Barnaby Rudge*, the only two earlier works that had shown signs of a desire to rise above pathos, or bathos, and melodrama. By looking at certain details of *Martin Chuzzlewit*, one perceives that Dickens was trying to adapt some rhetorical devices to the creation of a tragic atmosphere. Repetition can be used in all kinds of ways: in the description of Ruth Pinch's employer's house, for instance, the eight occurrences of *great*, from 'the great front gate; with a great bell' down to 'a great footman . . . at the great hall-door, with such great tags upon his liveried shoulder' (IX, 192/135)[22] are sinister without being in the least tragic, and serve in the main a satirical purpose. The rhetoric employed in the episode of the murder is based in part on the same simple device. It comprises other effects, like the capitalization of initial letters, as already seen, in 'Guilty

Deed' (XLVI, 791/712) and in 'Day . . . Night . . . Glory . . . Murder' (XLVII, 799/719), or like the more complex combination of procedures in the opening paragraph of chapter XLVII. For that begins with what can only be termed a sequence of three rhetorical questions, of which it will be enough to quote the first: 'Did no men passing through the dim streets shrink without knowing why, when he came stealing up behind them?' (XLVII, 797/718). And the paragraph ends with an extravagant kind of interrogative exclamation (showing blatantly how purely rhetorical the questions have been) and a reference to the earliest crime known to Judaeo-Christian culture, which lends a theological overtone to the passage: 'When he looked back, across his shoulder, was it to see if his quick footsteps still fell dry upon the dusty pavement, or were already moist and clogged with the red mire that stained the naked feet of Cain!' (XLVII, 797/718).[23] The connection does not bear close investigation; Tigg is not Jonas's brother, nor is he going to be killed because he has found favour in the eyes of God. All this is again somewhat overdone and not without crudeness, but the eerie atmosphere, the effect of ominousness are eventually created, or rather reinforced; for they had been created five chapters before, in the evocation of the stormy night at the beginning of chapter XLII. It was mentioned above that the rhetoric of that passage cleverly combined the advantages of repetition and of variation; to be more precise, the vocabulary accumulated through something like two and a half pages comprises *thunder* six times, *lightning* five, *flashed* three; *quivered* and *rain* twice each, while *night*, *lonely*, *storm*, *dark* and *murky* are only used once. No doubt this way of writing plays its part in the powerful, almost haunting effect the scene has on the reader's mind.

The overall quality of Dickens's writing in *Chuzzlewit* has been recognized by more than one critic, when sufficient attention has been paid to the nature of the writer's efforts to innovate. 'The greatness of *Martin Chuzzlewit* begins with its prose,' says Steven Marcus, who sees Shakespeare's influence all over the book, yet concludes that Dickens's mastery of language and style looks forward as well as back: 'Of all Dickens's novels, *Martin Chuzzlewit* is in one sense the most Joycean, for language itself is one of its subjects'.[24] And it is true, though not immediately obvious, that Dickens is no longer content to write happily, following the natural bent of his genius, but is henceforth developing an intelligent interest in the functioning or behaviour of language. That is, on the whole, the impression one derives from reading Patrick J. McCarthy's important article, 'The language of *Martin Chuzzlewit*'.[25] A complete analysis of this essay would be desirable, but there is no room for it here; mention must be made, however, of the six 'linguistic effects' which McCarthy sees Dickens using as 'means of heightening'; they are: animism, superlative expressions, odd collocations, lists, reworked clichés, and animal imagery. Examples of animism and animal imagery have been independently given above; the other categories are also of interest.

Yet the most striking, if not the most successful, innovation introduced by Dickens in *Chuzzlewit* is probably the grandiose inspired tone employed, mostly in connection with Tom Pinch. And that does not go down at all well with most modern critics. Earle Davis complains that 'this novel shows Dickens dropping into a questionable rhetorical habit. When he felt deeply about something, he wanted to exclaim about it in order to emphasize it . . . For some readers, this damages the style irretrievably.'[26] Influences have been looked for, and found. Like many of his contemporaries, Dickens can be seen as an all too willing disciple or victim of Carlyle; emulating Carlylese, when one isn't Carlyle (and sometimes even when one is), can be fraught with stylistic perils.

By 1843, Carlyle had achieved full recognition. *The French Revolution* had been acclaimed. His lectures on heroes and hero-worship had been well attended and highly appreciated. Dickens, in any case, had been an early admirer. He was to express his indebtedness to Carlyle by inscribing *Hard Times* to him in 1854 and by paying him a warm tribute in the preface to *A Tale of Two Cities* in 1859. But already, in the early 1840s, Dickens read Carlyle and attached great weight to the sage's opinions. He could not have escaped the impact of Carlyle's idosyncratic handling of English. Carlylese comprises, in addition to many Scotticisms and Germanisms, a fondness for unusual compound words, abstract terms, staccato exclamatoriness, rhetorical questioning, and vivid invective and apostrophe.

One expert on the relationship, Michael Goldberg, finds much resemblance with Carlyle in a moralizing and exclamatory paragraph of chapter XXXI ('Oh late-remembered, much-forgotten, mouthing, braggart duty, always owed, and seldom paid in any other coin than punishment and wrath') and especially in its concluding sentence: 'Oh magistrate, so rare a country gentleman and brave a squire, had you[27] no duty to society, before the ricks were blazing and the mob were mad; or did it spring up armed and booted from the earth, a corps of yeomanry, full-grown!' (XXXI, 567/495). Goldberg refers illuminatingly to another passage in *Chuzzlewit* that shows the complexity of the relationship between the great mid-Victorians; this is the extraordinarily brilliant parody of the transcendentalist style in the speech of the American 'literary ladies'. Goldberg writes:

> Dickens was as much aware as Carlyle of the excesses of his style and the pitfalls they could lead to. His wonderful passage in *Martin Chuzzlewit* on 'mind and matter' gliding into the 'vortex of immensity' to the accompanying 'howl' of the 'sublime' accurately hits off the kind of 'transcendental moonshine' Carlyle condemned in others but sometimes resorted to himself.[28]

This is interesting as proving that Dickens had a keen consciousness of the various levels of style. So, when he let himself go into the depths or the heights of the exalted and grandiose or the bathetic and the maudlin he must have been aware of what he was doing and what risks he ran. The apostrophes to Tom are not enjoyed nowadays, or not by many readers, but the value of the apostrophes is not nonexistent. Garrett Stewart explains:

> As much as the device of sentimental apostrophe is to be lamented in Dickens's addresses to Tom, its counterpart in the treatment of Pecksniff is most revealing . . . As a touchstone of sincerity, apostrophe is, like all rhetoric, unreliable . . . Pecksniff is in fact punished by that same form of apostrophe he has so often defiled; a reprisal by language alone.[29]

This is an enlightening commentary on the use and abuse of apostrophe. And the end of chapter X provides an excellent example of the phenomenon. Mr Pecksniff, on discovering that Mrs Todgers had made some mild compromise with her conscience in order to keep one of her boarders, exclaims: ' "Oh Calf, Calf!" cried Mr. Pecksniff mournfully. "Oh, Baal, Baal! Oh my friend, Mrs. Todgers! To barter away that precious jewel, self-esteem, and cringe to any mortal creature – for eighteen shillings a week!" ' (X, 229/170). Then does the narrator use apostrophe and exclamation in his turn to contradict Pecksniff with what is intended to be scathing irony: 'Eighteen shillings a week! Just, most just, thy censure, upright Pecksniff! Had it been for the sake of a ribbon, star, or garter; sleeves of lawn, a great man's smile . . . but to worship the golden calf for eighteen shillings a week! oh pitiful, pitiful!' So in this passage there are both the Pecksniffian and the anti-Pecksniffian kinds of apostrophe; the former is obviously insincere, the latter no less obviously sincere. Which doesn't mean that it is good literature and that its proper place is in a comic novel, or in a novel that is predominantly comic.

Dickens's absolute mastery over the English language is very much in evidence in *Martin Chuzzlewit*. I have long considered (and many times quoted) one sentence from *David Copperfield*, concerning Mrs Crupp, as the supreme illustration of this unique command, of this ability to force language to submit to the writer's imperious mood. But I had forgotten that one sentence about Mrs Gamp is built on the same principle and possibly even better; as the earlier example of the two, it is priceless:

And with innumerable leers, winks, coughs, nods, smiles, and curtseys, all tending to the establishment of a mysterious and confidential understanding between herself and the bride, Mrs. Gamp, invoking a blessing upon the house, leered, winked, coughed, nodded, smiled, and curtseyed herself out of the room. (XXVI, 492/422)

Or perhaps, though richer in verbs, this pre-Crupp example of Dickens's stylistic flexibility is not after all superior to the Cruppish gem itself:

Mrs. Crupp, who had been incessantly smiling to express sweet temper, and incessantly holding her head on one side, to express a general feebleness of constitution, and incessantly rubbing her hands, to express a desire to be of service to all deserving objects, gradually smiled herself, one-sided herself, and rubbed herself, out of the room.[30]

By reducing the number of the verbs, Dickens has been able to make the architecture of the sentence more harmonious, and he has achieved the acme of boldness or authoritativeness by using 'one-sided herself'.

Other examples of the novelist's great power might be listed. To select only one more, this little description of a rainy day in the country will serve:

> The day was dawning from a patch of watery light in the east, and sullen clouds came driving up before it, from which the rain descended in a thick, wet mist. It streamed from every twig and bramble in the hedge; made little gullies in the path; ran down a hundred channels in the road; and punched innumerable holes into the face of every pond and gutter. It fell with an oozy, slushy sound among the grass; and made a muddy kennel of every furrow in the ploughed fields. (XIII, 273–4/213)

This has little in common with the overelaborate pieces about the delights of nature and landscape. It is simple enough, genuine, not overdone, and it seems to be the result of shrewd observation. Some of the images are telling (*watery light*, *punched holes*, *muddy kennel*), and the language is in itself suggestive; the words *oozy* and *slushy* have themselves an oozy and slushy sound. In short, such a passage may well appear as unobtrusively but entirely successful.

Of course, in the eyes of Dickens's contemporaries, his real forte was the writing of dialogue; and even today, when Dickens is quoted, nine times out of ten it will be some fragment of a favourite character's speech, rather than description or narrative, that will come to mind. An expert on speech in the English novel, Norman Page, pays this tribute to Dickens:

> For Dickens . . . dialogue clearly exists to serve a purpose . . . to render not the real world but a fictional world that is amazingly vivid and varied. He does not appear to have been interested in persuading the reader . . . that anyone who ever lived spoke in the manner of Jingle or Mantalini or Mrs. Gamp. In these novels, speech is a matter of fictional convention – the author's own code of conventions, established and fairly consistently adhered to by him – rather than accurate observation.[31]

Norman Page, who has elsewhere demonstrated that the literal reproduction of real speech would be unreadable, deserves to be heard on his theme. But perhaps it should be added that the speech of Dickens's characters could not please and convince the reader as it undoubtedly does if the 'accurate observation' had not been called into play. Real speech, in Dickens's dialogue, is not ignored, even if it is heightened and stylized to a considerable extent.

## (iii)  FORMS OF THE COMIC

The forms and levels of the comic to be found in *Chuzzlewit* are extremely varied.[32] To begin with the least refined, it must be admitted that word-play occupies a prominent position in the book, though in its turn it operates in several ways. Punning pure and simple (though of course punning is never pure, as Freud has shown) is particularly frequent. The first chapter, about the Chuzzlewit genealogy, is entirely based on a series of elaborate puns, but that is only a preliminary exercise and not really part of the story. Yet once the story has got into its stride the reader is still faced with things like Tigg's physical description ('he can hardly be said to have been in any extremities, as his fingers were a long way out of his gloves, and the soles of his feet were at an inconvenient distance from the upper leather of his boots': IV, 97/44); or, to give a second example, a more elaborate comment on American drinkers in a bar-room ('some of whom (being thirsty souls as well as dirty) were pretty stale in one sense, and pretty fresh in another': XVI, 333/270) where there are really two puns, the second being emphasized by pointed commentary about the two senses of one word.

The malapropism is a close cousin of the pun; it has the advantage of not openly compromising the author or narrator, since the confusion is ascribed to one of the characters, like Mrs Todgers who speaks of a 'syrup' when she means a sylph or seraph, possibly because cookery is more in her professional line than myth or angelology (IX, 196/139). But Dickens was sufficiently enamoured of this joke to repeat it, or refer back to it, later on (XXXVI, 644/571). The confusion between 'chronic' and 'colic' is near the lowest conceivable level (IX, 208/151). Mr Pecksniff's own inability, in spite of all his linguistic pretensions and affectations, to distinguish between a calendar and a calender, and calling the latter an almanack (VI, 142/86–7) is rather more interesting, for it can reinforce the denunciation of the man as a complete sham in every respect. On the other hand, Mrs Gamp's implicit confusion between 'police' and 'pelisse', needlessly explained by the narrator ('The lady cried out fiercely, "Where's the pelisse!" meaning the constabulary': (XL, 698/623) is mostly either a mistake on Dickens's part or an example of bad faith; Mrs Gamp is supposed to be pronouncing 'police' in such a way that it comes to resemble 'pelisse', but, at least in twentieth-century English, the pronunciation of the two words is very similar.

It may not be necessary to spend too much time on another of the lower forms of the comic in *Chuzzlewit*, the scenes of mere farce. The comedy of Cherry Pecksniff's courtship, or storming, of Augustus Moddle, and especially the incident of what was to have been her wedding day and turns out to be the day of her desertion, is not of a refined order. The farcical element is stressed when Moddle's letter to her, announcing his desertion, is written from on board the ship that is taking him away from her, and her name is the 'CLIPPER SCHOONER, CUPID' (LIV, 914/828). That this occurs two pages before the exalted end of the novel may perhaps be regarded as a lapse of taste. There are several other farcical passages, including one in which it is possible to isolate the source of the reader's amusement, at the end of chapter IX (212/153–4), where Mr Pecksniff, after being generously wined and dined at Mrs Todgers's, refuses to be put to bed; he rises again, and each time the process of taking him to his bed has to be resumed, so that there is a clear case of the comedy of repetition, or of the farce of reiteration.

Other relatively undistinguished forms of the comic in *Chuzzlewit* include the use of the mock-heroic, generally in connection with Pecksniff, often treated as a great personage surrounded by rival ambitions and beset by 'enemies'. This yields effects of the following kind, when he has just told Mrs Lupin that her suspicion was very natural: 'Touching which remark, let it be written down to their confusion, that the enemies of this worthy man unblushingly maintained that he always said of what was very bad, that it was very natural; and that he unconsciously betrayed his own nature in doing so' (III, 86–7/34). The words 'confusion' and 'unblushingly' in particular introduce the parodic note of social and moral elevation; while pretending to refute the enemies, the narrator slyly denounces their victim. The enemies reappear time and again (for instance, 'some people said (and these were the old enemies again!)': VI, 143/88). A more elaborate pastiche of the dignified style is to be found in this:

Oh blessed star of Innocence, wherever you may be, how did you glitter in your home of ether, when the two Miss Pecksniffs put forth, each her lily hand, and gave the same, with mantling cheeks, to Martin! How did you twinkle, as if fluttering with sympathy, when Mercy, reminded of the bonnet in her hair, hid her fair face and turned her head aside: the while her gentle sister plucked it out, and smote her, with a sister's soft reproof, upon her buxom shoulder! (V, 135/80)

The reader having been invited to realize that the two girls in question were far from pretty, far from young, far from loving, far from sincere, the scene is clearly one of comedy and irony. But the mock-heroic mostly belongs to the early sections of the novel and clearly tends to decrease in frequency and importance as the story develops and as the genuinely heroic, or tragic, tends to take over.

The most striking idiosyncrasies of Dickens's humorous writing are to be looked for in other directions, and in great part in that of his highly distinctive relationship to language. He has a gift for the picturesque expression. Who else could have spoken of 'a faint gentleman' on board an American steamboat (XXXIV, 603/530) and thus suggested something precise and amusing? Who else could have been so eager to pounce on a ready-made phrase or idiom and demonstrate its absurdity by taking it quite literally? The Misses Pecksniff are again in the foreground, making a show of affection for Old Martin, and they 'embraced him with all their hearts – with all their arms at any rate' (X, 225/166). On the following page, Augustus Moddle (as yet known only as the youngest gentleman in company) complains of Mr Jinkins to Mrs Todgers, and says, threateningly, 'But let him look out! He'll find himself shaved, pretty close, before long, and so I tell him.' Upon which the narrator comes in with: 'The young gentleman was mistaken in this closing sentence, inasmuch as he never told it to Jinkins, and always to Mrs Todgers' (X, 226/168).

The higher the humorous effects rise, the more difficult they become to analyse rationally, the more arduous it is to trace the fun to its source. In the account of John Westlock's preparations for entertaining Tom and Ruth Pinch in his London chambers, and again in the very different context of a description of Mrs Gamp's room (XLV, 767/688 and XLIX, 824–5/742–4), there is a kind of infectious good-humour. Dickens's high spirits and verve communicate themselves to the reader, and amusement is thus created; the writer manipulates vocabulary in profusion, and his English becomes relaxed and almost journalistic, while remaining under artistic control and ordered to its purpose.

A note that is less characteristic of Dickens in general, but very noticeable in *Chuzzlewit*, is that of irony. Alexander Welsh writes that 'the most ironic (happily ironic) of Dickens's novels, *Martin Chuzzlewit*, portrays the builders of the earthly city in all their glory'.[33] That the irony is always happy may be questioned, especially where the criticism of America seems stridently angry, but on the whole Welsh is probably right. Examples of irony in its simplest form are easily found. When Tom Pinch, delightedly walking about the streets of London, steps out into the causeway in the middle of the traffic, in order to see the buildings better, he returns to the pavement 'wholly unconscious of the personal congratulations addressed to him by the drivers' (XXXIX, 690/616). Irony can also be observed in several chapter-headings, which are exemplary in the sense that a chapter-heading is a kind of label, and that thus the contrast between the goods and the label is placed before the eyes of readers, making the irony particularly flagrant: 'the most agreeable Family in the World' ushers in the acrimonious bickerings of the Chuzzlewits (IV); 'Mr. Pecksniff and his charming Daughters' (VIII); 'Mr. Pecksniff asserts the Dignity of outraged Virtue' (XII). It is obvious that Mr Pecksniff lends himself particularly well to ironical treatment. The irony consists, in his case, in affecting to take him at his face value, or at his own valuation; as he is always playing a part, the reality behind his words and attitudes will be emphasized, and amusement created, by the contrast between what he says on the one hand, what he is and does on the other. And indeed, whether in the chapter-headings or elsewhere, Pecksniff is a favourite butt of the narrator's irony. Jonas is another choice target, for other reasons. He is not a hypocrite and does not often pretend to be other than he is; on the contrary, he is a cynic and a bully. Thus the ironical treatment meted out to him need consist only of words of praise; in his case, any praise forms a visible contrast with the observable reality – 'the amiable Jonas' and other expressions of the same kind (XVIII, 361–5/298–302), or 'that amiable and worthy orphan' (XXXVIII, 662/586), are examples of, so to speak, simplistic double-dealing. When both Pecksniff and Jonas are involved, the irony becomes double-edged: Pecksniff's 'regard for that gentleman [Jonas] was founded, as we know, on pure esteem, and a knowledge of the excellence of his character' (XX, 395/331), a sentence which casts some light on the working of irony within the relationship between author or narrator and reader. 'As we know' is the revealing phrase in that respect; irony is useless and inefficient if what is really meant has not been made available, if the reader has not been initiated, taken into the author's confidence; irony is an esoteric process. There are all kinds of shades which require great attention from the reader; thus, when Pecksniff attempts to press his love upon Mary Graham, and she recoils from him, the narrator affects to exclaim in all innocence: 'A fantastic thing, that maiden affectation! She made believe to shudder' (XXX, 551/480). Of course, the narrator is not, cannot be, taken in; he is merely presenting to the reader the view of the incident that may be supposed to be going through Pecksniff's mind; and even that is insincere: the 'fantastic thing' is at something like three removes from reality, being what Pecksniff, not Mary, or the narrator, tries to persuade himself is in fact happening.

Irony is one of the instruments of satire. The satirical aspect of the comic is very prominent in *Chuzzlewit* and its targets are varied, as are also its value and quality. The American chapters are full of satirical thrusts, and perhaps the paragraph on dollars is the most striking example of their spirit and vividness: of the conversation of some American gentlemen we are told that

> It was rather barren of interest, to say the truth; and the greater part of it may be summed up in one word – dollars. All their cares, hopes, joys, affections, virtues, and associations, seemed to be melted down into dollars. Whatever the chance contributions that fell into the slow cauldron of their talk, they made the gruel thick and slab with dollars. Men were weighed by their dollars . . . Make commerce one huge lie and mighty theft. Deface the banner of the nation for an idle rag; pollute it star by star; and cut out stripe by stripe as from the arm of a degraded soldier. Do anything for dollars! What is a flag to *them*! (XVI, 336–7/273–4)

But British institutions, scenes and characters are not spared the satirical whip, even if it falls on the whole less heavily or less universally in their case: British snobbery is denounced (XXVIII, 522/451); the laying of the first stone for the grammar school is a ludicrous ceremony (XXXV, 624–5/550–3); nor is *Martin Chuzzlewit* free from the satirical gibe at Parliament which one looks for in every work by Dickens – it is particularly uncalled-for here, however, for the theme is the language of lovers, who

> can, in one way or another, give utterance to more language – eloquent language – in any given short space of time, than all the six

hundred and fifty-eight members in the Commons House of
Parliament of the United Kingdom of Great Britain and Ireland;
who are strong lovers, no doubt, but of their country only, which
makes all the difference; for in a passion of that kind (which is not
always returned), it is the custom to use as many words as possible,
and express nothing whatever. (XLIII, 750–1/673)

All the examples\of the comic given so far were relatively easy to
identify, characterize and classify. But they hardly bite into the major
question of Dickens's humour in *Chuzzlewit*. Perhaps, by now
examining a few more elusive specimens, some idea can be formed, if
not of the nature, at least of the mode in which Dickensian humour
presents itself in that novel. Its importance clearly decreases halfway
through the novel. Montague Tigg's attempt to borrow money from
Pecksniff is one of the most amusing scenes in the story, possibly
because it is a well-matched encounter between two unblushing,
undauntable antagonists: Pecksniff is piously uncharitable, Tigg
brazenly and divertingly (inventively) insistent (see IV, 104/50–1).
Next can be mentioned parts of the section devoted to Mr Pecksniff's
drunkenness at Mrs Todgers's. It has been seen that the end of it was
on the whole farcical, and based in part on a well-known device for
producing laughter, the use of repetition; but there is also the
analysis, or rather the display, of what happens when incipient
inebriation loosens some of the controls laid down by a man of strong
will and great experience in dissembling. His words still flow along the
channels he has created for them, but they come in shorter spirts and
with an admixture of involuntary eccentricities; and his amorousness
clamours for expression. Thus, when Mr Pecksniff asks Mrs Todgers
to let him hold both her hands he claims that this is the will of his
deceased wife, and that she is speaking through him:

'Don't suppose it's me: it's the voice; it's her voice'. Mrs. Pecksniff
deceased, must have had an unusually thick and husky voice for a
lady, and rather a stuttering voice; and to say the truth somewhat of
a drunken voice, if it had ever borne much resemblance to that in
which Mr. Pecksniff spoke just then. But perhaps this was delusion
on his part. (IX, 209/151)

The phenomenon might be described, anachronistically perhaps, as a
partial release of the id from the tyranny of the superego.

A less subtle, more characteristic, but entirely delightful example of Dickensian humour will be found in the denunciation of the inadequacies of representation in inferior art. Martin has had a meal in a wayside inn and raises his eyes to the walls:

> he looked at the highly-coloured scripture pieces on the walls, in little black frames like common shaving-glasses, and saw how the Wise Men (with a strong family likeness among them) worshipped in a pink manger; and how the Prodigal Son came home in red rags to a purple father, and already feasted in imagination on a sea-green calf. (XIII, 275/215)

This can go without comment of any kind: the prospect of feasting on a sea-green calf is dazzling in itself. A little later, without the least necessity, one finds Dickens creating one more of his hundreds of ephemeral characters of whom it is not enough to say that they are minor: they are minimal. They play no part in the story, they are gratuitous gifts to the reader by the way. This one is the driver of a light van, who gives Martin a paid lift to London, and entertains him with anecdotes of coaches and coachmen. He has brought into the conversation one 'Lummy Ned of the Light Salisbury' who was a musical guard of great distinction. On Martin asking whether he is dead, the driver replies, with what may be the all-time record of arbitrariness: 'Dead! . . . Not he. You won't catch Ned a dying easy. No, no. He knows better than that' (XIII, 278/217). There may be something indirectly gruesome in the notion of an exceptional man who is not of the dying kind; because, by contrast, all we unexceptional beings know what is awaiting us. But it is mostly, once more, the shock of pleasurable eccentricity that the reader experiences.

Among all the harshly satirical passages of the American episodes, there are a few touches of simple, enjoyable humour, like the following: ' "And do I then," cried the general, "once again behold the chicest spirits of my country!"/"Yes", said Mr. Norris the father. "Here we are, General" ' (XVII, 353/290). One of the most famous touches of humour in the later part of the book is to be found in the comment made by the butcher who sells steak to Tom Pinch: ' "meat", he said, with some emotion, "must be humoured, not drove" ' (XXXIX, 674/599). The emotion is understandable, but the sentiment is superbly conveyed; whether the faulty form 'drove' collaborates in the comic effect or not, the effect is achieved with perfect mastery and economy.

Not many of the characters appear as humorists in their own right. Most of the humorous effects are achieved at the expense of the characters, or of mankind in general; but Mrs Gamp displays a definite sense of humour, though not of the kindliest sort. Her humour is touched with sycophancy in her conversation with Mr and Mrs Mould (XXV, 472/404), and it is laced with grim contempt when she turns the ravings of diseased Lewsome into a comic dialogue (XXV, 482–3/412–13), but there is comic inventiveness and genuine humour in both cases.

On the whole, then, one can agree with Stephen Wall when he writes that 'Dickens was justified in feeling that there is a sustained comic exuberance in *Chuzzlewit* as great as in *Pickwick* and more original'.[34] Or with Barbara Hardy, who says of the comedy in that novel:

Together with the melodrama, and surpassing it in its variety and concreteness, it is the main source of vitality in *Martin Chuzzlewit* . . . The comedy provides its own special source of tension – we await the return to its self-contained comic farce and continued mannerism as the one firm line of interest in the novel.[35]

James R. Kincaid, one of the few serious recent writers on the comic in Dickens, also sees *Chuzzlewit* as

Dickens's funniest novel . . . It moves further than *Pickwick* towards an accommodation with a sophisticated world of experience and comes very close to building a comic society out of that world. It is very nearly Dickens's last attempt to present a comic solution.[36]

The author of *Martin Chuzzlewit*, then, with all his bewildering variety of stylistic capabilities, is still predominantly a humorous novelist, even if the vein of seriousness is steadily growing within him and his artistic ambitions are simultaneously rising to new heights. It might be claimed that he has not yet fully found himself and his way. But he has already achieved mastery and the power of conveying an astonishing diversity of meanings and effects.

## NOTES: CHAPTER 10

1   George Gissing, *Charles Dickens* (London, 1898), p. 54.
2   George Gissing, *The Immortal Dickens* (London, 1925), p. 113.
3   In J. Gross and G. Pearson (eds), *Dickens and the Twentieth Century* (London, 1962), p. 107.
4   Archibald C. Coolidge, *Charles Dickens as Serial Novelist* (Ames, Ia, 1967), p. 53.
5   Kathleen Tillotson, *Novels of the Eighteen-Forties* (London, 1954), p. 160.
6   In this section chapter-headings are quoted as they occur in the table of contents of the first and Clarendon editions, with capital initials to all nouns, most verbs, and some epithets.
7   Also Fieldingese in a different way. See *Tom Jones*, bk VI, ch. I.
8   Edgar Johnson, *Charles Dickens: His Tragedy and Triumph* (London, 1953), vol. 2, p. 807.
9   Geoffrey Thurley, *The Dickens Myth: Its Genesis and Structure* (London, 1976), p. 104.
10  See Wayne C. Booth, *The Rhetoric of Fiction* (Chicago, Ill., 1961); John Preston, *The Created Self: The Reader's Role in Eighteenth-Century Fiction* (London, 1970); and Wolfgang Iser, *The Implied Reader: Patterns of Communication in Prose Fiction from Bunyan to Beckett* (Baltimore, Md, 1974).
11  R. C. Churchill, 'Dickens, drama and tradition', *Scrutiny*, vol. 10, no. 4 (1942), p. 360.
12  Gissing, *The Immortal Dickens*, pp. 136–7.
13  See *Poetical Works*, ed. F. Page and J. Jump (1970), p. 847.
14  The Clarendon edition shows that Dickens had actually written *a great deal of* in this place.
15  See Coral Lansbury, 'Dickens' romanticism domesticated', *Dickens Studies Newsletter*, vol. 3, no. 2 (1972), p. 41.
16  'The sources of Dickens's comic art: from *American Notes* to *Martin Chuzzlewit*', *Nineteenth-Century Fiction*, vol. 24, no. 4 (1970), p. 476.
17  See Philip Collins (ed.), *Dickens: The Critical Heritage* (London, 1971), p. 185.
18  *Oliver Twist*, ch. XLVIII (Clarendon Dickens, ed. K. Tillotson (1966), p. 323).
19  Hippolyte Taine, *Histoire de la littérature anglaise*, 12th edn (Paris, 1911), Vol. 5, p. 15 ('One thinks of Hoffmann's fantasies; one becomes the prey of an obsession and of a headache. Such eccentricities belong to the style of illness rather than health').
20  'I have never observed any trace of the insane temperament in Dickens's works, or life', 'Dickens in relation to criticism', *Fortnightly Review*, XVII, 1872, reprinted in Alice R. Kaminsky (ed.), *Literary Criticism of George Henry Lewes* (Lincoln, Neb., 1964), p. 96.
21  The original manuscript added at that point more explicitly that Chuffey 'might have been stuffed and dried, and put into the glass case, half a century before at least'.
22  In the original manuscript, the great footman wore in addition a 'great waistcoat'.
23  The name *Cain* replaces in the first edition the original manuscript's periphrasis *him who took his brother's life*.
24  Steven Marcus, *Dickens from Pickwick to Dombey* (New York, 1965), pp. 214, 217.
25  See Patrick J. McCarthy, 'The language of *Martin Chuzzlewit*', *Studies in English Literature, 1500–1900*, vol. 20, no. 4 (1980), pp. 637–49. Unfortunately, there are a few mistakes (like calling Fagin Fagan) or examples of uncertain grammar in that article which shake the reader's confidence in the critic's authority in his own chosen field.
26  Earle Davis, *The Flint and the Flame: The Artistry of Charles Dickens* (Columbia, Mo., 1963), p. 146.

27  Here the Clarendon editor – questionably, in my opinion – restores *hadst thou*, a manuscript reading that had never got into print before.

28  Michael Goldberg, *Carlyle and Dickens* (Athens, Ga, 1972), pp. 174–6.

29  Garrett Stewart, *Dickens and the Trials of Imagination* (Cambridge, Mass., 1974), p. 122.

30  *David Copperfield*, ch. XXXIV (Clarendon Dickens, ed. Nina Burgis (1981), p. 424).

31  Norman Page, 'Eccentric speech in Dickens', *Critical Survey*, vol. 4, no. 2 (1968–70), p. 97.

32  They are studied with keen critical intelligence by Robert M. Polhemus in 'Dickens's *Martin Chuzzlewit* (1843–44): the comedy of expression', which is chapter 4 of his *Comic Faith: The Great Tradition from Austen to Joyce* (Chicago, Ill., 1980), pp. 88–123.

33  Alexander Welsh, *The City of Dickens* (London, 1971), p. 70.

34  See Stephen Wall (ed.), *Charles Dickens: A Critical Anthology*, (Harmondsworth, 1970), 'Introduction', p. 29.

35  '*Martin Chuzzlewit*', in Gross and Pearson, op. cit., p. 120.

36  *Dickens and the Rhetoric of Laughter*, (London, 1971), p. 132.

# CHAPTER 11

# External and Additional Material

The elements of *Martin Chuzzlewit* to be described and discussed in
the present chapter might be called, to pursue the culinary metaphor
initiated earlier on, the side-dishes of a plentiful meal. For, in addition
to the fifty-four chapters of the novel proper, the two most serious
editions available – the Penguin English Library and the Clarendon
Dickens volumes – include substantial supplements. They both
provide the text of Dickens's various prefaces and of his 'Postscript',
reproductions of the original illustrations by 'Phiz' (Hablot K.
Browne), and the cancelled beginning of chapter VI. The Clarendon
Dickens alone supplies a list of 'descriptive headlines' – the running
headlines introduced for the first time into the Charles Dickens
Edition of 1867. These are somewhat disparate items, but they cannot
be ignored, for they add something to the reader's knowledge and
understanding of Dickens's purpose and achievement. The prefaces,
for instance, express the author's own reaction to his book once he
had completed it, and to some comments on it he had already heard or
read. The cancelled fragment is more of a puzzle than a new light cast
on the novel, because the reason why it *was* cancelled is not clear. The
'Postscript' rounds off the American episodes of *Chuzzlewit* and the
history of Dickens's complex and passionate relationship with the
United States. The descriptive headlines contain a few interesting
side-lights and examples of the novelist's irony about his characters. As
to the illustrations, they were designed in close collaboration with the
author and they are unquestionably associated with the genesis of the
book.

The prefaces to *Martin Chuzzlewit*[1] form a body of writing which is
of unusual interest to the Dickens student. There are three author's
prefaces extant (37– 42/lxix and 846–8), written at long intervals of
time. The preface to the first edition was penned immediately after the
last number had been completed in 1844; it is the traditional gesture

of formal leave-taking. In the case of other novels, Dickens was often
content to leave it at that, and to go on reprinting the original preface,
with at best slight alterations. Not so for *Chuzzlewit*. Although there is
a certain amount of overlapping between the three prefaces, there are
also important innovations in the later ones. The second was written
in 1849 for the Cheap Edition of the novel; it was used again for the
Library Edition a few years later. But in 1867, when *Martin
Chuzzlewit* came to be included in the proudly named 'Charles
Dickens Edition of the Works of Charles Dickens', a new preface was
composed and printed. The date, 1867, is nowhere mentioned in the
volumes themselves; Chapman & Hall were shrewd businessmen and
they knew that dates make books age fast. But a reference in the third
preface to the first edition having appeared 'twenty-four years ago'
tallies with what is known of *Chuzzlewit*'s publishing history, and
provides internal evidence.

Each preface can now be succinctly described in its own right and
in comparison with the other two. The preface of 1844 contains the
following elements, in as many paragraphs (to which I append
numbers for purposes of later back-reference):

I.    The author says that he has nothing to say, but must say
      something because a preface is customary, and thus expected
      of him.
II.   He expresses his emotion at having finished his task.
III.  His purpose has been to exhibit the commonest of all vices, at
      the risk of being charged with exaggeration.
IV.   He has observed that nobody will recognize himself or herself
      when portrayed in his novels, but everybody is ready to
      recognize others under the same circumstances.[2]
V.    Dickens now explains that he has resisted the temptations of
      the current monthly number, endeavouring to keep firmer
      control over his story than in previous works of similar length.
VI.   And he liked doing that job.

The second preface, written for the Cheap Edition, when similarly
analysed, yields the following items:

I.    Dickens's object in that novel has been to attack 'the
      commonest of all the vices'. This repeats what had been said in
      section III of the first preface, but the phrasing is made much

more specific and pungent; detailed comparison is illuminating. First preface: 'I set out, on this journey which is now concluded; with the design of exhibiting in various aspects, the commonest of all the vices.' Second preface (in which this is the opening sentence): 'My main object in this story was, to exhibit in a variety of aspects the commonest of all vices; to show how Selfishness propagates itself; and to what a grim giant it may grow, from small beginnings.' Perhaps the second version is rather overwritten, but it is *bona fide* rewriting, not a mere perfunctory change of a word here and there.

II.  No plea will be made for the truth of Pecksniff's character (here Dickens dismisses the end of section III and the bulk of section IV of the previous version), but a few words about Jonas are in order.

III. Jonas's character must be appraised in connection with his education and parentage.

IV.  This case shows that, 'as we sow, we reap', which can also be verified by visiting children's quarters in prisons and work-houses.

V.   The American episodes illustrate only the ludicrous side of the United States; no softening of reality has been attempted (any more than in the case of British realities), but no exaggeration has been indulged in, even in the Watertoast scenes, which are a 'literal paraphrase' of published reports about a certain Brandywine case.

VI.  The characters of S. Gamp and B. Prig are part of Dickens's continued and much needed efforts in favour of sanitary improvement.

Thus, sections III–VI, or two-thirds of the second preface, are entirely new. The novelty lies in the ideas and arguments adduced, presumably in order to refute criticisms levelled at *Martin Chuzzlewit* between its first publication and the end of the decade.

The third preface provides further alterations, cancellations and additions. It is composed of eight sections, as follows:

I.   The charge of exaggeration may be unfair, and the fault may lie in the excessive weakness of the reader's perception rather than in the excessive vividness of the writer's. This resumes a line of argument already followed in sections III–IV of the first preface and in section III of the second, but the whole paragraph is newly written. It is also much more in the general style of a belletristic essay (as when Dickens now writes: 'What is exaggeration to one class of minds and perceptions, is plain truth to another. That which is commonly called a long-sight, perceives in a prospect innumerable features and bearings non-existent to a short-sighted person').

II. Dickens here resurrects, with new pungency, the point made at the end of section IV of the first preface, and omitted from the second (that people refuse to recognize themselves when portrayed in his works).

III. As in section III of the second preface, Dickens dismisses the notion of defending Pecksniff and points to the need for saying something about Jonas. This part of the third preface is not identical with its counterpart in the previous version, but close to it.

IV. The defence of Jonas is practically the same as before. Only one significant change is made, when 'the extreme exposition of a plain truth' becomes 'the extreme exposition of a direct truth', which seems to go beyond the substitution of one word for another. The emphasis is different: may not a truth be plain without being direct, and vice versa?

V. On the theme of 'as we sow, we reap', Dickens here merely repeats what he had said in section IV of the second preface.

VI. This section concerns the American episodes. It is on the same lines as the fifth paragraph in the second preface, but not without significant alterations. An allusion to Mr Bevan, the good American, as an exception among his compatriots, is introduced. The adverb *only* is added, and italicized for good measure, in a sentence which no longer speaks of 'the ludicrous side of the American character', but of 'a ludicrous side, *only*, of the American character'. Then, instead of adding 'that side which is, from its very nature, the most obtrusive, and the most likely to be seen by such travellers as Young Martin and Mark Tapley', Dickens now says 'that side which was, four-and-twenty years ago, the most obtrusive'. Finally, the two concluding sentences of that section contain a new tribute to 'the good-humoured people of the United States' and to 'that great nation'. This is more serious than anything we have come across so far. It is a change of attitude to the target of the satire in *Chuzzlewit*, and even to a certain extent a change of attitude, on the author's part, to the significance of his own novel.

VII. The comments on the Watertoast episode continue the resumption of section V from the previous version with relatively few changes; the most important are an allusion to the fact that the files of *The Times* are still available as evidence of the literalness of his paraphrase, and the cancellation of eight lines of details, protests, and allusion to Ireland.

VIII. This is about the sanitary improvements (based on section VI of the preceding preface). A certain amount of updating has been accomplished. Thus, instead of asserting that Mrs Gamp 'is a representation of the hired attendant', the paragraph now reads 'was, four-and-twenty years ago, a fair representation'. Similar changes of *tense* occur, for the same reason, later on. And the concluding sentence seems to introduce a reference to Florence Nightingale, for, after again deploring that it should have been left 'to private humanity and enterprise to enter on an attempt to improve that class of persons' (nurses), it now adds: '– since, greatly improved through the agency of good women'. Dickens, apparently, did not have time to do anything about the awkward collocation of *improve/improved* within less than a line of distance, but he took time to be fair to the class concerned by his former criticism, and perhaps to imply that his criticism had taken effect.

In one sense, the 'Postscript' of 1868 (919–20/855–6) continues the same process. This is a two-page appendage devoted to the American episodes and to Dickens's relationship with the United States. The bulk of this postscript consists of a substantial extract from a speech delivered by the novelist at a public dinner in New York on 18 April 1868. The dinner had been given in Dickens's honour (or honor) by 'two hundred representatives of the Press of the United States of America', that is, of a body of professional men who had fared exceedingly ill at his hands in *Martin Chuzzlewit*. The dinner and speech occurred in the course of Dickens's second visit to the States, delayed by the Civil War, and in some ways, when it did take place, much happier, or at any rate much less ambiguous, than the first. Dickens's status in 1842 had been that of a guest of honour travelling at his own expense, with nothing special to do, apart from seeing the country and being entertained. Breathing incense, not unmixed with harsher smells, had proved somewhat uncongenial to Dickens. In 1867–8 his visit was put on a commercial (and artistic) basis; he came to give public readings, by which he undisguisedly hoped to make a good deal of money. This sort of give-and-take – Dickens giving out aesthetic pleasure and emotion, his audiences giving dollars and applause – apparently suited both the visitor and the visited much better than the former vague arrangement, the kind of purposeless quasi-royal tour of 1842. Dickens might have suffered from loneliness in 1868; he had no wife with him, not even his friend or mistress Ellen Ternan had been enabled to join him; he was in very poor health, and he had to face the rigours of very harsh winter weather. Yet his speech to the pressmen breathes benevolence and enjoyment, or at any rate the determination to be pleased by the welcome accorded to him. The speech, or the long passage from it quoted in the postscript, is a tribute both to the second reception experienced by Dickens and to the improvements he had observed in American cities, twenty-four years after. He uses the superlative vocabulary of admiration that was so typical of him, words and phrases like: 'high and grateful sense of my second reception . . . the national generosity and magnanimity . . . astounded . . . by the amazing changes . . . on every side . . . gigantic changes . . . unsurpassable politeness, delicacy, sweet temper, hospitality, consideration . . . unsurpassable respect for the privacy'; and these words and phrases were used, he said, *not in mere love and thankfulness*, but *as an act of plain justice and honour*, and they were spoken *with the greatest earnestness*. Anyone acquainted with Dickens's style in his speeches and letters will here recognize two or three familiar modes of rhetorical emphasis: there are the duplicated abstractions (generosity and magnanimity, love and thankfulness, justice and honour), the other kinds of iteration or repetition (*astounded by/amazing, amazing changes/gigantic changes*), the proliferation of superlatives (*unsurpassable, the greatest*). The wording may be in excess of the emotion.

Apart from the compliments, the 1868 speech contained one assertion, or conjecture, of a very unusual nature. His hearers may well have been astounded by this amazing statement: 'Nor am I, believe me, so arrogant as to suppose that in five and twenty years there have been no changes in me, and that I had nothing to learn and no extreme impressions to correct when I was here first.' Dickens was not much given to questioning his own infallibility. This expression of humility is moving, and it is one of the rare signs of a maturing and mellowing of Dickens's personality at this late date.

The speech went on to point out, with much humour, that even an immensely improved press like that of New York could occasionally be misinformed and thus misinform the general public. Whoever said that Dickens intended to write a new book about America needed to be contradicted flatly, for nothing would induce him to do so. The only thing he was going to do was to have his tribute inserted as a postscript into every copy of either *American Notes* or *Martin Chuzzlewit* henceforth to be printed, as long as he or his heirs had any power over the contents of his books. That promise was made good, and the postscript is still reprinted where Dickens wanted it. It is a useful comment on the excessively harsh satire of the American episodes. It cannot quite restore the balance, but there is in it appreciable evidence of Dickens's intellectual honesty and goodwill.

The cancelled beginning of chapter VI is also a nearly unique phenomenon in the history of Dickens's writings. Instead of having the chapter as it now stands, the story branched off after a few lines into a quarrel between the two Pecksniff girls. The quarrel was occasioned by Charity's resentment of Mercy's attitude to Young Martin, the new pupil, on his arrival the night before: Charity thought her sister had been improperly coquettish, and let her know how she viewed that conduct. Merry insinuated that it was of her success that her sister jealously disapproved. The two young women soon came to blows and tears; that was the moment chosen by their father, who had been eavesdropping outside the room, to come in and effect a reconciliation between them, at the expense of Tom Pinch. They all three agreed that, for some mysterious reason, Pinch was the culprit. He was called in and duly admonished. And he was so meek that he almost believed in his own guilt.

Dickens never disclosed his motive for rejecting that episode. It may have appeared pointless to him. The scene led nowhere. The comedy was somewhat laborious and, although it did give an insight into the workings of family relationships in the Pecksniff home, its omission would in no way damage the novel. On the other hand, if the author was eager to engage the reader's interest in the story, he would be on safer ground with incidents marking a real progress, such as what he in fact substituted for the cancelled beginning – the announcement of, and preparations for, the Pecksniffs' immediate

departure for London. After all, the early sales of *Chuzzlewit* had
proved disappointing, and Dickens felt the need to get the novel off
the ground; in the same way as he was to send Martin to America, he
now dispatched the Pecksniffs to London – a felicitous move, it
turned out, since it gave birth to Todgers's – instead of letting them
stay and quarrel in the stale atmosphere of their village life.

The 'descriptive headlines' were a specific feature of the Charles
Dickens Edition. The amount of work done by the author for that
edition, whose name, and the golden signature that blazed on the
binding of every single copy, showed that it was dear to his heart, has
been diversely appraised. My own opinion, based on textual criticism
of both *Hard Times* and *Bleak House*,[3] is that there was very little
rewriting or stylistic improvement; possibly a word or two here and
there would be altered, largely for the purpose of renewing the
copyright. But in the main the Charles Dickens Edition of Dickens's
novels is greatly inferior to the first edition and does not deserve any
special respect; it is interesting mostly as one stage in the process of
deterioration of the text through reprint after reprint. What *is* of value
as a novelty, in *Chuzzlewit*'s case, is the preface, as has just been seen,
and in every case the running headlines. Not much is known about
the frequency of descriptive headlines in the printing of Victorian
fiction, or indeed of earlier or later English novels. What is apparent is
that the need for them was by no means taken for granted in
Dickens's days. No other contemporary edition of his novels has
them. No edition of Bulwer Lytton's novels that I have seen, for
instance, has them, either. It is also clear that Dickens and his
publishers felt that the Charles Dickens Edition must have some new
and attractive feature. The coining and insertion of 'descriptive
headlines' was a relatively undemanding way of catering for that need.
It was claimed in the prospectus for the Charles Dickens Edition – of
which almost a million and a half copies were circulated – that its
headlines had been written by Dickens himself;[4] and this has been
found to be the case at least for *Bleak House*. A copy of an earlier
edition is in existence with the headlines written in Dickens's own
hand. The previous editions had carried nothing similar. In the first
edition, for instance, every left-hand page had at its head LIFE AND
ADVENTURES OF, and every right-hand page MARTIN CHUZZLEWIT.
The running headlines coined in 1867 are of course of uneven value,
and they pose an embarrassing problem to the well-meaning editor of
a Dickens novel, who legitimately wishes to leave out nothing that the

author actually wrote in it. It is practically impossible to use the running heads *as* running heads,[5] because their number and placing depend on the distribution of the text in a volume. The Charles Dickens Edition had particularly full and close-set pages, running to 522 only, whereas the first edition (in spite of its fifty lines to the page) came to 624, and modern editions vary between 830 (Clarendon, and Oxford Illustrated) and over 900 (Penguin). A decision to print running headlines at the top of some pages would thus leave awkward gaps. An ingenious solution was found by the editors of the beautiful Nonesuch Library Dickens in the 1930s, who printed the running headlines in the margins of some pages, thus emphasizing their character, which is that of a marginal running commentary on the text. The Clarendon editors, however, like the Norton editors of other Dickens novels, adhering to their justified choice of the first edition as their copy-text, content themselves with reprinting the running headlines of 1867 consecutively, in an appendix (849–54). It must be admitted that, thus lumped together and read as one sequence (which was never their purpose), they make dull, or at best disconcerting, reading. A few attractive items, however, jump to one's attention even thus. There is the treatment of some proper names, for instance, such as Pecksniff's (in 'Pecksniffiana', II or 'Pecksniffian Domesticity', V) and Pogram's (in 'Pogrammania', XXXIV). The insistence on the theme of Self or selfishness is made obvious in 'Universal Self' (III) and in 'Discovery of Self' (XXXIII). And one may note the occasional literary allusion ('The Funeral Baked Meats' in the chapter dealing with Anthony Chuzzlewit's burial: XIX), the bold borrowing of a bold effect from the text (one headline reads merely 'Hush!' at the end of XLVI). But, in the main, the headlines provide an ironical commentary on the story; among many similar examples may be quoted 'The Art of Sick Nursing' (XXV), which faintly foreshadows the Whole Science of Government in *Little Dorrit*.

Altogether, then, the running headlines are of some historical interest, but cannot compare in importance, not only with the story – that goes without saying – but with the prefaces and postscript, or even the illustrations.

The original illustrations, supplied by Hablot K. Browne acting on Charles Dickens's detailed directions, have been reproduced in many later editions, including the Oxford Illustrated, of course, the Penguin English Library, and the Clarendon Dickens. But, for various technical reasons, an inevitable deterioration in quality is perceptible in recent reprintings. Copies of the first edition of 1843–4 still leave one under the impression that 'Phiz' was a major artist. Dickens's first illustrators, with Browne as the central figure, have been granted considerable attention in recent decades. It began with John Butt's article in the *Review of English Literature* in 1961 and went on to the major studies by Michael Steig (*Dickens and Phiz*, 1978) and Jane R. Cohen, (*Charles Dickens and His Original Illustrators*, 1980). In the meantime there had also been, in addition to Steig's earlier articles, an interesting chapter by Q. D. Leavis in *Dickens the Novelist* (1970), and the work of John R. Harvey, *Victorian Novelists and Their Illustrators* (1971). The most specific and elaborate discussion of Phiz's work for *Martin Chuzzlewit* is to be found in an essay of 1972 by Michael Steig, on which one chapter of his 1978 volume is based. '*Martin Chuzzlewit*'s progress by Dickens and Phiz' (*Dickens Studies Annual 2* (1972), pp. 119–50) leaves little, but none the less a little, to be added on its theme. Steig, and other students of the original illustrations, are in an excellent position to appraise the nature and limitations of the artists' contribution to the genesis of Dickens's novels when the novelist's letters specifying his wishes have been preserved. Two such letters are extant in the case of *Chuzzlewit*. One had been printed by John Butt; both are found in the Pilgrim Edition of the letters, as well as in an appendix to the Clarendon *Chuzzlewit* (843–5). But the expert can also work on a close comparison between text and plates and see whether there are details in the illustrations which are not mentioned in the story, and thus have been invented, or at least inferred, by the pictorial artist. Michael Steig has shown, most convincingly, that one of Browne's striking tendencies was the use of emblematic details: pictures on the walls, titles of books, resemblance of the characters' gestures and attitudes to famous scenes and paintings, all helped to emphasize not only the material or factual aspects of the incidents represented, but also their meaning and their moral significance. This, Steig contends, often turns Browne into a true collaborator of the novelist in the production of an 'illustrated novel' (which he sees as an important sub-genre of Victorian fiction). Browne, a disciple of Hogarth, may have been a lesser artist than his principal contender for the palm of excellence among Dickens's early illustrators, George Cruikshank, but he was probably a more adequate book-illustrator, especially during his great emblematic period (to which *Chuzzlewit* belongs). Steig summarizes Phiz's virtues as follows:

it is in his function as a genuine collaborator, helping to create works in the mixed media of words and pictures, that Browne is of greatest importance. When sufficiently inspired by the novelist, Browne was capable of producing virtual suites of illustrations, analogous to the satirical sequences of Hogarth. Through allegory and symbolism in the use of details, through design of subject, and through numerous parallels and contrasts between individual plates, Phiz created running commentaries upon the text, which may be considered an integral part of the novels.[6]

The major characteristic of Brown's work for *Chuzzlewit* is his adoption, for the first time, of a 'relative realism of character portrayal' (p. 123). There are reasons for believing that at least one of Phiz's plates had some influence on the writing of later episodes: the portrait of Pecksniff by Spiller and his bust by Spoker made their first appearance in the very first illustration without having been mentioned in the text; but they *are* mentioned in the second number (p. 126).

Michael Steig also usefully reminds his reader that symmetries and parallelisms between two plates printed in the same monthly instalment would be more likely to be perceived by contemporary purchasers when, instead of each plate facing the relevant section of the narrative, the two plates would be bound together at the beginning of the booklet (p. 129). Steig further points to various possible sources of Phiz's inspiration, such as French artists like David, Fragonard and Daumier. On the other hand, he courteously and irrefutably corrects the conjecture of an earlier French critic that Dickens himself had initiated the reference to *Tartuffe* in one of the last plates, presenting the discomfiture of Mr Pecksniff (pp. 139–41). This does not invalidate the notion that Dickens *was* influenced by Molière in the creation of Pecksniff. The resemblance between him and Tartuffe is great. Phiz recognized and proclaimed it. By leaving the plate unmodified, Dickens fully sanctioned this recognition.

What Steig seems less concerned to point out are some oddities of Browne's work. He does mention (p. 135) one slight inaccuracy in the plate entitled 'Mr Tapley succeeds in finding a Jolly Subject for Contemplation'; here the text says that Mark 'had employed a portion of his leisure in the decoration of the Rowdy Journal door, whereon his own initials now appeared in letters nearly half a foot long' (XVII, 344/280); in the plate it is the full name MARK TAPLEY that appears on the door. But there are at least two other discrepancies between plate and text which are not mentioned by Steig. In chapter XXXV there is an illustration called 'Martin is much gratified by an Imposing Ceremony'. The ceremony in question is the laying of the first stone of Mr Pecksniff's grammar school, after Martin's plans; the Member of Parliament is making a speech, and the reader is *told* that at a certain stage in his speech 'he pointed the trowel at Mr. Pecksniff, who was greeted with vociferous cheering, and laid his hand upon his heart' (XXXV, 626/554). On the page facing this statement, the reader is *shown* the orator pointing at the architect with his disengaged hand, gracefully holding the trowel in the air behind Mr Pecksniff's head. He may wonder which hand Pecksniff will lay on his breast, when he sees him holding his hat in one hand and a huge plan in the other (plus an additional roll of paper squeezed under his arm on the same side). This does not matter in the least, since taking off one's hat is fully as satisfactory as laying one's hand on one's breast. But the discrepancy in chapter XLII is rather more serious; this is when 'Mr. Jonas exhibits his Presence of Mind' after the carriage in which he was travelling during the stormy night with Montague Tigg has been 'crashing over'. Jonas is said, in the text, to have run to the horses' heads, and pulled at their bridles, in order to bring their hoofs nearer to the skull of Montague, who is lying senseless on the road. On the plate, Browne shows one horse lying on its back, entangled in the ruined chariot, while Jonas holds the bridle of the other horse, already free from the carriage, standing on its hind legs and backing towards Montague. Admittedly, there is a certain lack of coherence in the story itself, which seems to imply that Jonas is pushing both horses, still harnessed to the overthrown vehicle and not yet having found their legs. For, a little later, the driver will disengage the horses from the broken chariot and get them, 'cut and bleeding, on their legs again', and the driver will admonish Jonas: 'never you pull at the bridle of a horse that's down, when there's a man's head in the way' (XLII, 723–5/646–9). The text, in fact, tells two stories, but the plate tells a third, independent of both.

In *Dickens and Phiz*, Steig states that the moral theme of *Martin Chuzzlewit* suited Browne very well, and, while pointing out that nothing of the linguistic brilliance involved in the creation of Mrs Gamp could come through in the illustrations, he concludes that they do provide an efficient, though simplified, moral commentary.[7]

Mrs Leavis agreed that Browne was a good book-illustrator, gave warm praise to several of the *Chuzzlewit* plates (the family party of chapter IV, the scene at the pawnbroker's, and even the jilting of Charity Pecksniff, which she regarded as a congenial subject for the artist).[8] On the whole she fully confirms that the original illustrations are worthy of close examination, as forming a substantial part of a genetic study of *Martin Chuzzlewit*.

## NOTES: CHAPTER 11

1  No apology is required for dealing with them near the end of this book. They were all written after the novel had been completed, and some many years later.
2  cf. Swift, 'The Preface of the Author' to *The Battle of the Books*: 'Satyr is a sort of Glass, wherein Beholders do generally discover everybody's Face but their own.'
3  See Norton Critical editions of those two novels, ed. G. H. Ford and S. Monod (New York, 1966 and 1977).
4  See Robert L. Patten, *Charles Dickens and His Publishers* (Oxford, 1978), pp. 311–13.
5  The Penguin edition attempts to do that, but has to omit many of the 1867 headlines and to coin as many new ones.
6  Article in *Dickens Studies Annual 2* (1972), pp. 121–2. Subsequent quotations from the same essay are identified by page-number given parenthetically in my text.
7  See Michael Steig, *Dickens and Phiz* (Bloomington, Ind./London, 1978), pp. 51–85.
8  See F. R. and Q. D. Leavis, *Dickens the Novelist* (London, 1979), pp. 341–7.

# CHAPTER 12

# *Martin Chuzzlewit* and its Readers: Purpose and Achievement

Among the purposes assigned to Dickens, and, as appeared in his prefaces and sometimes in the text of the novel itself, in part stated by the author, is the expression of a theme.

Kathleen Tillotson, in her pioneering study of several novels of the 1840s, showed scepticism about the existence, or at least the efficient treatment, of a theme. She wrote: 'it is doubtful whether a reader lacking preface and biography would recognize that Selfishness, or even Hypocrisy (it is never quite clear which Dickens means) was its theme'.[1] But other respected Dickens scholars have felt differently. K. J. Fielding, for instance, considers that *Chuzzlewit*, as much as any of Dickens's books, 'is written with a moral purpose. It may be unnecessary to labour this point, but it is impossible to understand Dickens without it, and no one can question that this was his purpose in *Martin Chuzzlewit*.'[2] For John Butt, in one of his posthumously collected essays, 'In *Martin Chuzzlewit* and in each of the later novels, Dickens set out with a theme in mind and devised a plot to help him in expounding that theme. His success in *Chuzzlewit* is not so striking as in the later novels, but there is no doubting his intentions.'[3] And Michael Steig has roundly asserted that '*Martin Chuzzlewit* is built upon an essential superstructure of several moral progresses'.[4]

Whether or not Dickens's moral ideas cohered into a thematic superstructure, there can be no doubt that, in *Chuzzlewit* as in a large majority of Victorian novels, the author's moral ideas are abundantly expressed and are uninhibitedly made part and parcel of his central purpose.

Hippolyte Taine's summary of Dickens's moral message in *Chuzzlewit* is an amusing mixture of the straightforward and the satirical. It runs as follows:

Soyez bons et aimez; il n'y a de vraie joie que dans les émotions du
coeur: la sensibilité est tout l'homme. Laissez aux savants la
science, l'orgueil aux nobles, le luxe aux riches; ayez compassion
des humbles misères; l'être le plus petit et le plus méprisé peut
valoir seul autant que des milliers d'êtres puissants et superbes.
Prenez garde de froisser les âmes délicates qui fleurissent dans
toutes les conditions, sous tous les habits, à tous les âges. Croyez
que l'humanité, la pitié, le pardon, sont ce qu'il y a de plus beau
dans l'homme; croyez que l'intimité, les épanchements, la tendresse,
les larmes, sont ce qu'il y a de plus doux dans le monde. Ce n'est
rien que de vivre: c'est peu que d'être puissant, savant, illustre; ce
n'est pas assez d'être utile. Celui-là seul a vécu et est un homme,
qui a pleuré au souvenir d'un bienfait qu'il a rendu ou qu'il a reçu.[5]

Fair enough, one would say. But there is at the same time a great deal
of shrewdness in Steven Marcus's remark that

> In *Martin Chuzzlewit*, I must note, Dickens almost never uses the
> words 'moral' or 'morality' in any but an ironic sense: being a true
> moralist in an era of middle-class piety, propriety and prosperity, he
> regarded all claims made in the name of morality with skepticism.[6]

It is true that Dickens combines a defence of conventional morality
with a denunciation of its conventionality and deceptiveness. H. P.
Sucksmith has demonstrated that Dickens's moral preaching and
posturing, in the Pecksniff case in particular, fails when it is too
explicit, but can succeed otherwise.[7]

Among the other suggestions that have been put forward
concerning the thematic or intellectual centre of *Chuzzlewit*, the
notion of pastoralism has its attractive side, but must, I fear, be rather
summarily dismissed. The ode to the wind in chapter II ('Out upon
the angry wind! how from sighing, it began to bluster round the
merry forge, banging at the wicket, and grumbling in the chimney, as
if bullied by the jolly bellows!': 58–9/8) sounds conventional, childish
and curiously arch.[8] It is as though the relationship between the
novelist and Nature were of the same order as his attitude to sexuality;
the seductiveness of Nature, like that of a woman's body, must be
saluted from behind the safe barrier of comical language and imagery.
Yet Dickens's pastoral leanings in *Chuzzlewit* have been taken seriously
by one or two intelligent critics. Steven Marcus, for instance, writes:

special attention must be turned to Dickens's handling of the pastoral ideal in *Martin Chuzzlewit* . . . this conception holds a place of peculiar significance in Dickens's development as a novelist . . . Pecksniff is a monumental parody of the idea of pastoral innocence. For in *Martin Chuzzlewit* the pastoral vision is an illusion, an absurd identification of the self with nature, or a pretense of oneness with it. It is a relation to nature that is willed, wholly subjective, a mockery. In *Martin Chuzzlewit*, the promise the pastoral idea once held for him has given way to a view of the Pastoral as a microcosm of the corruption of society . . .[9]

Marcus goes on to show the impact of the American episodes, illustrating as they do the deterioration of the garden of Eden. All this is interesting and ingenious but one cannot refrain from observing that, if Pecksniff embodies a satire on pseudo-pastoralism, the narrator's brand seems hardly less spurious. John Lucas, on the other hand, compares Cobbett's notes on the misery prevailing in the countryside and Dickens's idealization in *Chuzzlewit*:

it is therefore worthwhile noting just how unrealistic Dickens's pastoralism is . . . We are forced to realize that the pastoral landscapes of *Martin Chuzzlewit* are not really views of rural England at all. As I remarked earlier, this novel is the least socially focussed of all Dickens's novels . . . in *Martin Chuzzlewit* nature is wholly mythic.[10]

It is difficult to make higher claims, in all seriousness, for Dickens's version of pastoralism in the book.

J. Hillis Miller's reading of *Martin Chuzzlewit* is more existentialist, and he sees as its theme, or at least as its 'arena', what he calls the present:

the arena of *Martin Chuzzlewit* is the present, a present which is irrevocably cut off from the past and in which society in the sense of an integrated community has been replaced by a fragmented collection of isolated self-seeking individuals.[11]

It is clear, from the various prefaces and from many passages in the text of the novel itself, that Dickens did intend selfishness to be his theme and his target. To a certain extent, the novel is a history of

selfishness in many forms within one family: Jonas and Pecksniff each
serve their own interests exclusively, the former being led to practise
cynicism and the latter hypocrisy for that single purpose; they are
flanked and set off by one or two almost incredibly selfless characters,
like Mary Graham, Mark Tapley and especially, of course, Tom
Pinch. But the most flagrant cases of selfishness, and those examined
with the greatest care, are those of the two Martins.

Of course, the importance of self as the central theme and purpose
of *Martin Chuzzlewit* has been subjected to a great deal of critical
examination and discussion. A few representative samples of the
comments it has elicited must include John Lucas's:

> Surely the novel has a perfectly plain subject, Self; or, to put it
> rather more fully, it is about the dire consequences of acting in the
> interests of Self, and these consequences stem mostly from seeing
> self-success in terms of financial acquisition and cover a whole range
> of personal disasters, failures of human relationships (marriage,
> friendship, etc.), the follies of great expectations, and so on and so
> on.[12]

And V. S. Pritchett's:

> A large number of Dickens's comic characters can be called *mad*
> because they live or speak as if they were the only self in the world.
> They live alone by some private idea. Mrs. Gamp lives by some
> fiction of the approval of her imaginary friend Mrs. Harris.
> Augustus Moddle lives by the fixed idea of a demon and by the
> profound psychological, even metaphysical truth that, in this life,
> everyone seems to belong to a person whom he calls 'another'. In
> our time Moddle would be reading Kierkegaard.[13]

That is a modern reading with a vengeance. For a twentieth-century
Moddle would hardly be likely to derive much pleasure or profit from
reading Kierkegaard, though a twentieth-century Kierkegaard might
find it interesting to read into Moddle's character. Selfishness as a
theme has not always been found to be working very efficiently.
H. M. Daleski, in his attempt to narrow down the moral core of the
novel, also has to dismiss first of all that notion of selfishness, as
something too vague to be a fit subject for precise exploration: 'the
theme of selfishness is itself developed without coherence, the term

"self" unavailingly being used in the set pieces to wed incompatible actions that constantly strain apart'.[14] Eventually, the readings which pronounce the central theme of *Chuzzlewit* satisfactory are those which associate the notion of self with the more modern obsession with isolation. That is the case of J. Hillis Miller's analysis, especially when he writes:

> selfishness exists in the novel not only as the ethical bent of the characters, but also as the state of isolation in which they live. The novel is full of people who are really enclosed in themselves, wholly secret, wholly intent on reflexive ends which are altogether mysterious to those around them.[15]

And of course the very title of Richard Shereikis's more recent essay lays stress on the same position: 'Selves at the center: the theme of isolation in Dickens's *Martin Chuzzlewit*'.[16] Shereikis sees the self-isolation of individuals as what *Chuzzlewit* is really about. Incommunicability, then, is not an invention of our own days.

From the above survey it can be seen that Dickens has not entirely succeeded, either by his explicit statements or by his treatment of his fictional materials, in creating a unanimous impression about his central purpose in the novel. This may in part account for the critical hesitancy which marks so many essays about it. People experience genuine difficulty in making up their minds; *Martin Chuzzlewit* is more complicated than it appears. The early reactions to the publication proved disappointing to the author. Robert L. Patten gives the most complete account of that initial period in the fortunes of the novel, beginning with the extraordinary agreement between Dickens and his publishers, which enabled the writer to travel in the United States at their – temporary – expense.[17] To the usual reasons adduced in order to account for the relatively low sales figures of *Chuzzlewit* in monthly instalments, Patten adds the contemporary economic crisis, which hit the publishing trade as well as others. The sales figures and the profits made by both publisher and author, even at that early stage, might have more than satisfied almost any other novelist. They justified, in any case, the organization of a celebratory dinner, when publication ceased, and it is interesting to note that the great painter Turner attended that dinner, though Turner is hardly the kind of artist that one spontaneously associates with Dickens. Finally, Patten gives all the figures of sales and profits for the period from 1846 and 1870, as well as information concerning American sales of *Chuzzlewit* in 1968. It thus appears that the novel rose to a better position than the initial results seemed to herald, but that its position in the latest count (in the United States, admittedly) was only eleventh on the list of Dickens's novels.[18] George H. Ford records some individual reactions of interest: Jeffrey, whom Dickens had come to regard, because of his enthusiasm over *The Old Curiosity Shop*, as his critic in ordinary, disapproved of *Chuzzlewit*; so did Angela Burdett-Coutts; there were few reviews, and those few were largely unfavourable; Ford thinks this was due to great part to the unfortunate effect produced by *American Notes*.[19]

Among the early reviews, there is one, unsigned, but known to have been written by J. Cleghorn, for the *North British Review*, which points to the moral perils of reading *Chuzzlewit*:

> We do not say that the chief evil to be apprehended from Mr. Dickens's works is that they will teach people, at least of the higher ranks, to commit crimes. Yet it is not impossible that they may give suggestions to vice . . . Another error is the undue prominence given to good temper and kindness, which are constantly made substitutes for all other virtues, and an atonement for want of them; while a defect in these good qualities is the signal for instant condemnation and the charge of hypocrisy.[20]

This can go without comment; but it seems that the need to write a novel like *Martin Chuzzlewit* was very urgent if many readers shared such a reviewer's opinions and prejudices. Some recent reactions have been just as surprising in other ways. Albert J. Guerard, one of the best recent critics of *Chuzzlewit*, calls it a 'serious entertainment', says that for nine of its nineteen months it 'offered little happiness and little goodness', because 'Dickens apparently could not escape this prevailing pessimism (in which he took, of course, great creative pleasure, as did Hardy with his gloomiest poems)'.[21] More surprising still is Coral Lansbury's reading of *Martin Chuzzlewit* as a religious novel, influenced by John Bunyan.[22] Finally, though it is not an eccentric view, it is worth noting here that William Faulkner was particularly fond of *Chuzzlewit* and placed 'Sairey Gamp (and Mrs. Harris) at the head of his lists of favorite characters'.[23] In short, admiration for that novel is like misery in that it acquaints a man (or a woman) with unexpected bedfellows.

Undoubtedly Steven Marcus has a point when he asserts that *Martin Chuzzlewit* 'is not an easy book to read' and that it 'makes an unremitting demand on the reader's attention'.[24] And, again, a spectrum of critical positions shows that *Chuzzlewit* challenges evaluation, has nothing obvious about it, can be appraised in more than one way. John Forster in his *Life of Dickens* already pointed to what he regarded as the unevenness of the book: 'In construction and conduct of story *Martin Chuzzlewit* is defective, character and description constituting the chief part of its strength'.[25]

George H. Ford is on sure critical ground when he distinguishes between the various strands of Dickens's inspiration; he says that 'An air of breezy confidence continues to blow throughout *Martin Chuzzlewit* even though the comic antagonist this time was more formidable and unlikely to be dislodged'.[26] On the contrary, H. M. Daleski sees both *Chuzzlewit* and *Dombey* (in which latter Ford saw a turning-point, the loss of mirthful assurance) as 'representative of [Dickens's] journeyman's work, that is, of his early maturity in which he is not yet a master'.[27] Which is also contradicted by Earle Davis's comments:

> *Martin Chuzzlewit* must be judged an artistic advance . . . the strong points of the story surely outweigh the flaws. If there were no later book which reached greater heights, this one would stand as effective accomplishment of a broad-scale novel with multiple plots developing a central theme, the first such masterpiece in the history of English fiction . . . it would seem to be obvious that *Dombey & Son* falls short of the total accomplishment of *Martin Chuzzlewit*.[28]

Perhaps 'it would seem to be obvious', but in fact it must be far from self-evident, since critical opinion is sharply divided on this very point, and there are at least two schools of thought: some prefer *Dombey* while others have a higher regard for *Chuzzlewit*.

Any preoccupation with thus 'placing' *Chuzzlewit* by assigning it its place in the hierarchy of the Dickens canon is bound to sound a little archaic nowadays, though it is not entirely illegitimate or sterile. There are indeed connections between *Chuzzlewit* and several other Dickensian works, though they have not all been observed. Thus, I do not remember any mention of the curious resemblance between the situation of Young Martin and Mark Tapley in Eden, and that of

Esther Summerson and her maid Charley Neckett in *Bleak House*.
The earlier episode foreshadows the later, in that in both cases master
or mistress and servant fall ill, dangerously ill, one after the other,
each being nursed by the other in his or her turn; but there is also a
significant difference between the two pairs, and the order of the
illnesses. In *Chuzzlewit* it is the servant who nurses the master/hero
before succumbing in his turn; in *Bleak House* the little servant is the
first to catch the disease, and it is made clear that Esther catches it
from her. This points to the radical difference between the characters
involved: Martin is a selfish young man, and needs what he gets from
the episode, a lesson in caring for others; Esther, of course, is a
paragon of self-denial.

Other accidental foreshadowings of future books include one page
of chapter XXVIII (520/449) in which there appears an insignificant
character called Pip – he is a fellow-guest of Jonas's at Tigg's dinner-
table, and is paired with one Mr Wolf! – and this Pip is said to be a
'theatrical man' and later occurs the striking combination: 'Pip is our
mutual friend.'

Dickens himself, though he had had a keen sense of his artistic
power while writing *Chuzzlewit* and of frustration at the disappointing
reactions of his audience, may not have given so high a place to the
novel in a general retrospect of his work. At any rate, when it came to
giving public readings, he selected only one passage from *Chuzzlewit*
for that purpose; not surprisingly, the single *Chuzzlewit* reading
staged Mrs Gamp, and was a sufficiently popular one to be given sixty
times, out of a total of 472 public readings by Dickens, thus taking
seventh rank in a body of sixteen items. But Dickens never read any
Pecksniff scenes, or anything connected with the assassination of Tigg
by Jonas, whereas Sikes's murder of Nancy (in *Oliver Twist*) had
become, by the end of Dickens's life, one of his favourite numbers.

Kathleeen Tillotson, in her admirable *Novels of the Eighteen-Forties*
(1954), had to make a choice in order to represent Dickens worthily.
She could have selected *Copperfield* (1849–50), but that was perhaps
too near the end of the decade, of which the more central products
had been *Chuzzlewit* and *Dombey*. She preferred *Dombey*, and her
book has not much to say about *Chuzzlewit*, of which she does not
appear to entertain a very high opinion. Edgar Johnson in his
biography expressed a similar preference:

Readers may prefer individual scenes in *Nickleby*, *Oliver*, or *Martin*

*Chuzzlewit* to individual scenes in *Dombey* – although it is debatable that they contain anything really better than Captain Cuttle and Mr. Toots – but no one could say critically that they are better books. The problem of building a unified plot around a central theme so imperfectly tackled in *Chuzzlewit* is triumphantly solved in *Dombey*.[29]

John Forster, on the contrary, had much praise to bestow on *Martin Chuzzlewit* as a whole, though he did so, as often, in more balanced terms than he is sometimes given credit for:

> *Martin Chuzzlewit* is Mr. Dickens's best work, taken as a whole. His characters have been more agreeable, but never so full of meaning thoroughly grasped and understood, or brought out with such wonderful force and ease.[30]

Of course, in a review published in 1844 Forster could only compare *Chuzzlewit* with Dickens's previous works, and he was so involved in his friend's professional life that he shared his exhilaration over any work in progress to a considerable extent; he believed that Dickens's art was indeed making continuous progress. Yet he was not perhaps too far wrong. And one sees with pleasure that Edgar Johnson, in an essay written sixteen years after his biography, seems to enjoy *Chuzzlewit* more wholeheartedly, writing now that 'its relative unpopularity is no measure of its achievement; Dickens's energies had never been more electric or his powers of comic criticism more glittering'.[31] There have been, and there are, *Chuzzlewit* enthusiasts who are ready to place that novel at the top, or near the top, of their preferential lists. Thus Geoffrey Thurley writing in 1976: 'No Dickens novel has quite such tempestuous energy . . . it is one of Dickens's most extraordinary and impressive achievements.'[32] One of the most rhapsodic recent evaluations of *Martin Chuzzlewit* is to be found in S. J. Newman's *Dickens at Play*. Newman calls *Chuzzlewit*, for instance, its author's 'deepest, most sustained and ambitious attempt to come to terms with' the world, or 'the culmination of Dickens's art . . . his greatest achievement . . . arguably his most far-reaching masterpiece . . . revolutionary in its mode and technique . . . the most blatantly brilliant expression of comic energy in Western fiction'.[33] But at the same time Newman is not unaware of some deficiencies, since he adds that '*Chuzzlewit* wears its art on its sleeve' or 'is badly marred by the fact that its virtuous characters, unlike its vices, are uncreative, unintelligent and woefully undramatic'.[34]

More to the point, perhaps, is the attempt to place *Chuzzlewit* along the line of Dickens's development as a novelist. This is what Richard Skereikis does when connecting the novel with what Edgar Johnson has called Dickens's 'grimmer gaze for human shortcomings':

> *Martin Chuzzlewit* is the first of his novels to reveal this important change in his view. As such, it stands at the threshold of his 'darker' phase, clearly anticipating the more sophisticated analyses of men and society that he undertook in such later works as *Bleak House*, *Little Dorrit* and *Our Mutual Friend*.[35]

To anyone unfamiliar with the course of Dickens criticism since the 1940s it may be necessary to point out that *dark* or *sophisticated* are intended in such a context as terms of praise, not of disparagement, and that by making of *Chuzzlewit* a forerunner of the three sombre masterpieces of the later period, rather than the last of the great comic achievements of the earlier days, the critic is intending to raise its status.

Again, very few judgements on *Martin Chuzzlewit* are all of one piece. Even in the most fervent appraisals reservations may creep in. Some of these are more specific than others and, of course, the more specific they are, the more helpful to a final evaluation of the novel. From R. C. Churchill's analysis in *Scrutiny* one gathers that

> If *Martin Chuzzlewit* be not universally thought Dickens's finest work . . . yet it has never been denied a place in the front rank . . . There can be few pieces of literature where the good and the bad jostle each other so closely.[36]

John Lucas is a little more precise when he speaks of

> the limits of inspiration that are reached in *Martin Chuzzlewit*, since it is in this novel that Dickens's fabulous imaginative gifts are put under the severest strain and finally crack. *Martin Chuzzlewit*, indeed, is a crucial novel in Dickens's development. To speak plainly, it is a crisis novel.[37]

The crisis in inspiration was to be later matched by a crisis in critical attention. As has become evident by this time, no comment by F. R.

and/or Q. D. Leavis has been found relevant to the present study: one understands why their joint book of 1970 contains no chapter on *Chuzzlewit*; the book has no index, but there are very few references to *Chuzzlewit* that could have been listed in it. There is nowhere in the book any clear evidence of the authors having read *Chuzzlewit*, but there is definite evidence by default (as they would have said) of their having disdained to think critically about it, of their not having found in it a sufficiently serious challenge to their imposing critical faculties.[38]

Altogether, a certain disappointment over *Martin Chuzzlewit* is perceptible through the comments of some of Dickens's warmest admirers. Ross H. Dabney points to the potentialities of the initial situation involving Mary Graham and the two Martins, before going on to assert that 'All these potentialities are missed; none of the three characters in this central situation comes alive'.[39] Geoffrey Tillotson's essay confirms this view of *Chuzzlewit* as a novel of potentialities missed, or of the gap between intention and achievement; Tillotson writes that 'Dickens's accounts of what he proposed, and what he in fact did, are wildly out . . . could there be a more genuine instance of the failure of a writer to grasp retrospectively what he had done?[40]

Finally, attention may be drawn to Garrett Stewart's definition, put forward tentatively: '*Chuzzlewit* might be called Dickens's most fully articulated novel-of-manners-of-speaking.'[41] That is not merely ingenious. There is food for thought in the connection thus established between the novels of manners and the part played by language and speech, and the gap between sincere feeling and outward expression, in *Martin Chuzzlewit*.

I have tried in this chapter to show how *Chuzzlewit* has been read, received, discussed, over the years, rather than impose my own final appreciation upon the reader. This suited my purpose all the better as I have great difficulty in stating what my position to that novel is at any given moment. Studying *Chuzzlewit* for several years, rereading it many times, organizing and writing this book, I have varied as many times in my attitude. *Chuzzlewit* seems to me to illustrate in an exemplary manner the complaint once made about Dickens in general, that his parts are greater than his wholes, in that Mrs Gamp is a masterpiece of characterization but the novel is not a harmonious and fully satisfactory work of art. Yet at the same time I have always found myself deeply engaged by this task, fascinated by even the least appetizing parts of the book and by the critical problems they raise. I have not resolved, even to myself, all of these problems, but I have become more convinced than ever that *Martin Chuzzlewit* deserves to be read and reread. It deserves, that is, and richly repays, the effort to surmount various obstacles in the reader's path. It is uneven, sometimes disappointing, but also often delightful, and occasionally great. It is true Dickens.

## NOTES: CHAPTER 12

1 Kathleen Tillotson, *Novels of the Eighteen-Forties* (London, 1954), p. 161.
2 K. J. Fielding, *Charles Dickens: A Critical Introduction* (London, 1958), p. 76.
3 John Butt, *Pope, Dickens, and Others: Essays and Addresses* (Edinburgh, 1969), p. 156.
4 Michael Steig, *Dickens and Phiz* (Bloomington, Ind./London, 1978), p. 61.
5 Hippolyte Taine, *Histoire de la littérature anglaise*, 12th edn (Paris, 1911), Vol. 5, p. 57 ('Be kind and loving; there is no true joy but in the emotions of the heart: sensibility is the whole of man. Leave science to the learned, pride to noblemen, luxury to the wealthy; take compassion on humble miseries; the slightest and most despised being may be worth as much in himself as thousands of mighty and haughty creatures. Beware of bruising the delicate souls that bloom in every station, under every garment, at every time of life. Believe that humaneness, pity, forgiveness, are the finest things in man; believe that intimacy, outpourings, tenderness, tears, are the sweetest things in the world. To live is nothing; to be powerful, learned, industrious, is little, to be useful is not enough. He alone has lived and is a man who has wept on remembering a benefit conferred or received by himself').
6 Steven Marcus, *Dickens from Pickwick to Dombey* (New York, 1965), p. 236.
7 H. P. Sucksmith, *The Narrative Art of Charles Dickens* (London, 1970), p. 228.
8 It was even more strikingly so in the original manuscript, when Dickens had called the wind 'vexed' instead of 'angry'.
9 Marcus, op. cit., 252–3.
10 John Lucas, *The Melancholy Man: A Study of Dickens's Novels* (London, 1970), p. 129.
11 J. Hillis Miller, *Charles Dickens: The World of His Novels* (Cambridge, Mass., 1958), p. 103.
12 Lucas, op. cit., p. 114.
13 See Ian Watt (ed.), *The Victorian Novel: Modern Essays in Criticism* (London, 1971), p. 31. V. S. Pritchett's essay on 'The comic world of Dickens' was written in 1954.
14 H. M. Daleski, *Dickens and the Art of Analogy* (London, 1970), p. 105.
15 Miller, op. cit., p. 104.
16 See *Dickens Studies Newletter*, vol. 7, no. 2 (1976), pp. 38–42.
17 Robert L. Patten, *Charles Dickens and His Publishers* (Oxford, 1978), pp. 123–7.
18 ibid., pp. 133, 136, 156, 332 and 343.
19 See George H. Ford, *Dickens and His Readers: Aspects of Novel-Criticism since 1836* (Princeton, NJ, 1955), pp. 36–49.
20 May 1845. Quoted in F. G. Kitton (ed.), *Dickensiana* (London, 1886), pp. 99–101.
21 See Albert J. Guerard, *The Triumph of the Novel: Dickens, Dostoevsky, Faulkner* (New York, 1976), pp. 15 and 236. Guerard is also an admirable critic of Hardy.

22  See Coral Lansbury, 'Dickens' romanticism domesticated', in *Dickens Studies Newletter*, vol. 3, no. 2 (1972), pp. 36–46.
23  Guerard, op. cit., p. 3.
24  Marcus, op. cit., p. 223.
25  Everyman's Library edition (1927), Vol. 1, p. 292.
26  Ford, op. cit., p. 84. The antagonist of Dickens's comic satire was the whole of British and American society.
27  Daleski, op. cit., p. 13.
28  Earle Davis, *The Flint and the Flame: The Artistry of Charles Dickens* (Columbia, Mo., 1963), pp. 148 and 156.
29  Edgar Johnson, *Charles Dickens: His Tragedy and Triumph* (London, 1953), Vol. 2, p. 643.
30  Unsigned review (1844) quoted in Philip Collins (ed.), *Dickens: The Critical Heritage* (London, 1971), p. 184.
31  See Edgar Johnson, 'The dark pilgrimage' in E. W. F. Tomlin (ed.), *Charles Dickens, 1812–1870: A Centenary Volume* (London, 1969), p. 50.
32  Geoffrey Thurley, *The Dickens Myth: Its Genesis and Structure* (London, 1976), p. 81.
33  S.J. Newman, *Dickens at Play* (London, 1981), p. 101.
34  ibid., p. 105.
35  Richard Shereikis, 'Selves at the center: the theme of isolation in Dickens's *Martin Chuzzlewit*', *Dickens Studies Newsletter*, vol. 7, no. 2 (1976), p. 38.
36  R. C. Churchill, 'Dickens, drama and tradition', *Scrutiny*, vol. 10, no. 4 (1942), p. 358.
37  Lucas, op. cit., p. 113.
38  See F. R. and Q. D. Leavis, *Dickens the Novelist* (London, 1970), passim.
39  Ross L. Dabney, *Love and Property in the Novels of Dickens* (London, 1967), pp. 38–9.
40  Geoffrey Tillotson, *A View of Victorian Literature* (Oxford, 1978), p. 133.
41  Garrett Stewart, *Dickens and the Trials of Imagination* (Cambridge, Mass., 1974), p. 125.

# BIBLIOGRAPHY

## (i)  EDITIONS

In addition to the editions published in the author's lifetime (first edition in nineteen/twenty instalments, 1843–4; then in one volume, Chapman & Hall, 1844; Cheap Edition, 1850; Library Edition, 1858; Charles Dickens Edition, 1867), *Martin Chuzzlewit* is conveniently available in at least three modern forms:

– as one volume of the Oxford Illustrated Dickens, with the forty original illustrations and an introduction by Geoffrey Russell (London, 1951), several times reprinted; uses the imperfect Charles Dickens Edition text;
– in the Penguin English Library, edited with an introduction and notes by P. N. Furbank and the original illustrations (Harmondsworth, 1968); also based, though with some discrimination, on the Charles Dickens Edition text;
– in the Clarendon Dickens (general editors: Kathleen Tillotson, James Kinsley and John Butt), edited by Margaret Cardwell (Oxford, 1982). Textually authoritative, and has a very valuable introduction, but provides no explanatory annotation and is inordinately expensive.

## (ii)  BIBLIOGRAPHY

In addition to the usual annual bibliographies (Modern Language Association, Modern Humanities Research Association), and the more recent *Annual Bibliography of Victorian Studies*, ed. Brahma Chaudhuri for Litir Database of Edmonton, Alberta (five yearly volumes and a cumulative volume covering 1976–80, all published in 1980–3), it will be useful to consult the following:

Stevenson, Lionel, (ed.), *Victorian Fiction: A Guide to Research* (Cambridge, Mass., 1964). The chapter on Dickens, pp. 44–153, is by Ada B. Nisbet.
Ford, George H. (ed.), *Victorian Fiction: a Second Guide to Research* (New York, 1978). The chapter on Dickens, pp. 34–113, is by Philip Collins.
Collins, Philip, *A Dickens Bibliography*, extract from *The New Cambridge Bibliography of English Literature*, ed. George Watson, Vol. 3 (Cambridge, 1970), printed for the Dickens Fellowship (London, 1970).
Gold, Joseph (ed.), *The Stature of Dickens: a Centenary Bibliography* (Toronto, 1970).
Cohn, Alan M., and Collins K. K., *The Cumulated Dickens Checklist, 1970–1979* (Troy, NY, 1982).

## (iii)  BIOGRAPHICAL AND HISTORICAL INFORMATION

The two greatest Dickens biographies remain particularly valuable. They are John Forster's *Life of Charles Dickens*, originally published 1872–4, and many times reprinted, and Edgar Johnson's *Charles Dickens: His Tragedy and*

*Triumph*, 2 vols (London, 1953), also reprinted, and of which an abridged version appeared in Penguin Books (Harmondsworth, 1978).

The more recent *Dickens: A Life* by Norman and Jeanne MacKenzie (Oxford, 1979) may be consulted. Also Philip Collins (ed.), *Dickens: Interviews and Recollections*, 2 vols (London, 1981).

Dickens's letters are of obvious relevance. *The Pilgrim Edition of the Letters of Charles Dickens* is in progress at the Clarendon Press under the general editorship of the late Madeline House and of Graham Storey. Vol. 3 (1842–3), ed. the general editors and Kathleen Tillotson, with the help of the late Noel C. Peyrouton, appeared in 1974; Vol. 4 (1844–6), ed. Kathleen Tillotson with the help of Nina Burgis, in 1977. Both are extremely valuable for the student of *Martin Chuzzlewit*. Vol. 5 (1847–9), ed. Graham Storey and K. J. Fielding, appeared in 1981. The complete edition is expected to comprise twelve volumes.

The history of the publication of *Martin Chuzzlewit* is detailed in Robert L. Patten, *Charles Dickens and His Publishers* (Oxford, 1978), especially ch. 7, 'Trouble in Eden: *American Notes* and *Martin Chuzzlewit*'. Dickens's troubles with 'pirates' (plagiarists and dishonest exploiters of his success) are the theme of E. T. Jaques, *Charles Dickens in Chancery* (London, 1914).

The critical reception given by the press to the novel is sampled by F. G. Kitton in *Dickensiana* (London, 1886), and at greater length in Philip Collins (ed.), *Dickens: The Critical Heritage* (London, 1971). The reputation of the novel over the years is analysed and discussed by George H. Ford in *Dickens and His Readers: Aspects of Novel-Criticism since 1836* (Princeton, NJ, 1955), and reasons for the lack of immediate popularity are propounded by Ada B. Nisbet in 'The Mystery of *Martin Chuzzlewit*' in *Essays Critical and Historical: Dedicated to Lilian B. Campbell* (Berkeley, Calif., 1950). The place occupied by *Martin Chuzzlewit* in Dickens's readings is examined in Philip Collins (ed.), *Charles Dickens: The Public Readings* (London, 1975).

Finally, among the studies of the original illustrations and their author, Michael Steig's article '*Martin Chuzzlewit*'s progress by Dickens and Phiz', *Dickens Studies Annual 2* (Carbondale/Edwardsville, Ill., 1972), and the same writer's exhaustive *Dickens and Phiz* (Bloomington, Ind./London, 1978) are the most usefully suggestive.

## (iv)   SPECIFIC CRITICISM

This section must be subdivided into two parts containing respectively the studies devoted to *Martin Chuzzlewit* specifically and propounding interpretations and readings of that novel as a whole, and essays on one particular aspect of the book. In the first category are to be found:

Benjamin, Edwin, B., 'The structure of *Martin Chuzzlewit*', *Philological Quarterly*, vol. 34, no. 1 (1955).

Burke, Alan R., 'The House of Chuzzlewit and the Architectural City', *Dickens Studies Annual 3*, ed. Robert B. Partlow, Jr (1974).

Butt, John, 'The serial publication of Dickens's novels *Martin Chuzzlewit* and

*Little Dorrit'*, in his *Pope, Dickens and Others: Essays and Addresses* (Edinburgh, 1969).

Chesterton, G. K., *Appreciations and Criticisms of the Works of Charles Dickens* (London, 1911).

Churchill, R. C., 'Dickens, drama and tradition', *Scrutiny*, vol. 10, no. 4 (1942).

Eigner, Edwin M., *The Metaphysical Novel in England and America* (Berkeley, Calif., 1978), pp. 34–8. On Dickens's degree of preconception in *Martin Chuzzlewit*.

Furbank, P. N., introduction to the Penguin English Library edition of the novel (Harmondsworth, 1968).

Gissing, George, *'Martin Chuzzlewit'*, in his *The Immortal Dickens* (London, 1925). An introduction written by Gissing for the Rochester Edition of the novel.

Guerard, Albert J., *'Martin Chuzzlewit*: the novel as comic entertainment', chapter 9 of his *The Triumph of the Novel: Dickens, Dostoevsky, Faulkner* (New York, 1976).

Hardy, Barbara, *'Martin Chuzzlewit'*, in John Gross and Gabriel Pearson (eds), *Dickens and the Twentieth Century* (London, 1962).

Lansbury, Coral, 'Dickens' romanticism domesticated', *Dickens Studies Newsletter*, vol. 3, no. 2 (1972).

Miller, J. Hillis, 'The sources of Dickens's comic art: from *American Notes* to *Martin Chuzzlewit'*, *Nineteenth-Century Fiction*, vol. 24, no. 4 (1970).

Newman, S. J., *'Martin Chuzzlewit*: the novel as play', chapter 8 of his *Dickens at Play* (London, 1981).

Scribner, Margo, 'Dickens's use of animals in *Martin Chuzzlewit'*, *Dickens Studies Newsletter*, vol 10, nos 2–3 (1979).

Shereikis, Richard, 'Selves at the center: the theme of isolation in Dickens's *Martin Chuzzlewit'*, *Dickens Studies Newsletter*, vol. 7, no. 2 (1976).

Van Ghent, Dorothy, 'The Dickens world: a view from Todgers's', *Sewanee Review*, vol. 58, no. 3 (1950).

Woodring, Carl, 'Change in *Chuzzlewit'*, in Clyde de L. Ryals (ed.), *Nineteenth-Century Literary Perspectives* (Durham, NC, 1974).

Among the studies of the American elements in *Martin Chuzzlewit* the following will be found useful:

Anon., *'Martin Chuzzlewit*: an American contemporary review', *Dickensian*, vol. 10, no. 4 (1914). The review is from *Brother Jonathan*, 29 July 1843.

Bishop, Joseph Bucklin (ed.), 'Theodore Roosevelt and Dickens', *Dickensian*, vol. 16, no. 1 (1920). Extracts from Roosevelt's letters to his children, written in 1906–8.

Blaisdell, Lowell L., 'The origins of the satire in the Watertoast episode of *Martin Chuzzlewit'*, *Dickensian*, vol. 77, no. 2 (1981).

Davis, Paul B., 'Dickens and the American press, 1842', *Dickens Studies*, vol. 4, no. 1 (1968).

Evans, Edward J., 'The established self: the American episodes of *Martin*

Chuzzlewit', Dickens Studies Annual 5, ed. Robert B. Partlow, Jr (1976).

Fielding, K.J., 'Martin Chuzzlewit and "The Liberator" ', Notes and Queries, vol. 198, no. 6 (1953).

Hughes, Dean, 'Great expectorations: Dickens on America', Dickensian, vol. 79, no. 400 (1983), pp. 66–76.

Johnson, Edgar, 'Dickens's anti-chauvinism', in Clyde de L. Ryals (ed.), Nineteenth-Century Literary Perspectives (Durham, NC, 1974).

Meckier, Jerome, 'Dickens discovers America, Dickens discovers Dickens: the first visit reconsidered', Modern Language Review, vol. 79 (1984).

Payne, Edward F., 'Dickens's first look at America', Dickensian, vol. 38, no. 261 (1942). This volume, issued a hundred years after the American tour, contains several other articles on its history.

Peyrouton, Noel C., 'Bozmania vs. Bozphobia: a Yankee pot-pourri', Dickens Studies, vol. 4, no. 1 (1968).

Slater, Michael (ed.), Dickens on America and the Americans (Brighton, 1979).

Stone, Harry, 'Dickens' use of his American experiences in Martin Chuzzlewit', PMLA, vol. 72, no. 3 (1957).

On some characters or on characterization in Martin Chuzzlewit:

Beasley, Jerry C., 'The role of Tom Pinch in "Martin Chuzzlewit" ', Ariel, vol. 5, no. 2 (1974).

Carlton, W.J., 'The barber of Dean Street', Dickensian, vol. 48, no. 301 (1952).

Chovil, A. S., 'Tom Pinch a failure?', Dickensian, vol. 28, no. 223 (1932).

Ganz, Margaret, 'The vulnerable ego: Dickens' humor in decline', Dickens Studies Annual 1, ed. Robert B. Partlow, Jr (1970).

Gold, Joseph, ' "Living in a wale": Martin Chuzzlewit', Dickens Studies Annual 2, ed. Robert B. Partlow, Jr (1972).

Hayward, Arthur L., 'Who was Chevy Slyme?', Dickensian, vol. 25, no. 212 (1929).

Kennedy, Veronica M. S., 'Mrs Gamp as the Great Mother: a Dickensian use of the archetype', Victorian Newsletter, no. 41 (1972). Something of a curiosity in Dickens criticism.

McCarron, Robert M., 'Folly and wisdom: three Dickensian wise fools', Dickens Studies Annual 6, ed. Robert B. Partlow, Jr (1977).

Manheim, Leonard F., 'Dickens heroes, heroes, and heroids', Dickens Studies Annual 5, ed. Robert B. Partlow, Jr (1976). Where one will learn that Tom Pinch, for instance, is a heroid.

Pratt, Branwen Bailey, 'Dickens and freedom: Young Bailey in Martin Chuzzlewit', Nineteenth-Century Fiction, vol. 30, no. 2 (1975).

Pratt, Branwen Bailey, 'A note on a character who does not appear in Martin Chuzzlewit', Dickens Studies Newsletter, vol. 8, no. 2 (1977).

Romano, John, Dickens and Reality (New York, 1978). Studies Augustus Moddle.

Some attention is given to chapter I of Martin Chuzzlewit in:

Kaplan, Fred, *Dickens and Mesmerism: The Hidden Springs of Fiction* (Princeton, NJ, 1975).
Rosner, Mary, 'The Siren-like delusions of art', *Dickens Studies Newsletter*, vol. 10, nos 2–3 (1979).
Ser, Cary D., 'The function of chapter I of *Martin Chuzzlewit*', *Dickens Studies Newsletter*, vol. 10, nos 2–3 (1979).

Finally, aspects of Dickens's language, style and speech are studied in the following:

McCarthy, Patrick J., 'The language of *Martin Chuzzlewit*', *Studies in English Literature, 1500–1900*, vol. 20, no. 4 (1980).
Page, Norman, 'Eccentric speech in Dickens', *Critical Survey*, vol. 4, no. 2 (1968–70).
Polhemus, Robert M., 'Dickens's *Martin Chuzzlewit* (1843–44): the comedy of expression', chapter 4 of his *Comic Faith: The Great Tradition from Austen to Joyce* (Chicago, Ill., 1980), pp. 88–123.
Pound, Louise, 'The American dialect of Charles Dickens', *American Speech*, vol. 22, no. 2 (1947).
Quirk, Randolph, 'Charles Dickens, linguist', in his *The Linguist and the English Language* (London, 1974).
Ward, A. W., 'Language and Charles Dickens', *Listener*, vol. 69, no. 1782 (1963).

## (v)  GENERAL CRITICISM

Among the innumerable critical studies on Dickens, the following have been found particularly useful, in various ways:

Alain, *En lisant Dickens* (Paris, 1945). Has an eight-page section on *Martin Chuzzlewit*, read only in French translation.
Bodelsen, C. A., *Essays and Papers* (Copenhagen, 1964). Contains a stimulating essay on Dickens's symbolism.
Carey, John, *The Violent Effigy: A Study of Dickens' Imagination* (London, 1973). The most brilliant recent overall view of Dickens's art.
Cazamian, Louis, *The Social Novel in England, 1830–1850: Dickens, Disraeli, Mrs Gaskell, Kingsley* (London, 1973). Martin Fido's translation of Cazamian's dissertation, originally published seventy years earlier.
Chesterton, G. K., *Charles Dickens* (London, 1906). One of the best critical studies of Dickens ever printed; still seems inexhaustibly fresh and stimulating.
Churchill, R. C., 'Charles Dickens', in Boris Ford (ed.), *The Pelican Guide to English Literature*, Vol. 6, *From Dickens to Hardy* (Harmondsworth, 1958). A twenty-five-page chapter embodying the *Scrutiny* approach with talent and discrimination.
Cockshut, A. O. J., *The Imagination of Charles Dickens* (London, 1961).

Collins, Philip, *Dickens and Crime* (London, 1962).

Collins, Philip, *Dickens and Education* (London, 1963).

Coolidge, Archibald C., Jr, *Charles Dickens as Serial Novelist* (Ames, Ia, 1967).

Dabney, Ross L., *Love and Property in the Novels of Dickens* (London, 1967). A thorough exploration of a central problem.

Daleski, H. M., *Dickens and the Art of Analogy* (London, 1970). A distinguished interpretation.

Darwin, Bernard, *Dickens* (London, 1933). Known in its day as a 'miniature masterpiece'.

Davis, Earle, *The Flint and the Flame: The Artistry of Charles Dickens* (Columbia, Mo., 1963).

Delattre, Floris, *Dickens* (Paris, n.d. [1929?]). An anthology with critical introduction fairly typical of the 1920s.

Fielding, K. J., *Charles Dickens: A Critical Introduction* (London, 1958). A compact, very well-informed volume; has one chapter on America and *Martin Chuzzlewit*. Second edition, revised and expanded, in 1965.

Garis, Robert, *The Dickens Theatre: A Reassessment of the Novels* (London, 1965).

Gissing, George, *Charles Dickens: A Critical Study* (London, 1898). An often shrewd, if occasionally biased, critical approach – but whose approach is not biased? – known to have sparked off Chesterton's book in protest against its excessive pessimism; but Chesterton himself admired Gissing's work.

Goldberg, Michael, *Carlyle and Dickens* (Athens, Ga, 1972). Deals with aspects of style, and the 'Nigger Question'.

Gomme, A. H., *Dickens* (London, 1971).

Hardy, Barbara, *The Moral Art of Dickens* (London, 1970).

Kincaid, James R., *Dickens and the Rhetoric of Laughter* (London, 1971). One of the few studies of the comic element in Dickens, with a substantial chapter on *Martin Chuzzlewit*.

Lary, N. M., *Dostoevsky and Dickens: A Study of Literary Influence* (London, 1973). Discusses the possible influence of Jonas and of Pecksniff on characters in Dostoevsky.

Leavis, F. R., *The Great Tradition* (London, 1948). Explicitly excludes Dickens from the great tradition of the English novel, but includes as an appendix an admiring essay on *Hard Times*.

Leavis, F. R. and Q. D., *Dickens the Novelist* (London, 1970). Significantly, almost pointedly, omits discussion of *Martin Chuzzlewit*.

Lucas, John, *The Melancholy Man: A Study of Dickens's Novels* (London, 1970). In one of the best general studies spawned by the centenary year, expresses many reservations about *Martin Chuzzlewit*.

Marcus, Steven, *Dickens from Pickwick to Dombey* (New York, 1965). Devotes fifty pages to *Martin Chuzzlewit*.

Maurois, André, *Etudes anglaises* (Paris, 1927). The first half of this volume is made up of four elegant lectures on Dickens.

Miller, J. Hillis, *Charles Dickens: The World of His Novels* (Cambridge, Mass., 1958). A pioneering study by a disciple of G. Poulet.

Monod, Sylvère, *Dickens romancier* (Paris, 1953); revised and translated as *Dickens the Novelist* (Norman, Okla, 1968).

Pope, Norris, *Dickens and Charity* (London, 1978). Treats of Pecksniff as an Evangelical.

Quiller-Couch, Sir Arthur, *Charles Dickens and Other Victorians* (Cambridge, 1925). In this book Dickens lords it over all other Victorians, and the lecturer, in his belletristic style, over his audience.

Schwarzbach, F. S., *Dickens and the City* (London, 1979). Sees *Martin Chuzzlewit* as a novel concerned with 'Architecture and Accommodation'.

Slater, Michael (ed.), *Dickens 1970* (London, 1970). A brilliant collection of centenary essays specially commissioned from well-known writers.

Slater, Michael, *Dickens and Women* (London, 1983).

Stewart, Garrett, *Dickens and the Trials of Imagination* (Cambridge, Mass., 1974).

Straus, Ralph, *Dickens: A Portrait in Pencil* (London, 1928). A good example of early biographical-cum-critical approach.

Sucksmith, Harvey Peter, *The Narrative Art of Charles Dickens* (London, 1970). One of the most thorough investigations of Dickens's craftsmanship.

Swinburne, Algernon Charles, *Charles Dickens* (London, 1913). Worth reading if only as a period-piece, but more gushing than critical.

Taine, Hippolyte, *Histoire de la littérature anglaise*, 12th edn (Paris, 1911). The fifth volume on 'Les contemporains' has sixty pages on Dickens, based on an article written as early as 1856, in which *Martin Chuzzlewit* played a great part.

Thurley, Geoffrey, *The Dickens Myth: Its Genesis and Structure* (London, 1976). A very interesting study of the workings of Dickens's imagination.

Tillotson, Geoffrey, *A View of Victorian Literature* (Oxford, 1978). This posthumous volume contains a forty-page essay on Dickens by the great Thackeray scholar.

Tillotson, Kathleen, *Novels of the Eighteen-Forties* (London, 1954). A classic.

Tomlin, E. W. F. (ed.), *Charles Dickens, 1812–1870: A Centenary Volume* (London, 1969). Another distinguished collection of centenary essays; finely produced and illustrated.

Walder, Dennis, *Dickens and Religion* (London, 1981).

Wall, Stephen (ed.), *Charles Dickens: A Critical Anthology* (Harmondsworth, 1970).

Watt, Ian (ed.), *The Victorian Novel: Modern Essays in Criticism* (London, 1971). Dickens has the lion's share in these reprinted pieces.

Welsh, Alexander, *The City of Dickens* (London, 1971). Original criticism and interpretation.

Wilson, Angus, *The World of Charles Dickens* (New York, 1970). Extremely readable, expert and stimulating.

Worth, George J., *Dickensian Melodrama: A Reading of the Novels* (Lawrence, Kan., 1978). Interesting, on a difficult and important aspect of Dickens's art.

# CHRONOLOGICAL TABLE

1812    Charles Dickens born in Landport, near Portsmouth.

1817    John Dickens, Charles's father, moved to Chatham.

1822    John Dickens moved to London. Charles left behind at Chatham.

1823    Charles joins his parents in London.

1824    Charles becomes a salaried worker in a blacking factory. John imprisoned for debt. On John's release, Charles is sent to school.

1827    Charles leaves school and works in a solicitor's office.

1828    Charles Dickens becomes a shorthand reporter at Doctors' Commons.

1832    Dickens becomes a parliamentary reporter.

1833    First stories published.

1836    Publication of *Sketches by Boz* and beginning of *Pickwick Papers*. Dickens marries Catherine Hogarth.

1837    Dickens begins *Oliver Twist* and completes *Pickwick*. First child born.

1838    Dickens completes *Oliver Twist* and begins *Nicholas Nickleby*.

1839    *Nickleby* completed.

1840    *The Old Curiosity Shop* published in weekly issues of *Master Humphrey's Clock*.

1841    *Barnaby Rudge* succeeds *The Old Curiosity Shop*.

1842    Dickens spends first six months of the year in the United States. Publishes *American Notes* shortly after his return.

1843    Beginning of *Martin Chuzzlewit*. Dickens writes his first 'Christmas Book', *A Christmas Carol*.

1844    Completion of *Martin Chuzzlewit*. The Dickens household transferred to Genoa.

1845    Back in England, Dickens acts in private theatricals and becomes interested in political journalism.

1846    After two weeks as the first editor of the *Daily News*, Dickens goes away again, this time to Lausanne and later Paris. Begins to write *Dombey and Son*.

1847    Return to London.

1848    End of *Dombey*. Publication of Dickens's fifth and last 'Christmas Book', *The Haunted Man*.

1849    Beginning of *David Copperfield*.

1850    Dickens launches *Household Words*, his own popular weekly, and completes *Copperfield*.

1851    Beginning of *A Child's History of England*.

1852    Beginning of *Bleak House*. Birth of the tenth and last child of Charles and Catherine Dickens.

1853    *Bleak House* and *Child's History* completed.

1854    *Hard Times* published in *Household Words*.

1855–6    *Little Dorrit* begun. Winter spent in Paris. Dickens buys Gad's Hill Place, a house near Rochester.

| 1857 | Dickens completes *Dorrit*, gets increasingly involved in theatricals, and becomes acquainted with Ellen Ternan, a young actress. |
| 1858 | Dickens is separated from his wife. He begins a long remunerative but exhausting series of public readings from his works. |
| 1859 | *Household Words* becomes *All the Year Round*, in which *A Tale of Two Cities* is published. |
| 1860 | Dickens begins to live permanently at Gad's Hill, writes essays (*The Uncommercial Traveller*), and begins to publish *Great Expectations* in his own weekly. |
| 1861 | *Great Expectations* completed. |
| 1864 | Dickens in poor health. Beginning of *Our Mutual Friend*. |
| 1865 | *Our Mutual Friend* completed. Dickens badly shaken by his involvement in the railway crash at Staplehurst (9 June). |
| 1867–8 | Winter spent on a reading tour in the United States. |
| 1870 | Dickens completes his farewell tour of readings in England, and begins the unfinished *Mystery of Edwin Drood*. He dies on 9 June and is buried in Westminster Abbey. |

# INDEX